MW00698457

MURDER BECOMES MIAMI

Dan:

I hope you find this crazy, creepy ride through Miami as scintillating as your trip across Manhattan was!

Jerry Eaton
aka Guy Herrington
12-12-15

MURDER BECOMES MIAMI

A DALTON LEE MYSTERY

JEFFREY EATON

The Cornet Group

This book is dedicated to:

James Feaster

Chet Flake

Linda Grimes

Sandi Mohler

George Rick

Beverly White

Shirl White

"If you're awake in this awful downpour,
then struggle free and paddle out the cellar door."
— Owl City

1

Shevonda Jackson stood along one side of the courtroom, arms crossed, eyes alert.

Intensely she studied the crowd assembled . . . the random assortment of diverse individuals with whom she was about to share this historic moment. There were the attorneys—celebrities now—immaculate in their designer suits and crisply ironed blouses and shirts. There were the family members—tense and quiet—sneaking brief, silent glances at one another. There were the onlookers—craning their necks like giraffes in a savanna. And there was, of course, the phalanx of reporters—entwined in wires and cords—bobbing and weaving for the perfect angle from which to capture the reactions to the upcoming verdicts.

She absorbed every detail around her without anyone taking notice—their attention, as always, was riveted up front. That's what she enjoyed most about working security at the courthouse . . . it allowed her (even as hefty as she was) to fade into the wallpaper and become the invisible observer when she wanted to, yet spring into action should the need arise.

"You're like a big ol' rattlesnake coiled against a rock," her cousin, Dante, had once suggested. She agreed with that assessment, took more than a little pride in it, in fact. She scanned the room again, slowly moving her gaze first right, then left. On the back row, a middle-aged woman pulled at a muffin she held in a napkin in her lap. In front of her, an elderly gentleman wearing a bolo tie leaned in to a college-aged girl who was whispering into his ear.

Shevonda's eyes traveled up to the defendant near the front of the room where she began to perform a detailed inventory of him. Perfectly coiffed, raven-black hair with a handsome hint of salt at the temples. Eyebrows that were impeccably tweezed, a nose that suggested a pedigree of privilege. A deep, smooth, unblemished tan. *What do you want to bet he uses moisturizer every night?* she thought.

She noted that like most defendants about to meet their destiny, he was trying a little too hard to appear blasé about it all. He shifted his glance around the room too much. Held his head a little too high. Moved the papers in front of him too often, shuffling them like a news anchor moving on to the next story. But then putting them right back to where they had been. Every so often he would blink rapidly, squint, then gingerly lick his lips—another sign of nervousness she recognized all too well.

You don't often see a man like that get nervous, she thought to herself. *He's the type who's usually throwing his earphones to the ground when someone blows a big play or jumping for joy when someone runs into the end zone.*

Intense? Yes. Nervous, though . . . ?

She studied him more closely. His jaw was rugged and his eyelashes were lush. He was quite a looker . . . *that* she had to admit. "But those are the ones you really have to watch out for," her mother had always warned her. "The pretty boys who gaze more into the mirror than into your eyes . . . avoid them like cockroaches, Shevonda," her mother had said. "Cuz they'll drop you like a pot of boiling water the minute someone younger and prettier walks by."

She sighed from fatigue and thought about everything she had heard over the past several weeks. She had no idea if he was guilty or not. The evidence and testimony hadn't swayed her one way or the other. Plus, she had worked in law enforcement long enough to know that often, verdicts had nothing to do with the testimony and evidence presented. Sometimes it just came down to how the defendant sat in a chair. Or whether his eyes evaded the most powerful jurors on the panel, or returned their looks with belligerence . . . or maybe even fear.

She also didn't know if she agreed with the Cuban women in her apartment building who said he was being railroaded because of his race. Because he was a Hispanic male who had succeeded in a white man's world and married a gorgeous young blonde to boot. Because he had a multimillion-dollar contract with a big university and even more lucrative endorsement deals from a host of sportswear companies.

All she knew for sure was that he was there because his wife had been stabbed multiple times inside the cabana next to their pool, and because a young man the police presumed to be her lover was found dying from stab wounds just a few feet away. And because the police had been called to the house four times during the previous eighteen months to restrain the defendant, whom they had always found to be in a violent rage. And because he had been arrested at Miami International Airport as he was boarding a plane for some country in South America she couldn't find on a map if her life depended on it.

She didn't really know if he was guilty or not. But she did know that from what the media was saying, the situation wasn't looking very good for him.

Suddenly, a rustle swept through the crowd as a door near the front of the courtroom swung open and the judge strode resolutely toward the bench. Everyone rose—then quickly sat back down again as the judge slid swiftly into her chair. She rifled through a few files in front of her, bent over to whisper to a bailiff at her side, then sat quickly upright and launched into the proceedings.

"All right, we are back on the record in regards to the Valenzuela matter," she said. "I see that Mr. Valenzuela is present before the court along with his counselors, Mr. Weiner and Mr. Consuelas. The jury is not present. Good morning everyone."

A low, "Good morning, your honor," rumbled in return.

"Let the record reflect that the jurors have indicated through the questionnaire distributed to them yesterday evening that they want their personal information to remain confidential. They also indicated they do not wish to speak either to the attorneys in this case or to the media. Does everyone here understand that and vow to respect that?"

Once again, a dutiful "Yes, your honor," was the reply.

"All right, summon the jurors please."

A deputy left for a couple of moments but soon returned with the jurors in tow. Shevonda scanned their faces as they entered the courtroom but did so with little enthusiasm, for she knew that contrary to popular thought, jurors rarely betrayed a verdict simply by their expressions . . . and sometimes their demeanor actually could mislead as to the verdict to come.

Once seated, everyone on the panel turned almost in unison and faced the judge at the front of the room.

"All right, jurors, I do want to thank you sincerely for the service you have provided over the past several weeks. I know it has been incredibly difficult at times for you and for your families but please do know your participation in these proceedings has been incredibly valuable." The judge then turned to a clerk on her right and asked, "Mr. Grantham, do you have the envelope with the sealed verdict forms, and if so, would you please hand them to Deputy Bryant?"

The clerk strode over to the deputy, clutching the envelope close to his abdomen. Once he had accepted it from the clerk, the deputy held it loose and fluttered it like a small fan.

"And Deputy Bryant, would you now hand the envelope to the foreperson of the jury, juror number one?" As the deputy came forward, the judge continued, "Madam Foreperson, would you review the verdict forms and check them to ensure they are the verdict forms you signed in the jury room?"

The foreperson took several moments reviewing each form. To Shevonda, this was always the most excruciating moment in a trial, made almost unbearable here by the many weeks of moment-by-moment media coverage that had turned the spectacle into a national obsession.

An eternity seemed to pass. Then the foreperson closed the flap on the envelope and said, "Your Honor, I attest that these forms are valid and contain the verdicts of the cases before us."

"Thank you," the judge replied. "All right, ladies and gentlemen of the jury, I'm going to ask that you carefully listen to the verdicts as they are being read by the clerk, for after Mr. Grantham has finished, I will ask you if these are, indeed, your verdicts. And I want to strongly warn the audience to remain calm during the reading of these verdicts. This has been a very emotional trial for many of you, I know. However, I have to emphasize that if anyone causes a disruption to these proceedings, I will instruct the bailiffs to have you removed immediately."

Shevonda tensed her muscles at this sentence—the rattlesnake coiled.

"All right, then, Mr. Grantham . . ." The judge nodded at the clerk to open the envelope, then turned forward. "Mr. Valenzuela would you please stand and face the jury?"

The clerk barreled into the reading of the verdicts more quickly than Shevonda had ever seen before—another example, she decided, of everyone's edginess and their desire to put a very quick end to a very silly circus.

"Superior Court of Florida, County of Miami-Dade. In the matter of People of the State of Florida versus Victor Xerxes Valenzuela, case number JH06655. We, the jury, in the above-entitled action, find the Defendant, Victor Xerxes Valenzuela of Coral Gables, NOT GUILTY . . ."

"Glory be!" exulted one of Valenzuela's attorneys. Quickly, however, the attorney reined himself in.

". . . of the crime of murder, in violation of penal code section 172(A), a felony, upon Erika Lindstrom Valenzuela, a human being, as charged in Count I of the information."

A soft gasp went up in the courtroom, followed by someone bursting into sobs. Shevonda scanned the room like a laser, but she focused not on people's faces but on their hands. Their hands . . . and nothing else.

The defendant slumped slightly, smiled, placed one hand on the shoulder of one of his attorneys and presented the palm of his other hand to the jury as a sign of appreciation for the verdict. Another defense attorney removed his glasses and slowly swept tears from the corners of his eyes.

The district attorneys sat stoic in their chairs, paralyzed and pale.

The clerk continued. "Superior Court of the State of Florida,

County of Dade, in the matter of People of the State of Florida versus Victor Xerxes Valenzuela. We, the jury, in the above-entitled action, find the Defendant, Victor Xerxes Valenzuela, NOT GUILTY of the crime of murder in violation of penal code section 172(A), a felony, upon Javier Alejandro Duran, a human being, as charged in Count II of the information."

The sobbing grew louder and the murmuring became more animated and widespread. The judge dropped her gavel quietly. "I will ask again for quiet in the courtroom, please."

"Signed this twenty-fourth day of May. Juror 115," the clerk concluded.

"Ladies and gentlemen of the jury, so say you all that this is your verdict?" the judge asked.

"We do," the jury replied in unison.

With that, one entire row occupied by members of the slain lover's family charged out of the courtroom, banging the door against the wall as they exited. Muffled sobbing continued from one of the back rows, but otherwise the room was silent.

Against the far wall, the serpent remained vigilant.

Once all the jurors had been polled as to the correctness of the verdict, the judge said, "All right. Ladies and gentlemen of the jury, I now excuse you from further service on this case. Thank you again for your contributions to this county's judicial process. I will be chatting with you shortly. These proceedings are officially adjourned."

As the crowd milled around slowly, as the reporters flashed pictures with their cell phones and surged toward the attorneys for interviews, as the defense attorneys clasped hands in the center of the table, Shevonda Jackson remained taut along the wall of the room, absorbing it all with dispassionate detachment.

However, after a few moments of watching the hubbub around her, after the many weeks of arguments, objections, recesses, and postponements, she could no longer remain completely silent on the matter.

As quietly as possible, in a soft, restrained fury, she muttered, "I can't believe that asshole got away with it."

2

GOTTEN WORD IT'S TIME FOR US 2 MOVE. HAVE U BEEN PROPERLY BRIEFED? ANY QUESTIONS?

The text message glared from the screen. Insistent. Unavoidable.

PROPERLY BRIEFED, came the reply. NO QUESTIONS.

GOOD. THEN B READY TO . . .

GOT 2 BE HONEST. A LITTLE NERVOUS HERE.

There was a pause at the other end. The sender wondered if making that confession would result in some sort of reprimand.

To the contrary, what came back was . . . understanding. Empathy, even.

OF COURSE U R NERVOUS. I WAS, TOO, BEFORE MY FIRST. NERVOUS IS NORMAL. WOULD WORRY IF U WERENT NERVOUS.

A short pause, followed by . . .

TAP INTO THAT NERVOUS ENERGY TO COMPLETE YOUR TASK AS SWIFTLY AS U POSSIBLY CAN. TAKE 2 QUICK STRIKES, MAYBE 3. U MUST B EFFICIENT. THEN, U MUST GET OUT OF THERE.

A moment to think about that. Then . . .

YOU DO KNOW HOW MUCH I WANT 2 DO THIS, DON'T

YOU? I'M NOT NERVOUS OUT OF FEAR. NERVOUS OUT OF . . . EXCITEMENT.

YES, WE KNOW. WE ARE VERY GRATEFUL FOR YOUR COMMITMENT TO THE TRANSFORMATION. WE ALL LOOK FORWARD TO WELCOMING U INTO THE FOLD. EVERYONE IS EAGER TO MEET U, TO SHARE OUR FELLOWSHIP WITH U. IT IS WONDERFUL HERE. U WILL LOVE BEING ONE WITH US. WE ARE EVEN PLANNING A PARTY FOR U, A WELCOME FOR OUR NEWEST SUPERSTAR!

A reflective sigh on the other end. Then, a smile, followed by thumbs flying.

CANT WAIT 2 MEET MY CONRADES EITHER! I WILL NOT DISAPPOINT!

There was a long pause. It seemed the conversation had ended.

But then . . .

GOOD. MAKE SURE THAT YOU DONT.

3

Lara Järvinen was the first to arrive at The Lee Group's conference room. She almost always was. On those rare instances when she wasn't, the firm's founder and lead architect, Dalton Lee, was certain to be the one to have preceded her.

Being the second-in-command, she took a minute to glance around the room to make sure everything was as it should be. She was gratified to see that the new administrative assistant had placed the correct number of chairs around the table and set the requisite bottles of water at each place. She was dismayed, however, to see a couple of remnants of copy paper, or torn napkin, scattered here or there on the carpet. Frowning, she bent over to collect the scraps and then tossed them into the recycle bin near the front door.

She knew that after Lee, the others would invariably, randomly, straggle in, signs of procrastination that irked her to no end yet resisted every effort she made to eliminate them. Of everyone on the team, Bree was the one she could rely on most for punctuality, but the junior architect also had the frustrating tendency of jumping up at the last minute and dashing back to her office for something that she MUST HAVE WITH HER in the meeting—her acrylic clipboard decorated with daisies, or her oversized mug of herbal tea, or her favorite pen with that ridiculous ponytail made of real horsehair that dangled from the eraser end, a souvenir she had brought back after a visit to her family in Arizona. On one occasion, Bree had left the room and gone back to her office to retrieve something THREE DIFFERENT TIMES before the meeting could get started. But Lara remembered with more than a whiff of satisfaction that the icy glare she had given the young woman the last time she had stepped back into the conference area had seemed to squelch *that* shtick forevermore.

Warren, the other junior architect, would usually come barreling in and dive-bomb into a chair at least three or four minutes after Lee had gotten things underway. He would always be muttering a heartfelt apology, but would *always* come barreling in, *always* a few minutes late. Irene would arrive shortly before or after Warren. Being the youngest and (dare Lara indulge in stereotype?) Asian, her head would always be buried in either her phone, her tablet or her oversized laptop computer, often to the point of having to be asked a question two or three times just to get a response out of her.

Roberto was the least predictable of them all. Well, she took that back. The talented designer was actually the *most* predictable in that he was *never* one of the first to arrive. When he did eventually saunter in, padding quietly along the farthest wall so as not to disturb, he often did so with his arms wrapped tightly around his torso, his head tilted downward, a scowl on his grizzled face. Lara had to give him credit for being respectful whenever he arrived. Her concern wasn't really with *how* he showed up at a meeting but with whether he would show up at all. These days, he frequently didn't.

She missed Jayden. The young Tennessean had always been on time, freshly pressed, sunny in disposition, cracking some corny joke he had read online somewhere that morning. He was the true Southern-American gentleman, a demeanor that, even though she was Scandinavian, she found heartwarming. But with Jayden's brother having been released from captivity after their adventure in Manhattan a year earlier, there was no longer any reason for him to stay with the firm.

Lara felt her soul dip toward sunset for a moment, darkened by the realization that everyone soon assembling was eager for the day they would no longer have to attend a meeting at The Lee Group. Especially a meeting such as this one.

Her thoughts turned to the new associate. *What was his name? Landon? Loren?* Lee had tossed it out so quickly in conversation she hadn't had a chance to absorb it. It was rumored he might join them for the meeting, but he wasn't really expected to, given that his flight from Sydney had arrived only that morning. To Lara's way of thinking, his qualifications were far from exemplary, but she had to trust Lee's judgment that they were solid enough. As an undergraduate at the University of Queensland, he'd pursued a concentration in microbiology (which probably wouldn't be of much use to the firm, she assumed), but he then had gone on to earn a graduate degree in something called Adaptive Architecture and Computation from the University of London.

And then, of course, there was his most relevant qualification of all—an older sister who had double-crossed an agent associated with The Organization and was soon abducted at knifepoint from the tennis resort outside Brisbane where she had been the club pro.

He was being brought on to the team to help Irene with whatever computer research—or hacking—they might need. Apparently he was an expert both at executing hacks and repelling them. A genius at something Irene referred to as *spear phishing*? And *logic bombs*?

She shook her head, sighed, began to rub the bony middle knuckle of her left hand with the thumb of her right. *I hope he isn't a dreadful bore,* she thought.

The door nudged open. It was her superior.

"Am I . . . disturbing you?" Lee asked.

"No, no, come on in. I had just drifted off into one of my reveries."

The head of The Lee Group strode in, his chest puffed out even more than usual.

"Good news?" Lara asked.

Lee raised both eyebrows and widened his eyes somewhat. "GREAT news, on the business front. It appears Harriman Tower is going to come in on time and a tad under budget. And I received an encouraging email from the development corporation in Hong Kong about the office tower project there that they contacted us about back in December." He removed the cap to the bottle of water in front of him and took from it a triumphant swig.

Lara nodded but said nothing. As the business manager for the firm, it was her role to ensure business flowed into the organization and projects got executed to a client's satisfaction. But in truth, those were the aspects of the job she cared least about. Design was her passion. She would much rather be working side by side with Lee, deciding how the lines of a building should reflect the function intended for it, engaging him in discussions about view corridors and rights of light . . .

"By the way, I think we may need to look for a new housekeeping firm," she suddenly announced. "I must have found three or four pieces of scrap paper on the carpet when I arrived here."

Lee wrinkled his nose. "Yes, I've been noticing more dust here and there as well. I know we've been dealing with Santa Ana winds recently, but that really shouldn't be an excuse."

Bree suddenly pushed through the glass door, and Lara noted with relief the younger architect was clutching to her breast the appliqued clipboard and numerous papers she usually went back for. "Sorry, I'm not late, am I?" she asked hesitantly.

"No, no, right on time," Lee replied.

Much to Lara's surprise, Warren stepped in immediately afterward, offering news rather than an apology. "Dalton, I just got a call from the facilities director with GlobeX Financial," he said in a rush. "They seem to be reconsidering some of the materials we recommended for their branches in Dubai and Abu Dhabi. Do you want me to handle it, or do you want to discuss it with them?"

The lead architect sighed and one side of his mouth slid southward a bit. "Well, in light of their most recent earnings report, I can't say I'm really surprised. No, I'll handle it. I'd rather they not compromise on the look of the finishes, but I can think of some alternatives that might work for them. I'll call them before the end of the day."

Warren slid into a seat next to Bree. "Is the new guy going to be here?" he tossed out to the whole room.

Lara looked for an answer from Lee, who shook his head. "Doubtful," he answered. "He took the nonstop from Sydney to L.A.

20

Fourteen hours. The jet lag from that trip is a real killer."

Everyone looked askance at their superior, who chuckled and winced at his ironic use of the word.

"Sorry," he offered, just as Irene skittered into the room and a chair all in one deft move. She was cradling her laptop and its power cord the way Bree had been embracing her clipboard and papers, and she spent the next couple of minutes with her head beneath the table in a labored effort to get the computer plugged into the floor outlet and Ethernet connection.

Lee looked around the table. "So, we are all here . . . except for Roberto?" He turned to look at Lara who shrugged her shoulders and gently shook her head. The architect nodded once, then said, "Well, then, let's go ahead and get this underway."

"Oh wait!"

It was Bree, leaping up from her seat. Across the table, Lara slumped and issued a none-too-discreet frown.

"I'm sorry, I meant to bring my knitting. Go ahead and start without me. I'll just be a sec."

Once Bree had cleared the door, Lee began to update the team about new projects that had come their way or likely would be. An office tower in Buenos Aires. A casino in Macau. A mixed-use development outside Washington, D.C. and possibly the headquarters of a financial firm based in Milan. "It's all good," he said, a boyish grin spreading across his face. He then clapped his hands dramatically. "It's all very, VERY good."

Bree ducked quietly back into the room and retook her seat, a pair of knitting needles and a ball of yarn tucked beneath one arm. Once Bree had gotten herself situated and had begun to slowly knit, Lara turned back toward her boss and noted how she hadn't seen him this upbeat in at least a year. He certainly seemed to have shaken off the torpor and gloom he had lugged around with him like a heavy knapsack when they were dealing with the situation in Manhattan last year.

But sure as she said that, she noticed his expression dip somewhat. He cleared his throat and scratched behind one ear.

"Before I ask you to give your updates on our current assignments, there is something I need to tell you," he began, seeming to rise up a couple of inches in his chair. "I know that our experience in New York last fall turned out to be far more unsettling than we anticipated. It reminded this group in particular, that as much as we wanted to believe that The Organization had been permanently subdued, and that the safe return of our friends and loved ones was months or perhaps only weeks away, it reminded us that, instead, they have regrouped and are now . . ." He trailed off, shifting his gaze from a point somewhere over one of Irene's shoulders to a spot beyond the conference room's glass walls where the other employees were advancing the firm's agendas.

Lara leaned forward slightly, placed one palm on his nearest forearm.

"Has something happened?" Warren asked. "What's going on? You would have called some of the other associates in here if there wasn't something going on with . . ."

Lee dipped his head to one side. "We're not sure," he replied slowly. "There's been chatter. About sleeper cells being activated. Of some sort of . . . initiative getting underway. Of their . . . relocating some of the hostages."

With that, everyone leaned forward and waited, to learn more about the circumstance of a sibling, a friend, a spouse—or in Lee's case—a mother and father.

The architect drew his lips into a tight thin line and rapidly shook his head several times as if clearing a shallow fog.

"We just don't know," he finally said. "But something, somewhere is poised to happen." He drew his lips together as if to whistle, but gently blew air out between them instead. "We don't want to acknowledge it, but these terrorists will likely be dogging us in some form or fashion for quite some time. They detest everything our society stands for and, as we've seen before, will stop at nothing to wrest control of our freedoms as well as our family members. They are angry, they are cagey, they are committed, and they know how to strike when we least expect them to." He was quiet for several seconds, mulling over the words with which to end his monologue.

Finally he nodded and simply said, "We must be vigilant."

His words floated there above them all for many seconds as they mused upon the possibilities and the frustration they felt at being confined to wondering . . . and waiting.

Over time, Lee allowed a smile to replace the concern on his face. "But I insist we focus on the positive side of things and rejoice in the fact we were able to locate the person responsible for the murders of Caitlyn and Cullen Drysdale in Manhattan and bring someone home from captivity as a result."

His employees echoed his comments, but the enthusiasm was muted.

Just then, the conference room door pushed open and a tall, broad-shouldered male in his early thirties stepped in. He was wearing a poncho-style shirt, jeans, flip-flops and a wide, movie-star smile. A necklace made of puka shells stood out against his dark tan. He reached up, ran a hand through a thick shock of wavy dark hair, then thrust both hands onto his hips, elbows jutting out to either side.

"Well, hello everybody. I was told this was where the meeting was taking place?"

Everyone sat silent, taking in and assessing the stranger. After a couple of seconds, his bright expression faded into a look of puzzlement as the room remained motionless. Suddenly, he brightened once more.

"Aw, I get it. You were probably expecting me to say, 'G'day mates,' weren't you?"

"Liam! Liam Wilding!" Lee exclaimed, rising from his chair and striding over to shake the young man's hand. "This is our new associate everyone. So you decided to join us, after all?"

The new employee nodded toward the team and turned back to Lee. "Yeah, well, I got a lot of sleep on the flight for a change. And I knew this was the most important meeting for the week, so I decided to shake off the old jet lag and haul myself up here to meet everybody."

Lee motioned Wilding closer to the table. "Let me introduce you," he said, but before he could begin, Liam extended a tanned forearm out across Lee's chest to stop his new boss from going any further.

"If you don't mind, Dalton. I'd like to test how well I did my homework on the flight over," he said, winking. Lee stepped back and made a sweeping gesture indicating his new employee should have at it. "Let's see, since she is face-deep into her laptop, I am assuming that the young lady back there is Irene, who I *very much* look forward to working with ..."

The young girl did not react until Warren leaned over and nudged her in the arm. At that, she turned, nodded, and flashed a quick grin before returning to her computer screen.

Liam scanned the room and landed on Lara. "You, of course, would be our trusted navigator and pilot, Ms. Järvinen," he said, nodding in her direction. She smiled and returned the nod emphatically. He wheeled around, pointed at Warren and squinted.

"You . . . don't look like a Roberto to me," he said, flashing another broad grin. "Which means you are probably . . . Warren."

"I am," the designer replied, smiling.

"When are we going to our first hockey game?" Liam countered quickly.

Warren looked around, bemused. "Tonight, I guess!" he said, chuckling. "Except, I think it's an away game."

"No worries! I'm happy to take a rain check on that," Liam answered.

The Australian placed his hands back on his hips, widened his stance some, scanned the room again, then turned to Lee.

"Roberto isn't here," he said more as a statement than a question.

"No . . . not yet, anyway," Lee replied. Liam waited for more but, not getting it, nodded and then slowly began to circumnavigate the front end of the table. He strolled over to Bree, took her free hand in his, cocked his head slightly and smiled gently at her. "So then this *has* to be the Bree I have heard *so much* about."

Bree looked up at the new recruit and blinked several times but said nothing.

From underneath the tabletop, however, she felt the ball of yarn roll off her lap and drop onto the carpet below.

4

Propped on all fours, the escort splayed her legs farther apart on the bed, enabling Jamal Culberson to move in a little closer from behind.

"Like this?" he said, looking over his shoulder at David Diaz, his reliable blocker who was framing the shot with his camera phone. Diaz exhaled loudly at what he saw and said, "Hell yes, dude. JUST like that." Culberson bumped his groin against the hooker, who giggled.

Leaning against the opposite wall, Drew Mendenhall threw an imaginary pass to his favorite target on the Miami A&M football team. "What do you know, Culberson?" he sneered. "For once, it looks like you might not be the premier wide receiver in the room." Once the quarterback had allowed his passing arm to drop to his side, he pushed himself away from the wall, stood up straight, edged closer to the bed and went back to stroking himself as his teammate began to fully penetrate the escort for the first time.

Diaz moved in closer as the wide receiver began to get serious. After a couple of moments, Mendenhall taunted, "You really seem to know what you're doing there, Jamal. Which animal on that farm of yours back in Mississippi taught you how to do that?" The quarterback scoffed a little after his remark, which the wide receiver answered with a middle finger upturned from his right hand. When Culberson lowered the gesture, he spanked the redhead lightly with his palm, then reached forward and collected several strands of her hair so he could pull her head back toward him.

"Better . . . some female sheep, Mendenhall . . . than one of them choir boys you probably played 'hide the corn cob' with . . . at that prep school you went to," he blurted out between breaths.

The jovial air soon evaporated; the sex became more earnest. The girl began to whimper and moan as Jamal now pumped seriously into her. Diaz lumbered his beefy nakedness in a semicircle around the pair, breathing heavily as he watched the action on his phone. Their quarterback inched nearer as well, until he stood right up against one side of the bed. In a low voice he sneered, "Give it to her, Jamal. Pound her hard. Make her want it. Get her ready for me."

Then, the room seemed to explode as the door flew open.

"What in the HELL do you guys think you are doing?!" the intruder bellowed. The action froze into a surreal form of suspended animation as the foursome tried to recalibrate from being participants of carnal sex to targets of frightful rage.

"Shit . . . Coach . . . we . . ." the quarterback stammered, backing away from the bed and dropping his hands in a frantic attempt at pointless modesty. Diaz let the camera lens dip toward the ground and stood terrified, his mouth agape. Jamal held tight to the hips of the escort but discreetly slid himself back out of her. His erection peeked out from above her buttocks but withdrew from sight when he lowered himself back onto his muscular haunches.

Assuming his familiar role as team leader, the quarterback stepped forward to plead their case. Then, remembering he was completely naked in front of the person most responsible for his four-year scholarship, he quickly backpedaled toward the wall.

"Coach . . . we're sorry. We're really, *really* sorry," he said. "You said we could use your guest house whenever we wanted to and your housekeeper told us that with the trial over and all, you planned to be in California through Sunday night, so . . . but . . . we shouldn't have . . . and . . ."

Valenzuela thrust his left palm out toward his quarterback as a sign for him to shut up. He maintained a sweeping stance just inside the doorway and intently surveyed the disheveled, sordid scene. He returned to his rant, although his face had lost the crimson it bore when he first stormed through the doorway.

"I SAID, what in the hell do you guys think you are doing?!" he repeated, but with only about half as much fury as before. Then, they watched as his grimace gradually transformed into a wicked smile. He softened his voice even more and his tone turned mocking. "What in the hell do all of you think you are doing . . . entertaining such a gorgeous babe like this and not inviting me to the party?"

For several moments, it felt as if someone had vacuumed all sound from the room. Eventually, one of the players quickly snorted. Valenzuela sauntered toward the hooker, who was looking doe-eyed at the coach. As he did, he yanked at his belt, whipped it through the loops, and tossed it into a distant corner.

"What's your name, beautiful?" he said softly, as he rapidly unbuttoned his heavily starched dress shirt. The fabric fell away, revealing solid, broad pecs blanketed with curly dark hair and a taut stomach with impressive abdominals beneath.

"Krystal," she replied, still not sure how she should actually respond to what was happening.

"Krystal," he repeated, his shirt now in a heap on the floor. "What a lovely name." He paused for a moment, then said, "Well . . . *Krystal . . .* have you ever . . . *done any*?"

He flashed another smile and, as he drew nearer, unconsciously (or subconsciously) flexed his bulging triceps.

"Once," she said, smiling up at him. "I didn't really like it."

He was standing a few inches away from her now. With his right hand he reached out and swept the lush, auburn hair away from her face.

"Ah. I see . . . I'm so sorry about that," he replied, his face assuming an exaggerated frown.

Then he went quiet again, held the room for several seconds in agonizing suspense. Slowly, however, he transformed his downcast expression into a lascivious smile.

"Well then, Krystal, tell me, have you ever puffed on a Fonseca Grande?"

Across the room his quarterback chuckled into his left fist; he understood the joke. Krystal, however, didn't have a clue.

"I . . . uh . . . don't think so," she said cautiously smiling at the punch line that still eluded her.

Vic Valenzuela swiveled his torso away from her and extended his arms out toward his players.

"Gentlemen, this young lady has never had the honor of tasting a Fonseca Grande," he announced with mock incredulity. "That is truly a shame. Don't all of you think this young lady should know at least once in her lifetime what's it like to puff on such a Cuban . . . delicacy?"

The players snickered, but more out of duty than conspiracy. They weren't entirely sure where this was headed . . . or whether they really should be going along with it.

The coach strode forward, stopping just a few inches from the prostitute. As he did so, he deftly undid the clasp on his waistband, quickly unzipped, inserted his extended fingers into the top of his waistband and thrust downward both his slacks and the crisp white boxers underneath, until gravity took over and sent both items tumbling to his ankles.

From behind the hooker, the team's wide receiver let out a low whistle. Leaning against the far wall again, his quarterback whispered, "Damn. . ."

The escort's eyes widened at the enormously long and thick appendage that bobbed just in front of her. Then she looked up at the leering coach and flirtatiously wet her lips.

"I thought you looked like the type who'd enjoy puffing on a big, fat Cuban cigar," he said, stepping out of the heap of clothing that now lay on the carpeting. He turned to the lineman on his right and nodded toward the camera. "Diaz, shut that thing off. Men, return to the formation you were in when I got here."

Mendenhall and Martinez looked at each other across the bed, shrugged, and cautiously circled in closer. The wide receiver lifted himself off of his haunches and waited for further instructions.

Vic Valenzuela widened his stance and moved right up to the escort's face. Pressing himself up against her, he looked down at her with thinly veiled disdain, took her chin in one hand, lightly slapped her left cheek and said, "Men, I think maybe it's time we show this little slut exactly what we Centurions mean when we say, 'All for one and one for all.'"

5

Later that night, in his billowy dream, Vic Valenzuela was floating. Not on some luxurious yacht, but on an elegantly simple, streamlined schooner with masts made of gold and sails spun from silk.

Across from him reclined a woman half his age, sporting languorous legs and oversized sunglasses. Maybachs, most likely, or maybe Chopard De Rigo. She gazed not at him but at some point on the horizon; her tresses stretched straight out behind her as if it were they, not the sails, that were propelling the boat forward.

He extended his right arm over the side of the boat and dipped two fingers into the water . . . felt the liquid race over them, around them, and sometimes in-between them.

Freedom.

He started to say something, decided not to. Instead, he studied the supple space at which her neck met her breastbone. Smooth, blemish-free, tight yet vulnerable.

So *very* vulnerable, it had been . . .

Serenity reigned as the boat whisked along the surface of the ocean. Obviously there were breezes about, but he did not hear them. If there were seabirds nearby, they soared past in silence. The craft cut through the water like a knife slicing through . . .

Suddenly, a click. He looked up. A sail detaching from the mast, perhaps?

Then a scraping sound and a soft thud. He stirred, sighed, confronted darkness and warmth. The coach rolled onto one side, exhaled deeply, and tried to recapture the glide of the sailboat, reconnect with the scent of the sea.

Another thud, slightly louder this time. He was fully awake now and detected another presence in the room. Raising himself onto his elbows, he blinked at the shadows to calibrate his vision.

"Hey. What's going on? What are *you* doing here? Is something the matter?"

The form sprinted across the room so spryly, revealed the dagger so rapidly, the coach didn't have time to react. The first stab was ill-aimed and ragged, grazing one ventricle at an obtuse angle. Blood first spurted like the arc from a water fountain, then settled into a low, steady gurgle as the winningest coach in all of football clutched the sheets and gasped for air.

The second strike was more precise, severing a lung almost completely in two.

The attacker first paused as the body sagged lifeless, then felt disgust surge up from within.

One more for good measure, a shallow pierce that trenched the spleen nonetheless. The assailant took a couple of moments to survey the outcome before reaching into a pocket, extracting the calling card so important to the assignment, and tossing it unceremoniously onto the now-soggy body.

Moments later, as the specter exited through the window it had entered, Victor Xerxes Valenzuela once again found himself floating out at sea.

Only this time the ocean was a viscous crimson, the sky above, a lackluster black.

6

"What's an eight-letter word for watercrafts? Begins with 'R.'"

Lee swiveled toward Lara, who was in the aisle seat beside him. They were somewhere over eastern Arkansas, or maybe the Mississippi Delta—he was never sure because that section of the country all looked the same to him. He thought he had noticed the plane crossing the Mississippi River a few minutes earlier. But then again, it might have been the Arkansas River. An expert on belfries and cantilevers, Lee was clueless when it came to rivers and tributaries.

Except, of course, for the River Cam, the graceful waterway he had cherished so as a graduate student of architecture at Cambridge.

"Another acrostic has you stumped, Dalton?" Lara replied, not taking her eyes off of the novel she was reading. "You're really off your game, these days, aren't you?"

Lee swallowed, looked back at the puzzle magazine on the seat tray in front of him.

"No," he said with much less confidence than he had intended. The architect quietly cleared his throat. "*No*," he said with more bravado. "I know the answer." He paused, waited for her to turn to him.

She finally did.

"I just wanted to see if *you* knew what it was," he added,

unconvincingly.

Over her glasses, she peered at him with a look that straddled bemusement and boredom. "Rowboats," she said directly. As she returned to the pages of her paperback, she shifted her weight in the leather seat, which Lee took as a subtle emphasis of her victory.

The architect bit his lower lip and silently counted the number of blanks in the answer. "Well, you're right, Lara!" he exhorted too enthusiastically. As discreetly as he could, he closed the cover of the magazine so she wouldn't see that, in fact, he hadn't yet filled in the blanks for that clue.

The architect clasped his hands together, situated them atop the puzzle book and looked back out the window. A thin layer of cirrus clouds lined the altitude at which they were flying; up ahead, however, they gradually diminished and the sky seemed to take on a deeper shade of blue. He turned back toward Lara, who was closing the cover of her book which, based on its cover, seemed to be a tale lodged somewhere between that of a bodice ripper and a spy thriller.

"Have you been to Miami before?" he asked his associate, taking a sip of the signature bourbon the flight attendant had served him.

She gave him a slightly softer version of the look she had offered him when he claimed he knew the answer to the acrostic clue.

"Miami is in Florida, correct?" she replied. Lee nodded.

"The first four things that come to mind when I hear 'Florida' are alligators, hurricanes, questionable election results, and outrageous real estate scams," she continued. "So, remind me why I would ever, intentionally, go to Miami."

Lee smiled and shook his head.

"Well," he began, raising one eyebrow. "For one thing, it's the only major city in the United States that was planned by a woman. I bet you didn't know that." Lara raised her eyebrows some in response, indicating she perhaps had some interest in this tidbit.

"I bet you also didn't know it was the city that installed the very first automated teller machine for rollerbladers." At that comment, she grimaced and shook her head.

Lee's smile became mischievous. "And, it has a lot of men over the age of fifty who are wealthy *and* single."

She replied with a *pffft* and turned away in mock disgust. She began to scrutinize the passengers across the aisle, pretend to be interested in what they were reading. Lee held his smile for several seconds, but when she did not turn back to him, he shook his head once more and opened once more the cover of his puzzle magazine.

She was back. "Why on earth would you think that because I am over fifty, the only men I would be interested in would be those who are also over fifty?"

He didn't have an answer for that. Not a good one, anyway. So he folded his right wrist over his left and turned to study the clouds once more.

But she wasn't finished.

"I've meant to ask you, Dalton, do you ever wish you hadn't solved the murder of Congresswoman Hirshhorn? Do you ever wonder what your life would be like . . . how all of *our* lives might be different . . . if you hadn't taken down their second-in-command back then? If you hadn't gotten us so enmeshed in this exasperating cat-and-mouse game we keep playing with them?" She had asked him everything in a whisper, but her tone was as fervent as could be.

Now, *he* held *her* suspense for several seconds, noticing more fully the sunshine that was brightening the cabin more and more as they hurtled eastward. When he finally refocused his attention on the woman he relied upon to run his business for him, he was smiling from ear to ear.

"But I did get us enmeshed, didn't I?" he replied.

***

Outside the baggage claim, two town cars were awaiting the team. Roberto, holding true to his commitment to create as small a carbon footprint as possible, opted to take a bus to the hotel. The designer was especially disappointed when he learned hotel reservations had been made for them not in Miami Beach, but in downtown Miami.

"*Chacho, man!*" he exclaimed as he plucked his canvas duffle from the carousel. "That's a good ten minutes from the beach!"

The head of The Lee Group gave his colleague a disapproving look.

"We're here to solve a murder, Roberto, not catch some rays," he said brusquely. The architect then lowered his head and his voice. "And, for all we know, to prevent another terrorist attack of some sort. Let's not forget that, shall we?"

That darkened the group's mood . . . until the town car emerged from the dark, exhaust-laden, lower-level arrival area and glided into a brilliant South Florida afternoon. Through the window next to him, Dalton Lee looked up at the sun, beamed, and reached into his breast pocket for his sunglasses. He lowered the window a couple of inches and was pleased to discover the air felt more "crisp Californian" than "thick Floridian"; the aqua-colored sky was almost cloud-free. The salsa tune that was blaring from the lowered windows of the car next to them provided a festive backdrop to their grand arrival.

But given what he had been told before they had left Southern California, Lee was certain their stay in South Florida would be anything but festive.

Lara turned toward her colleague and nudged his elbow.

"Is it just me, or is that the most depressing airport arrival area you've ever seen?" she said gravely.

Lee smiled, ducked his head some. "Well, maybe not the worst I have seen in *the entire world*," he replied, tugging at one ear. "But, yes, I would have to agree that it's pretty dreary. A bit more sunlight could do wonders for that place."

Rather than fade away, the discussion about architecture only accelerated as did the car on the Dolphin Expressway. Within moments, they were cruising past Marlins Park, the home of the city's major league baseball franchise and the first retractable-roof building in the world to receive an LEED Gold environmental certification. Like a young giraffe, Warren craned his head toward the structure. He found its futuristic, spaceship-like design exhilarating, but Lara deemed it, "just another hat box on steroids." She took the moment to also express her disappointment with the flora along the stretch of freeway they were travelling on.

"I was expecting many more palm trees than this," she sniffed.

They crossed the river and to their right, the buildings of downtown Miami and Brickell appeared before them, looking like the individual entries in a bar graph. On the left side of the highway, the cool, contemporary façade of the Gerstein Justice Building hugged the opposite guardrail, its square windows blocking their view north for several seconds. Once it retreated behind them, however, they felt themselves in the heart of the city, and within just a couple of minutes, they were cruising slowly through the streets of downtown.

Lara sat up alert as they slid past the glistening-white Adrienne Arsht Center for the Performing Arts. "That looks like it was designed by a Finn!" she exclaimed, marveling at the building's interesting juxtaposition of a tilted, flat wall of glass surrounded by jagged, iceberg-like wings.

They were headed south on Biscayne Boulevard now, and only a few blocks from their hotel. But the trip held one more delight for them, an architectural gem Lee found a special wonder in. Built in 1925 as the headquarters and printing plant for the *Miami News*, Freedom Tower resembled an elegant needle. Lee, Lara, and Warren all admired the building's Mediterranean Revival styling and the many design elements it borrowed from La Giralda in Seville, Spain. Warren was especially taken by the ornate cupola that perched atop the tower and housed a decorative beacon.

"We need to think about incorporating something like that into one of our next projects," he muttered softly.

Lee smiled and nodded. "I just hope everyone in the other car noticed and enjoyed those buildings as much as we did," he said as the car curved into their hotel's semi-circular entranceway.

The young man behind the registration desk handed Lee a note that sent askew their plans for the afternoon. A water pipe had burst inside the federal building in which their local contacts worked. So the decision was made to meet briefly that afternoon at a warehouse the Feds used periodically at the edge of downtown.

"I'm happy to host everyone in my suite," Lee offered the agents.

"Not a good idea, Mr. Lee," his contact told him on the phone. "We can't be sure your room wasn't bugged before your arrival."

That caused Lee to pull up short. *Someone might always be listening to me*, he mused. He gave that careful consideration for several seconds. *I'm not very comfortable with that*, he finally decided. *No, I don't like that AT ALL.*

***

Three hours later, as the sun was beginning its descent in the west, the team found itself standing in an empty parking lot littered with shattered glass and flattened paper cups. Everyone was gazing dubiously at the warehouse in front of them; at times Irene and Lara glanced over one shoulder with concern. Bree decided to be the first to broach the prevailing skepticism.

"I don't think this is it," she said to Lee, who was standing with his hands on his hips, his head tilted up at the hulking edifice.

"Well, it appears to be the right *address,*" he said tentatively, pointing to a series of numbers above the doorway in front of him. The two-story structure was anything but nondescript—graffiti covered most of the brick wall facing the parking lot that Bree and the rest of the team stood in. Those sections of the brick not covered with graffiti bore the faded remnants of once-colorful posters vaguely promoting some outdoor "*concierto*" or "*festival*" that had taken place several months—or even years—earlier. The building had two small rectangular windows, which were located above and on either side of the iron barricade that appeared to serve as the building's front door. But views into both were effectively blocked by either yellowed newspapers or soot-gray grime.

Lee glanced at the information he had called up on his phone, looked back at the door, stepped forward, and pressed a small pearl-white button barely visible to the right of the doorknob.

For several seconds, nothing happened. Lara tapped one foot impatiently and looked around the lot. Bree began to fan herself with a manila folder bearing documents she had brought for the meeting. Roberto quietly faded away from his associates and began to make slow circles in a far section of the lot, his arms wrapped around his torso. The rest of the team stood silent, studying the cracked asphalt beneath them.

"I hope someone comes soon," Lara finally said. "It's getting rather warm."

Lee balanced himself on one foot, leaned forward, extended a finger, and pressed the button again. Nothing . . . then, finally, they faintly detected a series of quick footsteps followed by the unlocking of several deadbolts from within. A thick wooden door behind the iron door opened, and a short, middle-aged Hispanic man nodded at them.

"Mr. Lee?" was all he said.

"Yes," was all the architect said in reply.

Immediately inside the door was a steep and narrow staircase they carefully ascended. "I don't know why you always insist on wearing heels to these meetings," Roberto said to Bree, poking her in the back as she wobbled up the stairs in front of him. She glanced back over one shoulder and flashed a quick smile. *Well, his humor seems to be returning to him,* she thought, followed by, *It's about damned time.*

The second floor of the warehouse completely belied the appearance of the exterior. It wasn't luxurious, but it was equipped with a brigade of sturdy metal desks almost camouflaged with power and Ethernet cords. A skylight stretched the length of the ceiling, allowing in natural light otherwise blocked by the papered-up windows. A variety of seating options were scattered throughout the long rectangular room—a love seat over here, a swivel chair over there.

But the room was void of human beings, save for one young man in a white short-sleeve dress shirt who was seated at a desk in a distant corner, leisurely turning the pages of a comic book.

A door in the back opened and a tall thin male in his early fifties with salt-and-pepper hair and onyx-black skin sauntered toward them, a blasé look on his face.

"Mr. Lee, I am Mackeson Sainclair," he said, slowly extending a hand toward the architect. From the precision with which the man enunciated his name, and the gentle lilt of his voice, Lee could tell their greeter was likely of Haitian descent. "I look forward to our working together."

Although their host was pleasant, he did not smile. "Did your flight go smoothly? Have you and your team gotten settled in at the hotel?"

As Lee nodded, he noticed the generous size of the agent's hands and how long and attenuated the fingers were. There were no watches or rings on display; the only evidence of any bling on Mackeson

Sainclair was the simple, gold-colored clasp at the bottom of his navy blue tie.

"Do people call you Mack?" the architect said jovially.

The agent looked down on Lee impassively. "No. They call me Mackeson," he replied. Lee's smile soured slightly. The agent then scanned the rest of the group, clapped his hands lightly in front of him, and said, "Well then, *kite yo ale*. This way."

As they paraded toward the door out of which Mackeson Sainclair had emerged, the federal agent glanced at a round wall clock like those once found in most any classroom. He stopped in his tracks.

"Marcus," he said to the young man who had been enjoying the comic book. "What time is the eighth race at Hialeah today?"

The young man scratched the bridge of his nose and ran the inside of his fingers back and forth across his lips as he considered the question.

"Four ten, I think. Maybe five after four. Something like that."

Sainclair looked back up at the clock, which read four fifteen. He grimaced and expelled a breath of frustration before resuming the march to the back of the warehouse.

Upon entering the spacious meeting area beyond the door, Lee and his colleagues were surprised by the presence of an agent they had worked with some on the case in New York.

"Hannah Weiss, isn't that correct?" Lee verified as he stepped forward to shake the hand of the diminutive young blonde.

"You have a very good memory," the agent replied, nodding at the rest of Lee's coterie as they assembled around her. Upon noticing Warren in the group, her expression became more serious. She walked over to him, extended one hand and patted him twice on the back of his arm.

"Mr. Jackson," she said with a definitive nod. "I'm so glad everything worked out the way it did in Central Park. That was . . . much too close for comfort."

Warren took in a deep breath, laughed nervously once. "Yes, I'm glad too," he replied. "And yes, it most definitely was." He gave her a strong nod of appreciation before Agent Sainclair communicated he was ready for things to get underway.

"Mr. Lee, we don't have much time this afternoon, and Agent Weiss and I apologize for the less-than-opulent surroundings here."

Lee took a chair and smiled to indicate he understood. "What do we know?" the architect said, taking on the federal agent's no-nonsense tone.

The question hung in the air for a few seconds before Agent Weiss responded by getting up out of her chair and taking a few steps toward Lee. "What we know is that we found *this* on Vic Valenzuela's body," she said, tossing a small card onto the architect's lap. As Lee reviewed the card, one side of his mouth twisted slightly downward.

Professor Humberto de la Cruz
Did It

"We've performed the routine analysis of it," Agent Weiss continued. "Like with all the others, there are no fingerprints. And you can feel the ridges in the paper. It's definitely from a first edition of *Wayward Colony*.

"We're certain it was someone connected to The Organization who committed the murder."

Lee turned the card over and over in his hand, as if it might suddenly, magically provide some additional explanation as to why a terrorist group determined to bring free nations under its domain would want to eliminate a college football coach.

"How did it happen . . . the murder, that is?" Lee asked.

Agent Sainclair had plucked a toothpick from a desk drawer and was using it to clean his teeth when the question arose. He took the toothpick from his mouth and raised up onto his toes a bit.

"Stabbed, in his sleep," he said matter-of-factly. The agent then checked himself. "Well, stabbed in his *bedroom* anyway. It appears the killer climbed up a trellis to the second floor and then entered the victim's bedroom through a balcony window. A partial footprint was found in some soil near the base of the trellis, and a little mud was on the trellis, which is why that is our dominant theory. But the footprint was very smooth. Extremely smooth. It's of little use, really."

Lee considered that for several seconds and nodded slowly.

"The plan is to go to Mr. Valenzuela's residence tomorrow to interview his assistant and some of the staff. I assume you'd like to be a part of that?" Gradually the federal agent resumed his oral-hygiene regimen.

Lee nodded, but said nothing for a few moments. Eventually he turned to Agent Weiss. "Anyone conveniently enter the coach's life recently? You know how they operate. Embed one of their own within the target's sphere of influence, execute their task, lay low long enough so the killer's departure doesn't draw much attention, then flee the scene. Or try to do all that, at least."

Agent Weiss was nodding as Lee spoke. "Yeah, well, that's going to be really difficult to determine in this case," she said. "This guy was a football coach. A *college* football coach. So there's players who've come and gone, assistant coaches and student trainers who have come and gone. And then add to that the fact he murdered his wife and her lover."

At that proclamation, everyone in the room turned their attention on her, well aware of the not guilty verdict that had been handed down a couple of weeks before. The agent cocked her head to one side, offered a look of calculated cynicism.

"He killed them. The prosecution may not have convinced the jury of that but . . ." She nodded decisively a couple of times. "Trust me, he killed them."

She returned to her basic thesis. "So, thanks to *that*, you can now add into the mix a whole platoon of attorneys and media handlers and the media reps themselves who shadowed him for at least a year . . ."

She sighed and dropped her right arm over the side of the chair she was sitting in. "The list of possible suspects is . . . enormous. And right now, we have no evidence. I mean, none whatsoever, unless you consider a nice little stash of cocaine inside a nightstand drawer 'evidence.' No one saw anything, no one heard anything, or at least if they did, no one is owning up to it. We haven't found a murder weapon. As Mackeson said, the partial footprint is of little use to us."

Her co-worker stood up straight again and leaned toward the group.

"There is a need to move quickly," he intoned. "You already know from your experience in Manhattan, Mr. Lee, that they tend to take an action like this right before they plan to launch one of their initiatives to . . ." The agent allowed the sentence to trail off, methodically resumed the flossing of his teeth with the toothpick.

The mood in the room went glum. For a few seconds, everyone looked down at the ground or into one of the far corners of the room. Eventually, Lee raised his left palm and began to stroke back and forth the area between his chin and his lower lip.

"The bedroom window . . . was it unlocked or had it been jimmied open?"

"There was no sign of forced entry," Agent Weiss replied. "The weather was nice. It was unusually cool, so we assume he had the window open to let in some fresh air."

Lee scowled.

"Given Mr. Valenzuela's recent notoriety . . ." He paused to choose his words carefully. "Given how so many people felt about Mr. Valenzuela after his being found not guilty of the murders, wouldn't you think he would have been a lot more concerned about his security than that seems to indicate? Doesn't that seem like a rather crazy thing for him to do?"

Agents Weiss and Sainclair exchanged a knowing look. Then Mackeson Sainclair painstakingly removed the toothpick from his mouth, looked intently at the architect, smiled ever so faintly, and said, "I can assure you, Mr. Lee, the more you come to learn about Vic Valenzuela, the more you'll agree that 'crazy' is probably an understatement for the man."

7

Bree was not about to let a new investigation get in the way of her enjoying this spectacular South Florida weather.

After all, she had the day off, sort of. Dalton planned to meet the federal agents at Vic Valenzuela's home that morning. She and the rest of the team were supposed to spend the day conducting background research. No reason why she couldn't spend an hour or two out in the sunshine . . . shopping, perhaps.

She opened the top dresser drawer and found the sunglasses she had purchased specifically for the trip. Okay, so maybe they were a little more "glam" than what she would typically wear. Probably not what she would have worn in Manhattan . . . and she wouldn't be caught dead in them back home in Arizona.

But this was Miami. And she was considering a quick little jaunt over to Miami Beach. Therefore . . .

Her phone buzzed. She removed the sunglasses and looked at the display. It was from . . . Liam? The new guy? She placed the phone back onto the dresser, inspected her reflection in the room's round mirror.

ARE YOU AVAILABLE? FOR A QUICK CHAT? the message had read.

She drummed her fingers on the top of the dresser. Considered the benefit of being at the shops in Miami Beach the moment they opened. But also considered . . . precisely what was it? A desire to be of help? Likely there was something connected to the investigation that he needed her to do for him. And he did say the chat would be a quick one. She took another quick glance at herself in the mirror, slowly drew one hand through her long, auburn hair.

YES, she texted back to him. AVAILABLE NOW.

A few minutes later, there was a tap on her door.

"Hey, Liam, come on in," she said breezily, extending one arm toward the chair situated across from her sofa. Instead, he strolled over to the sofa, sat down near the center of it and rested his arm on the back of it in a semicircular arc. Bree headed for the chair and thought maybe his posture on the sofa was what she had heard some of her friends refer to as "manspreading."

"It's a shame you have to be pressed into action so soon after joining us," she said with a wave of one hand. "You probably wish you could get to know everyone first. Go through some sort of orientation." She paused, her expression becoming more serious. "Then again, we don't really get to choose when we shift from working as architects to working on an assignment like this one."

Liam broke into a broad, brilliant grin and slunk another inch or so down the front of the cushion. "Aw, no worries, Bree, no worries. Besides, I like to think of myself more as a man of action anyway." His smile grew wider. Bree shifted slightly in her chair.

She waited for him to explain what it was he wanted to talk to her about. Instead, he tapped the back of the sofa with his fingertips and seemed to stare directly into her soul. And smiled.

She took a deep breath, gave a quick smile in return. "So . . ." she began. "What can I do you for?"

Liam's expression dimmed a bit. "Sorry?"

Bree cleared her throat, looked off across the room. Then returned her attention to her new associate, who had somehow found a way to smile even more broadly than before. She admired his tan—it was natural, she decided—and she was impressed that he had obviously not ignored his legs in developing his physique. She noted that his thighs were like those of a rugby player.

She shook her head, realizing he was awaiting a response from her. "I meant . . . what's up? Why did you want to get together? Is there something you need me to do for you? A question you need me to answer?"

His expression brightened again. "Aw, sorry for the confusion, Bree. Actually, I just thought it'd be good for us to have a little chat, that's all. Get to know one another a little better. Actually, I wanted to know if there was anything I could do for *you*."

Had his expression not appeared so genuine, were his tone not quite so earnest, she would swear that he was . . . "Oh! Okay. Yeah, sure. That's good. Chatting is good. Well, let me see . . ." She looked toward the ceiling, trying to summon up some way he might be of service to her.

She finally landed on, "Well, maybe you can tell me a little bit about yourself. I didn't really get much information about you before we left Southern California."

He took his arm off the back of the sofa and moved it to his left thigh, hunched forward, and placed his other arm on his other thigh. That made it appear as though he was vigorously flexing his biceps. Only he wasn't.

"Well, there's not that much to tell, really," he said, taking on a thoughtful look. "Not that much that's interesting, anyway. Grew up in Queensland—that's where Brisbane is. I was a bit of a surfie growing up. When I wasn't surfing, I was teaching myself how to hack into just about any type of computer on the planet."

He stopped for a moment and delivered another of his abundant smiles. When she smiled faintly in return, he decided to plow forward.

"A lot of my rellies back in Australia are in the health care field, so I went to uni in Queensland and got my degree in biology, but I realized I was a lot more interested in marine biology than anything having to do with medicine. Then I even got bored with *that*, so I decided to go to architecture school."

"Right. University of London, wasn't it?" Bree said. "How did you end up there?"

The Australian let out a short laugh. "Same reason most guys end up at whatever college they go to," he replied. "A sheila." He raised two fingers on each hand and made air quotes as he said the name.

Bree leaned forward. "I'm sorry, what? You were dating some girl named Sheila?"

At that, Liam threw his head back and chortled. When his eyes locked in with Bree's again, she thought she detected a genuine glint of joy in them.

"Aw, Bree, you are everything they told me you were," he said. Then he added, "Nah, a sheila is how a lot of Aussie guys back in the day referred to a girl. So, yeah, it was a girl who lured me to London. But her *name* wasn't 'Sheila.' She *was* a sheila. Sorry, outdated reference I probably shouldn't use with an American."

Bree nodded, but in truth, she was having a hard time keeping up. She decided it was probably best to change the subject to something that wasn't so . . . Australian. "If you don't mind my asking . . . your sister?" she said.

"My sister?" Another massive grin creased Liam's face. "Nah, her name wasn't Sheila either. It was Caryn, rhymes with foreign," he replied, now guffawing. Bree fell into a chuckle with him. It was hard for her not to. *It would be hard for anyone not to*, she thought.

And then, suddenly, there was that look in his eyes again.

He nodded slowly, as if he were making up his mind that very moment that it would be all right for him to confide in her. "Yeah, well, my sister was quite the tennis star in Australia when she was younger. Made it to the quarterfinals at the Australian Open twenty years ago. After she retired from playing tennis competitively, she settled in at Sanctuary Cove. There's quite a tennis community there. Anyway, she started giving lessons at the tennis center." At this point, his smile narrowed and his brow furrowed some. "There was this bloke who was taking lessons from her. Seemed nice enough. They dated for about a year." He stopped and looked up at Bree with a searching look in his eyes.

"That's all right, Liam, you don't have to give me the details if you don't want to," she said. His gaze shifted to a place somewhere over Bree's left shoulder.

"Nah, it's all right. It's just . . . I don't really know a whole lot more. Apparently, he was one of . . . them . . . you know. And he told her something that she then spilled to the local authorities, and . . ."

Bree raised her right palm to let him know she understood the rest. After her hand returned to her lap, she gave him a compassionate look. "Do we have any idea where she is, where they're keeping her?" she asked him.

He returned his gaze to her, suddenly looking very much like a ten-year-old boy, which, Bree guessed, was probably about the age he had been when his sister had been kidnapped.

"Borneo," was all he said in reply.

Bree nodded gently and sighed. Slowly, she began to consider what details about her own life he might be interested in hearing. And just how much information she was comfortable sharing. However, he interrupted her thoughts before she came to a conclusion on either point.

"Actually, Bree, there *is* something you might be able to help me with."

"Sure, what is it?"

He paused for a minute. "Um, this Irene. What do you know about her? Since she and I are going to be working together, I thought I should probably learn more about her. She looks heaps young to me."

Bree recalibrated her thoughts. "Irene? Oh, right, well . . . she is young but she's not really all *that* young. I mean, she's probably twenty-two or twenty-three, something like that. She's graduated from college, I do know that. Graduated with honors from some technical university in British Columbia. She's very smart. Knows a lot about technology. But . . ."

Liam's mind seemed elsewhere. "Really? Twenty-two? I could have sworn she was still in her teens," he said. "More like sixteen or *maybe* seventeen." His brow was furrowed again. Whatever it was he was deep in thought about, it seemed to annoy him.

"Huh, what do ya' know," he eventually said.

Bree waited for him to ask what it was she had intended to say about Irene when he had interrupted her. Or to ask something about her.

But he didn't. Instead, he leapt from the sofa, brushing his palms down the front of his jeans as he took a few steps forward. "Well, that's probably enough earbashing for one morning," he said. "You were probably diving into some important research when I texted you. Hope I didn't hold you up too long. I'll check back in with you in a fair bit."

With that, he marched to her door. But rather than leave immediately, he turned to her, winked, made a clicking sound with his mouth, and delivered yet another enormous, brilliant grin. Then, with gusto, he turned the doorknob to the left and was gone.

Bree continued to sit in the chair, looking over her shoulder at the door he had just exited, her arms crossed in front of her abdomen. She had to concede he was incredibly charming. And she would be lying if she didn't admit she found him a little bit attractive.

And yet, she thought to herself, *there's something about that guy* . . .

8

"Investigators are continuing to comb the house and grounds of former Miami A&M football coach Vic Valenzuela for clues into the former coach's murder. Valenzuela's body was found Tuesday morning in the bedroom of his estate, located in one of Coral Gables's most exclusive neighborhoods. Police are refusing to say what if any leads they have, but they did tell Action News they found multiple stab wounds on the body and believe the winner of three national football championships likely died instantly."

The viewer of the newscast snickered and adjusted the tablet computer some to reduce the glare that was making it hard to see the screen.

Well, I wouldn't say 'instantly.' But, yeah, pretty quick. Quicker than I expected, anyway.

One hand traveled over to the canister of sunflower seeds to the right, but the eyes never left the screen of the tablet computer and the local station's coverage of the murder investigation. It had, of course, been twenty-four-seven, given the coach's notoriety and the fact his own exoneration on murder charges had taken place only a few weeks earlier.

The newspapers were absolutely *saturated* with stories about his death . . . and life. His hardscrabble life as the son of Cuban immigrants. His turn as an all-state fullback in high school and his successful shift into coaching a few years later. His commitment to helping inner-city youth fend off obesity. His almost maniacal commitment to being fit himself. His turbulent marriage to local debutante Erika Lindstrom and, of course, his being arrested and put on trial for her murder and the murder of her young boyfriend.

But reading the newspaper coverage of it all held no interest, here.

Watching this is a lot more fun. I can talk back to you people.

"Police say they believe the intruder gained access through a second story window that was unlocked."

That's right. And trust me, that wasn't as easy as it looked.

"And that a murder weapon has not been found."

Of course it hasn't. Probably won't be, unless you idiots look under every pile of leaves, branches, and twigs in Miami-Dade County.

"However, investigators do say they have discovered a few pieces of evidence at the murder scene they are sorting through."

The hand traveled cautiously back toward the sunflower seeds, but knocked the canister over in the process.

Shit!

"But that, as of now, they have no suspects in the murder of the high-profile and highly controversial coach."

Of course they don't. I followed my instructions to the letter. I knew exactly what I was doing. I always do. Those of us working to bring about The Transformation are so much smarter than you people take us for. Power to the cause.

"But the police also want to emphasize they do not believe the general public is in any danger. Reporting from police headquarters, this is Celeste Saucedo, Action 9 News."

Another snicker. Both palms placed over the mouth. A shake of the head.

Ha ha. You must be kidding. What a bunch of dumbasses you all are. The general public is in extreme danger.

Only . . . not quite yet.

9

Lee was relieved when Agents Sainclair and Weiss told him they were more than happy for him and his team to accompany them during the interviews they conducted, but that they preferred to conduct the interviews themselves.

His fabricated story that he was designing a memorial to the victims in the Manhattan murders had worked in giving him access to many of the suspects. But he had gotten exhausted trying to remember that he was talking to those people in the role of an architect trying to learn more about the victims instead of a detective trying to assess their guilt or innocence.

So he was more than happy this time to just tag along, examine things . . . and listen.

The town car he was in was heading south on Brickell Avenue toward the river on its way to its eventual destination—Vic Valenzuela's home in Coral Gables. But given the way Agent Sainclair had described it, the place built five years earlier by the university sounded more like a compound than a home. Eleven thousand square feet. Five bedrooms and five-and-a-half baths. Indoor tennis court. Outdoor spa. Combination game room and sports pub with scoreboards above the bar providing real-time updates of college football and basketball games from around the country. A spa, complete with its own eucalyptus room. And a six-car garage in which Valenzuela kept the restored 1950s-era automobiles he had brought over from (smuggled out of?) his native Cuba.

When Agent Sainclair had finished with his itemized description of the estate, Lee thought, *Even I consider that a bit much.*

Lee pushed himself deeper against the leather of the back seat and scanned the bustle of Brickell Avenue from the car's tinted windows. Warren and Roberto would meet Lee at the Valenzuela home; Bree, Liam, Lara, and Irene were to stay at the hotel to begin their research. It was one of the rare moments during the course of his work that he got to savor the serenity of solitude.

Fortunately, he was in high spirits (for a change). His mood was perhaps the rosiest it had been in months, perhaps a year. The firm could hardly keep up with all the architectural commissions coming its way. His health was solid. Thanks to his cutting out most of the red meat in his diet, the joint pain in his left knee had almost vanished. And, his creative spark was at an all-time high.

True, the murder of Vic Valenzuela meant The Organization and its contorted definitions of freedom and liberation had intruded into his life yet again. But when the group had resumed its campaign in Manhattan just over a year ago, it was after a twenty-year hiatus. So it seemed like a defeat for everything he had achieved in the interim. Now, it just felt like a nagging headache that required close attention, but most likely could be relieved.

Or could it?

His thoughts shifted to the motley crew of angry misfits who made up the worldwide terrorist group known as The Organization. What was it—or who was it, *really*—that they felt such anger toward? How was it that a group of individuals who by day were financiers, entrepreneurs, hedge fund managers or (in the case of Lara's father) iconic architects and urban planners, could by night coalesce around a terrorist manifesto driven by a classic science fiction novel? He told himself it might be prudent for him to reread *Wayward Colony* to refresh his memory of the actions undertaken in the book by the resistance fighters that The Organization had modeled themselves after.

Despite the threat the group represented, Lee was smiling peacefully as the limousine approached the Brickell Avenue Bridge.

Maybe all I've needed in my life is a lot more sunshine, he told himself.

The limousine began to traverse the crossing, and Lee was temporarily startled by the sudden grinding created by the tires connecting with the metal grate that made up the drawbridge portion of the structure. A hundred feet further, the vehicle eased to a stop as the cars ahead waited for a light to change. He turned to his left to admire the bronze monument known as the Pillar of History, which soared more than fifty feet into the air from the bridge's east pedestrian walkway. Lee had read about the monument when it had been completed a few years earlier by Cuban-born sculptor Manuel Carbonell. At the time, he had admired both its graceful lines and the fact that the sculptor had completed the monument with only his right hand after having suffered a stroke halfway through its execution.

Lee's eyes traveled up to the statue atop the pillar, a stirring homage to Miami's first inhabitants that was simply called Tequesta Family. A Tequesta warrior stood majestic, one knee bent, his bow and arrow aimed toward the sky. His wife sat beside his left foot. In her arms, she cradled their infant child, who covered its face with its tiny hands.

So compelling, Lee said to himself as the limo continued to idle beside the monument. *Such an epic testament to our innate urge to reach for the stars and seek our place somewhere in eternity.*

The warrior's wife turned her head slightly, peered down at the architect through the tinted windows. "Dalton, you *do* realize, don't you, that the reason this child is covering its face is because it sees the coming extinction of our people?" she said. Obviously, she was mildly put out with him.

"No, no, I *didn't* realize that," he stammered softly in reply. In the front seat, the driver of the town car cast a quick, wary glance into the rearview mirror.

"Well it is," the warrior's wife said with conviction. "*It is.* That's something you and your team ought to think about over the days and weeks ahead."

Lee nodded obediently at the statue as the traffic jam slowly unknotted and the town car glided forward and off the southern end of the bridge. He sat back against the seat again, emitted a long, deep sigh.

Well . . . great, he said to himself as the car gradually accelerated southward. *That's just really, really, great.*

***

Lee was the last to arrive at the house in Coral Gables. The goal had been to keep the investigation from disturbing the upscale neighborhood as little as possible. But Lee felt pretty sure that given the number of cars arriving, and the people in suits traipsing across the front lawn, the neighbors could not help but stand at their front windows, binoculars aimed toward the house.

He met up with Agents Sainclair and Weiss, who indicated with a discreet tilt of their heads that they wanted him to follow them around to a side of the house that was shielded from the street by an eight-foot-tall masonry wall. Roberto and Warren straggled behind, both dressed more professionally than Lee had seen them dressed in some time.

Agent Sainclair nodded as the architect joined up with them.

"*Bonjou,* Mr. Lee, trusting you had a pleasant evening in the hotel?"

Lee indicated to Sainclair that he had. "Why did you lead us around here?" he asked the agent.

Agent Weiss stepped in to answer. "Given Valenzuela's profile, we suspect the tabloids are paying some of the neighbors or lawn crews to tip them off when there is any activity here," she replied. "The faster we get out of sight the better. And . . ." She rotated her torso around toward the house. ". . . we believe this to have been the point of entry for the killer. That up there is Valenzuela's bedroom window."

Everyone looked up at the tall French windows located behind a dark iron railing, windows that now were most definitely closed and appeared not just locked, but fortified from within.

Agent Weiss pointed to a smaller masonry wall that rose between them and the house. On the other side of it were several small trees and shrubs intended to provide additional security to the ground floor of the home.

"As best we can tell, the killer somehow first accessed the lawn we're standing on, then scaled that smaller wall into that garden area," Agent Weiss continued. "After that, they climbed up that trellis you see with the ivy growing on it, and climbed onto the bedroom balcony from there. It was at the base of that trellis where we found the partial footprint."

From the ground, Lee examined the route the killer was presumed to have taken, and calculating the distance between the trellis and the balcony, decided the intruder must have had extensive background as a cat burglar.

He turned to Warren, whose expertise at clambering around and breaking into structures had been renowned throughout Canada before he changed his ways and headed off to architecture school. "What do you think?" he asked.

His associate squinted at the sky, took a few step forwards, took another few steps to the side, and returned to his boss.

"Doable," he replied. "Not *easily* doable, but doable."

The federal agents indicated to Lee that Valenzuela's personal assistant was waiting for them inside. A housekeeper answered the door and opened it wide for the group to file in. They immediately found themselves in a spacious foyer furnished with voluminous, hacienda-style furniture that ranged from solid mahogany buffets to an upright vitrine whose shelves were stocked with a variety of earthenware cups and goblets. Lee was no expert when it came to home furnishings, but to his eye, all the furnishings and accessories appeared to be originals rather than reproductions.

The housekeeper put an index finger into the air. "*Un momento,*" she said softly as she turned and disappeared through a pair of sturdy oak doors that appeared to lead to the back of the house. Lee kept his head down, intently studying the large, square, terra cotta tiles that comprised the foyer's floor. He thought he detected short but wide fissures in some of the tiles, which he thought rather odd given the house had been built only a few years earlier.

No one in the entourage said anything, save for Roberto who, after looking wide-eyed at the entrance area for several seconds, muttered, "Boy, did I go into the wrong business."

Soon, the grand doors opened again and a young blonde woman marched toward them, one hand extended. She resembled Agent Weiss in coloring and stature but where the federal agent exuded a background that was definitively "street," this woman exuded one that was definitively "Swarthmore."

"Good morning, everyone. I'm Ashley Taymore, Mr. Valenzuela's assistant. I would say it is good to see you, but given the circumstances . . ." She wore a taut, khaki-colored skirt, a sky-blue blouse, simple jewelry, and an airy silk scarf around her neck. Agent Sainclair made introductions all around and asked where they could have a private conversation.

"Let's go into the conference room," she answered, leading them toward the door she had just entered through.

They proceeded down a narrow hallway decorated with framed photographs of the coach posed with celebrities from all walks of life—a woman who was the emcee of one of South America's most popular daytime talk shows, a major league baseball most valuable player from the Dominican Republic . . . even a Hispanic astronaut who had commanded one of the space shuttles. The hallway led to another grand door, which opened onto an open-air courtyard filled with ornate wrought-iron furniture. As they trekked across the courtyard toward yet another door that apparently would take them to the back of the house, Roberto caught the eye of the housekeeper, who was standing quietly to his left. The housekeeper's expression was stoic, but she lifted her chin slightly and squinted at him. He narrowed his gaze at her . . . and she lifted her chin once again.

That's . . . interesting, he said to himself.

Moments later, everyone was seated casually in a conference room far more snug than Lee had expected. So snug that Warren and Agent Weiss had to sit on one end of the conference table.

Five-and-a-half baths and this is the best he could do for a conference room? Lee thought, subconsciously doing what he could to make himself skinnier.

Valenzuela's assistant sat in a high-backed, black leather chair at the opposite end of the table. "Despite the circumstances that were . . . swirling . . . around Coach Valenzuela at the time of his murder, we are of course shocked and saddened by his loss," she began. "I am happy to answer whatever questions you have, help you however I can."

Mackeson Sainclair reached up and moved the toothpick he had been chewing on from one side of his mouth to the other. "Thank you, Ms. Taymore," he said. "We appreciate the cooperation. Please describe what, if any, interaction you had with Mr. Valenzuela on the day of the murder. Did you see him that day, talk to him at all?"

The blonde parted her lips to say something, stopped, looked around the room for a second, then chose to proceed.

"Yes, I saw him *and* spoke with him that day," she said. "I arrived here around my normal time, about eight thirty in the morning, I believe. He had planned to be in California on vacation through Sunday, but he cut short his trip and arrived here at the house about four in the afternoon instead. He asked me to update him on some things that had come up while he was gone. I left around five fifteen, maybe five twenty. That was the last interaction we had."

"What sort of 'things' had come up while he was gone?" Agent Weiss asked.

The assistant took a moment to reflect on the question, shook her head slightly. "Nothing critical, really," she answered. "He had received a lot of messages since the verdict came in, so we went through those. He was supposed to have some minor skin surgery performed right after he got back, but his doctor had called asking to reschedule it. Of course, his most prominent, endorsement-related appearances have been canceled for some time now, but a longtime friend of his had inquired about Coach Valenzuela appearing at a charity golf tournament in the fall. And another asked if he might give a speech at a coaching convention in North Carolina later this year. So we discussed all of that, as well."

"Somebody actually asked him to be part of a *charity* golf tournament?" Agent Sainclair shot out.

Valenzuela's assistant returned his cynical look with one of cool equanimity. "Yes. Someone did," she said very slowly. "If you will recall, the coach was found *not* guilty."

Agent Weiss turned to Warren, nudged his shoulder, and whispered, "What do you want to bet she has a crush on him?"

Warren smiled, but said nothing.

"And, I might as well say it right now, no, I don't have a crush on Coach Valenzuela, he and I weren't having an affair, nothing else along those lines was going on," the assistant continued, seemingly oblivious to what Agent Weiss had just said. "I'm well aware of what people can think, especially given his well-publicized interest in . . ."

She paused, set her lips tight for a moment. ". . . women with blonde hair. However, *our* relationship was always completely professional. I am engaged to be married this fall, and my fiancée and I are quite content."

With that, Warren nudged the shoulder of Agent Weiss, who widened her eyes and nudged him back as discreetly as possible.

"Thank you, Ms. Taymore," Agent Sainclair said. "You said the deceased cut short his trip to California. Any idea as to why?"

She looked up at the agent, blinked several times. "No. He didn't really say. I know that while he was out there, he told me he was getting frustrated with the progress of the repairs being made to the house, but I can't really say that's what caused him to return early."

"What sort of repairs are being made?"

The assistant rolled her eyes toward the ceiling. "He and the university have been trying to keep it quiet, but a lot of the original construction of the house a few years ago turned out to be substandard. Most of it, actually. The university agreed as part of its settlement with Mr. Valenzuela to manage all of the repairs."

"The contractors, have they been working near the scene of the murder . . . by Mr. Valenzuela's bedroom?" Agent Sainclair asked.

"No. All the work has been at the opposite end of the house. For about the past two or three months. They haven't been working anywhere near his bedroom."

Agent Weiss shifted her position on the edge of the table so she could lean forward. "So you really have *no* idea as to why he returned early from California?" she said.

The assistant looked down at the tabletop. "Well, no, I don't know *for certain*," she replied slowly. "I mean . . . he was meeting with a lady friend while he was out there, and . . ."

Everyone waited.

". . . and I did get the impression that hadn't gone very well."

Agent Sainclair pressed further. "This lady friend . . . who is she?"

"Her first name is Samantha. I can't recall her last name. I do know she is a sideline reporter for one of the cable networks."

"What gave you the impression their . . . get-together . . . hadn't gone well?"

Ashley Taymore continued to look at the tabletop, her expression becoming more skittish.

"Oh, I am probably speaking way beyond my authority here," she said. "Really, I don't know that was the case at all. I just know he was pretty irritable when he arrived here from the airport. And then, while I was updating him, he got a phone call. And I am assuming it was from her, because I heard him say 'Sam' more than once."

"Their phone call, do you know what was it about?" Sainclair asked.

The assistant shook her head slowly. "No, not really. He got up and walked to the far corner of the room during the call. I only heard him stress that whoever he was talking to definitely shouldn't fly here that evening."

She stopped short, looked up at the agents. "I'm sorry. Really, that's all I heard. It was a very brief conversation. And I'm probably making way too much of it."

Agent Weiss slid off her post next to Warren and walked around the side of the table toward the assistant. "Can you tell us what you did after you left here that evening?" she asked.

Again, the assistant opened her mouth to respond, then hesitated. "Am I being . . . do I need to have my attorney here?" she asked.

"Well, you do have a right to contact an attorney, Ms. Taymore," said Agent Weiss. "But it's really not necessary. The question is just standard procedure. You didn't tell us where you went after you left here, so . . ."

"I was in my condominium," the assistant interrupted. "All evening."

Agent Sainclair cleared his throat. "With your fiancée?"

A pinched look overtook her face. "No, she is . . . on an assignment in Paris. I was . . . alone that evening, drinking some wine and watching a movie."

The room grew quiet. Agent Sainclair turned and gave his co-worker a look that indicated both that they probably needed to wrap up the investigation and that the assistant hadn't provided all the information he was hoping she would.

"Well, thank you for the time, Ms. Taymore," he said. "One more thing. Are you aware of anyone who has entered Mr. Valenzuela's life over the past year or two, anyone who might want to . . . cause him some harm?"

The assistant gave the federal agent a quizzical look, then scoffed.

"Of course. Pretty much everyone. Coach Valenzuela was not . . ." She paused again. The public relations training she had received at Swarthmore had kicked in.

"There were many people who didn't like Coach Valenzuela, who were unhappy with some of his activities," she said more methodically. "A *lot* of people. I've had to deal with those people on a daily basis for the last year and a half or so."

The assistant leaned forward slightly and lowered her voice. "I can't even begin to narrow the list of all the people who might have wanted harm to come to him."

She stopped, and Lee noted her jaw tighten significantly.

"But if I had to, I would suggest you start with the parents of the young man who was found murdered here with Mr. Valenzuela's wife, as well as Mr. Valenzuela's sister-in-law, Astrid. Given the horrible threats he was receiving from all of them during the trial, I have to believe it was one of them, or someone associated with them, who murdered him."

As the assistant was leading the detectives back through the courtyard on their way to the foyer, Roberto looked for the housekeeper who had nodded discreetly to him earlier. But all he saw was an abandoned vacuum cleaner, its cord wrapped tightly around a drooping potted plant.

At the front door, Ashley Taymore's manner reverted to that of the gracious host they had met when they had first arrived.

"I hope I didn't confuse you more than I helped you, Mr. Sainclair," she said with a short chuckle. "And, please don't hesitate to let me know if I can be of further assistance." She smiled, but seemed to want to say something more.

She leaned closer to the detectives. "I truly hope you find who did this," she said, softly. "The coach may not have been . . . a saint." Her mouth twitched slightly. "But no one deserves to have happen what happened to him."

As they headed across the front lawn toward their town cars, Lee was scratching a spot just behind his left ear. "Well, *she* seemed genuine enough," he said to Agent Sainclair who was trudging slightly behind the architect, his hands in his pockets. "True, she doesn't have an alibi for where *she* was when Valenzuela was murdered, but she couldn't possibly have been more cooperative with us. It's not The Organization's style to be so forthcoming and friendly."

The federal agent clamped down on the toothpick, which caused it to tilt upward from between his teeth. Then he plucked it from his mouth and turned toward the architect. "Mr. Lee, in Haiti, there is a saying that is especially appropriate at a time like this. *Bèl dan pa di zanmi.*"

Lee lowered his head and arched his eyebrows at Sainclair. "Translation?" he asked.

The agent lifted his chin a bit and peered at his companion through narrowed eyes.

"In English," he said, "it means, 'Always remember that not all smiles are friendly.'"

10

The coach's sister-in-law, Astrid Lindstrom Steinberg, agreed to meet with the detectives that afternoon at her art gallery in Coconut Grove, so long as her attorney could be present. The parents of Javier Duran agreed to come in for questioning, but it would have to be after they closed their furniture store in Little Havana for the day.

Over lunch, Agent Sainclair turned to Dalton Lee, who was looking skeptically at his plate. "You were very quiet during our interview with Ms. Taymore," the agent said. "Please know, Mr. Lee, that you and your colleagues are welcome to ask a question if you feel the need to. We need to direct the questioning, but your input and insights *are* valued here."

Across from the architect, Agent Weiss nodded vigorously. "Warren tells me . . . he has contacts with some of . . . the cable networks," she said as best as possible in between chews of her Reuben sandwich. "He's agreed to help me . . . look into that 'Samantha' person . . . that Ashley Taymore told us about." A small piece of corned beef plopped onto the tabletop in front of Agent Weiss. She gathered it up with her napkin and placed the wad on the edge of her paper plate.

"I didn't know you knew anyone with the cable networks," Lee said as he set down the grilled cheese sandwich he had just taken a nibble of.

Warren nodded vigorously. "I've gotten to know some of the guys who cover the hockey teams in Southern California. I figure Hannah and I should be able to figure out who this Samantha is, and her connection to Valenzuela, with a few phone calls."

Roberto, seated on the other side of Lee, was focused on the finicky eating style of his boss. "You don't like your grilled cheese sandwich, do you, Dalton?" he said with a faint smile.

Lee answered by scrunching his mouth up and to the left a couple of inches.

"Oh, you're into grilled cheese sandwiches?" Agent Weiss asked, using two fingers to nudge back into her mouth a strand of sauerkraut that had tried to escape during a chew. "You need to have one of the Cuban grilled cheeses at Valentina's over on Twenty-Ninth. They give you a choice of sweet or dill pickles, the mayo is low fat, and they spritz both sides of the sandwich with cooking spray. It's really delicious."

Roberto glanced at his boss, who looked as though he were watching the climactic scene of a horror film.

"I'll . . . give that some thought," he finally said, taking another even-more-tentative nibble of the sandwich he was holding.

***

"Zamira, would you please watch the gallery while I meet with our visitors?"

The young woman in a tight white dress accented with a turquoise and coral necklace smiled and nodded. She pushed back the roller chair she was in, stepped out from behind the computer desk, and moved more centrally into the gallery space. The gallery owner then said, "Please follow me," to the detectives and began to glide toward a back room whose walls were as taupe as the tunic she was wearing. Roberto turned to glance back at the assistant, almost walking into a gallery wall in the process.

"Would anyone like some water, or some herbal tea?" Astrid Steinberg asked. They had filed into a room which, Lee noted, was as big (if not slightly larger than) the conference room in Victor

Valenzuela's home in Coral Gables. "By the way, this is my attorney, Eli Golden."

Everyone nodded at the fit, middle-aged male in a dark gray suit, then politely declined the invitation for a beverage.

"Thank you for your time, Ms. Steinberg," Agent Sainclair began. "This shouldn't take very long. As you know, this is about the murder of Victor Valenzuela. I think you understand this is just an information-gathering exercise at this point."

"Of course," she responded softly. Her short dark hair descended to a soft point just below her ears and she wore minimal makeup. She sat composed, the fingers of her manicured and moisturized hands intertwined in front of her on the Plexiglas conference table. Her elbows pointed outward, her posture was perfect.

"You sent threats to Mr. Valenzuela while he was on trial. Can you . . ."

"Excuse me, but Ms. Steinberg doesn't have to answer that," the lawyer said. "She . . ."

His client graciously extended her right arm and placed her palm firmly on his forearm. "Eli, it's all right. I want to address this," she said.

She delicately cleared her throat, licked her lips lightly, and looked directly at Agent Sainclair. "Yes, I sent one long and very threatening letter to Mr. Valenzuela," she intoned, matter-of-factly. "He murdered my sister. The evidence of that is indisputable, as far as I am concerned," she said. "I was *very, very* angry, and I think we all appreciate the fact that anger is a perfectly normal and understandable stage of the grieving process."

Quietly, she took in a deep breath.

"However, I am no longer that person. I have come to peace with what happened. I had to. It was corroding my soul. And at some point, I realized that my dear sister would never abide the sort of person I was becoming. She was no saint herself, but her heart was huge; her spirit was generous and forgiving. I realized that if I truly wanted to honor her life, I had to change. I felt *obliged* to change. For her. I needed to quell the vindictive impulses I was grappling with, tame the fury that was churning inside me.

"So a couple of months ago, I spent a couple of weeks at a spiritual retreat in Oregon. And . . . it helped. Enormously. When you sit meditating on a mountaintop, marveling at a verdant valley below you, and you come face-to-face with the immense power that must be at play in the universe to make the rivers flow as they do and the fruits and vegetables flourish as they do . . . when you come to respect the intricate relationship between the sun and the rain and the farmers and the land, you realize how worthless hatred really is as an emotion. And how insignificant your emotions are in the grander ecosystem around you."

Agent Sainclair studied the woman for several seconds. "So you acknowledge you've had vengeful feelings for Mr. Valenzuela?" he said.

The attorney sat up quickly. "Astrid . . ."

"Eli!" Her interjection was soft but tinged with rebuke. After a few seconds, the gallery owner regained her composure and turned back to the federal agent.

"Yes, Mr. Sainclair, I have felt a great deal of vengeance toward Vic Valenzuela *in . . . the . . . past*. However, I locked all those feelings in a box and tossed them into the ocean some time ago. I have at one time felt ill will toward Mr. Valenzuela, but I no longer do. And I most certainly did not kill him."

From across the table, Agent Weiss shot, "Do you know who did?"

Astrid Sainclair turned toward Hannah, considered her for the very first time.

"Of course I know," she said simply and quietly.

The room fell quiet as everyone waited for Astrid Steinberg to render her verdict in the case.

"I have not the slightest doubt at all," she finally said, a wispy smile forming at her lips, "that it was karma that killed Vic Valenzuela."

***

If Astrid Steinberg was the embodiment of composure, Danielo Duran was the epitome of outrage.

"I no kill that son of a bitch, but if I know who did, I'd give him every last cent I have because thanks to him, my family finally get the justice we deserve, the justice we never got in the courtroom!"

The furniture store owner sat belligerent in his chair, eyes on fire, shoulders taut. His wife, Yolanda, sat slump-shouldered in the chair beside him, a morose expression controlling her face, a tissue crumpled between her fists. Warren and Agent Weiss had peeled off from the team to research the sportscaster in California, so Agent Sainclair was to go it alone with the couple while Lee and Roberto sat next door, watching the interview from behind a one-way glass in the federal agency's satellite office in South Miami.

"Mr. Duran, can you tell us where you were on the night Mr. Valenzuela was murdered?"

The seething father was quick with his response. "I with my wife. In our home. We finish watching television, go to bed."

Agent Sainclair looked to Yolanda Duran who said nothing, nodded slightly. "Is there anyone else, any other family member, who will attest to that?"

Danielo Duran's chest began to heave. His wife looked at him with concern in her eyes; she worked the tissue between her fingers.

"No, there is no one else because *our son is all we have!*" he bellowed as he thrust his torso toward the investigator. The surge was so intense, Dalton Lee tensed his body behind the glass for what felt like a full-fledged assault. But the store owner suddenly softened, redirected his upset into jabbing the tabletop with his index finger.

"I am sorry. It's just . . . please understand . . . Javier was our only child. He was a great kid. He make good grades in school. He go to community college. Make—how do you say it? —honors list. He have a good job at a country club. He work hard.

"My wife and I, we are sixty and we only have a few more years to work. We no have much, a small house, a little in the bank. That's all. The rest of our family is in Puerto Rico. But we no want to go back there. We want to stay here. We looking to our Javi . . . we *relying* on him . . ."

The vitriol surged back. "And then this *cabron*, he take my Javi's life! And no pay anything for it! Not one day in prison. *Nada!*"

His wife put her right hand out toward her husband to calm him down, but Lee noticed her jaw get more rigid, and her look more agitated, as her husband's outbursts grew increasingly raucous.

"No, I no kill the bastard!" he shouted as if trying to persuade the creator above. "But I very, very happy somebody did!"

Suddenly, he was spent, the way a lawn mower dies after sputtering on its last pint of gasoline. No one said anything for a moment or two.

Behind the glass, Lee felt a quivering in his coat pocket. He extracted his phone. It was a text.

IN MIAMI NOW. WOULD LIKE TO MEET ASAP. THIS EVENING?

Lee texted back: YES. SEND LOCATION. SOMEWHERE DISCREET PLEASE.

Then he deftly dropped the phone back into his pocket.

Agent Sainclair decided to push forward. "So, you and your wife were home the entire evening?" he asked the pair.

"*Si*—well, I go to the drugstore to get antacid for her when she wake up with the heartburn. But yes, other than that, yes, we in our home all evening."

The agent squinted at Danielo Duran. "This drugstore. What time did you go there? And how long were you gone?"

The furniture store owner looked up at the ceiling, counted on his fingers. "No more than fifteen minutes," he said. "Twenty maybe. I leave at around eleven, just before the store closed."

His wife touched her husband on the arm and rattled something off to him in Spanish. He smiled, replied to her in a patient tone, looked back at the investigator. She said something else to him, this time with slightly more passion. He shook his head, waved her off, turned his attention back to Agent Sainclair.

Lee cast a quick look at Roberto, who had not taken his eyes off the couple during the exchange. The associate turned and met Lee's glance, nodded once, and then refocused his attention onto the Durans.

"We'll need the name and address of the drugstore, if you don't mind, Mr. Duran." Agent Sainclair jotted a few notes in a lined notebook he had open in front of him.

"Sure, sure," Danielo Duran replied hurriedly. Then he looked up at Agent Sainclair and grinned from ear to ear. "I very sorry for my behavior," he said, suddenly the chivalrous gentleman. "Please understand, this been a terrible time for the two of us." He paused and his grin dimmed somewhat. "Please understand I completely honest with you when I say I no kill that *hijo de puta*, and I hope you no find who did."

Agent Sainclair began rummaging inside his coat, hunting around the inside pocket for a toothpick. "So, can you think of anyone else who might have done this, Mr. Duran? Did anyone say anything during the trial, indicate in any way they might actually go so far as to . . . ?"

The shop owner raised one finger in the air and methodically began to nod.

"When I hear that Señor Valenzuela was murdered," he said, "I tell my wife that I wouldn't be surprised if the coach did it." He looked at his wife, spat out a couple of sentences in Spanish, which she returned in kind, nodding heavily at Agent Sainclair.

"What coach?" the agent probed.

"I no remember his name. But he say he was an assistant with Valenzuela."

"What made you think he might be the one who murdered Mr. Valenzuela?"

"Well, he sit next to us a lot during the trial," Duran answered. "He next to me the day the verdict come out. And all I remember—please, I very much in shock then—I just remember him rubbing my back and saying, 'He shouldn't get away with this. I promise you, Señor Duran, he won't get away with this.'"

The furniture store owner sighed and stared blankly at the agent across from him. For the first time during the interview, Danielo Duran seemed grounded in reality rather than driven by fury.

"He seem—you know—very sure of what he says," he said to Sainclair. "It give us much comfort . . . and we really need it then." He paused and took hold of his wife's hand. "Something about how he say it . . . it made me really believe it."

Agent Sainclair chewed on his upper lip and rocked gently in his chair a few times as he thought about what Duran had just told him. He had found a toothpick in his pocket and started to extract it, but decided instead to leave it where it was. He then scribbled a bit more in his notebook and glanced at his watch. He probably wouldn't have enough time to get to the final race at Hialeah, he decided.

Once Agent Sainclair had wrapped things up with the Durans, and the pair had left the interview room, Lee looked at Roberto and arched one eyebrow. "What was that little drama about . . . the one between the Durans?"

Roberto smiled, pushed his chair onto its back legs, and placed the palms of both hands on the back of his head. "Well, Yolanda Duran was reminding her husband he had a flat tire when he went out for antacids," he said, "and telling him she thought he should inform Sainclair that he hadn't been gone for just fifteen minutes but for more than an hour."

11

After the interview with the Durans, Lee shooed the others back to the city and promised he would reconnect with them the following day. He told them a personal issue had arisen and he would take a cab back to the hotel once it had been attended to.

One look from Roberto was all it took, however, for Lee to know the designer wasn't buying it.

It was the beginning of rush hour, so the traffic on Dixie Highway was excruciatingly slow. It didn't help that he had to travel through the throngs trying to squeeze their way into Dadeland Mall. *I need to remember to give this cabdriver a really big tip*, he told himself.

Eventually the traffic thinned, but that only meant the cab got to cruise along the boulevard rather than lurch along in stop-and-go fashion. They rolled past one fast-food restaurant and bank branch and furniture warehouse after another, the elevated Metrorail tracks looming parallel to them on their left. Lee smiled at the irony of how his destination was literally only a few minutes up the road, yet figuratively miles away from the bland suburban landscape that currently surrounded him.

His attention was temporarily arrested by the citrus-colored signage of the Shops at Sunset Place, an outdoor shopping mall that reminded him of many of the open-air emporiums back in Southern California. At that point, the taxi was able to pick up even more speed. It carried Lee past the baseball stadium on the Miami A&M campus, past the contemporary, two-story office buildings in the heart of Coral Gables, past the designer-centric ambience of the Village of Merrick Park, past even the Coconut Grove rail station, depositing him eventually at his glorious meeting place with his mysterious friend—the Vizcaya Museum and Gardens overlooking Biscayne Bay.

Built by James Deering, one of the founding executives of International Harvester, the landmark estate had always been a favorite of Lee's. Part Italianate villa, part playboy mansion, part seaside museum, the building had represented both a nod to the past and an embrace of the future when it was completed in 1922. Its Mediterranean Revival architecture summoned up one of the eighteenth-century estates outside of Venice, with stucco walls, a red-tile roof, and windows in the shapes of arches and circles. But the home was also quite modern for the day, having been both built from reinforced concrete *and* equipped with generators, a water-filtration system, a central vacuum-cleaning system, a dumbwaiter and not one, but *two* elevators.

He loved how the formal gardens surrounding the Main House masterfully reimagined the spirit of those created for country mansions in eighteenth-century France and Italy. And yet, at the same time, they had been quite innovative in how they wove subtropical plants that could stand Florida's climate (like palm trees and birds of paradise) into a scheme that otherwise was entirely European. Scattered throughout the grounds were numerous fountains, as well as sculptures made of a soft and porous coral stone designed to weather soon after the gardens were completed.

By the time Lee arrived at the estate, a low bank of clouds had crept over the region and a faint mist began to nip at Lee. *Well, if my string of beautiful weather had to come to an end*, he thought, *this would, of course, be the likely time for that to happen.*

It was after five o'clock so the estate was closed to visitors. A stolid sentry wearing a vest with POLICE emblazoned across the front eased his way from behind the front gate and strode toward him. "I'm sorry sir," he said, raising one hand to halt Lee's advance. "The estate . . ."

"The estate is often referred to as the Hearst Castle of the East, I believe," Lee said in a muted monotone.

The guard stopped short, like a dog that had suddenly been told to heel. "Yes, you're right. It is, Mr. Lee," he said. "Please. Follow me."

The pair carefully scaled the steps leading to the house's front entrance. There Lee's escort nodded once at the doorman, who allowed the pair entry into the building.

"I will lead you to the back of the house," the guard said softly. "Beyond that . . . I know nothing."

They wound their way past the cloakrooms and through the entrance hall, and followed the north arcade toward the back of the building. There Lee turned to his left and looked into the grand living room with its Renaissance-era furniture and monumental organ, the pipes of which were concealed by doors that were installed by cutting a religious painting in half.

At the back of the house, Lee could see—beyond the broad East Terrace on his left—both Biscayne Bay and the concrete breakwater just offshore, a monumental work that had been designed to look like a Spanish sailing caravel from the sixteenth century. Lee thought that in the gloom and the mist, the artificial sea vessel looked more like an ominous alien from some sci-fi flick than an inspired architectural element designed to calm the sea.

He and the guard next paraded past the golden-hued Music Room, which was resplendent with furnishings and decorations inspired by the city of Milan. Lee took a moment to marvel at the elegant piano and harp that shared stage center, and the painted panels that covered the room's wall and ceiling, panels derived from the palace of a noble family from Northern Italy.

Finally, they stood along the southern edge of what represented the heart of Deering's winter home, the courtyard, which at one time had opened to the sky. It was now completely enclosed to protect the house from storms and sun, and was capped with a state-of-the-art, pyramid-shaped skylight.

"I will leave you here," the sentry told Lee, gesturing toward the door that would lead the architect out to the gardens on the south side of the house.

Lee glanced at the follow-up message he had received on his phone:

IN THE GARDEN RESERVED FOR COMEDY AND TRAGEDY
A BEFEATHERED YOUNG MAN WILL SHOW YOU THE WAY

He sighed. He remembered that one of the many green spaces beyond the South Terrace bore the name the Theater Garden and that it evoked the feel of an outdoor stage. But he had no idea where it was located . . . or the easiest way to find it.

He wandered onto the terrace and toward the concrete sarcophagus that held watch above the lush gardens in the distance. To the left, he spotted a sunken, verdant nook and ambled off in that direction. But the moment he spotted the pineland heliotrope, yellow geiger, and lignum vitae meandering alongside limestone pavers, he knew this was that part of the estate known as Secret Garden, a place relatives could retreat to for privacy while the head of the house entertained on the terrace above.

He turned, trudged back up the steps, and meandered around to the perimeter of the grounds, which were populated with a diverse assortment of sculptures and balustrades.

Quite quickly, he came upon a roughly landscaped area shaped like a vase, and his antennae quivered. Directly before him were two statues made of lead that stood atop marble columns. Lee recognized the statue on the right to be a tribute to Punchinello from Italy's *commedia dell'arte* tradition, a character who was predictably vicious and pretended to be too stupid to know what was really going on. His counterpart on the left was Harlequin, the jovial trickster in a checkered costume.

The architect breathed in sharply. Harlequin was wearing a wide-brimmed hat accented by a long feather. His face was a theatrical mask with a maniacal grin. His right arm crossed around his torso; one finger seemed to point to a spot behind him. Lee followed the arc of the joker's gesture and it directed his gaze to a simple stone bench that was surrounded by a cluster of mangroves and flanked by statues of a shepherd and shepherdess.

Sitting motionless on the bench, dressed all in gray, was the person he had come to meet.

"Well, you definitely look a lot better than the last time I saw you, Dalton. But you might want to consider applying some sunblock. You're getting pink."

The pair smiled. Lee took a seat, crossed his legs, and scanned the landscape in the distance.

After a moment, his friend said, "Such a lovely place, I've always thought. We tend to meet in such . . . *dismal* locations. I thought a change of scenery might do us some good. So sorry the weather chose not to cooperate."

The architect leaned over, rested his forearms on his thighs, looked over his shoulder at the person in gray. "Does that mean you have some cheerful news for me?"

His companion grimaced slightly. "No. They are both still very fragile, Dalton. *Quite* fragile. I don't imagine anything will happen in the next few days . . . but I can't guarantee it *won't* either."

Lee turned away, raised his hands into a praying position and cradled his fingers just beneath his nose. "I'm curious . . . of the two of them, who is in . . . the *better* health?"

A breath in. "Oh, your mother, definitely. Her disposition is fairly agreeable most of the time. *Her* decline has been more . . . cerebral than physical."

Lee continued to study the regimented shrubs and hedges that made up the garden's Center Island. At the remark, he dropped his head, shifted the positioning of his fingertips so they now rested against his forehead.

"What's wrong, Dalton? Isn't that what you wanted to hear? That your father is in worse shape than your mother? I wouldn't really call his condition dire, but his heart really can't . . ."

"Stop it," Lee said, his rebuke coated with irritation. "I don't want *either* of them to be suffering, or in pain. To be honest with you, regardless of our relationship, I'm probably much less prepared for *his* passing than hers."

Silence overtook them for several seconds. A flock of birds flapped gracefully across the sky like show planes gliding perfectly on autopilot.

The sun dipped to that angle at which children begin to sense it might be time to start heading home from play.

Lee decided to shift into business mode. "Why are we here? What did you need to tell me?"

"It's . . . a paperwork situation. They want your permission to . . . remove any and all forms of life support, if need be. For your father in particular. They don't *have* to request this of course. It's being done as a courtesy . . ."

"A COURTESY?" Lee's exclamation caused a flock of pigeons clustered near his feet to scatter. He dialed down the volume of his voice, but not its passion. "You have GOT to be KIDDING ME!" he whispered. "They are holding them *hostage*, for God's sakes! Do they also consider *that* to be some sort of courtesy, as well?"

The other person looked at Lee, swallowed heavily, waited for the architect's anger to subside. Dalton merely fumed, his chest heaving.

"Wait, this has nothing to do with being courteous, does it?" he said suddenly. "This has everything to do with them wanting to avoid any culpability if . . ."

The person did not reply for a while. Then, "Am I to take that, Dalton, to mean the answer is no?"

Lee ran his tongue around the surface of his teeth. Thinking.

"If they do remove life support . . . does that mean he will die peacefully? Will it be like . . . falling asleep?"

His companion took some time to consider the question and how to present the answer. "Possibly. That's very possible. Especially if your father is unable to swallow and you choose to withhold fluids. That would lead to ketosis setting in, and at that point, he likely wouldn't feel hunger or thirst or pain. Eventually, he would suffer arrhythmia, and then die."

Lee was nodding as the information was relayed to him.

"Then again . . ."

The architect stopped nodding. "Then again . . . what?"

A heavy sigh. "Dalton, you know I have always been forthright with you. I have always tried to provide you with whatever information you need . . . whatever information you need that I can deliver, that is."

"Yes."

A long pause. Then . . . "Given your father's condition, a stroke isn't just a possibility, but a *very likely* possibility. And if he has a stroke, and there is no directive mandating that life support be removed . . ."

"Yes?"

The other person turned, stared intently at Lee. "Have you ever heard of Terri Schiavo?"

Lee thought for a minute. "The name is vaguely familiar."

A nod. "You were probably in high school when it happened. Maybe middle school. She was a young woman, about the age you are now. Her heart failed and that caused her to suffer major brain damage. Over time she went into what is called a persistent vegetative state. Your eyes are open and you are aware of everything around you but your motor skills are destroyed so you cannot say anything and you cannot move. You feel pain . . . but you can't communicate that to anyone else who is with you. Maybe you can breathe on your own, maybe not. You can't be fed, so they force nutrients into you through a feeding tube."

Another long pause.

"If your father has a stroke, goes into a vegetative state, and there is no directive mandating life support be removed . . . they *could* choose . . . to just leave him that way. To let him . . . languish, in that condition, if you will. It's not out of the question. They've done it before."

Lee stared in disbelief. Almost imperceptibly, he shook his head. "Why? For what *possible* reason?"

His companion let out a soft, indignant scoff. "Oh, Dalton, your biggest flaw is that you assume everything has logic attached to it. It doesn't. I suppose they *could* think it worthwhile to keep your father in a vegetative state because they consider him to be a more valuable asset to them alive than dead. Or, because he might yet deliver some information that could prove enormously beneficial to them in some way."

The person paused, turned away from Dalton, began to gaze at some specific shrub in the distance. "Most likely, however, they would do it out of spite. To spite *you*, specifically."

Lee felt one temple throbbing, a slight ache developing behind his right eye. *This is madness*, he thought. *With my thumb perfectly pressed against the top of the larynx, I could . . .*

He stopped himself. That route took him only into a cul de sac, and he knew it. As much as it troubled him, this person was one of the few emotional crutches he had at the moment. And then, there was someone else's welfare to consider . . .

"Do you have the papers on you? Give them to me," he demanded suddenly. "I'll sign them right now."

"We'll have them drawn up. I'll contact you when we have them ready."

It was deep into dusk now. Lee needed to get back to the hotel. He *yearned* to get back to the hotel.

"What did Victor Valenzuela have to do with The Organization? How did he get in their way? What's this all about?"

His companion clucked once. "You know better than to try that, Dalton."

Lee didn't realize that his teeth were clenched, that one hand had balled into a fist. "They're on the verge of another attack, aren't they? What is it? Give me *something*."

Just then, a gentle breeze rustled the mangroves behind them, carried the scent of the sea their way. Lee's antagonist closed both eyes, breathed in deeply.

"Ah, the ocean. Such a magnificent, mysterious puddle, isn't it, Dalton? So often, the origin of so much life. And yet, at other times, the cause of so much death, as well."

The speaker patted Lee on the knee and rose from the bench. "Time for me to go. Don't worry. We'll be in touch."

12

It was going to be a busy day.

Lee, Lara, Bree, and Liam had committed to accompanying Agent Sainclair that morning when he went to interview the athletic director at Miami A&M. Lee had a feeling that would lead to even more interviews, as the web of people who could have stepped into Vic Valenzuela's life—and murdered him—continued to spiral outward.

Warren and Agent Weiss would continue their research on the female sports reporter with whom the coach had quarreled in California. Irene was consumed with conducting online research about the coach, Astrid Steinberg, and the Durans. Roberto had come up with his own assignment, which he had proposed to Lee in a phone call the night before.

"That housekeeper at the Valenzuela home, there's some good reason why she wanted my attention, Dalton," he told his boss. "If I can somehow get her to meet me away from that compound, she might open up to me. I could be wrong, but I think it's worth a shot."

Lee agreed to Roberto's request. He decided that given everything the young man had gone through in Manhattan, the designer deserved to feel a little more in control of his life these days.

"But first, I have . . . one of my appointments tonight," Roberto told Lee. "Once I have that out of the way, I'll do what I can to learn something from the housekeeper, I promise."

Lee told Roberto that would be fine. Despite the ominous message the architect had received from the wife of the Tequesta warrior, his mood was buoyant. He had received word from the office in Southern California that an architectural commission in Mendocino was a go. Agent Sainclair had arranged for him to give a tour of the Deco architecture in Miami Beach as a means of earning his keep when the murder investigation flagged. And for now, The Organization remained an abstract threat, although he knew that feeling of distance would probably start closing in on them sooner rather than later.

He was, however, more than a little nervous. He knew next to nothing about sports and he was about to walk into the offices of arguably the most successful college football program in the country. He wasn't even sure he would understand what they were saying. "I know what a touchdown is," he said to Lara. "And I know they run and pass the ball. Do they kick it? I'm not sure. It is called *football*, so probably, right?"

Lara sighed and patted his hand. "The rest of us will fill in the gaps for you when you need us to, Dalton," she replied.

Lee was flabbergasted when they arrived at the Miami A&M athletic complex, which occupied an entire city block on the west side of the campus—more than that, actually, if one included the practice fields for the football and soccer teams, the baseball field, *and* the tennis center. And that didn't even include the stadium in which the football team played, which was located across town.

"We are completely landlocked here," athletic director Stuart Wilbanks told the group as he ushered them into his office. "When we needed a bigger stadium, the university decided it just made sense to share one with the professional team. It doesn't pose any inconvenience for us, and the kids think it's cool they're playing in the same stadium as their idols."

Lee thought if they had tried, they could have easily shoehorned a stadium into the area taken up just by the Concourse of Champions, the huge multimedia museum that paid tribute to the university's many national championships in football, men's diving, and women's golf. Or, perhaps they could have plopped it on the site now occupied by the department's academic center, which teemed with more than one hundred and fifty computer terminals reserved exclusively for the university's athletes.

"Do they even *have* an architecture school here?" Lee whispered to Lara as they took their seats in Stuart Wilbanks's office.

"Yes, remember that tiny little two-story building with the cute cupola on top that we drove past a few minutes ago?"

Lee nodded.

"Well, that was it," Lara deadpanned.

The athletic director plopped into his leather-backed chair with a significant "Oof." He wore sand-colored slacks and a short-sleeve, forest-green polo shirt with the university's centurion emblem printed on it in white. The polo pulled tight against his broad shoulders and ample abdomen, but he was otherwise well-groomed and seemed relatively fit for a man of fifty-two. Lee surmised Wilbanks had played football himself, and sure enough, on the wall behind the man's desk were two photos of him from his playing days, artificially posed in a running stance, a ball cradled in his arm. But there were no meaningful trophies or certificates on the wall, which told Lee the athletic director probably sat on the bench more than he starred on the field.

Today his expression was one of a man who had been through a lot, but who could still, somehow, find some humor in it all. "So it takes this many people to solve a murder these days, does it?" he said, scanning the entourage. "Well, it *is* Vic Valenzuela we're talking about here, so I guess I shouldn't be surprised."

He laughed lightly and shook his head. "Let me tell you, everyone at some point in their career should be forced to supervise somebody like Vic Valenzuela," he said, leaning back in his chair. He stopped short to address a female assistant who had brought the group in, but was now leaving his office.

"Um, Tamryn, would you bring everyone here some water, please?" He blew air out through his mouth. "Sorry about that. Now what was I talking about? Oh, right, supervising Vic. Except, one does not really *supervise* Vic Valenzuela so much as . . ." He tapped the desktop with a pen he held in his left hand. "You don't supervise Vic so much as you toss some recommendations his way, stand back, and pray to God your liability insurance is paid up."

Nervous chuckles filtered through the room. After all, the object of their laughter *had* been murdered just a few days earlier.

Mackeson Sainclair used his tongue to navigate a toothpick from one side of his mouth to the other. "So, does that mean you had a difficult relationship with Mr. Valenzuela?" Lee glanced at Lara with a look that said, *Well, he's certainly not wasting any time, is he?*

Wilbanks scoffed a bit. "Oh, Vic and I got along okay," he answered, leaning over his desk toward the detective. "I knew that, given his stature, I only had so much sway over Vic, and he knew I could help him a lot behind the scenes with the university administration when he needed it. I wasn't crazy about some of his antics, but I was never much of a choirboy myself, so . . ." He started drumming the pen on his desktop as if the frantic tempo somehow completed the sentence for him.

"What sort of antics?" asked Sainclair.

The athletic director took on a wistful grin, as if he and Valenzuela had been fraternity brothers, and he had just remembered one of their most outrageous, pledge-week escapades.

"Let's just say that Vic—may he rest in peace—always viewed rules as . . . suggestions," the athletic director said, pulling himself back in a bit. "His appreciation for women was pretty well-known. His appreciation for drinking was *most definitely* well known. I had to pull him out of one or more bar fights. Sometimes, those bar fights were with women."

From out of the corner of his eye, Lee noticed Liam smile broadly . . . and Bree reconfigure her mouth into a judgmental frown.

"Fortunately, Vic's record as a coach always saved his ass," Wilbanks continued. "No one can ever argue with Vic's record." The athletic director's smile suddenly fell apart. "*Could* argue with it, I mean."

The room stayed quiet for a couple of moments. Sainclair uncrossed his legs and looked at a legal pad he had in his lap. He seemed to be reading some notes he had made to himself.

The assistant returned with a tray full of bottled waters. Everyone but Lara took one. As they were uncapping their beverages, Sainclair looked up.

"Can you think of anyone who had been shadowing him over the past few months? Anyone who seemed a little too interested in his business, had been following his whereabouts a little too closely?"

Wilbanks's grin transformed into a look of serious contemplation. "Well, he always had female students who were groupies of his, but none of them stands out really as being, you know, a real kook about it, or anything. He had a tendency to piss people off on a fairly regular basis, but again, I can't think of anyone who ever notched things up a level in any way." He paused. "I just assumed . . . his death probably stemmed from, you know, what he was on trial for, which I *cannot discuss at all.*" He had both hands up in front of his face and was waving them quickly back and forth like windshield wipers set to high.

"Understood," Agent Sainclair said quietly. "So, no one recently has demonstrated any sort of unusual behavior toward the coach?"

The athletic director went to thinking again, slowly shook his head. "No, not really. You might talk to the sportswriter who was working on the biography of Vic before he died. Vic might have told him something that would help you."

"He was writing a biography?" Sainclair said.

"No, he wasn't writing it himself. Some writer with one of the national sports magazines got in touch with him about a year ago and suggested Vic let him ghostwrite his life story. Apparently, after you've won a national championship, everybody wants to read what you have to say, regardless of whether it is intelligent or not."

At that comment, Lee exchanged looks with Liam and Bree. Noticing Lee's response, the athletic director lifted his hands again.

"I shouldn't have said that. What I meant to say was I'm not sure Vic really has anything to share with the general public that would be all that . . . insightful, you know what I mean? But, hey, I get it. He was the alpha male's alpha male. He was the sort of guy every guy out there wants to be. And given all the colorful stories there are out there about Vic, I can understand why people would pay twenty bucks, maybe more, to read a biography about him. Hell, I know most of those stories myself and *I'd* probably pay to read about them."

Agent Sainclair nodded slowly and thought about what Wilbanks had said. "This sportswriter who was working on the book . . . what's his name?"

Wilbanks breathed in, looked up at the ceiling, and then swiveled around to his laptop and punched a few keys. "Todd . . . something," he said, hitting a few more keys before finally dropping his wrists onto the desktop in exasperation. "This damned computer," he said, swiveling back to the group in front of him. "It's Todd something. I'll have Tamryn get it for you before you leave. She'll have it."

"Thank you," Sainclair said.

Lee raised one hand in the air. "Excuse me," he said tentatively, glancing over at Sainclair who nodded for him to go ahead. "I was just wondering . . . Mr. Valenzuela's assistant told us the university had built the home he was living in when he died, but that there had been a lot of problems with the construction."

Wilbanks sighed and frowned. "Yeah. We don't like to talk about it, but it turns out the contractor hired for the job had just arrived here after abandoning several projects in Texas. A lot of the work was substandard, so we've been paying to have it redone."

Lee thought about that, raised his hand again, about half as high as before. "The substandard work . . . was it confined to a certain part of the house or was it throughout?"

The athletic director set a firm line with his lips. "Pretty much throughout," he replied. "I'm not sure what we'll do with the house now that Vic is gone. Maybe just sell it for a loss. Whatever new coach we hire won't want to live in it, that's for sure."

Sainclair looked at Lee, who let the agent know he was finished.

The federal agent turned a page in his notebook, looked up at the athletic director. "Earlier today, we spoke with Danielo Duran, the father of the young man who was found murdered on the estate along with Mr. Valenzuela's wife. Mr. Duran mentioned that at the trial, he was comforted by someone who used to coach here, someone who was fired after a run-in with Valenzuela. Know anything about that?"

Wilbanks sat back in his chair. His expression was first one of someone rapidly scanning an internal hard drive, then one of someone who had possibly landed on exactly the data point he had been looking for.

"Wow, I hadn't even thought of Hayden Haas," he finally said. "It's been a couple of years at least, but it would make sense. He *did* behave sort of odd for a while after he was fired, although at the time, I couldn't really say that I blamed him. Yeah, Hayden was an assistant coach under Vic for a couple of years. Not a particularly good one. Came here from Maryland State. His wife taught in our chemistry department while he was here. A couple of our trustees recommended him when we had an opening for an offensive coordinator."

Lee leaned over to Lara and whispered, "Why would they want someone on their staff who was offensive?" She shook her head vigorously at him and waved him off.

"Anyway, he and Vic never got along," Wilbanks continued. "After one big row they had, Vic said either Haas had to go or he would. I never understood why Vic disliked him so—all he would tell me is that when it came to football, the guy didn't know his ass from a hole in the ground. The trustees who had recommended Haas when he came here went to Vic, talked to him, and after a couple of weeks, everything seemed back to normal. But around the end of that season, Haas apparently did something else that pissed Vic off, and this time Vic wouldn't back down. He said if Haas wasn't fired immediately, he'd accept an offer he had on the table from Oklahoma Tech. A majority of the trustees agreed the university couldn't let that happen, so I had to let Haas go."

Wilbanks paused to catch his breath, began to move around some file folders on his desk. "The guy seemed nice enough, but I saw the writing on the wall. My hands were tied."

Sainclair used his tongue to shift the toothpick back to the other side of his mouth. "How did this Mr. Haas act oddly after he got fired? What exactly did he do?"

The athletic director gazed off in the distance. More than he had at any other time in the conversation, he seemed to pick his words with exquisite care. "Well, he sent a *lot* of emails to Vic, a lot of emails, and he sent them to him for several months after he had been fired," he replied.

"The emails . . . were they threatening?"

Wilbanks shook his head, kept gazing off into the distance. "No," he eventually said. "They weren't threatening, they were more . . . pleading. He was begging Vic to give him his job back. Said he would do everything Vic told him to do, whatever Vic wanted. As far as I know, Vic never responded to the guy. But he did have to call security once to have Haas removed from campus when he showed up unannounced at Vic's office. But then that was that. Vic didn't hear from Haas again. Or if he did, he never told me about it."

Sainclair was scribbling on his legal pad. "Can you tell us where this Mr. Haas is now?" he asked.

"Yeah, he's out in Kendall. Coaching high school ball out there I believe. Or, no, wait, *middle school*." The athletic director shook his head. "If *that* weren't bad enough, apparently his wife left him soon after we fired him." He paused and chuckled again. "But that's coaches' wives for you. Those of us who have coached have a saying, "Nothing strengthens a marriage more than a long-term coaching contract."

He glanced at a small clock next to his desk lamp and slowly stood up, his way of indicating to Sainclair and the others that the interview was over. "Kind of sad, isn't it?" he continued, lightly bouncing his fingertips on the desktop. "The nice guys like him always seem to end up in pitiful circumstances, while the jackasses like Vic get to live the good life."

Sainclair removed the toothpick from his mouth and stared at the athletic director. "You mean the jackass who just got murdered?" he slowly said.

The athletic director thrust his shoulders back and lifted his chin to where he was looking down his nose at the federal agent.

"Oh yeah, right," he said without batting an eye. "There is that, isn't there?

***

Lee's prediction that it would be a long day came true. Agent Sainclair made a phone call, and soon they were off to Kendall to speak with Hayden Haas. The coach was worried he needed an attorney present when he learned they wanted to speak with him about the murder of Vic Valenzuela, but Sainclair assured him they were only interested in asking him some routine questions.

Twenty minutes later, they pulled onto a tidy, mundane subdivision populated with homes that were only slight variations on a theme of identical. They were all two-story structures. They all had two-car garages and all had at least one car sitting in the driveway. They were all the color of either a sheet of bond paper or a vanilla wafer. They all were shaded by one or two palm trees. Some of them might have a metal mailbox standing beside the roadway, others might sport a circular driveway paved with sand-colored bricks. But *all* of the houses, every single one of them, had Spanish-style roofs made of rounded clay tiles in the ubiquitous color of the region—terra cotta.

The coach's home was the largest on the block and slightly more manicured than the rest. But Lee noted the back bumper of the car in the driveway was fairly banged up, and the light fixture beside the front door seemed slightly askew.

A middle-aged Latina, wearing a simple white apron over a colorful flower-patterned blouse, answered the door.

"We're here to see Mr. Haas," Sainclair told her. "He's expecting us."

She smiled gently, ushered them in, and led them to a heavily windowed sunroom where a sea of indoor plants flourished. Haas was bent over, using a white plastic can to water the base of a dieffenbachia.

"Ah, thank you, Lupita," he said to the woman. But instead of leaving the room, she motioned that she wanted to tell him something before the questioning got underway.

"Heather is to go to ballet soon, so I drive her there," she said. "Then I go to the grocery store and then pick up the cleaning you said is waiting for you."

After he nodded that he understood, she scurried to pull into the room a couple of small chairs for Bree and Liam. Dalton Lee and Lara took the two armchairs that were in one corner; Agent Sainclair elected to stand.

"So, this is about Valenzuela, is it?" Haas said, turning his attention back to all the foliage. "I assume somebody told you about our history and that's why you're here."

The coach was wearing a thin, dark flannel shirt, jeans, and black sneakers. He was a few years younger than Stewart Wilbanks but twenty pounds heavier. Whereas Wilbanks bore a joviality along with his world-weariness, Haas seemed to bear just more world-weariness. Although he brandished a full head of hair, it was mostly white; his eyeglasses were slid as far south onto the bridge of his nose as they could be without falling off. He did not saunter from plant to plant so much as lumber between them, and several of them had leaves that seemed as sad as the person doing his best to replenish them.

"Thank you for making time for us," Sainclair began.

Haas interrupted him with an ironic chuckle. "Not a problem," he said, shaking his head a bit. "Time I have plenty of these days." The coach turned his attention from the taller plants in pots on the floor, to a series of smaller plants tucked into colorful containers that rested on one of the floor-to-ceiling bookshelves that lined the far wall.

As Lee might have expected, the shelves contained a wealth of books on football, football players and football coaches, but also a few devoted to such topics as contemporary dance and—of particular interest to Lee—Szechuan cuisine.

"As I said on the phone, Mr. Haas, we're just here to ask you some routine questions. If you would, please describe how it was you came to coach at Miami A&M."

Haas seemed to perk up a bit—probably because he was being given a chance to relive his glory days, Lee assumed.

"Well, I was the quarterbacks coach at Maryland State when Wilbanks called me to say they were looking for an offensive coordinator and that some of his trustees thought I might fit the bill." He stopped to inspect a fern he was watering. "Surprised the hell out of me, to be honest."

"Why is that?" Sainclair countered.

Haas sighed and turned to look at the agent. "Well, in this business, there's sort of a pecking order of coaches. I didn't really see myself as being in the . . . stratosphere . . . of those they might consider for a position like that. I'd done okay at Maryland State. We won a few more games than we lost and we went to two bowl games in the five years I was there. But I wouldn't have thought that was a record that would really make anybody at a school like Miami A&M sit up and take notice."

The coach suddenly leaned forward and squinted at one of the floor plants next to Liam and Bree. "I swear no matter what I do to that cat palm, it doesn't seem to want to respond," he said, beleaguered.

Liam glanced at the plant, turned back to the coach. "Um, if I might, I think it might be getting *too much* water."

The coach pushed his glasses back up the bridge of his nose and inspected Liam more closely. "Huh. Too much, you say?" The coach peered back over at the plant. Sighed. "Well, you might just be right on that."

Liam gave Bree one of his toothpaste smiles; she gave him a "well-look-at-you-Mr.-smarty-pants" expression.

Coach Haas sighed heavily. "Now, where were we? Ah, the job offer. And then there was that weird thing about the trustees." He turned and arched onto his toes to water a series of small philodendrons on a high shelf.

"What weird thing?" Sainclair asked.

The coach waited until he had tilted the watering can back to a level position before answering. "The fact I'd never met any of them, never heard of them," he replied.

He headed over to a small metal shelf next to the bookcases and carefully set the watering can upon it. "Usually you know the people who are recommending you for a job. Maybe you went to college with them, or they're the brother of another coach you've worked with somewhere. I'd never heard of those guys. But, I wasn't going to look a gift horse in the mouth, as they say. They promised that Madeline—she was my second wife—could have a faculty position in the chemistry department, use their world-class laboratories to further her research. My daughter would be able to get a great education for a substantial discount. They were going to increase my salary by about twenty percent. The perks were great . . . so it was like a dream come true." He chuckled to himself. "I take that back, it wasn't *like* a dream come true . . . it *was* a dream come true."

"Dad?"

Everyone turned to see standing in the doorway a reedy, delicate, young woman in leotards, a canvas backpack slung over one shoulder.

"Sorry," she continued, holding on to the doorway with her right hand. Her torso was tilted forward and balanced over one leg. "Lupita's driving me to dance class. I'm going over to Natalie's after that for dinner, and either she or her mom will bring me home about nine."

Her father nodded, then his expression changed slightly. "Come here for a second," he said, beckoning with one hand.

She danced on tiptoes over to her father, who put his arm around her bony shoulders. "Everyone, this is my daughter, Heather. Honey, these are . . . officials . . . who are looking into the . . . Valenzuela matter."

She crinkled up her nose. "Ugh," she said softly. The detectives smiled and acknowledged her as she scrunched closer to her father.

Lee could tell he had just received a message. He slid his hand into his pocket, edged the phone out of it, and glanced at the screen.

HAVING THE DOCUMENTS DRAWN UP NOW.
WILL CONTACT YOU IN A COUPLE OF DAYS
TO HAND THEM OFF TO YOU FOR SIGNATURE.

Lee frowned and dropped the phone back into his pocket. The coach was giving his daughter a peck on the forehead. "Make sure you're home no later than nine-thirty, okay? Don't forget, you have a psychology test tomorrow."

She nodded and pranced back toward and out the doorway, waving briskly at those assembled as she departed. Bree noticed Liam following the young woman's gait all the way to the front door.

"And tell Natalie's mother I said it wouldn't hurt you to have second helpings," he called out after her.

When she was out of sight, he sighed, trudged over to a small desk in the room, and slowly dropped himself onto the nearest corner of it. "Sorry, being a single parent isn't easy," he muttered to no one in particular.

"I thought you mentioned a wife—who was teaching at the university while you were coaching there," Sainclair said.

The coach's expression shifted from one that was foggy, to one that was forlorn. "I did," he replied, casting a quick, embarrassed look at Sainclair. "After I lost my job and we moved out here, she left me. Just walked out. No note. Haven't seen or heard from her since."

He stopped and drummed the front of his desk with his fingertips. "But I feel bad for Heather, mostly. Her mother—my first wife—passed away from leukemia when Heather was three. She hasn't had a female role model for most of her life. Then a few months before I got the job at A&M, Madeline strolled into this little bar I used to frequent near the Maryland State campus. We had this whirlwind romance that she pretty much drove from the start. Soon after, we decided to get married. I figured Heather was finally going to be part of a happy family. But then . . ."

He looked sheepish again. "I'm guessing that's why she's thrown herself into dance the way she has. She practices at least every day. I used to worry about her being addicted to it." The coach waddled back over to his desk and dropped down on one corner of it. "Now I'm just glad she has something in her life she's passionate about."

"Mr. Haas?" It was Lupita this time, keys in her hand and a purse slung over one wrist. "I leave now. There is a casserole on kitchen counter. Put it in the oven at three fifty for . . . thirty minutes. Set out the dark gray suit so you don't forget to take it to the cleaners. And you need to call Heather's principal tonight. She called a few minutes ago."

Lee leaned in Lara's direction. "I think she's the first person I've seen who's even bossier than you are," he whispered, grinning impishly. Lara didn't flinch, except to recross her legs away from Lee.

"So, why was the relationship with Vic Valenzuela . . . so strained?" Agent Sainclair was asking the question of Haas, but his attention seemed to have trailed over to one of the bookshelves behind the coach.

Haas took in a deep breath, twisted his mouth somewhat. "You know, I've finally come to the conclusion that Vic really was the problem child there," he eventually replied. "For a long time, I beat myself up trying to figure out what I had done wrong, what I could have done to make things different. But the fact is, Vic was the issue. Vic was *always* the issue.

"On Monday, he would tell me to come up with some new plays that would give us a more powerful running game. On Thursday, he would say he wanted our quarterback to scramble more and throw deeper passes. One week our offense was too uptight, the next it needed to be more conservative. He'd slap me on the back after a victory and tell me I was the best offensive coordinator he had ever worked with, and then the very next morning would call me into his office and ream my ass for not clearing with him some of the offensive plays I had called.

"On a personal level, he was often friendly . . . even charming. He'd make sure my parents had great seats at a game when they came to town. He was always nice to Heather—he even brought his wife to one of Heather's dance concerts. But professionally, he was completely unpredictable. Vic was dysfunctional for sure, maybe even psychopathic. That's the conclusion I've finally reached, anyway."

Sinclair crossed his arms in front of him. "Something happened that caused him to go to the trustees and ask them to dismiss you, but then he reversed himself. What was that about?"

Lee noticed Sinclair was gazing at the bookcase behind Haas again.

The coach chuckled and focused on a spot just to the left of Sinclair's head. "You know, I remember that, but I really can't remember for sure what it was about. If I remember correctly, it had something to do with a series of plays I had designed that *did* result in a fumble, but we won the game anyway. I think that's what it was, and I have no idea why Vic backed down once the trustees talked to him.

"But I do remember *vividly* what led to my finally getting fired," the coach continued.

"What was that?" Sinclair asked, his attention riveted back onto the coach.

The coach's expression turned distant and dour. "During a game against Alabama Southern, Vic's wife came down to the sidelines. We were ahead something like forty-eight to ten with three minutes left, so we were all pretty loose and joking around, having a fun time. Erika and I had been chatting, and she was standing near me when a play came our direction fast. *Real* fast. I reached out, grabbed her just above the waist, and yanked her out of the way about two seconds before a five-foot-eleven, two-hundred-and-fifteen-pound running back came charging across the sideline right where she'd been standing.

"In the locker room afterward, Vic was livid. Screaming at me like never before. Called me a two-timing, disloyal, son of a bitch. *In front of the players.* And one week later, I was no longer the offensive coordinator for the Miami A&M Centurions."

He stared at each person in the room for at least a couple of seconds. "I mean, really, how much of a sicko does a person have to be to fire somebody who probably had just prevented his wife from getting a broken neck?"

No one said a word. No one breathed for what seemed a full minute.

Lee could tell something was nettling Sainclair. The agent kept tweaking his mouth, glancing through his notes on the legal pad, looking back up at Hayden Haas.

"Mr. Haas, earlier today we spoke to Danielo Duran. He is the father of the young man who was found murdered the same night as Erika Valenzuela."

"Yes, I know who he is," the coach replied, his expression becoming steely.

"He told us that at the trial, you told him Vic Valenzuela shouldn't get away with the murders of his wife and Mr. Duran's son. He told us you said, and I quote, 'I promise you he won't get away with them.' Is that correct?"

Hayden Haas stared blankly at Sainclair for some time, his jaw rigid, his look intense. But then after a couple of moments, it suddenly all broke, as if he were an actor who had just finished his audition.

"No, of course not . . . I mean, I didn't mean it *literally*," the coach scoffed, looked off at a distant corner of the room. "No, I was just trying to be helpful to the guy. He had just learned that the man who had murdered his son was going to get away with it, for god's sakes. He was devastated."

The coach reached down, plucked a shred of lint from his jeans, and flicked it onto the floor. "I just said what anybody would have said in the situation. I wanted to help him feel better, that's all."

Sainclair sniffed. "I know I told the questions here would just be routine, but I have to ask, Mr. Haas, where were you on the night of the murder?"

Haas had been looking at the floor. But when Sainclair finished the question, he slowly raised his head and looked the federal agent straight in the eyes. "I was at a coaching clinic up in West Palm," he said matter-of-factly.

"Is there someone who can verify that?"

Hayden Haas nodded. "Sure," he said. "But I know where you're going to go with this. And I might as well save you some time. Yes, someone can verify I attended the clinic. But no, there is nobody who can verify I was in my hotel room around eleven thirty on the night that Vic Valenzuela got exactly what he deserved."

13

Well this is definitely an upgrade from before.

Roberto stood on the sidewalk in front of the imposing condo building whose opposite side looked out on Biscayne Bay. This building didn't have a name like all the other condo buildings in the neighborhood, but the address loomed prominent over the entrance, in chrome-colored numerals that vaguely suggested the Deco era.

I'm thinking that font is Gloria, the designer said to himself, his head slightly atilt. *Or maybe it's Mouse Deco?*

Even if he were mistaken about the typeface, he knew he had the right location. That's what mattered most.

He suspected the particular condo unit they had summoned him to was vacant; the way they operated, probably the entire floor was. Since twilight was well underway, he hoped the unit had working electricity. Even a luxury apartment seems creepy when vacant, but it becomes especially so when it's completely dark inside and its view is nothing but a vast, shadowy sea.

He trotted up the marble staircase to the tall glass doors beneath the address. There, a concierge acknowledged him and smiled while holding open the door.

"Which floor are you headed to, sir?" the thirty-something male asked.

Roberto glanced down at his phone. "The . . . ninth," he replied.

The concierge's expression clouded some; he suddenly began to look down at the floor more than at Roberto. "Ah yes, well, then, you'll want to take that bank of elevators on the far left."

Roberto at first chuckled to himself when the porter reacted the way he did. He had become used to the quizzical glances and sudden shifts in behavior his requests at times like this elicited. Then he felt that familiar little quiver of anger erupt inside him. *An eleven-year-old girl shouldn't have to be going through something like this,* he lectured himself. *The plight of an eleven-year-old girl being held hostage shouldn't be the cause for weird looks and cloak-and-dagger meetings like this.*

But he had come up with a plan—if not a plan that would rescue his younger sister from these monsters, then at least one that might help him and the rest of the team determine where The Organization was keeping her.

He pressed the button inside the elevator car. Nothing.

Pressed again. Still nothing.

The designer glanced up at the digital screen that displayed what floor the car was on, tried to spur the elevator into action by telekinesis. *Nada.* He sensed a tiny wave of claustrophobia beginning to creep through his nervous system. *Claustrophobia hell,* he thought. *Who am I kidding? This is the beginning of one of my freak-outs.*

Suddenly, he heard a whirring sound, and the elevator doors magically opened. A man standing perhaps three-and-a-half-feet-tall, and wearing a gray, pinstripe suit accented by a coral-colored dress shirt, strode confidently into the car. He was holding a cell phone horizontally in his hand. Once he was fully inside the car, he turned, pointed the device in the direction of the control panel, and pressed a key on the phone's touchscreen. The whirring sound returned and the doors to the elevator car slowly closed.

Roberto turned and studied the man, who was staring straight ahead. A mere wisp of a moustache arced over the man's upper lip, but his eyebrows were black and bushy. He also was sporting a comb-over, which Roberto found particularly unflattering from above.

Then, like one of those animatronic characters in a theme park ride, the little man slowly rotated his head toward Roberto and his simper elongated into a full-fledged smile. A silver tooth peeked out from the bottom tier of teeth.

"Good evening, Mr. Bermudez," he said in a voice that sounded as if it were mildly influenced by an intake of helium. "Sorry for that delay. We wanted to be certain no one had followed you here."

Roberto considered this for a couple of seconds, decided to have some fun with his companion. "Well, if someone *was* following me," he said, "I'm pretty sure you scared them off."

From below, the diminutive man allowed his smile to retreat inch by inch until his expression became chilly and impassive. He turned back toward the front and seemed to be studying their distorted reflections in the highly polished elevator door.

Soon the car glided to a stop and the doors opened without the man taking the cell phone out of his pocket. The hallway bombarded Roberto with a hazy mixture of periwinkle and powder blue. The wallpaper bore a pattern that was something between a flame stitch and a paisley—a psychedelic mash-up Roberto felt certain they had chosen for its ability to disorient anyone who might venture onto the floor. He stood still in the center of the hallway in an effort to orient himself, but veered left only when he felt his escort brush his wrist in passing and mutter, "This way." They walked to the end of the hall but just as they were approaching it, a door on the right opened automatically.

Roberto was in a playful mood. "That's some wrist action you've got there," he said to his consort, who somehow managed a high-pitched twitter despite not having moved a single facial muscle.

The condo was amazingly like Roberto had imagined it . . . in his worst-case scenario. The only way it varied from his vision of bleakness was that the desk in the center of the room sported a chrome pharmacy lamp equipped with a forty-watt, LED bulb. And the windows affording one a vista of a dead-calm Biscayne Bay were flanked by soft, gauzy sheers that billowed gently despite the absence of any breeze.

"There," his escort said, extending his left arm toward a simple, straight-backed chair with a caned seat. His guide waddled around the desk and over to the window. There, he leaned over and squinted through the glass like a dentist inspecting a filling.

The laptop was sitting open immediately beside the lamp; its desktop background comprised a squadron of automatons standing shoulder to shoulder, the phrase "I AM A WAYWARD COLONIST" superimposed over them.

Roberto plopped himself into the erect, uncomfortable chair and raised his right hand to tap the space bar.

"Not yet!" the small man whispered, his voice now huskier. Roberto arched both eyebrows, held his hand in midtap, awaited further instruction. Slowly, his guide closed the sheers toward the center, then almost immediately opened them back just as slowly to their original position. A moment later, the room was awash with a pale red light that seemed to be emanating from some sloop out at sea. The vermilion hue inched first along the wall to Roberto's right, then along the wall behind him (bathing him, in the process in a faded-out red), then along the wall on his left, shifting both in size and geometry depending on which canvas it was traveling along. Once it had made a full run of the room, the light snuffed out like a candle on a birthday cake.

"Okay, *now*," the small man said, tugging on the bottom of his suit coat as he turned from the window.

Roberto tapped the space bar once and the screen glowed with the color of the beacon that had just filled the room. In the center, a yellow wheel spun repeatedly, and then (much faster than it ever had before, he noticed) the gleaming face of his little sister appeared.

"*Hola, mi pequeña mariposa. ¿Qué más?*"

Isabela shrugged her shoulders and smiled a toothy grin. "I'm OK," she replied. "Why do you always first speak to me in Spanish, 'Berto? I speak English, too, you know. Mostly English . . . now."

He chuckled. She was getting so mature, so quickly. He wondered if she had any sort of female figure there to help her through the puberty she was on the threshold of, a puberty she may have already entered, for all he knew.

"Yes, I know that," he said to her. "But I don't want you to lose touch with your heritage. *Tu cultura*. In fact, I thought maybe the next time we get the opportunity to chat, we'd start playing a little game that will help you with your Spanish."

"What is it?" she said, shooting him a look that made it clear she thought she was far too grown up to still be playing games with her older brother.

Roberto opened his mouth, then demurred. At the far right of the screen, he spotted the slimmest of shadows grow slightly larger as the person casting it edged closer to Isabela.

"Um . . . we'll get to that in a minute," he replied. "But first, I have some good news. Remember our cousin, Necha?"

Isabela squinted some; seemed to be having trouble remembering.

"*Necha.* She used to babysit you on the weekend and throw *guanábanas* at you while you ran around in the yard."

Isabela's face brightened with remembrance. She nodded. "Oh yeah, I liked her a lot. She used to tell me ghost stories under the sheets late at night."

"Exactly. Well, guess what, she had a baby!"

Her face brightened even more. "A boy or a girl?"

"A girl," Roberto replied. "And they named her Bella. After you."

Isabela's eyes got wide and her smile exploded. "That is so cool!" she exclaimed. "I can't wait . . ." Then her face dimmed and Roberto's pulse galloped.

He bit down on his lower lip for several seconds. He did not want to blow this. He could not allow his anger to screw up this opportunity. As he had with so many other opportunities in the past.

He took a moment to study her more closely. "You doing okay?" he queried, his head down, but his eyes tilted up toward the screen in search of any scar or scratch she might not want to acknowledge to him.

She pursed her lips at him, shrugged and bobbed her head up and down.

"Any illness? Are you eating your vegetables?"

She nodded again, only more mechanically this time, which told him most likely, they still were not feeding her any vegetables at all.

"Good, okay," he said, feeling his nerves catch up with his pulse. "So, like I was saying a minute ago, I thought maybe the next time we got to talk, we'd play a little game. One of the games we used to play back in Puerto Rico."

She nodded, waited for more.

"Remember how we used to play *Veo, veo?*"

She nodded again only now she looked directly at him, her eyes did not move from his.

"Here in America, they call it, I Spy. But we will play it in Spanish, so you can practice the language."

She continued to blaze a hole into the back of his head.

He chose to slow down his speech in hopes his intent would get through.

"First, you will say, '*Veo, veo,*' and then you will say, 'Something . . . something what?'"

"*Algo que empieza con . . .*"

"Right, 'something beginning with,' and then you'll say what the first letter is in whatever it is you see . . . there."

Her eyes bulged a bit, her lips twisted into a discreet smile.

"Understand, Isabela? And then I will try to guess what the thing, or the many things that you spy, are. And you will tell me if I am right or not. And then vice versa."

He could tell from the vaguely conspiratorial look on her face. She understood.

"Wonderful," he said hurriedly. He glanced at his phone, which was sitting beside a stained mouse pad to the left of the laptop. "We don't have very much time left. So is there anything you want me to say to Mama Minga and Tio Santos?"

She looked down at her smock, played with the top button for a minute, suddenly got an idea. "Tell them to send me some corn ice cream!" she said, giggling.

Roberto nodded with recognition at the exotic ice cream flavor he and Isabela would share at the *heladeria*, the flavor they would choose when they weren't eating the salt-cod version of the dessert.

"I'll be sure to tell them that. That's the very first thing we'll do once we . . ."

The computer didn't shut off so much as grind to a halt. Regardless, she was gone.

But she had understood. *Maybe this will work, after all*, he thought. He turned to look behind him. The door to the room had somehow reopened, the light in the hallway beckoned him from the room. He stood up, assuming his chaperone would want to accompany him at least to the bank of the elevators.

But his escort was sleeping in a chair by the window, his mouth agape, a soft snore filling the room. His baby-like head was plopped to one side, resting precariously in the palm of one tiny, cupped hand.

14

Intermittent showers arrived the following morning, dampening Lee's mood. And the architect was still trying to recover from the conversation that had taken place at Vizcaya. Lee had never been afraid of death. But neither had he been forced—as he had during the conversation at that estate—to so vividly confront the unpleasantness that can accompany the end-of-life experience.

He wasn't depressed, really. But he was feeling pretty sour.

Much to Lee's chagrin, Agent Sainclair was the antithesis of sour when he called the architect that morning.

"*Bonjou!* Mr. Lee. *Kijan ou ye?* Are you ready for more investigating?" Sainclair seemed beyond enthusiastic—he was ecstatic.

What have you done with the real Mackeson Sainclair? was all Lee could think. "Yes, of course," he replied. "And how are you . . . Mackeson?"

"Wonderful! *Mwen byen!* Poseidon's Prince came through in the ninth. Came from four lengths behind in the final stretch. It was *enkwayab!*"

Lee shook his head. "Excuse me?" Then the architect deduced that the agent must have been at Hialeah Park the night before. "Ah, well, congratulations, Mackeson. Was it a big wager?"

"Quite big," Sainclair replied. "Will buy us a nice lunch today! But first, the writer who was working on the biography about Vic Valenzuela has agreed to an interview. Put on your running shoes."

"My running shoes?"

"Yes, running shoes, sneakers," the agent urged. "He is to be questioned while he takes a run along the river. He leaves this afternoon for a week in Little Duck Key, so this is our one chance to talk to him."

Lee blew out some air. He had been fairly regular with his exercise regimen prior to their leaving for Miami. But his workout revolved solely around a medicine ball, a barbell, a Chinese wand, and an Indian club. The benefits they brought him were greater strength and agility. He hadn't undertaken a serious cardio program in months.

"Okay," he said weakly into his phone. The architect decided it might be good to have Liam come along. He felt he needed to be including the young man more in the investigation . . . and he figured Liam could probably keep up with the others if Lee's stamina started to wane.

"Sure thing, Dalton," Liam said when his boss gave him marching orders. "I'll meet you in the lobby fifteen of."

The sportswriter, whose name was Todd Cavender, suggested they run along North River Drive, starting not far from Lee's hotel. Cavender turned out to be more of a committed runner than Lee had expected. He was dressed in ultrashort running shorts that were navy blue with a fuchsia stripe up the sides; his lime-green tank top bore the motto RUN RAGGED in tall capital letters, and his legs possessed the wiry muscularity associated with marathoners (although the sportswriter told them he had never attempted one).

"I'm not really into all that competitive crap," he said, jogging in place to warm up. "I run against myself. Against my watch."

He yanked his head in one direction. "Let's go."

The quartet trotted off along North River Drive, heading northwest. The showers had abated, but the clouds were charcoal and threatening. Lee found he was also impressed with Mackeson Sainclair's athleticism. Although the agent was the oldest of the four, he had a commanding gait, as though he had run track for many years. Liam, in contrast, ran like a linebacker, and had to slow himself repeatedly so as not to leave the others in his dust. Lee held up well at first, but after a quarter mile, the humidity began to press on his chest. His choosing to run in a hefty white t-shirt was already proving to be a bad idea.

"So, the book on Vic Valenzuela . . . how did that come about?" Sainclair asked the writer.

From his post next to Sainclair, but closer to the river, Cavender shot the federal agent an ironic look. "What else? Money. Some independent publisher contacted me, told me they had inked a deal with him, and that they had read my stuff and thought I might be a good fit for the project. We went from there."

"What's the name of the publishing company?"

Cavender looked up to the sky to think on that. "Iberá. Ibero. Something like that. I think it means 'Spanish.'"

"Nah, it's the name of a series of wetlands," Liam tossed over one shoulder. "In Argentina."

Everyone's breathing became more labored. Lee was getting a second wind but was also slowly beginning to fall behind. On their right stood a midrise building that on one hand looked residential but on the other possessed the efficient sterility of an office building. It was a brilliant white, and Lee could not find any identifying markers on it. Quickly he calculated the number of floors—there were thirteen.

Now that's odd, he thought as he struggled to catch back up with the others.

"What exactly . . . was the book to be about?" Sainclair asked Cavender. "Is it still going to get published?"

"No, it's not and that's just *idiotic*," the sportswriter responded. "It was really going to be a puff piece. How Vic brought himself up by the bootstraps to become the winningest college football coach in modern history, yadda, yadda." He let out a huff. "I mean, I understand I was only able to get about a third of the information we needed for a full biography before he was murdered. But the guy is now the most talked about sports personality of the year. Maybe the *decade*. The book really should get published anyway. I'm still working on that."

"In the course of doing the research that you *were* able to conduct . . . did you come across anyone who just suddenly appeared in Mr.

Valenzuela's life? Out of the blue? Someone who seemed like the sort of person who wanted to harm him or might have indicated they'd like to get him out of their way?"

Lee noticed that Sainclair was dropping about half a pace behind Cavender. Liam was a hundred feet or so ahead of the group. A young woman with long brown hair walking toward them with an afghan hound on a leash slowed as they approached. Just before they met, all the men edged to the right to let her comfortably pass—all of them, that is, except for Cavender, who kept his stride and brushed against her side as he passed. She frowned at him over one shoulder.

"Yeah, sure, lots of people," the journalist replied. "One of the things . . . I came to learn about Vic in the time I spent with him . . . was that he was one of those people who makes friends easily and makes enemies just as easily. And everybody *wanted* to be . . . his friend . . . his wingman, if it were.

"Like, once, I met him at this sports bar . . . in the Grove. When I walked in, he had two guys on one side of him buying him drinks. And three on the other. They were doing shots . . . and singing some Cuban folk song Vic had taught them. A song like 'Guantanamera,' only faster. He was both a babe magnet *and* a bro' magnet.

"But then, all it would take . . . was someone delivering a word with the wrong inflection . . . and Vic would be swinging them around, above his head, the way some sports fans twirl a towel to egg their team on." The writer paused, caught his breath, gave a short laugh. "He was the *perfect* subject for a biography."

The more Cavender talked, the more Lee began to feel the writer himself missed being the wingman to Vic Valenzuela's top gun.

"Anyone . . . in particular . . . stand out?" Sainclair asked. The agent had surged to where he was running alongside the journalist, but the effort had obviously taken the wind out of him.

"No, I can't say *that*," the writer replied. They stopped and ran in place for a few seconds at an intersection, waiting for the stoplight to change. "I mean, if you're looking for suspects, I think the best candidates are staring you in the face, really." The light went green, but they held up for a moment to let a kid on a skateboard glide past them.

"Best candidates?" Sainclair probed as they jogged across the avenue.

The writer lowered his voice as they prepared to ascend the curb on the opposite side of the street. "Well, take Astrid, for example, his sister-in-law. I shouldn't tell you this, but—oh, what the hell does it matter now?—Vic insisted to me they went to bed together once."

Agent Sainclair glanced back at Lee and raised one eyebrow. "Vic Valenzuela . . . and Astrid Steinberg?"

"Yeah. And the best part of it? He swears *she* came on to *him*."

Sainclair exchanged another look with Lee, who shrugged his shoulders and picked up the pace a bit to be in a better position to keep up with the gossip.

"Then there's the chick out in California—the sideline reporter."

"What about her?" Sainclair said.

"Well, she did seem to just dive-bomb out of nowhere. She was very aggressive with Vic. Which was all well and good, except, well, he was under indictment at the time. I mean, I can understand the whole gold digger thing. But this girl has a great job with a primo network. She's making at least a high-six-figure salary every year. Why would somebody like that make a serious run at a guy who might be in prison for the next fifty years of his life? And from what Vic told me, she seemed a little, you know, cra-cra."

Sainclair scrunched his nose. "Weird? Weird how?"

The writer glanced over at the federal agent, quickly brushed sweat from his brow with his right forearm. "You know, bipolar, manic-explosive, whatever it is they call it. Vic told me once he thought he'd probably marry her. I assumed that's why he went out to California right before his murder. He was going to propose to her, I'm pretty sure. So, who knows . . .?"

Sainclair was starting to flag again. Lee suspected the deluge of information and well-qualified suspects was more than a little to blame for the agent's fatigue. Fortunately for Sainclair, the sky chose to open up with a sudden downpour. Lee called out to Liam, who was still many yards ahead. The younger architect circled back and joined them as they ducked into a Mexican restaurant that conveniently appeared on their left.

The restaurant was dark and cool, overly air-conditioned, Lee thought. Tiny replicas of the Mexican flag hung on a thin cord that stretched across the back wall; knockoff versions of the hacienda-style furniture they had seen at Vic Valenzuela's estate cluttered the long, horizontal room. High on the wall to their right, a large television monitor broadcast a soccer game from somewhere in Latin America. There was outdoor seating in the back that faced the river, but it had just been cordoned off because of the rain. So they commandeered a mint-green vinyl booth at the opposite end of the room, sitting beneath a neon ad for one of the cheap Mexican beers the restaurant sold.

In the spirit of healthiness, the three detectives ordered iced teas and a small basket of chips and salsa.

"I'll have a top-shelf margarita on the rocks," Cavender said briskly.

Agent Sainclair glanced yet again at Lee, who returned the detective's look with a faint, Cheshire-cat grin.

"To be honest, I don't know how I can be of much help to you," the writer said, after taking a big gulp of the ice water in front of him. He set the glass back down and twirled the bottom of it in the moisture that had collected on the tabletop. "The more one gets to know Vic Valenzuela, the more people you bump into who might have wanted to do him in. He was just that sort of personality. He used women. He used business associates. He pissed off co-workers left and right. And when you have organized gambling interests angry at you, well . . ."

The writer picked up his tumbler again, but this time took only a quick sip.

"Organized gambling interests.' What does that mean?" Agent Sainclair was pulling a napkin toward him. When the restaurant's paunchy proprietor brought the table its beverages and chips, he asked him, "Do you have an extra pen or pencil?" The owner nodded once and said, "*Si*. I will get one."

The writer smiled with his arcane knowledge. "First, I really don't if this is true or not. It very well might not be. But I've been told by more than one source that Vic was approached a year or two ago to—um, how should we say it?—*influence* the outcome of some of his team's games. And that he went along with it—for a while. Vic would always dodge the topic when I'd bring it up. With a wink. Said there was no way he could affect how a bunch of nineteen- and twenty-year-olds perform on a football field on any given day. That he couldn't *possibly* dictate when a fumble, or an interception, or an errant pass, might happen."

The writer paused to toss to the side the straw poking out of his margarita, to lift the heavy glass to his lips, and then take a long, luxuriating drink. Once he had set the glass back down, he added, "Of course, we all know that's a bunch of bullshit."

Lee noticed that Liam, who was sitting on the opposite side of Cavender, had extracted his phone from a pocket in his shorts. He was squinting at the screen and appeared to be flipping through several messages. When he had finished reading, he set the phone on the table and with two fingers, nudged it away from his paper placemat. The phone slid to a rest adjacent to Cavender's.

The proprietor returned and handed Sainclair a cheap ballpoint pen without its cap. "These gambling interests. Can you identify any of them?" the detective said, flipping the pen around so he could write with it.

Cavender shook his head, took another ample sip from his drink. "No, I never pursued that story. I value my life too much to get myself in the middle of that sort of shit."

They munched on a few chips; Cavender glanced at his sports watch. Lee decided he had better ask the journalist a question that had been twisting around in his mind for some time.

"We were told that Valenzuela's house was having a lot of problems. Structural issues, that sort of thing. You know anything about that?"

Cavender contemplated the information for a second. "Yeah, I seem to remember Vic mentioning something about that. Apparently the contractors were pretty shady. I think he told me once they were going to have to repair or replace stuff from one end of the house to the other over the next couple of years."

Lee thought on that. "I'm wondering . . . don't you think it a little odd that a major university would hire contractors who were so inept at their job?"

The writer looked off in the distance, tapped the side of his margarita glass. "I guess so," he replied. "I don't know. Probably happens all the time. Their business is education, not construction, right?"

The table grew quiet, almost somber. Then, out of the blue, the writer perked up, as if someone had plugged him into a nearby outlet.

"But, if you ask me," he said, reclaiming his keys and phone from the tabletop, "it's probably too late for you to find your murderer. Whoever did it is probably all the way to the West Coast by now. Or, deep into Mexico or South America. Or, they're lying on a beach in the Caymans or on Bora Bora . . . if they're smart, anyway." He sat up straight. "Sorry, I have to go. I have a romantic dinner scheduled tonight down in the Keys. A nice start to a well-deserved vacation. I'll need to hit the road soon."

The foursome paid their bill and filed out of the restaurant. The sun had emerged while they were inside, elevating the temperature in the process.

"There are usually a lot of taxis waiting for fares just up the street there," Cavender said, as he darted toward a bridge in the opposite direction that would take him to the south side of the river. "Hope I was helpful."

He sped off, disappearing quickly around a grove of bamboo shoots that shielded part of the restaurant from the road.

The trio trudged toward a point several yards up where a cab or two appeared to be idling.

"Well, he certainly supplied us with a lot of data," Lee finally said to Sainclair. "I'm not sure though that it was all that helpful in our narrowing the focus of the investigation."

Sainclair was sucking intently on a toothpick he had plucked from an oval wicker basket that was sitting on a vending machine near the restaurant's front door. Liam had his head down into his phone again; Lee presumed he was scanning more messages.

"Maybe," the federal agent replied, gazing straight ahead. "Mr. Cavender is a curious man, I believe. *Li pale franse.*" The agent pivoted his head and smiled directly at Lee. "Literally, it means, 'He speaks French.' In Haiti, that is what we mean by, 'He can't be trusted.'"

"You're telling me," Liam suddenly said, still studying the screen on his phone.

"What do you mean?" Lee asked his associate.

The young architect took a deep breath. "Didn't Cavender just say he was having dinner down in the Keys tonight?" The other detectives nodded.

Liam held up his phone and turned the screen around so Sainclair and Lee could read it. "I bumped his phone while we were sitting in the restaurant and downloaded most of what was on it. According to this itinerary his travel agent sent him a couple of days ago, he's scheduled to be on a plane for Anchorage in about four hours."

15

Irene stared at the phone as it shimmied next to her on the floor. The hotel room had been a blissful oasis all day and she had been savoring her afternoon of research. She didn't appreciate her concentration being interrupted.

She picked up the phone, looked to see who was calling her.

What does HE want with ME? she wondered.

For several seconds, she stared at both the IGNORE and ACCEPT options. Chose to accept.

"Hello?"

"Irene? This *is* Irene, right? It's Liam. The new guy on the team."

"Right. Yeah, I saw that on the phone."

He let out an embarrassed laugh. "Right. I should have known that. Sorry. Hey I was wondering if you were available to chat for a few minutes. Since we're going to be working together so much, I thought it might be nice to . . . get to know one another better."

Irene chewed the inside of one cheek. "Right now?" she replied. She glanced over at her tablet computer; she had hoped to spend some time catching up with her friends on CyWorld.

"If you can, that would be spiffy. Probably only take fifteen or twenty."

She pulled her phone away from her ear to see what time it was. It wasn't that late; she could afford a few minutes. "Okay, you can stop by if you want," she finally said.

"Aw . . . yeah, I was wondering if maybe I could get you to come up here to my room," he replied. "There's something I'd like to show you."

She hesitated. *That's a little odd*, she thought. But then she recalled Lara telling her all about the guy's credentials and about his sister and what a superb technogeek he was beneath his surfer-boy exterior. *I'm sure it's fine*, she decided.

"Okay, I'll be up in a few minutes," she said as she began to disentangle herself from the many cords around her and lift herself up off the carpet.

When he opened the door, she thought at first that she had caught him just out of the shower. He was wearing only a pair of robin's-egg-blue surf shorts that were, well, *very short*, and a white tank top (or, as Liam referred to it, a "singlet") with some rock band tour logo on it. That was it. No socks, no shoes. And, for some reason, his hair was wet.

"Sorry, I just threw some gel in it," he told her when she couldn't seem to stop gawking at it. "Hope it's okay I'm just in me togs this morning. I sort of felt like being really casual today. Florida's a really casual place, right?"

She nodded and made a conscientious effort to close her gaping mouth. It wasn't that she found him attractive. She didn't. He wasn't her type at all, even though he was the sort of guy most girls find *very* attractive. She had just never met anyone who so effortlessly carried around with them so much—"personal magnetism."

"So, Irene, take a seat here," he said, quickly clearing a haphazard stack of shorts, sandals, and—she noted—very skimpy underwear from a chair in his room. She sat on the very front edge of the chair, her ankles crossed in front of her, her fingers fiddling with the bottom hem of her blouse.

"Would you like some water?" he asked, suddenly the compliant host. He jumped up before she answered and charged over to the minifridge under the sink in the suite's pseudo kitchen, where he extracted a bottle of still water the size of a small carton of milk. "No worries, the tab's on me," he said, flashing a smile that Irene guessed he had used to start more than one bushfire back home in Australia.

"So, tell me all about yourself," he said, plopping himself horizontally onto the sofa.

She looked around the room, tried to reconstruct any chapter of her life she thought he might find even remotely interesting. Didn't he know Asian girls don't like to talk about themselves? Well they like to talk about themselves, but not to guys. Especially guys like *him*. Asian girls were trained to listen. To nod a lot, and smile. And listen. Or, pretend to listen, anyway. And nod a lot.

And smile a lot.

"Well . . ." she began, pulling at the fabric on the chair she sat in, "um . . ."

"How much of Korea do you remember?" he suddenly shot out, a smile still dominating his face.

She looked at him, transfixed. *How does somebody get such confidence?* she thought.

"Uh, not a lot," she replied. "Some. But I think maybe a lot of what I remember may really be from some of the visits I've had there since we left."

He closed his grin into a firm line but nodded solidly at what she was saying.

"I mean, I remember *some* things. The subway system was pretty new when we left there, but I remember riding it all of the time. Korean barbecue is really good. But I also remember it really stinks there. I mean, a lot of the sewers are open and there are all the fish markets, so . . ." She stopped, suddenly aware that she was doing all of the talking.

"Have you ever been there?" she finally asked him.

He was smiling again, shook his head.

"Nah," he replied. "Been to Japan once, but that was only for a few days. Went there to study the biology of some of the anemones around the islands in the south. Got totally rotten the one night I spent in Tokyo. Can't remember a thing about that." They both laughed and she took a swig of the water.

"But no, never set foot in Korea."

He was quiet for a second, contemplating the carpet. Then, out of nowhere, "So who's *your* hostage? They never really told me."

Suddenly she felt as if she had a sore throat, or as if the lozenge she had taken for her sore throat had gotten stuck in . . . her throat. She also felt a little peaked. That's what Westerners called it, wasn't it? "Peaked?"

"Well, he's a friend from school," she began, although she instantly wondered if she had already misspoken. Meaning, did he really consider her a friend? How could someone who is being held hostage by terrorists think of the person responsible for that (even if it was accidental) as a *friend*?

"Did you know him in Korea?" Liam prodded.

"No, um, we met in Vancouver," she replied. *Getting this out of me is NOT going to be easy, no matter how nice you are,* she told herself.

"I love Vancouver!" he suddenly erupted. "I've actually surfed off the coast there! Well, Vancouver Island, anyway!"

"Really?" she replied. She didn't really care; she was back to her usual practice of deferring to the male in the room. She had never understood this thing guys had for sports, for always having to beat somebody else at something, or as was the case here, conquering nature somehow. *Why couldn't guys just get along with everyone and everything around them?* she wondered.

"Yeah, I mean, the surf there's nowhere near as awesome as Australia or Hawaii, but we made a go of it," he said. Then his look became more serious. "Anyway, sorry, back to you, and your story."

She gulped quietly. *Wow,* she thought. *He seems to really care.* She felt an odd flutter inside her. She wasn't attracted to him, but she *was* beginning to come to the conclusion that she liked him. That she liked him a lot.

She focused upon a location in the carpet near the one he seemed to have been zeroed in on.

"We were in school together and I had been reading about this weird cult and how they had tried to assassinate an American congresswoman several years ago. I thought it was kind of interesting and so did he . . . Sung-min, that is. That's his name. Anyway, I started doing some research on the side, and I realized the group wasn't all that sophisticated when it came to things like encryption and password managers and authentication protocols."

He was silent, nodding at her slowly again as encouragement to continue.

She took a deep breath. "So, I started poking around. And I learned a lot about them . . . especially about their technology assets and how they use technology."

Liam was still reclining on the sofa like Olympia in the painting by Manet.

"And . . .?" he asked her, looking more deeply into her than she felt comfortable with. And yet, she somehow felt completely comfortable with it.

"And . . . I had been doing all of my research . . . on *his* computer. While he was in class, or while he was sleeping, or while he was out with his friends. He was a part-time teacher's assistant, so the Wi-Fi access on his computer was a whole lot more sophisticated than the ones I had on mine.

"And eventually The Organization caught on to me, discovered what I was doing. I was stupid, really. It turned out they were a lot smarter about tracking software than they were with the rest of their technology. At the time, I didn't think it would make much of a difference. But one night, he was walking back to campus from a bar and they pulled up beside him in this huge black van and threw him into the back of it at gunpoint."

Her breaths were coming almost in heaves at this point. She had never fully relayed the story like this before. Certainly not to someone whom she knew as little as she did this guy.

"Whoa. Were you with him when that happened, Irene?" Liam asked softly.

The question suspended over both of them for some time. Finally, she gently, and sadly, nodded.

She expected him to laugh, or to say something like, "You're kidding me!" or tell some story he thought topped hers, or do one of the many goofball things that guys tend to do at such a moment.

Instead, he just looked at her. Quietly. For a very long time. And eventually just said, "Wow." Then he rose from the couch, padded over to her, bent down and put his arms around her.

In any other situation, she would have evaded the embrace the way a cat darts away from an overly affectionate stranger. But for some reason, this felt . . . okay. And maybe she needed it. And he wasn't getting icky. He just hugged her. Gradually, almost without realizing it, she allowed herself to accept his comfort. She locked her hands together along the top of his back and was amazed at how broad and solid it felt.

"That must have been horrible, Irene," he eventually whispered into her ear. "Must still be horrible. I hope you know that it wasn't your fault. You can't let yourself feel any guilt about it." He squeezed her tightly once, for good measure. "You just can't," he said. "You shouldn't. No need to, understand?"

He held her for a moment longer, and then, just as suddenly as he had been there for her, he was away and off on another topic.

"Come here, I want you to take a look at this," he beckoned.

He was standing in front of the work desk, his back to her. And looking at him there, standing there in that way, in *those* shorts, she felt for the first time a stirring she really didn't want to feel.

"What is it?" she replied, sauntering over next to where he stood. He had made a few quick taps on the keyboard of his laptop and was gazing into the screen, which bathed the room in a blue-green glow.

"You told me something very private about you," he said, "so I feel an obligation to do the same in return. I respect the fact you shared something that matters a lot to you. Well, here is something that matters a great deal to me."

In the husky twilight of a Miami night, Irene glared into her co-worker's computer screen, which was filled with poorly lit photographs of girls younger than her in various stages of seductive undress. Some were on their stomachs with their ankles coiled in the air behind them, others stood with one hand on a hip, a finger posed suggestively in their mouth.

She took a step or two closer to the screen, read a few words posted on either side of the photos, took a large step back, and slowly put one hand to her mouth.

All she could think was, *Oh my god . . .*

16

"Here kitty, kitty."

She navigated her way through the jungle of philodendrons, bromeliads, and palmettos that dominated the tiny back yard. Her visitor remained on the small, rotting porch, fiddling subconsciously with the drawstrings on his windbreaker.

"Want some help?" he called out to her.

She stopped for a moment, considered the offer. "Oh, I've got it," she answered. "Besides, these cats are a lot more likely to come to me than to you."

She paused, gave some thought as to where she wanted to set the saucer of milk she was balancing in her right hand. "You know, most people here don't realize how bad the feral cat problem is in Miami," she went on. "There's so many of them, the authorities here call the groups that they congregate in 'colonies.' Ain't that somethin'?"

"Yes, it is," the silver-haired gentleman replied quietly. "And, for our purposes, appropriate."

The woman swiveled slowly around to him, flashed a knowing smile that briefly revealed a glint of silver embedded within her lower row of teeth.

"Yes, I guess that's right. I hadn't really thought of it like that. But you're right."

He winked at her once; she winked back, then returned her focus to the cluttered yard. She took another couple of steps forward, then (with more than a little effort) bent over and placed the milk next to an edging formed by a cluster of bright-red plants.

"Here, kitty kitty," she repeated in a singsong voice. "Here, kitty kitty. Come on, cat!"

Suddenly, a luminous black feline hopped onto the old stone wall that outlined the boundaries of the yard. It lifted its head, surveyed the scene, stretched some, then dropped onto the ground beside the barrier. Deftly, it slunk its way through the foliage until it was only a foot or two from the milk.

The woman gave a short cackle.

"That one there's Zeus. Or that's what I call him anyway. Thinks he has full reign of the place, he does. Most of the other cats around here are scared of him. I'm not really all that crazy about him myself, but he keeps the rat population down, so I keep him fat and happy and otherwise, try to leave him alone."

The cat slithered between the woman's legs, brushing up against her calves in a quick show of gratitude. Then it darted toward the milk, lapping it from the saucer with several fast flicks of the tongue. The woman leaned her head to the right, crossed her pudgy arms in front of her, and smiled sweetly as the cat made a few final laps at the saucer.

She exhaled heavily and waited. Her visitor stepped off the porch and sauntered forward, watching the cat move away from the milk.

Zeus advanced on a gazing ball a few feet in front of them, but suddenly doddered off to the right. A moment later it was back where it had been, but seemed to become confused when it first circled around itself counterclockwise, then repeated the maneuver in the opposite direction.

The animal's decline was rapid and fierce. Within seconds, it tossed its head first one way then the other like a condemned man avoiding a noose. Soon, the torso and head jerks became more frequent and violent. At one point, the cat's mouth widened and locked open, revealing fangs that were jagged and yellow. Finally, falling to one side, Zeus stiffened then vibrated, as if he were undergoing rounds of electrical shocks.

Seconds later, the cat lost all its bodily functions, issued a final heave of breath.

Nothing.

Frozen.

Gone.

The old woman tilted her head toward her opposite shoulder, lifted her right leg, and kicked the almost rigid corpse with her toes. Then she swiveled around to her visitor and arched her eyebrows.

"What do you think?" she asked, with an air of efficiency. He thrust his fists into the pockets of his running shorts, hunched his shoulders, gave the woman a fast, soldierly nod.

"I think we're there," was all he said.

17

They might be eavesdropping.

Dalton Lee didn't relish the possibility that the planning sessions with his team might be overheard. It had never dawned on him The Organization might go to such lengths. But it made sense that they could. And that they might.

Place a bug beneath one of the drawers in his dresser. Affix a microphone behind a piece of artwork. Run wires from an air duct to a van outside or just register one of their associates into the suite next door and have them listen through a drinking glass pressed firmly against the wall.

The options were endless, and they all made him skittish.

So he devised a Plan B for the meeting that he felt it important they now have—convene in the lobby bar of the renowned Fontainebleau Hotel in Miami Beach.

Opened in 1954, the hotel was the crowning achievement of Morris Lapidus, the son of Orthodox Jews who fled Ukraine to New York with his family when he was an infant. Over time, it became not just the iconic symbol for the Miami Modern (MiMo) style that Lapidus unveiled throughout the region, it became the emblem of the cool, glamorous lifestyle of those who vacationed in Miami Beach in the mid-twentieth century. It served as the backdrop for such movies as Frank Sinatra's *A Hole in the Head*, Jerry Lewis's *The Bellboy*, and the James Bond classic, *Goldfinger*.

But Lee felt the hotel had truly proven itself to be iconic architecture in the way it had achieved an equally colorful reputation in real life. Law enforcement knew the Fontainebleau as the place in the 1970s from which the Black Tuna Gang ran one of the largest marijuana distribution rings at the time. To the architecture community, it was enshrined as the building that won a groundbreaking lawsuit that helped repudiate in the United States the centuries-old "ancient lights" concept. Dating back to the start of English Common Law, the doctrine said that the owner of a building with windows that had received natural daylight for twenty years or more was entitled to forbid any construction or obstruction that would deprive the building of that light. But when the owners of the Eden Roc Hotel next door tried to use that as grounds for a lawsuit designed to stop an addition to the Fontainebleau that would block all of the sunlight coming to its pool and cabana, the Fontainebleau prevailed and the expansion went forward.

Lee was especially pleased to see that the hotel's most recent renovation had preserved many of the quirky details of Lapidus's original design. The curvilinear hallways that had outraged critics when the hotel debuted were still curvilinear but no longer outrageous. Still embedded into the floor of the hotel's lobby were the multiple marble renditions of the black papillon bow tie the architect had worn almost every day. And the famed "Floating Stairway" (now called the "Stairway to Nowhere") still ascended from that hotel lobby to a petite, mezzanine-level platform that provides guests panoramic views of the ground-floor pandemonium . . . and no other option than to descend back down the stairway.

But Lee had chosen to stage the meeting at the Fontainebleau not so much for its architectural heritage but for the philosophy with which its architect had envisioned it. Morris Lapidus once wrote, "If you create a stage and it is grand, everyone who enters will play their part." The hotel was most certainly grand . . . *and* it was fun *and* it was frivolous, *and* it sparked a mood of merriment and glee.

Lee wanted that *joie de vivre* to override the fact that he and his team were about to consider who might have shredded the vital organs of Vic Valenzuela, and how that butchery might relate to the insidious plans of a dangerous cult.

"When we're finished, I might pop into the spa for a treatment or two," Bree said, sliding in next to Liam in the white leather booth that Lee had snared for the team.

The Australian laughed heartily. "Now that you mention it, Bree, a massage sounds like something that just might hit the spot," he replied. Their boss was on the verge of admonishing the pair when he realized the banter was an indication he had definitely selected the right spot for their confab.

Soon enough, everyone else filtered in . . . except for Warren and Agent Weiss, who had messaged Lee they were polishing up some last-minute research and would probably arrive a few minutes later than planned. Lee glanced at his watch. Since even Roberto had made it to the Fontainebleau—by cobbling together trips by shuttle tram, by bus, *and* on foot—Lee was eager to get the discussion underway.

"Ah, here they are," Lara exclaimed as the pair pushed through the front door and scrambled across the lobby toward them.

"Sorry, Dalton," Warren said, a sheepish look on his face. "We—I mean *I*—let the clock get away from me."

"*And* the cabdriver didn't take the easiest route here," added Agent Weiss who— for the first time in the many months that Lee had known her—appeared more ruffled than rested.

"Okay, let's get started," Lee said.

Liam quickly set down his phone and pushed it away from him so it slid to the far end of the table, near where Irene was sitting.

"What's that for?" said Bree.

"You never know," he replied. "Lots of people have listening devices on their phones these days. That woman over there . . ." He pointed to a heavyset woman in a silk pantsuit sitting at a table a few feet away from them. "Or that bloke over there . . ." He nodded toward a college-age male with shoulder-length hair. "Either one of them could be planning to listen in on our conversation. *Fortunately,* I have an app on my phone that scrambles signals like that up to a hundred and fifty feet away."

Lee looked at his protégé with amazement. He hadn't even considered such a possibility. *This kid is going to be a nice add to the team, after all,* he told himself.

"Can I bring all of you something to drink?" A lithe young woman in a sleeveless black shift and low heels stood beside Roberto, smiling expectantly. Irene ordered a soft drink, and Roberto, Warren, and Liam all opted for fruit juices.

"I'll have a vesper martini with a twist," Bree chimed in confidently.

"Oooh, that sounds good, I'll have one as well," Lara said.

Lee turned slowly and arched an eyebrow at his second-in-command. The server cocked her head toward him.

"I believe you carry a special Chinese jie tea here?" he said quietly.

"Yes, we do," she replied. "It may take a few minutes for me to assemble all the items, if you'll bear with me."

"So *that's* why we're meeting here," Warren said, shaking his head. "You sly dog you."

Their boss grinned impishly. "Well, if you can kill two birds with one stone . . ." The architect then straightened in his chair and rubbed his palms together. "All right, Irene, what have you found out through *your* research?"

No answer. Bree glanced at Lara, who reached out and placed a palm on Irene's forearm. "Irene, dear, Dalton asked you a question."

The youngest associate glanced up. "What? I'm sorry? What did you say?"

Dalton narrowed his look at her. "I was just wondering what your research has turned up."

She nudged her glasses up the bridge of her nose. "Well, quite a bit, actually," she replied. "I contacted the convenience store where Mr. Duran claimed to have purchased the antacids for his wife and was able to get them to send me the feed from their surveillance cameras."

"*Claimed?*" Lee repeated. "He didn't go there after all?"

"Oh, he went there. But the films show him walking into the store a few minutes after eleven. He is in there for about three or four minutes and then he walks out, eating a slice of pizza. And then he drives off . . . in a direction *opposite* of the one he came from."

"No antacids?" Lee probed.

Irene shook her head. "No antacids, no sack that the antacids could be in. He didn't purchase any antacids, unless he had them stuffed in his pants, which would be pretty difficult."

"That's . . . fascinating," Lee said.

"Maybe he stopped there for pizza and then drove to another store to get the antacids?" Bree offered. "Maybe that store was . . . out of them?" She sunk back into her seat as she realized the absurdity of her supposition.

"We're going to want to talk to him again, that's for certain," Lee said. "There's also the issue of his wife saying he told *her* he had a flat tire and was gone for much longer than ten or fifteen minutes. But all that said, I have a hard time seeing Mr. Duran as a member of The Organization, carrying out the murder of Vic Valenzuela. True, he would have been an easy person to recruit after his son was murdered. But he has *too good* a reason for killing the coach. He is *too prime* a suspect. Usually, their operatives are somewhere in the background. Someone with no personal vendetta against the victim. By the same token, it's also unlikely that Astrid Steinberg is the assassin."

Irene put a finger in the air. "About that," she began. "I stumbled on something really juicy about her and Vic Valenzuela."

"That they were having an affair? We already knew that," Bree said.

"No. I knew that too. This is something else. Apparently, their interactions weren't just sexual, they were financial, as well."

"What do you mean?" Lara asked, leaning forward.

Irene paused. Rarely did she have such an opportunity to sculpt such a moment of suspense as this one.

"Well . . . I was able to hack into her banking accounts, and guess who wrote Astrid Steinberg a check for two hundred and fifty thousand dollars about six months before she began to spend two hundred and fifty thousand dollars to open her gallery."

"Wait?!" Warren exclaimed. Now he was leaning forward. "You're saying the man who murdered her sister, the man she was calling every name in the book in every press conference that took place for a year—*he* turned around and wrote her a quarter-million-dollar check to fund her business? Say what?!"

"I wish one of my enemies would be that friendly to *me*," Roberto said, sliding down into his chair.

"Sounds like some sort of payoff, if you ask me," Liam added.

"Maybe," Lee countered. "But one has to wonder . . . a payoff for *what?*"

No one had an answer for that. The server returned with their beverages and everyone took a moment to stir their soft drinks, sip their martinis or, in the case of Lee, steep their tea. After his first slurp, Lee settled back in his chair, an almost coquettish smile crossing his lips.

"To your satisfaction, is it?" Lara asked.

"Perfect," he replied. He drank once more from the cup, carefully placed it on the saucer. "So, what else do we know?" he said.

Liam raised a hand. "Um . . . if I may, Dalton." His boss nodded for him to go ahead. "I've been scanning The Organization's usual chat rooms and underground messaging sites for activity. Not only has the volume picked up quite a bit in the past week or two . . ." He looked around the table, took on a more troubled look. "But also . . . the activity has begun to . . . swarm around here. South Florida, that is. Miami in particular."

Everyone waited for him to divulge more information, provide additional analysis. Bree tilted back her martini glass, held it there for a couple of seconds before swallowing.

"I'm not sure what it means," he continued. "I haven't been able to fully decode any of the messages. I'm seeing lots of references to 305 and 786, which are the primary area codes here. More than one reference to 'flamingos,' things like that. It's all fairly general. But, seems to me, that if they *are* plotting something, it'll likely take place either here, or someplace near here. And soon."

"Isn't that just our luck," Lara said, casting a glance tinged with fear toward Lee.

Roberto sat up. "I'm going to try to reconnect with the Valenzuela housekeeper this week. I'm not sure what if anything I'll get from her, but she seemed pretty desperate to get my attention for some reason. And I'm looking into the angle that Valenzuela was fixing the games he coached . . . what the biographer told you guys. Maybe whoever was encouraging him to do that was a member of The Organization. Maybe the money they earned from it was going to fuel whatever initiative they plan to launch. And then, when he bailed . . ."

"That's a good theory, Roberto. A very good theory," Lee said. "Keep pursuing that."

"What about the biographer, the sportswriter?" Bree asked. "Did we stop him before he got to Alaska?"

Agent Weiss shook her head. "We have no grounds for doing so. He hasn't broken any laws . . . yet. He lied to Mackeson and Dalton and . . ."

She peered at Liam for a couple of seconds and squinted.

"Liam," he prompted her.

"Right," she said, snapping her fingers. "He lied to . . . the guys. But that's all. We do have people monitoring his activities while he is on the road. If he tries something funny, they'll be on him like a permanent tattoo."

Lee smiled at Agent Weiss's colorful simile.

"So to sum everything up, the people we've had a chance to interview, the people who intrigue us, include Astrid Steinberg, Javier Duran's father, Todd Cavender, and, of course, Hayden Haas," Lee said, counting gently on his fingers.

"I wouldn't rule out Valenzuela's assistant, the blonde," Warren said. "Remember, she doesn't really have an alibi for where she was that night." He looked over at Agent Weiss. "Besides, we all know how blondes can be."

The agent returned his joke with a "what-does-that-mean" sneer, followed by a roll of the eyes and a quick grin.

"Speaking of blondes, what did you and Agent Weiss find out about the sportscaster?" Lara asked. "The one he apparently had the fight with in California."

Agent Weiss leaned forward. "Thank you for bringing that up, Lara. It appears we can eliminate her as a suspect. There's no record that she ever boarded a flight from any of the airports in Southern California to any of the airports here. And her claim that she attended an awards banquet that night checks out. Several people say they are confident they remember seeing her there. However . . ."

Lee was mid-sip when Weiss dropped in the conjunctive adverb. He kept the cup in the air, peered at her over its rim.

She looked at Warren. "Do *you* want to tell them, or . . ."

"Go ahead," he said softly.

She picked up her beverage and began to tilt her glass but suddenly set it back down.

"Well, it turns out that they had been dating for about six months or so. She was really into him, his felony indictment for first-degree murder notwithstanding. He was confident he was going to be found innocent of the murders and she says his bravado convinced her as well. She even said the fight they had in California wasn't that big a deal—she wasn't particularly crazy about the guy who was writing the book about him, and she was urging Valenzuela to drop the project. But his ego being what it was, that was the last thing he wanted and it just kinda pissed him off that she had suggested it.

"Anyway, everything about their courtship was pretty rosy, she said, except for one little thing."

"What was that?" Lee asked, still peering at her over the rim of his teacup.

Agent Weiss turned again to Warren who nodded once. "Because of their schedules, they'd meet up whenever they could. Some place where he was coaching a game, or a city in which she was covering one. And she said that more than once, they'd be at either a jazz club in Kansas City, or a cafe in New Orleans, or maybe a bookstore in Chapel Hill, and they'd look up and standing or sitting somewhere nearby was somebody Valenzuela knew. And, regardless of the city, and regardless of the venue they were in, it was always the same person spying on them, every single time."

"Who was it?" the team barked in unison.

Hannah Weiss smiled with the inner joy of someone about to reveal a tantalizing secret. She took a quick swig of her beer and quickly wiped her lips with a sleeve.

"It was Hayden Haas," she said dramatically. "The coach that Valenzuela got fired from Miami A&M."

18

Scanning . . . scanning . . . scanning . . .

ROOMMATE WANTED for DUPLEX

Nope, that's not it . . .

RIDE NEEDED TO JACKSONVILLE . . .

No . . .

FOR LEASE, 2 BR, 1 BA, Duplex, $2,400 mo. Water included.

Really? There are people out there who can afford that?

The bulletin board was chaotic. But for some reason, they had insisted on leaving the message on a college campus bulletin board, so that was probably to be expected. Index cards with information written in pen were pinned on top of colored flyers that had been run off at the nearest copy shop.

What dim bulb thinks black type on dark purple is a good idea for an ad?

Scanning . . . scanning . . .

Where is it? I don't have much time.

Many of the notices resembled video game monsters with missing teeth, thanks to the detached email addresses or phone numbers that had been pulled from the bottom of the flyer. Finding anything worthwhile in this visual assault would be difficult enough; spotting something very specific was going to take forever.

HELP WANTED. Grill cook. Late night or early morning shift. $10.50/hr.

Noooo wayyyyy.

A big sigh. Hands on hips, head tilted back.

Scanning . . . scanning . . . sca . . .

And then, there it was:

**FOR SALE, 4 X 4, Good shape, Original paint,
Cloth seats, $80,000 AS IS**

Pay close attention, now. The first number in the headline will be your guide, they had said.

**You can now meet the outdoors on your own terms.
Make contact with nature right at your door. Used 4-by-4 that's in
good shape delivers the adventure to your afternoon. Will be gone
this weekend, maybe before Thursday. Body color is green, needs
a refresher coat perhaps. One stain on otherwise immaculate
vehicle's bench-seat upholstery. None on driver's seat.
No other defects. See other side for phone number of owner.
Thanks. Jake Pond. Hurry to ride in what is the women's favorite
vehicle to park in!**

Scanning closely to get the real message, the *intended* message.

Okay, understood. Yep . . . okay. But . . . where?

The person in front of the bulletin board reached the end of the ad, gave a quick sigh and a definitive nod.

Ah, so THERE. Hmm. Interesting choice.

A perfect choice, really . . .

19

Hockey season was over. And Miami's professional team hadn't made the playoffs. So a night out at the ice arena wasn't going to happen.

But Warren had another option in mind that he thought could be just as satisfying.

"Jai alai?" Liam said, his brow furrowed. "I've heard of it. But I must say, I don't know a thing about it."

"It probably enjoyed its biggest popularity in the sixties and seventies," Warren replied. "It isn't as hot today, but the fronton here *is* the largest in the world. They call it, 'the Yankee Stadium of jai alai.'"

"Sounds right to me," his co-worker responded.

Warren looked away for a second, then back at his colleague. "Would you mind . . . if Hannah, Agent Weiss, came along? Actually, the jai alai was *her* idea."

Liam pulled his head back, shot one of his Hollywood smiles. "Sure, mate. The more the merrier. Now that you mention it, I'll see if maybe Bree wants to come along."

Warren nodded. "Yeah, that would be good, the four of us," he replied returning Liam's smile.

Bree scrunched her nose as the quartet tramped through the lobby of the fronton toward their seats. It was bad enough that the facility sat in a bleak neighborhood of warehouses and metal shops just east of the airport and that it sported a seedy casino as an afterthought attachment. Then they walked inside, where she became keenly aware that whatever glamour once accompanied the sport had long ago vanished. Betting receipts littered the floor the way ticker tape covers the streets after a parade. To their left, three men in wheelchairs watched the action on big-screen television monitors whose picture quality harked back to broadcasts from the 1950s. Graffiti suffocated the large cement columns that provided structural support to the upper deck. Here and there, her sneakers stuck to some gooey substance on the floor.

"Isn't it great?!" Agent Weiss said, swinging her arms around her like a schoolgirl on a playground.

They trudged up the ridged ramp that led to the auditorium, which was a sea of forest green offset by salmon-colored tiles. The cement floor contained even more discarded tickets than the lobby did; on either side of the gallery, large backlit advertisements for beer, chewing tobacco, and a rental car agency flickered intermittently.

"No one is going to mistake jai alai for the sport of kings, are they?" Bree said, almost (but not quite) beneath her breath.

As it was late afternoon, most of the place was empty, but they chose to take four seats near the back of the gallery anyway. Somewhere nearby, a walkie-talkie squawked with instructions for the security guard who was carrying it. To their right, an older woman wearing a thin purple coat and a black beret chattered into her phone in Creole French.

It was in between matches when they arrived, so Warren took a minute to bring Liam and Bree up to speed on the game.

"Basically, the first team to score seven points wins. You can score a point in a lot of different ways, but usually it happens when someone on the other team fails to catch the ball with their cesta, the basket thing they hold in their hands. Or when they send the ball out of bounds. The ball's called a pelota. There's a bunch of teams and they rotate—when one team loses a point, they move to the back of the line and the next team moves onto the court to play the team that won the point. And like I said, the first team to win seven points wins the match."

"He's so smart," Agent Weiss said, nudging Warren in the arm.

"So basically what you're saying is, you don't really *win* a match so much as the other team loses it for you," Liam said.

Warren opened his mouth to say something, then closed it. "Yeah, I suppose that's right," he said, giving thought to that.

"I like footy more already," Liam replied, chuckling. "You have more control over your destiny, seems to me."

A trumpet flourish sounded over the weak intercom and several players dressed in white emerged from a tattered metal cage at the left end of the court. An elegant Spanish tune accented by the sound of castanets played as the athletes sauntered lackadaisically to the center of the playing area. On cue, they turned toward the chain link fence that protected spectators from errant balls, lifted their cestas halfheartedly toward the sparse crowd then trudged back to the cage, their ceremonial obligation apparently complete.

"So, does anyone have any worthwhile theories as to who offed the football coach?" Liam asked the others. As he waited for their response, three referees in zebra-striped uniforms walked onto the court and assumed their positions for the first point.

Everyone remained quiet for a moment. Finally, Bree spoke up.

"It's way too early to say," she began. "I'm still torn. On one hand, Señor Duran definitely seems to have the rage to do the deed, doesn't he? But I agree with Dalton that he doesn't seem like the type who would be connected to The Organization. I mean he was already drawn into Valenzuela's circle through the murder of his son. Normally, I would be more inclined to suspect Astrid Steinberg. Her zen act seems a little too phony, if you ask me. But then, her connection to Valenzuela is exactly the same as the Durans' so . . ."

Warren was chewing his fingernails, stopped to respond. "My money is still on his assistant. I'm thinking he wanted to have a three-way with her and her fiancée, they turned him down, and he was going to retaliate by firing her. So she 'fired' him first."

Agent Weiss laughed and hit him on the shoulder. "You're like a sixteen-year-old!" she cried. "Besides, your theory has nothing to do with The Organization. Remember? The calling card? On Valenzuela's body?"

Thwack!

One of the players, wearing a number six on his jersey, had slammed the pelota against the granite wall to the far right of the audience. It ricocheted up and off the ceiling and then angled downward toward the players. Someone in the backcourt rushed forward, caught the ball in his cesta, and hurled it like a bullet back toward the wall on the spectators' right. The orb slapped the wall, then sped back low toward the players, but it dribbled twice on the floor before the opposing team could reach it. That caused a buzzer to sound and the emcee to announce a point for the team in orange.

Bree looked at Liam. "You haven't said anything. And you're the one who *started* this whole line of questioning. What's *your* thinking?"

Liam was sunk in his chair, his chin lodged firmly onto his chest. He twiddled the fingertips of both hands on the armrests and said nothing for a few seconds. Then he sighed loudly.

"I'm thinking we don't have anywhere near enough information yet," he said. "We may have met the murderer . . . but then again, we very well may *not* have. Like Hannah said, we need to be giving a lot of thought as to *why* Valenzuela was killed. 'Cause if we do, that ought to lead us to *who* killed him."

"I like the gambling angle," Warren offered. "He was throwing games and The Organization was making a lot of money off of the results to fund their terrorist activities. One day he decides he doesn't want to do their bidding anymore, so they kill him."

Agent Weiss put one finger in the air. "*Except*, all the information we've accumulated indicates The Organization is not in the least bit short on funds."

"Maybe they planned some sort of attack at one of the Miami A&M games," Liam suggested. "And maybe Valenzuela got wind of it and was heading to the authorities—to you guys—to warn them about it."

Another round was about to begin. The two players representing the purple team emerged from the cage, and as they took the court one could sense the pitch of this round would be more ferocious than the previous one. The posture of the new combatants was more belligerent, their expression far more menacing.

The shorter player on the orange team served the pelota, swiftly sweeping the sphere toward the granite wall. But rather than gracefully addressing the rebound, the backcourt player for the purple team attacked it, swooping it up into his cesta with a fierce flick of the wrist and then brutally smashing it against the ceiling. The opposing team volleyed it successfully, but with a puny lob that caromed gently off the far wall. This time, both players for the purple team charged toward the pelota like savage hunters racing toward felled elk.

Whack! Thwack! THWACK! The ball resounded, spinning ever and ever more violently. With each return, the players' grunts turned into groans then became primordial shouts, the ball missing a player's head or torso only because of some miraculous dive to safety. It was as if the purple team had a blood vendetta toward their adversaries and would settle for nothing less than their annihilation.

Gradually, those in the gallery became caught up in the frenzy, first prodding the players individually to "Kill the others!" and "Smash the pelota!" Over time, however, their yells coalesced into an eerie incantation, a feral chant one would more likely expect from people holding torches and pitchforks.

And still, the pelota whizzed past at a now-incomprehensible speed.

Slap! Slam! SMASH!

A tormented scream erupted from the court and one of the players crumpled in agony, gripping his thigh where the ball had smacked into it. The referees blew their whistles and trotted over to the player to closely inspect the extent of his injury. The chanting in the gallery became a dissonant murmur; the unruly mob turned dull and disinterested.

Bree took a big breath. "Well that was . . . nerve-racking," she said, her eyes saucer-like and a forearm across her chest.

As the medical diagnosis continued, a teenager walking in front of the foursome halted suddenly. He turned, hiked one leg onto the railing in front of them, bent forward and began to retie his shoelace.

"Ah, that reminds me, there *is* a bit of positive news on the forensics front," Agent Weiss announced. "Apparently, a trace of soil was found on the floor of Valenzuela's bedroom carpet yesterday. We're having it analyzed now to see what it might reveal. We're assuming it was brought into the room by the intruder when they stepped through the garden. But we don't know that for sure. It could have belonged to someone else in the house . . . or Valenzuela himself, for that matter.

"What *is* odd about it . . . is that it's just a trace . . . a very small clump. One would think if the killer tracked in some mud from the garden, we would have found a lot more of it. It's almost as if some of the mud had been vacuumed up before our investigators got there."

"Or the killer cleaned their shoes before they entered the room and just didn't quite get it all," Warren added.

The match was being suspended; the player's injury was serious enough to warrant his being assisted off the court, his arms draped over two referees' shoulders.

Agent Weiss exhaled and stood up. "I'm going to go get a beer." She looked at Warren. "You want anything? It's on me. Or on the American taxpayer, I guess I should say."

Warren mulled the offer, looked at his watch. "Yeah, I'll have one," he answered.

"Anyone else?"

Both Liam and Bree shook their head, but Bree rose from her seat as well. "As much as the thought terrifies me," she said, "I think I need to go find a ladies' room."

For a few minutes, the boys canvassed the sad scene around them. A man in his seventies proceeded at a snail's pace along the walkway in front of them, urging his walker forward with a steady grunt. Two Latinas, whose abdomens overflowed their tight jeans, strolled past, chewing gum and chatting nonstop without listening to what the other was saying. The lighted billboard that promoted economy car rentals flickered once then lost its illumination, as if it knew the fronton's days were numbered and decided to flee the scene before the wrecking ball showed up.

Finally, Liam turned to his left and looked sheepishly at Warren. "So . . ." he began hesitantly.

Warren turned toward Liam, raised his eyebrows, waited for more.

"So . . . you and Agent Weiss?" Liam was tilting his head in the direction toward which the federal agent had walked.

The question suspended over the empty seats between them for several seconds. Warren sniffed, looked in the direction Liam was nodding toward, dug down into his seat. Then he jumped. "What . . . me and her? No. NO! I'm married, remember?"

"Right," Liam said, turning forward. Quiet ensued for several more seconds. Then, "I do have to say she sure seems keen on you."

Warren didn't respond. He set his elbows on his knees, clasped the fingers of one hand into the spaces between the fingers on the other and pushed his face forward into the large fist he had formed. "She *is* interesting," was all he said.

Another long quiet played out. Liam returned his attention to the empty court in front of them, glanced back over his shoulder at the smattering of spectators behind them.

Then, without provocation, Warren added, "But as I said, I'm a married man."

Liam looked at Warren and nodded several times slowly as he watched him. But Warren said nothing else.

Eventually, Warren released his pose and leaned back in his chair. Glanced over at his colleague. "And what about you . . . and Bree? Anything going on there?"

Liam's face lit up, but more from embarrassment than joy. "Aw, Bree's great, really great," he said somewhat robotically. "But . . . nah . . . she, um . . ."

Warren smiled. "She's . . . what? . . . too old for you?" he said quietly.

Liam frowned, looked in the direction of the restrooms, then back at Warren. "Nah, mate. What I was going to say was that it's pretty obvious she's the type of woman who doesn't really need me."

20

Roberto had a hunch. He wasn't sure it would work, but he was pretty certain it would. Especially since the housekeeper had seemed not just *interested* in speaking with him but *anxious* to.

All he needed was a housepainter's outfit. But he could pick that up at most any uniform shop, so . . .

"*Buenos dias, señora.* I am here to repaint the bedroom?" Roberto took off the white cap he was wearing so there wouldn't be a shadow on his face. He raised his eyebrows.

It took a moment, but a spark of recognition illuminated within her. "*Si, si, por favor venga, venga.*"

She ushered him in, placed one hand behind his shoulder blade, and rapidly nudged him down a side hallway.

"I thought there would be more painters," she announced in Spanish, apparently in an attempt to shield their agenda from any of the other workers on the estate who spoke or understood the language.

"I can do the job of three people in half the time," he replied, going along with the charade.

With the fingertips of her right hand, she prodded him down the long hall, like a teacher marching an uncooperative student to the principal's office. Then she cupped the outside of his right shoulder and tapped several times, indicating he should turn left. They careened into a small room that appeared to double as both a maintenance area and the housekeeper's office, although the only indication of it being a place where things were managed was a makeshift desk composed of a plank of wood sitting atop two file cabinets.

Once they were both inside the room, she swiveled around and deftly locked the door. Roberto started to sit in a simple wooden chair next to an ironing board beside the room's one window, but seeing no other seat in the room, offered it to the housekeeper instead. Wearily, she lowered herself into the chair and cupped one hand into the palm of the other.

"*Me llamo Roberto. ¿Cómo te llamas?*"

"Margarida," she replied softly.

"Is something wrong? Are you in danger?"

The housekeeper turned and looked over toward the far corner of the room. "I no think so . . . I . . . don't know."

Roberto kept his gaze on the woman, whom he guessed was about fifty. He was betting she was undocumented. "*¿Tienes tus papeles?*"

She glared at him momentarily, looked down at her lap. "No."

When she lifted her head, her eyes were damp. She began to wring the fingers of her left hand inside a fist she had made with the right.

Suddenly, there was a commotion outside the door that made them both start—husky voices and the clang of metal. *Probably just workers transporting a ladder through the house*, Roberto thought. He breathed in through his nose.

"What is it you want to tell me? Why were you trying to get my attention the other day?"

Gradually, her expression of fear transformed into a sense of mild distrust. "*¿Es usted un policía?*"

Roberto shook his head vigorously. "No. Not the police. You are safe with me. I am investigating what happened to Señor Valenzuela but I am not a policeman. *Un detective*. He paused, studied her. "Isn't that why you wanted to talk to me?"

She nodded gently, wrung her finger some more.

"Do you know anything about what happened to Señor Valenzuela?"

She studied him closely. Studied the back of the file cabinets for a moment. Considered a calendar that hung on the wall. Eventually decided that she could trust him. "Maybe," she said weakly.

He waited. She looked at the tiles on the floor.

"What, Margarida? What do you know?"

She set her lips tight together. Began to chew lightly on the lower one. "I . . . not sure. Except . . . there was a party that night."

"A party? What kind of party?"

Her look turned fearful. "I . . . don't want to say. A party. Some of the boys . . . with a girl . . ."

"What boys? What kind of girl?" Roberto had to struggle to keep his tone soothing; he was giddy with the possibility that she may hold the clue . . . be able to provide some identification . . . that might help them solve the murder.

"The boys. *Fútbol*," she said. "The girl . . . she . . ." Margarida made a disdainful face.

Roberto was trying to follow. Then it came together for him. Some of the football players. And . . . "*¿Ellos estaban teniendo relaciones sexuales?*"

She nodded. Flashed a brief, embarrassed smile that quickly melted into a worrisome frown.

"How do you know this, Margarida?"

Her look turned fearful again. "My casita . . . it is close," she replied haltingly.

Roberto considered the information she had provided thus far. He couldn't really see how it related to Valenzuela's murder, but his instincts told him not to rule out the possibility that it was.

"What time did the party stop?" he asked her.

"About ten o'clock," she replied instantly. Her immediate response told Roberto she must have looked at some sort of timepiece just as everyone was leaving.

Another bang resonated from the hallway. She turned and flashed a look at him that indicated she needed to end the interview as soon as possible. He decided to change course for a moment.

"*Señora*, don't worry. You are safe. I will make sure no one knows about your status."

Suddenly she became quite chatty, although for good reason.

"*Gracias.* I don't know what I do. I work for Mr. Valenzuela since I came here, six years ago. Now he is dead, I hear that they are going to sell the house, I don't know what . . ." She teared up again. One pudgy hand flew up to her face.

"Shh, shh," he said. He looked in his pockets for a kerchief or tissue, but wasn't sure why he did that since he knew he never carried any. "It will be okay, Margarida. I promise. Somehow, it will all turn out fine."

She sniffed some. Nodded. Looked at him for more.

"Here is what I need you to do," he said. "I need you to listen. To every conversation you hear around here. Watch everything that is going on. It is very possible . . ." He realized he needed to tread carefully here. "It is possible you will hear something or see something that will help us figure out who killed *Señor* Valenzuela. If you do, you let me know, okay?"

Although she nodded slowly, he could tell her consent was genuine. He breathed deeply with relief. Then, he recalled he had allowed a previous thread of conversation to drop. And that he needed to pursue it before he left.

"Margarida, the party . . . you say it ended about ten o'clock?"

She nodded.

"And everyone left after that?"

Her face froze some. She shook her head.

"Not all the boys left?"

She nodded. "*Si . . . los muchachos . . .* they leave." Her face went pale again. "But . . . the girl . . . she . . . not with them when they go."

Roberto was confused. "Wait, you're saying that all the football players left?"

Margarida nodded.

"But the girl . . . *la prostituta* . . . she didn't leave when they did?"

The housekeeper nodded again. "*Si, correcto.* I see the boys go in the cabana, and then the girl come. Then the boys leave . . . and I watch . . . but she no leave with them.

"I no see her leave cabana at all."

21

"You're good to go, Mr. Lee. We have performed as thorough a sweep of your room as we can, and we can't find anything. Of course, we can't guarantee *one-hundred-percent* that there's not a listening device in the room. But I feel pretty confident in telling you it's highly unlikely anyone is eavesdropping on you."

Lee thanked the surveillance team that Agent Sainclair had sent over at his request and walked them to the door. He noticed that almost instantaneously, a low-grade throbbing behind his left temple miraculously vanished.

Slowly, he looked up, and around, the tops of the walls of his suite.

"I love to have sex with pygmies and elephants," he shouted with bravado. Waited. Nothing. Smiled. Waited a little longer.

"Preferably at the same time," he added, even more loudly.

All he could hear was the gentle whoosh of air through the room's numerous vents.

He smiled once more. "Good," he whispered. "Much better."

***

For a change, the rest of his team arrived almost on top of one another. Liam and Irene arrived first, with the former trying in vain to have a conversation with the latter. Lee noticed that just as Liam would lengthen his stride, Irene would speed up. The junior associate eventually claimed a chair right next to Lee. Which was odd, he thought, since she customarily chose to sit on the floor.

Lara, Warren, and Bree all arrived next. Lara—seeing that her usual position next to Lee had been captured by Irene—sat in an armchair across the way. Warren plopped himself in a second armchair while Bree chose to stand, her back to the rest of the group, her arms extended behind her and holding onto the top of the chair Lara sat in. Liam leaned against a wall a few feet away from her.

Which meant when Roberto arrived soon afterward, there was very little perimeter of the room for him to navigate. So he stopped short, just inside the door, arms to his side, and waited for the proceedings to begin.

"Roberto, how nice of you to join us," Lee proclaimed. "I know we all look forward to your report about what took place at the Valenzuela estate." The designer smiled quickly and nodded, but did not move. Still, everyone turned toward him. And waited.

He blinked a few times, realized they expected him to deliver . . . immediately. "Well . . . I was right, she did have . . . something to share," he stammered. He went on to relate how the housekeeper had never seen the young woman leave the premises. And that the housekeeper was worried about her future, given Valenzuela's demise and the household being dismantled over the coming weeks.

"Did she have any other information about the young woman?" Lee asked. "Did she give a name? A description?"

Roberto shook his head. "No. Nothing. But she did say she could probably identify the football players who were involved. She said she had seen a couple of them before. I'm guessing they can probably lead us to the hooker."

Lee nodded emphatically at Roberto's summary then clapped his hands. "All right, this will be brief," he announced. "We all have some assignments today, given the new information that has been uncovered."

Lara watched the architect from across the room and wondered,

What is this hand clapping thing of his? It's like he thinks he's a maestro and we are his orchestra.

"First, some news," Lee began. "The sportswriter who was working on the biography of the victim did make it to Alaska, but authorities there have located him and he has agreed to be interviewed by remote. Lara and I will join Agent Sainclair for that interview, as well as one Mr. Sainclair intends to conduct afterward with Danielo Duran.

"Bree, I want you and Warren to go with Agent Weiss when she reinterviews Astrid Steinberg later today. Remember, if you can think of a pertinent question to ask, it's okay to ask it. But our objective is mostly to stay in the background, listen, and watch closely." The pair nodded.

"Roberto, you are going to follow up on your conversation with Valenzuela's housekeeper and see if you can determine the identity of the hook . . ." Lee shot a quick glance at Lara, whose brow flinched just a tad. "The prostitute," he concluded, and Lara's brow returned to its original position.

Lee felt his phone buzz. He smoothed it out of his pocket, saw a text.

THE DOCUMENTS ARE READY FOR YOU TO SIGN.
LET ME KNOW WHEN YOU CAN MEET.

The architect felt a knot twist somewhere along his spine. He took a deep breath, shoved his chin downward.

This is it, he thought. *I guess this is really it.*

Discreetly he typed a reply and hit SEND.

Lara, sensing something was up, was filling in for him as drill sergeant, asking questions of the team and suggesting some plans of action. Filling in seamlessly, as she always did.

I should give her a raise, or take her out for a nice dinner, or something, Lee told himself.

He returned his attention to the group. "Now where was I?" he asked, once Lara had filled him in on what he had missed. "Ah, Irene and Liam, you two need something to do. I think the two of you should remain here at the hotel and probe into Valenzuela's financials,

Astrid Steinberg's financials . . . *everyone's* financials. And whatever else worthwhile you can find, for that matter."

Irene released a sound that was something between a sigh and a gasp. The others in the room turned in her direction.

"Something wrong, Irene?" Lee asked.

She glanced up and looked at her boss like a toddler who had come upon a tiger. After a moment, she replied, almost inaudibly, "No. I'm fine."

***

On the laptop screen, Todd Cavender looked more annoyed than cowed.

"You can see, can't you Mr. Cavender, how your actions raise suspicions about your intent?" Agent Sainclair was in no mood for it today. Lee noticed he seemed more disheveled and brusque than usual.

Cavender rolled his eyes and sighed. "I suppose so," he said. "But it's all very easy to explain. I mean, it's not *my* fault that I wanted to go into hiding. It's his. Vic's. Actually, I should bill his estate for pain and suffering. I might just do that."

Although he sniffed ironically after expressing the opinion, Cavender came across as mostly serious. Which caused Lara to turn to Lee and roll *her* eyes.

Sainclair leaned closer to the monitor. "Why do you believe you have to go into hiding, Mr. Cavender?"

The writer sighed again. "Look, I've been getting death threats ever since it was announced I was taking on Vic's biography. Almost every week. Sure, I know most of them are from kooks who never intend to follow through with them. But you never know. It only takes one. And then, after Vic was found not guilty, the threats got a *lot* worse. A lot worse. I didn't sign up for that sort of shit. Look, I just wanted to write a book. About a hugely successful college football coach. That's all."

Now Sainclair sniffed. "Why Alaska? Why not the Keys, where you said you were going? Isn't Alaska taking things to the extreme?"

Sarcasm shined through the smile Cavender delivered.

"Yeah, well, I can see how that might look to *you*. But the reality is, I have a college friend up here who runs a salmon farm. He offered me a one-year gig and it sounded good to me. Thought it would at least give me a chance to sort out what I want to do next. And who knows, maybe I'll like it and keep at it for a while. I figure if it doesn't suit me, maybe I can use it as a base from which to write some articles for the outdoor sports magazines. Whatever it takes for me to get away from all the drama down there. I don't need it."

Sainclair now sighed, leaned back in his chair. Lee looked at the federal agent and indicated to him to mute their side of the conversation.

"I don't know, I think his story sounds sort of . . . *fishy*." Lee chuckled at himself, but Sainclair remained stoic.

"There's not that much that we can do right now, that I can see," he mumbled. "There's nothing we can arrest him on. His contact in Alaska contends he had invited Mr. Cavender up there. Offered him a job. Still, they could be in on this together, for all we know.

"But if that's the case, I'm most certain we'll learn that soon enough. *Ak pasyans w ap wè tete pis.*"

The agent, realizing Lee would ask for a translation, beat him to the punch. "With patience, you will see even the breast of the ant," he said, smiling at Lee for the first time.

***

"Raul. That headboard. *Muévelo allá.*"

Danielo Duran was pointing toward a far corner of the furniture store, which was crammed with chairs, tables, lamps, and bedding. One entire wall featured mattresses and box springs standing on end. Sofas in a variety of fabrics—including every faux leather on the market—sat chock-a-block, like soldiers in line for inspection. Signs proclaiming ¡Venta! and ¡Pague en mensualidades! were affixed to the wall with masking tape, heralding the fact that a sale was underway and financing was available. Duran wore a long-sleeve blue work shirt with a white t-shirt underneath, and blue jeans.

"We go back to the loading area to talk," he said quietly to Sainclair, his chin tucked into his chest. Trailing close behind Sainclair were Lee and Lara, who regarded the furniture she passed with more than a bit of disappointment.

At the back of the store, an extra-wide garage door was open, allowing natural light to bathe what was otherwise a bleak interior. "Hey, go take lunch early, eh?" he said to a middle-aged man in a gray jumpsuit who was sitting on the dock, both legs dangling outside the loading area. The worker pushed himself off the dock and onto the concrete below, then skittered off around one corner of the building.

Duran sauntered toward the open door, reached into his back pocket, and extracted a pack of cigarettes. "Okay I smoke?" he said to Agent Sainclair.

The agent nodded, dove into the interview. "Mr. Duran, you weren't entirely truthful with us a couple of days ago, were you?"

The furniture store owner took a long drag, scuffed the concrete floor with the toe of one shoe. "I . . . no understand what you mean," he replied, looking warily at the detective.

"You didn't buy any antacids for your wife that night, did you?"

Danielo Duran thought for a moment, then a look of sudden confidence crossed his face. "*Sí!* Yes! I buy some for her!" He scratched behind one ear, then held up one hand. "Wait. Somewhere I have receipt."

He dug into his back pocket and pulled out a bulging, bifold wallet held tight by a rubber band. After a minute of sifting through receipts and ticket stubs, he exclaimed, "*Ah, aquí!*" Then he unfolded a piece of paper that was longer than the typical receipt and handed it to Sainclair.

The agent clamped down on a newly inserted toothpick and inspected the piece of paper Duran had handed him. The purchase was for antacids, it said, and the date was correct; the time it showed was just before midnight. Sainclair continued to scrutinize the receipt word for word.

"This shows you purchased the antacids at a store on Southwest Eighth. You told us the other day you purchased them at a store on Flagler. And the surveillance cameras there show you coming out of *that* store, eating a slice of pizza."

Duran looked befuddled at the detectives for a moment. Suddenly, he smiled and nodded as if his memories of the evening had suddenly returned to him in a torrent.

"*Sí!* I go to store on Flagler. When I walk in, I see pizza and I am hungry so I buy a slice, then I leave. I forget antacids. Then, I remember a friend who imports furniture, he tells me a couple of days ago he has some tables he wants to sell me and that they are in a pickup truck at his house. I know he live nearby, so I drive past to see if they are still there and take a look at them. I am going home when I remember I forget my wife's antacids. So I stop there . . ." He nodded toward the receipt in Sainclair's hand, "And I buy some. Then I go home."

Lara leaned over to Lee. "Either this guy has the world's worst case of attention deficit disorder or he is the world's worst liar," she whispered.

Sainclair turned the receipt over and over again in his hand, then shoved it in the right pocket of his slacks. Took the toothpick out of his mouth, looked around, and tossed it into a tall plastic trash can nearby.

"All right, we will explore that," he said with a sigh. "Your friend who has the tables you were interested in . . . did you speak with him that night? Can he verify that you were there?"

Duran licked his lips. "No. I just go by his house, stop, look at the tables in his truck, and then leave."

"Why did you say earlier that you were only gone from your house for ten or fifteen minutes?"

Duran took on a sheepish look. "My wife, she is very jealous," he said. "I tell her I have flat tire so she not think I am having, you know, relations with another woman. I . . ." He glanced at Lara, then back at Sainclair. "I have one, three years ago and she find out."

Sainclair considered this, looked at Lara, who shrugged her shoulders as if to say, "Why is everyone looking at *me?*"

"So, at what time did you return to your house, Mr. Duran? What time, *really?*"

The store owner looked up to the ceiling, but only for a moment. "About twelve thirty," he replied with a nod.

Late enough for you to have gone to Valenzuela's house and murdered him instead of looking at tables in a friend's pickup truck, Lee thought to himself.

***

The Astrid Steinberg encountered by Warren, Agent Weiss, and Bree was a very different one from the one interviewed by Agent Sainclair a few days earlier.

This Astrid Steinberg was more on edge. More harried. Less serene . . . and much less cooperative in answering their questions.

"I really don't see why this is turning into such an interrogation," she told the trio as soon as they arrived. "I thought I made my feelings perfectly clear to your colleagues the other day. How long will this take?"

"It's as if whatever medication she was on the last time she got interviewed has worn off," Agent Weiss whispered to Warren just before she began to interview the gallery owner.

"It may have," Bree chimed in, under her breath.

Agent Weiss directed the conversation. "Now, Ms. Steinberg, I need to ask you some questions that are . . . fairly delicate."

The sister-in-law of Vic Valenzuela was standing in the center of one of the main exhibition rooms in her gallery, having declined a suggestion by Agent Weiss that they retire to a more private location. She was eyeing a sculpture that had just been placed in position by her assistant. She cradled her right elbow in the palm of her left hand; her index finger extended to a point just below her nose.

"No, let's move it just a few inches to the right, Zamira," she said. Her assistant complied with the request. The gallery owner took one step to the right and tapped the side of her nose in contemplation.

"I'm sorry, a *delicate* question did you say?" she responded without looking at the detectives. She raised her chin a couple of inches. "Yes, Zamira, I think that's fine." At that point, Astrid Steinberg turned her head slightly toward Agent Weiss but continued to focus her gaze predominantly on the statue.

"Go ahead and ask whatever you want," she said. "We both know I'm not obliged to answer."

Agent Weiss shared a look with Bree. "Um, it has come to our attention," she began slowly, "that you and Vic Valenzuela had a . . .

business partnership, is that right?"

With that, Agent Weiss received Astrid Steinberg's full attention.

"Zamira, that will be all for now. We'll finish the installation a little later." Once the assistant had left the exhibition room, the gallery owner looked her interrogator down and up.

"Define business partnership," she said warily.

"To be precise, we understand Mr. Valenzuela wrote you a check for a quarter of a million dollars shortly before you opened this business. Is that correct?"

The gallery owner tried unsuccessfully to look nonplussed. "How did you come upon that information?" she asked. "It's accurate, yes, but I want to know how you learned that."

Agent Weiss felt the steel walls closing in, decided playing hardball was her best option of keeping Astrid Steinberg from running right over her. "We have an excellent research department," she said with a taut smile. "They hardly ever miss a beat."

The art patron turned slowly and began to saunter back toward the sculpture that had been behind her, studying it yet again. As she approached it, she arced to its right and then strolled behind it, never taking her eyes off it.

"Yes, Vic was very kind to write that check," she suddenly said, gazing at the textured marble the artist had carved to suggest a woman's dress. Deep indentations in the alabaster gave the impression of folds in the fabric. Above the dress, a young woman was focused on some point in the distance, a look of shock, or terror, on her face. "He was gracious to me during the buildup to the trial. And during."

"And yet, you called him quite a few ugly names during that time . . . in public, I might add," Agent Weiss reminded her. "I was especially impressed with this one." The agent consulted notes she had secured to her clipboard. "At some point, you called him a 'vile, opportunistic loser.'"

Astrid Steinberg flashed a brief look of disgust at Agent Weiss, then returned her concentration to the statue.

"You have to understand," she said, condescension seeping into her tone, "I couldn't possibly allow the public to think that I might harbor kind feelings for Vic. If I had, someone might have begun to wonder whether I had conspired with him somehow in Erika's murder. I might have been asked to testify, if I had appeared even the slightest bit sympathetic to him.

"Or, at least, that's how I was counseled."

Agent Weiss put her questioning on hold for a moment as the woman began to glide around the other side of the sculpture and back toward them. This time, however, the federal agent noticed her rival was keeping one eye on the artwork, the other on her.

"So you didn't really mean those things you said about him?" Agent Weiss offered.

Astrid Steinberg smiled, met the agent's glare head on.

"Oh, I meant them . . . most of them, anyway," she intoned. "Besides, I just assumed the check was a payment proffered from a place of guilt. I didn't see any reason why I *shouldn't* accept it. Doing so was just my way of paying tribute to Erika. Making him *pay* for what he did to her, *literally*, if you will. Everyone focuses on her murder. What they overlook is that before the murder, he beat her repeatedly—at least five or six times. That during one of the more violent episodes, he dislocated her shoulder. That for almost a full year, she tried to leave him but couldn't because he had her shackled psychologically as well as financially.

"On the other hand, I have to say, Vic treated our mother and father like royalty. Sent them on a trip to Hawaii. Paid for all of it. And he really did work tirelessly to see kids throughout the country embrace a healthier lifestyle.

"But, see, that was the thing. I knew that Vic was always a master of the grandiose gesture that would burnish his public persona. So, when I finally had an opportunity to, I was delighted to personally dismantle that public image. And then take his money . . . *away* from the public spotlight.

"Besides, it wasn't as if that money was going to suddenly motivate me to become best friends with Vic."

Just then the detectives heard a sound from the other room—the gentle bell attached to the front door tinkling as Zamira let someone in. Footsteps slowly approached them from behind.

"Well, that's very interesting," Agent Weiss replied, "because we also have some new information leading us to believe your relationship with Mr. Valenzuela was intimate as well as financial."

The gallery owner's expression instantly became more rigid than the marble in the sculpture behind her. However, as the footsteps behind them drew closer, she raised her eyebrows and smiled almost theatrically at the person who had just entered the room.

"Eli, you're here!" she cooed, like an abandoned lover whose prodigal beau had finally returned. "Yes, yes, I know, you're a few minutes late, but actually, your timing is impeccable. You're just in time to see these people out."

***

At the hotel, Liam and Irene had a wealth of new information for the rest of the team.

"It's *that* interesting, is it?" Lee asked.

"Yes, it's *that* interesting," Liam replied, grinning broadly. "Who do you want to hear about first—the sportswriter, Astrid Steinberg, or the Duran guy?"

Lara decided to interject into the proceedings. "Todd Cavender," she said quickly. "I thought he was much too smug."

Irene was grinning now. "Well, we did a little checking into his finances and found them *very* interesting, indeed," she said. "He was the hardest to find because Todd Cavender isn't his birth name; it's the name he writes under. His real name is Carlton Cavender Todd II. Once we figured that out, we were able to unlock his accounts with a nice little piece of code Liam scripted, and what we learned was . . ."

Lee and Lara raised their eyebrows in anticipation.

"We learned that he's been making regular payments of about twenty-five hundred a month to a group called DXR9 Enterprises," Liam responded.

"Who's that?" Lee crossed his arms and smiled; he already liked how this collaboration was panning out.

"Well, that took some more digging," Irene said, "but we were finally able to figure out . . . that it's one of the largest gambling syndicates along the East Coast. Perhaps *the* largest."

"Gambling?!" Lara exclaimed. "Didn't we hear that the coach might have been involved with a syndicate somehow?"

"Yes, we most certainly did," Lee confirmed. "I wonder just how that might be connected to this, although I can think of a couple of possibilities. What else have you learned?"

Liam hopped up from his seat and brought his laptop over so his superior could see the screen.

"Well, Dalton, it turns out those aren't the only large money transfers that have been taking place lately," he said. "We knew Astrid Steinberg had received a check for a quarter of a million from Valenzuela just before she opened her gallery, right?" The architect nodded. "Well, we thought it might be interesting to look at her outflows as well . . . and, boy, were they *ever* interesting."

"How so?" Lara inquired.

The Australian tapped a few keys and pointed at a location on the screen. "Look here, see these withdrawals?" Lee saw five references to checks, each written about two weeks apart, each for twenty-five thousand dollars. Each written to some company called WLC Enterprises. Not much public about that business, but I was able to triangulate some legal filings that company was in the middle of and discovered WLC Enterprises is a shell company set up by three men better known as Noah Weiner, Sidney Lanier, and Antonio Consuelas.

"That's . . ." Lee began.

Liam finished the sentence for him. "Valenzuela's defense team. Exactly."

"Oh, my stars!" Lara exclaimed. "She and Valenzuela were in bed with each other in more ways than one, weren't they?"

Lee examined the figures on the screen and nodded. "Nice work, you two. Very solid work. Now if we can just figure out what it all means. Why on earth would Astrid Steinberg have been paying money to the lawyers hired to defend the man who murdered her sister?"

"But wait, Dalton, there's more," Liam said excitedly.

Lara placed one arm across her breast. "I'm not sure my heart can take it," she said sarcastically.

"It may not," Irene said, a comment that made even Lara pull up, given it was likely the first time the youngest associate had ever cracked a joke at work, much less one directed at her.

"It appears something is up with Mr. Duran," Irene continued, using an index finger to push her glasses up the bridge of her nose. "Not only did he receive a large sum of money out of the clear blue, he received it the day *after* Vic Valenzuela was murdered."

"How large?" Lee asked.

Irene kept her two superiors in suspense for several seconds before answering. "Fifty thousand dollars," she finally said, beaming.

"Fifty thousand dollars! That's an awful lot of money for a furniture store owner to earn in one day," Lara said.

"Depends on how he earned it," Lee said. "Do we know where he got it?"

Irene shook her head. "No. Because he deposited it all as cash. Split up over six different checking accounts he has at six different banks throughout the area."

For a while, everyone was speechless. Lee considered all the data, decided it was too much to sort through just then. "Plus, I need to get ready for the Art Deco tour of Miami Beach that I am supposed to lead tomorrow," he said.

Lee noticed that as they were departing his room, Liam and Irene seemed engaged in some strange form of cat and mouse. The Australian seemed almost desperate to talk to his colleague.

She, on the other hand, was having none of it.

22

Irene tried to skedaddle to her room before Liam could accost her. But their rooms were on higher floors, so he caught up with her in front of the elevator bank.

"Have you given it some thought? Will you consider it? I can make sure you earn heaps extra money."

She swung away from his intense glare, her expression having rapidly fallen from one of adolescent-like bliss to adolescent-like angst.

"I don't know," she whispered back to him. "I'm not really comfortable about it. It's not really me. Plus, I'm terrified of what Dalton and Lara would do if they found out." She tried to focus on her reflection in the elevator doors. "I'm not saying, like, *absolutely* no, I just need some more time to think about it."

Liam was quiet for several seconds, but continued to stare at her. "Okay," he finally said. "I'll give you some more time. But only a day or two. Our window of opportunity for doing this is pretty short."

She swung her laptop bag around her legs. Lifted the toe of her right shoe and banged the heel against the floor a couple of times. "It just feels really weird, you know? I'm not sure I have the confidence to pull it off. I mean, I can't really see anyone caring that much about what I . . ."

"Trust me," Liam interrupted. "They will. You're perfect. You'll be a rock star. Seriously, Irene. I know this stuff. You'll be great. Maybe even ... an international sensation."

She smiled quickly, chewed on her lower lip for a while. Eventually, she glanced up at him. "How much did you say I could make?"

He smiled, like a salesman who has just realized the customer is on the verge of buying after all. "About the same as what you make working for Dalton. But you would only have to put in an hour a day. If that. And I can arrange it so you do it late at night, after you're finished with your investigative work."

She looked down at her shoes. Wished the elevator would hurry up.

"But you know it's not just about the money," he added. "It's about the esteem you'll gain. You'd be bringing a whole lot of pleasure to a whole lot of people if you do this." His tone was silky now, seductive as sin. She glanced up at him again; he winked back at her. Smiled that smile of his.

"You click on the link I sent you?" he asked.

She nodded.

"You hear what the other girls said about it? How it turned out to be a lot more satisfying than they thought it would be?"

She didn't answer him. Just then, the elevator arrived. She stepped into the car first, scurried into a back corner.

As the car was ascending, he pivoted toward her. "To be honest, Irene, in a year, maybe even in a few months, you'll probably be too old for it. So I really need you to decide ASAP." The silk was gone; he was all business now.

Soon the elevator doors opened and he left her alone inside the car.

She would never have let him know it, but she was already trying to decide exactly which outfit of hers would work best for the photography session and how best to conceal the new hearing aid she planned to pick up later that day.

23

Sunshine again. Sunshine brilliant to the point of brittle. Sunshine demanding sunglasses, otherwise your retinas will fry. Even better . . . dry air and a lilt of a breeze to accompany all that sunshine.

Now, if only Dalton would show up, Lara thought, notebook clutched tightly against her breasts. *These tourists are getting edgy.*

"I'm sorry, do you know when we will begin?" asked a short, stocky woman in a hat like those worn by people who work the rice paddies of Southeast Asia. "The hotel told us this tour would begin at ten."

"Yes, I know, I understand," Lara replied, growing increasingly irritated at her superior. "Mr. Lee is usually very punctual. I am sure he will be here momentarily."

She had barely finished her sentence when a gunmetal-gray scooter with a cherry-red seat came roaring up next to the sidewalk in front of them and screeched to a stop behind a parking meter. Lee briskly removed his helmet and broke out into a broad grin as he dismounted the Maicoletta that he had just had brought in from California.

"I am so sorry, everyone, but I just thought that a tour about stylish architecture, being given to such stylish visitors to Miami Beach, deserved nothing less than a stylish beginning. Dalton Lee, at your service. Is everyone ready to learn about one of the most eclectic collections of architecture in the world? Did everyone do the homework I asked them to do?"

Suddenly, it was as if someone had unloaded a basketful of puppies onto the sidewalk. The mood shifted from fretful to festive. Grinning replaced grousing, and everyone rushed forward to smile at Dalton Lee, coo at Dalton Lee, shake the hand or pat the back of Dalton Lee.

A few feet away, Lara surveyed the camaraderie and allowed the subtlest of smiles to form on her lips.

Lee clapped his hands boisterously.

There it is AGAIN! Lara remarked to herself, rolling her eyes.

"All right, everyone, gather round. Before we head off, I want to provide you with some background about what influenced the architecture you are going to see." The dozen or so individuals who had signed up for the tour dropped their conversations and shuffled closer to the architect so they could take in every word.

"Now, South Florida has a lot of wonderful architecture, but this tour will focus on the Art Deco style for which Miami Beach is so renown," he began. "Can anyone tell me when the term 'Art Deco' came about?"

Those in the crowd turned and looked at one another quizzically for a few seconds before a middle-aged woman in a striped blouse ventured, "The twenties?" A male in the crowd quickly followed up with "The thirties."

Lee smiled teasingly. "Actually, I think you will be surprised to learn that although the architectural style is from the twenties and thirties, the term 'Art Deco' didn't appear until the late 1960s."

This revelation sent a murmur through the crowd, and Lee pushed himself up onto his toes with pride at the prestige he had already established with his audience.

"It was a trendy phrase used by a British art historian to describe the style's emphasis on decoration over function," he continued. "And the term just stuck."

More people nodded their head and edged closer to their host for the tour.

"What's really ironic," Lee continued, "is that many of us look at Art Deco today as a retro style from a simpler time. But back then, it was seen as the exact opposite—as a statement of how automobiles and assembly lines were making everything faster, sleeker and more streamlined. That idea only intensified during the thirties, when Art Deco evolved into what we now call Streamline Moderne, a term that also didn't show up until the late 1960s, by the way."

More "oohs" filtered through those listening to Lee. Lara nodded discreetly at the architect, indicating that he might want to pick up the pace.

"So, quickly, Art Deco in the twenties was all about straight lines—especially vertical lines—and angles. Art Deco structures emphasized ornamentation—especially sculptural ornamentation. Big influences included, in archaeology, the discovery in 1922 of King Tut's tomb, and in art, Cubism. You can really see that in a building a couple of miles from here that was constructed in 1930 to house the Miami Beach Public Library and Art Center, but now houses the Bass Museum of Art."

"Are we going to see the hotels they showed all the time on *South Beach Vice*?" an older woman called out.

"Oh, I really hope so, I *loved* that show," her companion echoed. Lee paused, flummoxed for a moment.

"Um, yes," he replied, wincing. "We will . . . see *some* of them, anyway. But that is actually an excellent segue to my next point, which is that many of the hotels here in Miami Beach actually reflect the Streamline Moderne style of the thirties. Art Deco referenced the past, but Streamline Moderne was all about the future. If the inspiration for Art Deco buildings was the cube, then the inspiration for Streamline Moderne buildings was the teardrop. Where Art Deco was about vertical lines and angles, Streamline Moderne was about horizontal lines and curves. And the architects here took the trend one step further, creating a regional style called Tropical Deco, which added into the mix such Florida-related design elements and motifs as sunbursts, portholes, sea horses, and flamingos."

Just then, a loud pop came from somewhere deep within the group. Everyone jolted, thinking a gun had gone off.

"Sorry," said a younger woman with frizzed hair. She grinned sheepishly and held up a plastic water bottle she was drinking out of to indicate that it, not a gun, had been responsible for the outburst.

A fortyish woman in designer sunglasses now spoke up. "My mother told me she and my grandparents vacationed here once when she was little and that their hotel was a real dump."

From several feet away, Lara could easily hear the irritation bubbling beneath the chuckle Lee offered the woman.

"Yes, well, I'm *getting* to that," he said. "See, most of the hotels on our agenda today were built to appeal to people in the Northern United States who were lucky enough to get away to Florida for the winter. You can see that in many of their names— the Park Central, Essex House, the Palmer House, and the Carlyle—which were merely stolen from fashionable New York hotels.

"But by 1941, the military had commandeered most of the hotels to house the soldiers who trained on the beach just before our entry into World War Two. After the war, these hotels and their surrounding neighborhood became a destination for retired poor people. It declined to the point it took on the nickname 'God's Waiting Room.'

"And the area pretty much stayed that way until the late seventies, which is when the preservation and restoration efforts began. What's been done since then is really remarkable. In fact, it would probably be impossible to try to undertake such a widespread preservation and restoration effort today. And now, let's go check out some of the spectacular results of all that restoration, shall we?"

Lee guided the team toward the curb so they could cross the street to the first hotel on their stop. At the back of the throng, two women in their sixties leaned in toward one another. Both wore khaki slacks and tropical shirts and had cameras dangling around their necks. The only difference between the two women was one had hair that was tinted red, and the other had hair as white as the facades of the hotels they were about to explore.

"He certainly has an impressive knowledge on the topic, doesn't he?" whispered the redhead to her friend. The other woman nodded. "He does, but you know, he's a lot shorter than I thought he'd be."

The group collected in front of the Breakwater, a hotel opened in 1939 with a prominent, vertical nameplate featuring bold white letters on a sky-blue background.

"This is a really sublime example of the tropical flavor of Art Deco," Lee began, extending one arm upward with a flourish as he spoke. "You have to remember, there was no central air conditioning back in the thirties and forties. So, the architects had to infuse these buildings with features that would help the rooms stay cool."

Almost on cue, a few in the crowd began to fan themselves with their tour brochures.

"In the Breakwater, we see two of those features very clearly," Lee continued. "First, note the long, vertical ledges over the windows that resemble eyebrows—see them there, and there, in blue? Those ledges cast shadows in front of the windows so the sunlight doesn't enter them directly. The second feature is the use of windows that wrap around the corners. Those allow for cross breezes to help cool all the corner rooms."

"Was this one of the hotels they used to show on *South Beach Vice*? It looks like one of them to me."

Lara shot a nervous look at Lee, who was smiling through what appeared to be not just gritted teeth but *grinding* teeth.

"Yes, as a matter of fact, it is," he replied more graciously than she expected. "You can tell that because of how vivid the colors are. The original colors were white or softer shades of beige and gray, as those colors reflect the harsh sun the best. But by the time that show came here to film, color televisions had become the norm. The producers decided to repaint the hotels in much brighter—some would say *more garish*—colors, so they would 'pop' more for the cameras. And, yes, the Breakwater was one of those hotels."

Half of the crowd seemed impressed by what they had learned about the color change; the other half appeared disappointed. Lee, however, was undeterred.

"Of course, the other feature that makes this hotel so special is that vertical spire with the Breakwater name on it. Do all of you see how the architects designed that to look like the bow of a ship, and how the entire hotel resembles an ocean liner getting ready to sail out onto the Atlantic?"

The crowd suddenly perked up, issuing a chorus of "yeses" and "uh-huhs" in support of Lee's assessment. The architect then turned his back on the crowd and put two fingers in the air. "Follow me," he said briskly, bending both fingers rapidly in the direction he was heading. They marched north on Ocean, but at the first intersection, they found themselves assaulted by a phalanx of video screens broadcasting soccer and baseball games, as well as rock music blasting from loudspeakers positioned at various locations throughout a sprawling patio.

Lee grimaced. "That's the bar of the Clevelander," he said, sighing. "Definitely not in keeping with the spirit of the Deco era." He sighed once more. "*And*, I'm told, it is just about the highest grossing bar in the entire state of Florida."

The architect suddenly veered left and directed those following him to a quieter spot in front of a hotel at Tenth and Collins. He stood there stolidly for a couple of moments, waiting for one woman in the group to finish emptying sand from one of her shoes, and for two of the young men who had signed up for the tour to stop texting whatever they were texting to whomever they were texting it. When everyone had reassembled, he resumed his spiel.

"We're now looking at Essex House, one of the most exquisite examples of Streamline Moderne here in Miami Beach," he announced majestically. "Once again, you can see the nautical motif of a ship setting sail, only this time, it looks like a tugboat rather than a cruise ship, and we have porthole-like windows running down one side. To see the third signature element of the Tropical Deco style, we'll need to take a quick peek inside the lobby."

Lee led the way, holding the door open for everyone in the entourage. "How are we doing timewise?" he whispered to Lara as she passed by him.

"Better," she replied. "Do you want me to strangle the woman who keeps asking about *South Beach Vice*?"

"Please, no!" he whispered back, laughing. "We have enough murder to deal with as it is!"

By the time Lee joined everyone inside the lobby, they were already marveling at the lush mural over the faux-marble fireplace, with its romanticized depiction of an Everglades from several centuries ago.

"Now, Essex House was built in 1937 and was, as you can see, exceptionally restored in 1992. What I especially want to point out here are the remarkable terrazzo floors, the third element that architects relied on to make the hotels cooler than they might have been." Everyone looked down, but one woman slid a bare foot out of the moccasin she was wearing and proceeded to run her toes gently back and forth along the tile, nodding at her friends as she did so.

Lee slowly turned to Lara and bugged his eyes out in horror. Quickly, he darted off to a different part of the lobby.

"IF YOU'LL JOIN ME OVER HERE," he quickly commanded, "I will tell you a fun story. Back in the day, gambling was both illegal and common in South Florida. Those who gambled knew which hotels hosted such activities, but they couldn't just walk up to one of the staff members and ask them where the gambling was taking place."

"I would," one of the older husbands interjected. A smattering of giggles ensued, but evaporated quickly when Lee made it clear he wanted to move the story forward.

"Yes, well, the architects found a *very* clever way to clue those people interested in gambling just where within the hotel they might find the action." The crowd waited for Lee to finish the thought, but he just stood in one spot, smiling. They waited another couple of seconds, and still he did nothing but smile, rocking to and fro on his heels. Finally, the architect slowly tilted his head downward and everyone responded with delight when they saw, embedded within the terrazzo floor's design motif, three bold red arrows pointing toward a room at the far end of the lobby.

"No one ever had to say a thing," Lee said, lifting his eyebrows mischievously. "But gamblers instantly knew exactly where to go."

After everyone had explored the hotel's historic lounge, complete with several Deco-era furnishings, they filed back out in front of the hotel. But Lee stopped everyone before they had made it out to the street corner.

"Before we move on, I want to point out to all of you this swimming pool on your left," he announced. Everyone collected at one edge of an intimate, rectangular courtyard that was surrounded by towering palms and accented by a handful of colorful lounge chairs. "For several years, this was actually a patio with a terrazzo dance floor where guests would dance the big apple or the fox-trot," Lee told them. "However, after World War II, more and more tourists to Miami wanted a swimming pool at their hotel, despite the fact one of the world's great oceans was just two blocks away.

"Miami and Miami Beach are cities blessed with almost unlimited access to water, yet for some reason, water keeps becoming more and more important to the people here."

From there, they trudged north on Collins, past the white, pink, and blue Webster to the eleven-thousand-square-foot building at the corner of Collins and Espanola Way that for many years had housed a New York-style delicatessen. Built in 1939—when Streamline Moderne was at its zenith—the structure was one of only a few Deco-era buildings in Miami Beach, Lee said, that had been crafted by a truly renowned architect, Henry Hohauser.

"It's another tug boat!" someone in the crowd shouted. Lee laughed; he was in a better mood now that he saw that he had succeeded at educating at least a few of the tourists to look at the buildings here in an entirely different way.

"Yes! It most certainly is, isn't it?" he answered. "Again we see the jutting tower in the front. And note that this 'ship' has three porthole motifs on either side, although in this case, they don't serve as windows and each one is a different size than the one beside it."

Like a wrangler corralling wayward mavericks, Lee herded the tourists back east to Ocean Drive.

"I'm sorry, Mr. Lee?"

The questioner wore tan corduroys and a blue, button-down, Oxford-cloth shirt. Lee wondered if the younger man might be a budding architect himself.

"I don't know if this is right or not, but I seem to recall reading somewhere that the phrase, 'in the pink' is connected to Art Deco. Is that right, or am I getting two things confused with one another?"

The tour guide brightened considerably. *Now this is how an architecture tour should roll*, he said to himself.

"Yes, you read correctly," Lee responded. "In many Art Deco-era buildings throughout the world, neon lighting was often recessed behind ceiling panels. Many of the more glamorous spots used pink lighting, because it gave their patrons a more attractive glow. And that's why when we now see someone who looks really healthy, we say they look like they are 'in the pink.'"

The tour continued down Ocean Drive past the McAlpin, which Lee pointed out to be one of the signature accomplishments of the other noted architect to design hotels in Miami Beach during the thirties, L. Murray Dixon. He went on to tell them the McAlpin was perhaps the purest distillation of Miami Beach art deco. "The perfectly symmetrical facade, the wrap-around eyebrows, the sea-foam-green and peach accents—they all come together in this one simple building," he said. "And does anyone see the face in the center of the building?" The crowd stood silent for only a moment before someone said, "Yes, there!" pointing to three windows and a spire which, together, denoted the eyes, nose, and mouth of what could be construed as a Mayan warrior bedecked with war paint.

They now found themselves walking single file, shoulders squeezed forward, to navigate the gauntlet of restaurants that dominated both sides of the sidewalk. And sometimes even *that* wasn't enough to avoid an unintended encounter with a circular tray of sandwiches or cocktails that some server was rushing pell-mell to the tables.

"Ooh, that dessert looks *really* yummy! You want to share that?" the red-haired woman said to a heavyset male who had just received an enormous slab of key lime pie. He guffawed heartily in response. "Sure, sit down, ladies. There's enough here for all of us to share."

The awnings that extended over the sidewalks, from the hotel entrances to the curb, provided those dining underneath with a sense of shady intimacy. But they also amplified the din of raucous laughter, clattering dishes, and thumping hip-hop that provided a constant backdrop to all the chaos. Somewhere nearby, a deep fat fryer was hard at work, causing Lara to scrunch her nose.

Eventually, the crowd came upon the Cardozo Hotel, another Streamline Moderne gem from 1939 that had been named for the former Supreme Court justice Benjamin Cardozo of New York. Whereas many of the hotels they had seen faced the street in the form of a square, the Cardozo had the shape of a long, rectangular diner, its ocean liner-like curves pushing out at either end. Along the roofline, giving off the impression of portholes, were a series of oculus windows like those found in the domes of the Pantheon and in Byzantine structures.

"Ah! And some of you might find it interesting to know that the lobby of the Cardozo was used in the filming of a movie called . . ." Lee reached into his back pocket, pulled out a large index card and squinted at it. "*There's Something About Mary.*" The crowd didn't react much to that, looked at one another for help. "Oh, and also a movie called *Scarface*, with Al Pacino." That elicited a much bigger reaction, although Lee couldn't be sure if it was because of the film or because of the name of an actor most everyone was familiar with.

They crossed Thirteenth and suddenly someone from the group shouted, "*The Birdcage!*"

Lee glanced to where the woman was pointing, which was at the Carlyle. Drenched in white and seafoam green, the hotel had once sported green curtains that locals considered a poor choice until the architect Michael Graves referred to them as "charming."

"Um . . . okay?" Lee said, bewildered by the woman's comment.

"*The Birdcage*. That movie about the two gay guys with the nightclub," she said more urgently. "Robin Williams. Somebody else I can't remember. This is it. Their nightclub."

Slowly, others in the group began to nod and point. Lee looked helplessly at Lara who offered only a pained smile in return.

They had just two quick stops left on the tour. Lee turned toward the entrance of the next hotel on their itinerary, and his face froze. It hadn't struck him until this very moment the significance this particular structure shared with the very reason he and the rest of the team were in South Florida.

"This is the Hotel . . . *Victor*," he said, turning to wink at Lara as he emphasized the name. Lara looked at him quizzically for a moment, then the import of the name registered on her face. She shook her head slowly and smiled back at him.

"The Victor is another of L. Murray Dixon's masterpieces," Lee continued. "Built in 1937, so a little earlier than the other buildings we've seen. You see two sections, and the original hotel is actually the taller of the two. The five-story structure you see down there is actually a masterful addition that opened in 2003." Several in the tour group went "ohhh" upon learning how contemporary the smaller wing of the hotel actually was.

"Now, we won't be going into this hotel, but if we did, you would see—as we did at Essex House—a glorious terrazzo floor in burgundy, cream, and sea green, as well as another Everglades-inspired mural by the artist, Earl LaPan. This was one of the first hotels to enjoy the benefits of restoration, and I think you can understand why."

As though they had rehearsed it relentlessly, Lee and Lara turned to one another and nodded simultaneously. The architect began to slowly walk backward.

"Now we are going to end our tour with one last stop—a fascinating one but not one that has anything whatsoever to do with Art Deco architecture." After walking another twenty yards, Lee turned toward a Mediterranean-style villa that from certain angles could have been mistaken for Vic Valenzuela's home in Coral Gables. A terra-cotta tile roof slanted precipitously toward the sidewalk; imposing iron gates flanked by potted palms kept the visitors at bay from the towering wooden door set within a Gothic arch.

"*This* is the Villa by Barton G, originally named Casa Casuarina, but more widely known as the mansion in which renowned fashion designer Gianni Versace lived for four years. It is the third most photographed home in the United States, after the White House and Elvis Presley's Graceland." Lee's data sent a charge through the group, and they pressed closer to peek through the dense foliage and ironwork that separated the structure from the street.

"Now the city of Miami has a very Latino population, but in Miami Beach you are more likely to meet Europeans, or possibly—as the locals call them—the Brazilians with their bazillions."

Like a sitcom audience responding to a studio sign, Lee's entourage erupted with laughter.

"One of the glamorous Europeans to land here was Versace, who moved here in the early nineties. The hotel restorations were well underway by then, but the neighborhood still was mostly populated by a few nightclubs and modeling agencies, as well as a few hotels occupied by snowbirds. Versace's arrival riveted everyone's attention on what was happening here. Before you knew it, Elton John was staying here, Madonna was staying here, Princess Diana was staying here, and top writers and architects and fashion models from all over the world were descending here, sometimes for work but sometimes just to party with Versace."

Lee pivoted toward the building and extended his left hand.

"Twenty-three thousand square feet. Ten bedrooms. Eleven bathrooms." At this point, the architect paused and put one finger vertically into the air. His audience waited breathlessly, giddy with suspense.

"*And* a fifty-four-foot-long mosaic pool lined with *24-karat gold tiles.*"

"No!" one woman exclaimed. The others followed up with comments like, "Shut up!" and "Can you believe it?"

Like an accomplished thespian, Lee waited for the audience reaction to diminish before delivering the next lines of his script.

"Versace purchased the mansion for just under three million dollars. Recently, it was purchased at auction for more than *forty million.*" More scoffs of amazement and expressions of astonishment rippled through the crowd.

"And, of course, it was right here on the steps of this structure that Versace was gunned down on a July morning in 1997 after reading newspapers at a nearby cafe. The man who shot Versace, Andrew Cunanan, shot himself eight days later in the upstairs bedroom of a houseboat he had taken refuge in. No one has ever been able to come up with a definite reason why Cunanan killed Versace. But the authorities did determine later that Cunanan had murdered at least five other people over the previous three months, in a spree that ranged from Minnesota to Chicago to New Jersey. It seems he was a young drifter who despised older, wealthier gay men like Versace. He may have stalked the fashion designer for a few days before the killing, learned his daily habits, and then gunned him down when he saw an opportunity to do so."

The crowd was bolted to Lee's calm yet captivating telling of the saga.

"And that concludes our tour, everyone," Lee said abruptly. "We will email you a summary in about a week or so. Thank you so much for coming." There was a smattering of applause and several on the tour stepped forward to shake Lee's hand and have their picture taken alongside the architect.

As the crowd began to disperse, the man who had earlier professed his love of gambling turned to his wife and shook his head.

"Can you believe that, Barbara?" he boomed. "Here we thought we were just going to be spending the morning with a world-renowned architect. Who knew he'd also be somebody who knows all the details about an unsolved murder?!"

Lee pivoted and looked at Lara, who had both palms pressed over her mouth and was shaking her head slowly from side to side.

24

Roberto decided the morning that Dalton was off giving his tour of Miami Beach might be a good time for him to pay another call on Vic Valenzuela's housekeeper. It took her only a couple of minutes to identify two of the football players she had seen entering the cabana the night of his murder.

"*Aquél!*" she exclaimed, pointing a finger at a head-and-shoulder shot of the quarterback in a team brochure Roberto was tilting in her direction.

"You're sure?" he confirmed.

"*Si,*" she replied. "*Estoy segurísima.*"

He turned the page.

"*Y él también,*" she suddenly said, pointing this time at a photo of David Diaz, who had been the cameraman for their escapade. She reiterated to Roberto she had seen three players—not two—go into the cabana with the girl. But she wasn't sure which black player in the brochure was the one that had attended the party that night. Roberto didn't worry about that. He knew either Drew Mendenhall or David Diaz would give up the other player easily enough.

In one quick phone call, the quarterback proved correct Roberto's hunch.

"Yes sir, we'll all meet you downtown," Mendenhall told Agent Sainclair matter-of-factly. "With our attorneys."

Given the sensitive nature of the conversation, and Lee being preoccupied with his tour of Miami Beach, Sainclair said he'd like for either Warren, Roberto, or Liam to come watch the interview. Roberto and Liam accepted the invitation; Warren indicated he and Agent Weiss had some additional research they wanted to conduct that day.

"Research—so that's what they're calling it now," Liam said to Roberto, winking. Roberto gave Liam but a wisp of a smile before sobering himself. "I think they really are doing more research," he replied, without the slightest hint of irony.

***

At the agency's offices, Sainclair was in anything but a joyous mood. "*Tout pa bon,*" he said to Roberto, shaking his head. "These *bébés* are more lawyered up than a drug cartel."

"Bad night at Hialeah, Mackeson?" Roberto asked.

Sainclair didn't say anything for a time. His head was bowed as he collected from his desk his notes and a couple of manila folders containing background information. Then, eventually, he answered Roberto's question.

"*Wi,*" he answered, almost imperceptibly.

Two attorneys representing the university had accompanied the players to the office. The quarterback had brought along a family attorney as additional counsel. Liam and Roberto assumed perches behind a one-way mirror that gave them a view of everything taking place in the room.

Sainclair sighed heavily as he dropped into a metal chair that was opposite the assembly. "This . . ." he began, sweeping one arm out across the group, ". . . is entirely unnecessary. I'm just going to ask a few routine questions."

The group remained silent. After reviewing the contents of one of the manila folders, Sainclair cleared his throat. "So, exactly who was it who organized this party?"

The football players looked at each other blankly. Eventually they all nodded, anointed the quarterback as their spokesperson.

"I guess I did," Mendenhall said. "Well, we *all* did really, but I had the key to the coach's cabana and I'm the one . . ."

"You have a key to the victim's cabana?" Sainclair interrupted.

Mendenhall looked frustrated. "I *did*," he said. "The coach gave one to me last year after I made second-team all-American. But I had to give it up when you guys contacted us." He flashed a look at the attorney beside him, who didn't react.

"*Bon*. Okay, how did you find this prostitute?"

All three players turned in different directions to seek out the guidance of those beside them. The attorney sitting next to the quarterback spoke up. "Do you intend to charge my client with solicitation?" he asked.

Sainclair stared the lawyer down. "We *might* charge all three of them with that . . . if they do not cooperate with us," he intoned.

The attorney sighed, looked down, readjusted the bottom of his tie, then turned and nodded at Mendenhall.

"We found her on gregslust.com," he said.

Sainclair peered at the quarterback. "Greg's . . . ?"

The attorney seated next to Jamal Culberson sat up. "Gregslust. It's an online bulletin board for people looking for . . . sexual situations. It has this whole area devoted exclusively to masseuses, escorts, etc. Pretty much anything you're looking for you can find there."

Sainclair squinted at the attorney for a moment, nodded, then swiveled to his left to resume his questioning of the quarterback. "All right," he said, returning to his notes. "You found her on this bulletin board and . . ."

"Well, we didn't really find *her*," Mendenhall interrupted.

"What do you mean?"

"Well, we actually called for another girl. A brunette. With really huge tits." His lawyer reached out and clamped one hand on the quarterback's forearm. The athlete quickly swiveled around to look at the attorney, then shrunk back into his seat. "Sorry. What? I should say . . . much larger . . . breasts?"

His counsel propped one elbow on the arm of his chair, dropped his forehead into the open space between his thumb and forefinger, and began to slowly massage his brow.

"Anyway, this other girl showed up. Told us the brunette had gotten another call and couldn't come. We didn't really care all that much because the one who came, Krystal, was, like, even *more . . .*"

The attorney glanced up quickly at his client, widened his eyes a bit. The quarterback dropped his head down into his chest, blew out some air.

"She . . . well . . ." He turned toward his attorney briefly, then returned his attention to Sainclair. "Anyway she wasn't the one we originally planned to . . . be with."

In the anteroom, Liam turned to Roberto. "You thinking what I'm thinking, mate?" he asked.

"That maybe The Organization had some connections with the prostitution agency, and when they learned there had been a call out to the Valenzuela estate, they saw it as an opportunity to get one of their operatives near him?"

Liam nodded slowly.

"I wouldn't be at all surprised," the designer whispered back.

Sainclair was shuffling through his notes. "This young woman . . . you said her name was Krystal? Had you ever seen her before? Hired her before? Do you still have the phone number of the agency you procured her through?"

The attorney beside Jamal Culberson sat forward again. "I can tell you right now, it's highly unlikely you're going to find her. These girls, they're on the move. Constantly. One week, they're turning tricks here in Miami. The next, they're working in Tampa or Orlando. Two weeks after that, they're temping at a law firm in Jacksonville or Atlanta. Another two weeks go by and they're hostessing in the lobby bar of some hotel in D.C. or Nashville. You can call around all you want to and you might find a few Krystals, but trust me, they won't be the Krystal you're looking for."

Sainclair turned and studied the attorney more intently, and for a longer time, than he had before. "I must say, *mesye*, your encyclopedic knowledge of the industry is both impressive and incredibly helpful."

Roberto and Liam snickered behind the mirror; the attorney retreated and began to discreetly chew on the inside of one cheek.

"Now, back to Mr. Mendenhall," Sainclair announced, looking at the quarterback. "A witness claims the young woman did not leave the cabana when the rest of you did. Is that correct? If so, why didn't she?"

The quarterback's jaw slackened some. "You mean somebody was watching us do her? Like, a peeping tom, or something?"

Sainclair took on a pained expression. "Let me guess, young man," he said. "You're attending Miami A&M on a full *athletic* scholarship, aren't you?"

The gridiron star nodded, his mouth still agape.

"No, son. No one was watching you . . . doing . . . whatever it was you were doing. Someone saw all of you go into the cabana, and then they saw you come out. But not the girl. They say she never came out. Why is that?"

Again, the threesome consulted each other silently. Now, it was Jamal Culberson's time to speak.

"I'll tell you why. It's 'cause she told me she wanted me to come back there later and finish what I started." A lurid smile crept across his lips. "She wanted a whole lot more of what Jamal had been giving her."

The attorney next to him cleared his throat loudly. The wide receiver winced with irritation at the rebuke. "What, dude? It's the truth! Bitch couldn't get enough of it!" His attorney merely shook his head and looked at the ceiling.

"Anyways, I was the one who drove us over there. So when the party was over, I takes Drew and Diaz back to the dorm. After I drops them off, I goes back to coach's to get me some more of that sweet stuff." The star player turned sullen. "Only the bitch wasn't there when I get back. She'd up and gone."

"Did you see any sign of her? Was there a door open? Did she leave anything behind?"

The running back looked down at the table, shook his head. "No. The door wasn't locked or nuthin', but it wasn't open, neither. And, no, I didn't see nuthin' of hers laying around on the floor. I mean she was *outta there.*"

The interview room fell quiet. But after a moment, Culberson suddenly looked up. "But . . ."

Everyone turned toward him.

"I did notice one of them windows back in the bedroom *was* up a little bit. Like maybe three or four inches."

Roberto looked at Liam and frowned. "*That* would explain why Margarida didn't see her leave the cabana," he said. "She snuck out the back."

"I knows that window was up," Culberson continued, "'cause I remember feelin' a little bit of a breeze when I go back there, and I was worried somebody might have overheard it when I was making her moan real loud and all . . ."

Culberson's attorney shot forward. "Are we done here? Do you need anything else?"

Agent Sainclair smiled a tad, then let it fall. "Yes. I do. A description of the girl, if someone can provide it."

The quarterback decided to reclaim control of the conversation. "I can give you that," he said. "She had reddish-brown hair, she was maybe about five-seven, five-eight. She wasn't fat or anything, but she was kind of . . . big-boned."

Sainclair was scribbling quickly. "How old would you say she was?"

In the adjacent room, Liam sat up and leaned closer to the mirror.

Mendenhall shrugged. "I don't know. Twenties for sure. She seemed a little older than us."

Sainclair was scribbling faster now. "Any distinguishing marks? A mole? A tattoo of any kind?"

For the first time, David Diaz spoke up. "She had a little tattoo on the inside of one thigh," he said, almost in a whisper. "Of a lizard, or something like that. I noticed it when I was looking through the viewfinder of the video camera."

The lawyer of Diaz leaned forward and swiveled in his client's direction. "Oh, Jesus, you guys *filmed* the damned thing? I want that camera in my office by the end of the day, *do you hear me?*"

The lineman nodded like a bobblehead on amphetamines.

Sainclair sighed again, glanced at his watch. "All right, so I just need to know where all of you were around eleven thirty, eleven forty-five, on the night Mr. Valenzuela was murdered."

They exchanged glances again.

"I was back at the dorm, David was at the dorm," the quarterback said, pointing one thumb at his teammate. "Jamal dropped us off there around eleven."

"Are there people in the dorm who can confirm that?"

Both football players said "yeah" simultaneously.

The group then turned to the star running back, waited for him to articulate his whereabouts.

He said nothing.

"And where were you, Mr. Culberson?" Sainclair asked.

The football player stared directly at the federal agent before his look veered off toward a side wall. "On my ways back to my apartment, I guess," he said softly.

Sainclair nodded slowly a few times. "So you hadn't returned to the dorm yet. By eleven thirty or so."

Culberson indicated the agent had the story right. Looked off toward a different wall.

"What *time* did you get back to your apartment? Do you have a roommate?"

The running back's expression shifted from one of caginess to one of edginess. "No. I lives alone."

Sainclair began to stare the athlete down. With painstaking care, he repeated, "And at what time did you arrive back at your apartment, Mr. Culberson?"

Sainclair couldn't tell whether the running back was giving some thought to the question or giving thought of how he was going to evade it. Finally, the football player shrugged.

"Beats me. Midnight maybe. Maybe a little after."

"Can you think of anyone who might have seen you in your car? Did you pass a patrol officer? Someone you know from school? Anyone who can verify you were in your car when you say you were?"

Culberson's face grew sullen again. He blinked several times at the federal agent, set his jaw firm.

"Nope," he replied almost defiantly. "I didn't see nobody, and nobody seen me."

25

As the storm clouds began to gather, so, too, did they.

First, the silver-haired athlete wearing a purple windbreaker and dark running shorts. Then, the serene woman of Middle Eastern descent with a paisley scarf around her hair. Next, two Hispanic men, natty in their tailored suits, followed by a Rasta-musician type, colorfully bedecked in a striped serape.

The last to arrive was a thirty-something brunette in a tautly tailored business suit. Under one arm, she carried a zippered, burgundy-colored case . . . a case containing a high-powered computer that would help them set their plot into motion.

The nameplate on the door of the sixth-floor office suite said GIANT HORIZON TEA, a jab that would bring a smile to anyone familiar with the group's fondness for anagrams. Or—given what their motive was—not a smile, perhaps, but an arched eyebrow at the least.

"Congratulations, Grant, on finishing the Ironman competition in St. Croix," said the woman carrying the small portfolio. "That's quite an achievement."

Murmurs of appreciation filtered around the table. However, Grant did not acknowledge the accolades. Instead, he stared at a point on the tabletop in front of him. "Well, I didn't beat my personal best like I was hoping to. Maybe next time," he replied briskly.

Like a slow-moving satellite radar, the brunette scanned the rest of the table until her gaze fell upon her colleague in dreadlocks. "Ah, Rodney, your children are all doing fine, I take it?"

He smiled widely, revealing a narrow gap between two teeth in the upper front. "Yes, thank you, Aiisha. They are becoming like sailfish in the sea. I can't keep up with them. They exhaust me."

Everyone laughed and nodded that they understood Rodney's predicament.

"Don't expect them to slow down anytime soon," Grant said, still preoccupied with the tabletop. "When they get to be teenagers, they'll be moving even faster, only then they'll be behind the wheel of a car you're paying insurance on."

Another round of hearty chuckles filled the room. When they subsided, Aiisha smiled even more broadly, but her tone became more businesslike.

"We are here today to formally launch the next stage of The Transformation. We have received from our compatriots in New Zealand both the funds and the supplies we need to advance the cause." She waited a few beats before continuing.

"Are we all in agreement that now is the time for us to light the torch and begin our quest to help our fellow citizens bask in the joy of living flawless lives in this very flawed world?"

In unison, the group chanted, "We are." Grant had responded enthusiastically but continued to look only at the surface of the table.

"Excellent," Aiisha responded. She unzipped the portfolio in front of her, pushed back the leather cover and pressed the power button on the computer. "While we are waiting for this to boot up . . . do I understand correctly, Dimah, that you have made contact with the agent who will activate the plan? The one responsible for removing the football coach who interfered with our initiative?"

The woman in the headscarf nodded gently.

"Yes, my sister. I connected with the agent through the bulletin board, as we discussed. On Thursday we are to meet, and I will hand over at that time the vials containing the toxins for the trial run, as well as the details the agent will need to ensure they are properly distributed into the regional water system."

For several seconds, all one could hear in the room was the steady hum of the air- conditioning system. Then, Aiisha gently dropped one forearm onto the conference table and inhaled deeply. "Perfect," she said softly. "Wonderfully perfect. It sounds like everything is advancing precisely as we want it to."

Just then, a rolling rumble reverberated through the building. They could tell the afternoon sea breeze storms were kicking into full force.

"Damn it, I knew I should have brought an umbrella," said one of the two young men wearing a suit.

"It'll blow over by the time we're done," Grant replied. The triathlete had removed his gaze from the table and was staring at the young man intently. "There might still be showers around but, don't worry, you're not going to get hit by lightning, son."

There was an odd silence as the triathlete continued to glare at the younger man as though a response of some sort was expected. His counterpart tugged on the lapels of his suit, smiled meekly in return, and nodded. Grant, however, did not look away.

"I . . . have a question."

It was the other young man in business attire. Whereas his colleague was smooth- shaven and sitting back in his chair with one ankle resting on the other knee, this Dapper Dan sported a trimmed beard and had both elbows resting on the conference table, his chin cupped in both hands.

"Yes, Tomás?"

"I was wondering . . . what will the effects of the toxin be? How will we know when they've started to manifest? What exactly should we expect?"

The beam on Aiisha's face dimmed; she now began to scrutinize the tabletop the way Grant had earlier. Methodically she moistened her lips with her tongue, then shot a quick look at the woman across the table from her.

"Dimah, you are more intimately acquainted with the science of it all. Do you want to take this one?"

Her colleague nodded, then leaned forward into the table.

"The mechanisms we are using are called diatoms. Diatoms are single-celled, aquatic organisms that fall under the category of golden-brown algae. As algae go, they are unique in that their walls are composed of silica . . . glass, which actually makes them very beneficial to society. They get used a lot in dental paste, shoe polish, silver polish . . . things like that.

"But when diatoms absorb too many nutrients, they become lethal. The algae starts to grow out of control, sometimes creating what scientists call algal blooms. Diatoms by themselves are not usually toxic, but the algal blooms they can form contain compounds that will kill most fish, birds, and mammals, including humans . . . Yes, Ramón?"

The businessman who had forgotten his umbrella had his hand in the air.

"Excuse me for interrupting, sister. You said they *sometimes* form these algal blooms. I don't understand how *sometimes* is going to work for us. Don't we need to be absolutely certain that happens? How are we going to be sure these diatoms do what we need them to do?"

There was another rattle of thunder, which was shorter but more intense than the first. Dimah exchanged discreet smiles with Aiisha, who nodded for her to continue.

"Actually, comrade, the question you ask is most verily an astute one. And you are correct. Normally, the development of algal blooms is accidental and sporadic. However . . . we have been working for some time to engineer a form of diatom that we could program to mutate into an algal bloom almost immediately after it has been introduced into water. As you all know, our research was unexpectedly interrupted a couple of years ago. But since then, we've been able to get those studies back on track, and I am happy to say we've been successful at creating, *en masse*, diatoms that behave like perfectly programmed time-release capsules.

"Except that, when someone ingests a time-release capsule, it usually is to relieve pain. These time-release capsules will *inflict* pain. Great pain. And suffering. And then, eventually, death."

The mood around the table was reverent, with an undercurrent of excitement.

"But . . ." It was Tomás, sitting forward in his chair now. "But . . .

I thought our goal is to liberate our fellow citizens, not kill them. To free them from the oppressive institutions that govern their lives and squelch their individuality."

A brief tic flickered across Aiisha's face; the left side of her mouth arced downward slightly. She recovered quickly, however, and pushed out another wide smile.

"It's good that you broach that issue, my brother, it really is," she replied calmly. "It's very easy to sometimes misunderstand or misinterpret our initiative, or the means by which we intend to advance it."

Everyone at the table quickly turned to look at Tomás; however, he showed no response to the remark.

"You are correct . . . *liberation* is our primary objective. Most of the uninitiated around the world trudge through their day suppressed by the selfish actions of multinational cartels and corporate oligarchies that are completely indifferent to the hopes and desires of those they enslave. When we achieve *full* liberation, when we assume complete *control*, the individual will become the decision-maker. Boundaries, regulations, and ownership of private property will all become quaint, meaningless concepts. Any one person will always supersede the group."

She paused, glanced down at the table for a moment.

"With a few sensible exceptions, of course, that the Grand Council will determine as the liberation evolves. Power to the cause."

Instantly, everyone around the table echoed the incantation. "Power to the cause."

Aiisha braved another broad smile. "But, to your point, Tomás. Severe disruption of the established power structure is critical to our ability to roll out the initiative. We are most likely to assert our goals, manage the liberation from a place of strength, if we first cause havoc with the institutions in place."

She tilted her head slightly, put one palm in the air. "Let me rephrase that. Havoc is not sufficient. Our goal, really, is to generate hysteria. And this plan is the catalyst for precisely that. *Hysteria.*"

Dimah decided it was time for her to step back into the conversation. But her tone, which had been factual and scientific before, now seemed more personal. And more impassioned.

"We cannot predict with absolutely certainty what effect the diatoms will have," she said. "We expect the consequences will vary from children, to adults, to the very elderly. But we will probably notice the fruits of our labor taking hold quite quickly. First, we'll hear of some people experiencing milder symptoms—lethargy and memory loss for example. Those will quickly be followed by intense muscle aches and, within twenty-four hours of that, we should notice people coming down with very serious neurological disorders, including seizures. As our toxin mutates within the body, we'll know our work has been successful when damage begins to manifest in the liver and kidneys of those who have absorbed it. With the vital organs collapsing like a row of dominoes, we can then be confident it's just a matter of hours before we will witness mortalities on a massive scale."

Everyone at the table quietly indicated their satisfaction with the answer.

Aiisha referred to the computer on the table, swept the screen a couple of times, pressed a few keys.

"Now, the version of the toxin that our agent will distribute in the next couple of days is—how should I put it?—Toxin Light. It's a milder form of the toxin and we will ensure it reaches only a limited population. It's a test run to verify that our research was indeed successful.

"Once we know for certain that we have the toxin where we want it to be, we'll increase its potency and expand its distribution considerably in the final run a day or two later. Within a few hours of that more comprehensive distribution, the effects should manifest in devastating ways. There no doubt will be mass casualties, which in turn, will lead to chaos region-wide. At that time, each of you will be playing a pivotal role in helping to secure our management of the region. I show that Grant is going to lead reinforcements that will take over the regional health department and oversight of most of the private medical centers here?"

He acknowledged her assessment was correct. She went back to reading from the screen. "Tomás and Ramón will be using the connections they've established at City Hall over the past couple of years to assume command there . . ."

She used three fingers to sweep the screen, put a hand out to stop it, silently read some more, then nodded. "Ah, Rodney. Of course, you will be stepping in to direct all of the first responder groups."

Rodney again revealed the gap between his front teeth. "Yes, I am very pleased at the respect that's been shown here for my experience as third-in-command of the Jamaican police force," he replied.

Aiisha looked up from the screen. "That leaves Dimah and me, who will be mobilizing the community and neighborhood organizations we've infiltrated over the past eighteen months. The funds we've funneled into all of those groups have given us even more leverage with them than I had hoped."

An emphatic crack, followed immediately by a roaring boom, lifted everyone a couple of inches off their seats. As the roll of thunder that ensued gradually diminished, they all laughed nervously at one another.

"I hope that's not the universe making a statement about its displeasure with our plan," Rodney said.

Aiisha slowly shook her head and greeted her colleagues with yet another boulevard-wide smile. "Not at all, my brother, not at all," she quietly replied. "I interpret that as the universe enthusiastically telling us it considers our plan to be nothing short of brilliant."

Grant leaned far over his end of the table and engaged Aiisha with an intense look. "The plan *is* brilliant," he said, a smirk appearing beneath his seriousness. "Now, let's move it along, make sure the test run goes well, and make damned sure we don't fuck things up the way our comrades in Manhattan did."

26

With her right hand, Bree drew from the deck on the table in front of her. Slowly she made duck lips at the new card as she tentatively slid it between those fanned out in her left hand. Then she sighed, grimaced some, sighed again.

"How did the Art Deco tour go this morning?" she asked perkily, glancing up at Lara.

"Pretty well, I guess. When it came to the hotels, some of the tourists were more interested in their film credits than their architectural significance. But I suppose that is to be expected. And, of course, Dalton was his effervescent self."

Bree smiled, scrutinized Lara some. "Which joke did he tell this time? The one about how many architects does it take to screw in a light bulb? Or the one about why the architect crossed the road?"

The firm's second-in-command narrowed her eyes at the architect.

"Oh, no you don't," she said warily. "Play your hand. Every time you lure me into a conversation like this, you end up discarding something that doesn't match either the suit or number, and I don't notice until it's much too late. My mother used to play cards like that with me so I'm on to you. You're a card shark, plain and simple, Bree Westerman."

The younger woman feigned offense for a moment before

transforming her look of shock into a sly grin.

"That's why it's called *Crazy* Eights, Lara," she said, a devious lilt in her voice. She plucked a card out of those she held and dropped it onto the discard pile with exaggerated élan. "Eight of clubs!" she announced dramatically. "And I am changing the suit to . . . diamonds!"

Now it was Lara's turn to frown. Her shoulders sagged and Bree could tell from the furrows in her adversary's brow there wasn't a card bearing a diamond anywhere in her already-voluminous holdings.

"Why are guys such dopes?"

The question came from the floor nearby, where Irene sat cross-legged, her chin in her hands, her elbows planted firmly on her thighs. She was staring at her laptop screen (which was not unusual) but she was not tapping any keys (which for her *was very* unusual).

Lara let out a high titter. "Have you been conversing with Sung-min again?" she asked, shooting a furtive look at her cards every now and then in the hopes they had magically changed since the last time she had studied them. Discreetly, she extended her right hand and drew another card. Her expression did not change.

"No, not him," Irene replied glumly. "He's probably the only guy I know who *isn't* a dope."

She said nothing more, continued to gaze into her laptop.

Bree looked at the young associate. "Then, who?"

Irene didn't respond at first. Finally, she reached out and tapped a couple of keys on her computer. "Never mind," she offered. "It doesn't matter."

Bree and Lara had entered a frantic spate of draws and discards, but both stopped at the same moment.

"Is it Liam?" Bree said, urgency in her voice. "Are things between you and Liam all right?" The architect looked over at Lara and silently communicated some concern.

Again, Irene was quiet for several seconds, as if the question hadn't been asked. But eventually, she touched her keyboard once and said, "I'm talking about this Vic Valenzuela guy. The coach. What a complete dope he was."

Lara looked at Bree, who dipped her head and chuckled slightly. "Oh, right. The murder victim. Of course." Then she sobered some.

"What do you mean? Why do you think he was a dope?"

Irene blew out some air and rapidly began to type, launching a few windows on her monitor simultaneously. "What I mean is, if the guy didn't want people to know he was throwing games for a while, he did a terrible job of hiding it."

She pointed toward one of the windows she had just opened. "Up until four years ago, there wasn't any connection—that I can find anyway—between the spread on the games Miami A&M played in and the actual scores." She reached toward the computer again and pounded on a few keys. Pointed at a new window. "But then a couple of years ago, something changed."

Lara peered at the younger associate. "What changed?" she asked, covertly dropping a card onto the discard pile and sneaking a look at Bree to see if she had noticed.

Irene sighed again. "Well, take their first game three years ago against Alabama Western. The spread was twenty-four points, with Miami A&M supposed to win. At the end of the third quarter, Valenzuela's team was ahead thirty-four to nothing. But then, one of the best defenses in the country suddenly gave up seventeen points in the fourth quarter, making the final score thirty-four to seventeen."

Lara turned to Bree and shook her head. "I don't . . . understand how this football gambling works."

Bree smiled at her colleague.

"Alabama Western was expected to lose the game by at least twenty-four points—that's the spread Irene was talking about. So gamblers betting on the game were basically asked, if twenty-four points get added to Alabama Western's final score, who do you think will win *then*?

"Since Miami A&M was ahead by thirty-four points at the end of the third quarter, those who bet on them would have won their bet, had that been the final score. But since Alabama Western narrowed the gap to seventeen points, and they were being given an additional twenty-four points, those who bet on Alabama Western ended up winning instead. Irene's saying it looks like our murder victim might have allowed the other team to score a bunch of points so those betting on that team won. It's called 'throwing a game'—sometimes the coaches and even the players can have money riding on the other team winning, and they'd rather lose a game and win a lot of money from their bets, than win a game that isn't really that all that important."

Lara nodded slowly, indicating she sort of understood. Bree let her smile drop some and pointed at the discard pile. "And oh, by the way, you just dropped the six of diamonds on top of the nine of hearts."

Lara allowed her eyes to travel down toward the pile. "Oh my, now how did *that* happen?" she said softly.

Bree continued to look directly at her rival, and when their eyes met once again, she said, "Nice try. Didn't work."

Lara scowled at her colleague. She extended one hand slowly and with a pained expression drew a card from the stack.

"And the same thing happened in just about every game that year." Irene was getting revved up now; not once during the conversation had she looked at either Bree or Lara. She made a few more clicks and opened up yet another window on her computer.

"Ahead by twenty-one over South Carolina Tech going into the last quarter," she said. "But gave up ten points in the final two minutes, resulting in a score of thirty-one to twenty, when the spread was thirteen. Next game. Against Louisiana A&M. Ahead twenty to ten with five minutes left but gave up eight points to still win twenty to eighteen, but the spread was three. Same thing happened in pretty much every game that year *and* the following year. In fact, although they won every game those two seasons, they actually lost every game except one to the spread.

"However, this past season . . ." She hit one key with the flourish of a conductor indicating the need for a dramatic cymbal crash from the orchestra. "They lost just one game overall but suddenly they started winning a lot more games against the spread. It is pretty hard to believe that was just a coincidence."

The room fell silent, no cards were played.

Eventually, Bree sighed. "Let's say we determine without a shadow of a doubt that he was helping The Organization rake in a lot of money by throwing games for a while. And then, for some reason, he decided to stop doing it. Let's even say we figure out who, specifically, was most upset by his having such a change of heart. I'm not clear that helps us identify who killed him, or what The Organization's next plot is."

Bree paused, then she seemed to fret. "It's good research, Irene, it really is," she continued. "But we either need to figure out exactly who did Valenzuela in . . . or exactly what sort of scheme The Organization has planned."

Lara played a card and then turned her attention to the junior associate. "I'm curious, which game was the first one in which it appears the coach stopped—what was it you called it?—tossing the outcome?"

Both Bree and Irene chuckled.

"It's *throwing* the outcome but you know, that's a really good question, Lara. Maybe if we can pinpoint when he started disobeying instructions from The Organization, and we dig into his emails and texts around that time, we might find out who if anybody was particularly upset about what was going on."

Irene began to type furiously on her laptop's keyboard, then came to an immediate stop and ducked her head closer to the monitor. Bree could tell from the movement of Irene's lips she was doing some quick analysis of game scores.

"Looks like it was the second game of last year," the junior associate finally announced, tapping a couple more keys. She moved her vision closer to the monitor once again. "They were playing Southern Kentucky State. The spread was sixteen. Miami A&M was ahead fourteen to nothing going into the final quarter so if they wanted to lose against the spread, they were already doing it. But then they scored ten more points and won the game twenty-four to seven, beating the spread. They also beat the spread on the next game, lost to the spread on the game after that but turned around and beat it again on the next two games."

"Nice," Bree said, returning to her hand. "When you get a chance, see if you can poke around into Valenzuela's emails around that time. Maybe we can find somebody who was expressing some serious dismay over how well Valenzuela's team was suddenly performing."

When she was finished giving instructions to Irene, the architect began to place the five of hearts on the discard pile, held up, then took the five of spades out of her hand and laid *it* on the stack instead.

"And, by the way, you never answered my question about how things are going with Liam," she said to the junior associate. "You two getting along okay? You teaching him a thing or two?"

Irene sat back from her computer, scratched behind one ear, then turned and smiled back at her colleague.

And said nothing.

Just then, Lara's phone buzzed. She pulled it from a skirt pocket and held it to her ear, listened. Bree could faintly hear someone chattering emotionally on the other end.

"What! When!?" Lara exclaimed. The vigor used by the typically placid administrator caused even Irene to look up from her computer with alarm.

More squawking on the other end. To Bree, it sounded vaguely like Dalton. But if it was him, he was in a dither like one she had never seen or heard before.

"I understand, calm down, Dalton," Lara said. "When do you expect to be finished with your appointment this afternoon?" Lara listened to the reply, then nodded. "All right, I will meet Agents Sainclair and Weiss at their offices downtown in an hour or so. You can just meet me there when you can." She quickly ended the call, turned to Bree, her mouth agape.

"That was Dalton," she said, not realizing Bree had already deduced that. "Remember that personal assistant we met the day after we got here, Ashley Taymore? She called Agent Sainclair this afternoon and told him she wanted to turn herself in for the murder of Vic Valenzuela."

No one said a word for several seconds as they absorbed what Lara had just revealed. Then, from the floor, Irene said, "Okay, so that makes, like, *no* sense *whatsoever.*"

27

Dalton Lee stood before the low rock wall that separated Erwin Road from the cemetery. Although the wall bore the appearance of antiquity, he knew it was relatively modern, constructed in 1989 by the City of Coral Gables as part of its campaign to restore the burial site into a place of peaceful repose.

A cemetery, Lee thought to himself. *Of all the places for me to have to sign these damned documents.*

He wasn't clear what was going on with his contact. This really seemed to Lee like a thoughtless choice, and, prior to now, his confidant had seemed to be (if anything) a paragon of *thoughtfulness*. The architect scanned the diverse, discreet headstones he could make out through the vegetation, an assortment of tributes to early South Florida pioneers with names like Dowling, Larkin, Brooke, Mitchell, and Plummer. Tributes that just thirty years earlier had been overgrown, vandalized, and (in some instances) obliterated.

And that's when it struck him that his contact had, in fact, given supreme thought to the selection of the location of their meeting. It was as if the overriding message Lee was supposed to receive was that the most meaningful gift we can offer our parents is a death somehow memorialized with dignity.

A cool tremor ran through him. *Can't be the weather*, he thought. *It's almost summer.*

He stepped through a gap in the stone wall and took a moment to study the bronze marker that had been placed at the simple entrance by the Coral Gables chapter of the Daughters of the American Revolution. The plaque explained that although it was now called Pinewood Cemetery, the burial ground had once borne the name *Cocoplum*, after the evergreen shrub that grows abundantly throughout the state. Another ten yards inside the entrance, a second plaque on a tall metal standard provided further detail about the heritage site, including the fact it comprised more than two hundred and sixty plots and had not hosted a burial since the 1940s.

It looks like it, Lee thought. *If I wanted to film a cemetery scene for a horror movie, this would be the place to do it.*

He strolled farther into the space and was taken aback at the juxtaposition of elegance and simplicity that pervaded the grounds. Some of the gravestones were spare and square, bearing no ornamentation but the name of the deceased. Others rose perhaps a foot or two from the ground and featured personal insignias, like a horseshoe or a cross. But although he was an architect, he was pleased to see no grandiose temples here, no emblems of extravagant ego.

Sunlight kept appearing and then vanishing as dense clouds raced across the sky, creating the effect of an erratic spotlight put there to guide him to his eventual meeting spot. The deeper he pushed into the cemetery, the less comfortable he became. The grounds seemed completely absent of any other being. The wind abruptly went flat, and the color of the air shifted from sun-dappled to green-gray. Each step seemed to resound off some nearby tree trunk, each breath echoed with an eerie, jagged edge.

When a sudden gust scattered the leaves about his feet, he swore he heard a voice traveling along the current.

"Do you fear death, Dalton?" it asked.

The architect stopped short. He realized he had never seriously considered the issue. He was fairly certain he wasn't afraid of death, but the *process* of dying might be another thing altogether. Which is what made this encounter today so unappealing to him. For he was about to seal the dying process for someone else, and he wasn't at all certain his decision was the right one.

"Perhaps," he quietly said to the wind.

After a moment, the architect trudged on past a cluster of gnarled cypresses. On his left, a shrub seemed to quiver despite the absence now of any breeze. On his right, a tombstone appeared to bow toward him slightly.

Eventually, he made his way into a small clearing. And there, beyond a slight rise, he saw his contact sitting on a flat stone bench. It was similar to the one they had occupied at Vizcaya. Only, this bench looked more primitive than man-made, offered no armrests or back for him to relax against.

"I thought you said you had grown weary of meeting in dismal places," Lee said, staring off into the distance after he had taken a seat.

The other person sat with hands clasped in front; propped against one hip was a large accordion file that sat partially open.

"Dismal? I'm sorry you view this locale that way, Dalton. To be frank, where you see death and desiccation, I see life and vegetation."

Dalton turned to look at his companion. "How poetic," he responded, his tone dripping with irony.

The other person sniffed. "I've never really been one for poetry, Dalton. Too . . . sing-songy or melancholy, wouldn't you agree?"

The speaker waited some time for a response, but realizing none was forthcoming, sighed then shifted to the one side and began to rummage in the file box that rested between them.

"You seem a little anxious, Dalton. Not to worry, this shouldn't take very long. They need your signature and initials on every page, but the entire document is only ten or eleven pages, I believe."

Dalton felt his stomach flip as he accepted the stapled-together papers that were handed to him. *How can such life-and-death matters get reduced to eleven point type on sulfite paper?* he wondered.

On his way to the cemetery, he had committed to studying the document closely, to ensuring every humane protocol would be followed to the letter. But now, with the papers before him, he could not bring himself to confront the possible demise of his parent with such precision and concentration. He rapidly reviewed each page, saw terms like "execute a do-not-resuscitate order," and "make any and all health care decisions," and "incurable or irreversible mental or physical condition."

He looked off into the distant trees for some signal of what to do. He heard a faint snap and then saw a short brittle branch separate from a limb above and topple to the pine needles below.

As if suddenly electrified, his right hand flew across the blanks that asked for some form of identification. He flipped from one page to the next as if this were his hundredth (rather than first) time to review the document. After he scribbled his initials on the final page, he allowed the first several pages to flop back on top of it, thrust the package toward his contact, jumped up from the bench, and marched several paces toward the sunlight that now filtered through the lush canopy of leaves above.

His contact called out to him, but he ignored the appeal; stood instead with his hands buried in his pockets, fingering the few coins that lay within. He drifted, back, through folds of time, to a day when he was six, maybe seven. They were at a neighborhood lake, somewhere in San Diego (to this day he was haunted by the fragrance of the evening primrose that surrounded that body of water). His father had bought him a wooden toy sailboat and it was his first attempt at being its skipper. Which meant standing beside the lake, his tiny right hand positioned against his forehead, salute-style, to shield his eyes from the glare coming off the water. Watching the small craft skim one way, then the other, as the steady breeze switched directions.

Once, the boat sailed several feet from shore, and he felt his heart gallop at the thought he was about to lose forever the project on which they had teamed together for hours. He stepped toward the edge of the water to retrieve the boat, but his father placed an arm across his small chest and said, "Wait. Let it come to you. It will. The water and the wind will bring it to you. When they are ready."

And, after a few moments, they did.

Lee was cloaked in sadness, yet felt no urge to cry. Was he heavyhearted because of his father's condition? Or because of his lack of control over the situation? Or his sense that his life these days seemed to be nothing more than one interminable wait—a wait to know whether he would ever find a lifelong companion to settle with, whether he would rescue his parents or say goodbye to them forever from afar. Whether he could prevent whatever lurid scheme The Organization was about to set forth.

He whirled around and stomped back to the bench. The other person looked up at him placidly.

"I get that you can't reveal what it is they have up their sleeve," he said, fuming. "At least tell me when. *When* are they going to launch whatever it is they have planned?"

He could tell he had made his contact uncomfortable with the request. And he could also tell he was going to get his wish.

The person turned and clasped the accordion file shut. Then quickly glanced up at the architect.

"Soon, Dalton. They are bringing it forward soon. When they are ready. But only when *they* are ready."

28

On their way to Ashley Taymore's interrogation, Lee and Lara had a spat.

"What do you think of our new associate?" Lara asked her superior.

Lee sniffed, swept some lint off one pant leg. He could guess where this was headed. Lara rarely asked a question to obtain information that might actually inform her opinion on the topic. Usually, her perspective about the situation was already set, and her inquiry was merely a means of starting a conversation so she could convey it. The "it" usually being something negative.

"Oh, I'm rather pleased, really," the architect replied, deciding he was in the mood for a little fracas. "Liam's agility with technology is really impressive, and he's already been an awesome help to the investigation more than once. And, he seems to be getting along with everyone else on the team, so . . ."

Lee swept a curl of lint from his other pant leg, waited, smiled to himself.

Lara sniffed, discreetly cleared her throat. "I wonder . . ." she began. "I wonder if he might be getting along a little *too* well . . . with Irene."

That made the architect pull up.

"What . . . what do you mean?"

His second-in-command smoothed her skirt toward her knees, her lips flattening into a narrow horizontal line.

"Bree says she has overheard . . . some conversations . . . and . . . he seems . . . inordinately concerned with girls who are Irene's age. He follows her around a great deal, whispering into her ear." She paused, turned to look out the window of the town car. "It just all seems . . . rather inappropriate."

Lee considered the data Lara was providing him, retraced his encounters with the two, searched for any corroborating evidence. Finally, he shook his head.

"They're working together, Lara," he said. "They're like a team within the team. I would almost expect them . . . *want them* . . . to develop a bond of some sort. The way you and . . ." He pulled up. Lara turned and looked at him. Quickly, he glanced away. "Anyway, *I'm* not seeing it. I'm certainly not seeing anything . . . unseemly. You don't *seriously* believe that . . ."

"Are you implying, Dalton, I am not being serious?" The snap in Lara's tone sent a quiver through the architect. He thrust himself fully against the back of the seat, bracing himself for whatever was to come. "Perhaps the issue is not whether I am being serious, but whether *you* are taking things seriously enough!"

One didn't need a knife to cut the tension as the limousine crept through the late-afternoon traffic . . . a slightly ragged fingernail would suffice. The pair in the back seat stared out their respective windows for some time. Neither uttered a simple syllable or shifted a single centimeter.

The car banked a corner and glided down a less congested side street. They passed a street vendor selling oranges and grapefruit, a boutique hotel under construction, a pocket park highlighted by a fountain that cascaded water vertically down a pink marble slab.

Gradually, and for the first time since they had entered the limousine, Lee turned and looked straight at his associate.

"My parents are dying, Lara," he said. "Both of them. My father will probably pass away first, but they tell me they can't even be certain of that." He paused briefly, but with the gate now flung open, he decided to barrel through it. "They asked me to give them the power to remove life support, or withhold it, or whatever it is one does at a time like this. I didn't really read the wording that closely. I couldn't. I just can't . . ."

He stopped, bit into his upper lip. Forced himself to push forward.

"I wonder if I did the right thing, Lara. My entire life, I've been proud of my ability to always know the right thing to do, and yet, when it's your own parents, and they have given you so much, and sacrificed even more, and then suddenly you're being asked to take something *away* from them, force the *worst possible* sacrifice on them, without even knowing if that's what they want, if it is something they are ready for . . ."

He was looking out the window again, breathing heavily now. His right leg bounced vigorously up and down.

"I don't know. How does one choose the compassionate approach when the only options presented to you are prolonging someone's pain and ensuring someone's death? Oh God, I have no idea if I made the right choice or not. And how do you live with yourself if, after all is said and done, you decide you made the *wrong* choice? What would *you* have done, Lara, if it had been *your* parents?"

His assistant stared straight ahead, slightly slack-jawed, trying to catch up with all that had just transpired, with having been whipsawed from a sense of self-righteousness to her current worry for Lee's well-being. It took her several moments to comprehend his questions, much less come up with an articulate answer to them.

"First of all, I am terribly sorry, Dalton, I am so very, very sorry. I am sorry for your parents and what they are going through, and I am sorry for this awful predicament you find yourself in. I wouldn't wish it on anyone. And to be honest, I hope I'm never confronted with it—although, being an only child like you are, I most likely will. It's dreadful, there's just no two ways around it.

"If it were my mother, the decision would be particularly difficult. She taught me not just how to live life but also to value life above all else. So, I would be inclined, I think, to prolong her life as much as possible and not set myself up as the agent for her passing. But then, to see someone that sweet and that nurturing experiencing any form of discomfort might very likely make the decision to end things— if not actually *simple*—at least a little simpler, I believe."

195

She paused, then breathed in deeply. "However, if it were my father, well, that would be the simplest decision of all. For I see *no benefit, whatsoever*, in prolonging the existence of an egocentric backstabber. I have not the slightest doubt in my mind that were the situation reversed, he would step forward and unplug the power cords to all the life-sustaining equipment in *my* hospital room, especially if someone were paying him handsomely to do so. Therefore . . ."

It became quiet again, except for the clang they experienced when the car traversed a large metal plate in the middle of the street. Once the limo had cleared the plate, the driver slowed the vehicle and began to edge it toward the curb.

Lara peered at Dalton, reached over and placed one hand firmly on his forearm. She suddenly became composed and focused.

"But here is what I think matters most, Dalton," she intoned. "Have your parents *ever* given you any indication that they distrusted your decision-making abilities? Have they ever *once* caused you to feel as though you were being foolhardy, rash, or unwise in how you were directing your own life?"

The architect considered the question intently for a moment.

"No," he finally said. "They haven't. Not once. If anything, they've done nothing but endorse every decision I have made."

They looked at each other and exchanged silent smiles across the back seat as their limo rolled to a stop.

Lee exhaled heavily. "And *that*, my dear Lara, is why I cherish your counsel and companionship so." The architect sat up and straightened his tie in preparation for exiting the car.

Beside him, Lara was gazing through her window at a dapper, older couple savoring a late-afternoon meal at a sidewalk cafe, a champagne bucket situated between them.

***

Ashley Taymore wore an impassive expression, her hands placed across each other. She nodded slightly at her attorney, who looked like someone who might have attended Swarthmore a decade or so before her client.

"The reason Ms. Taymore did not come forward earlier is that she feared for her safety and for her privacy," the lawyer said. "She thought if she waited a couple of weeks, the media frenzy might not be so . . . intense." She quickly glanced over at the young assistant to Vic Valenzuela and returned the nod. "She realizes now that was probably a mistake."

With his tongue, Mackeson Sainclair edged a toothpick from one side of his mouth to the other. He had his chair balanced on its back legs, an uncharacteristically casual stance for the agent to take during an interrogation, Lee thought.

The architect turned to Lara, who was watching the proceedings with him in a room behind a one-way mirror. "Why confess now to a murder she didn't commit?" he wondered aloud.

Lara continued to stare into the room in front of them. "What makes you so sure she didn't commit it?" was all she said in reply.

Agent Weiss, who sat beside her colleague in the interrogation room, decided to thrust herself into the questioning.

"So, Ms. Taymore, exactly *why* did you murder Vic Valenzuela?" She hurled the question at the young blonde as if to say, "Hurry up, I have a massage booked in thirty minutes."

Ashley Taymore shot a glance at her lawyer, then sat forward in her chair. "I killed him because he raped my fiancée."

Everyone sat still, absorbing the unexpected comment.

"When did this happen?" Agent Weiss countered.

The assistant to Vic Valenzuela thought for a moment. "About a year ago. He had invited the two of us to have dinner with him one evening on his yacht. I thought he just wanted to reward me for my service—I had been working for him almost exactly a year. But it didn't take very long for us to realize he had something else in mind. He made it clear pretty quickly that he wanted to have a three-way. Or watch two lesbians with each other. Something along those lines, anyway."

She sighed heavily. "Anyway, we politely declined. He seemed fine with that at the time, although I did notice he got that little thing he gets when he is angry and trying to suppress it. I noticed it, but I didn't really think much about it."

"What little thing?" Agent Sainclair prodded.

She pointed toward her temple. "His vein. It gets more prominent. And purple. Not dark purple like a bruise. Just . . . more prominent. I noticed it, but he smiled and said, 'No problem.' Poured us all some more champagne. The moment passed.

"I'd already had three or four glasses of champagne and suddenly I was feeling it, so I went into the cabin to lie down. That's when he attacked Suzanne. He raped her on deck."

"Did you witness this attack?" It was Agent Weiss again.

"No, I . . . she told me about it afterward. I slept through it."

The two agents looked at each other, then Agent Weiss began to flip lackadaisically through the pages of a legal pad in front of her.

Ashley Taymore leaned forward. Glared at the two detectives. "I have no reason, whatsoever, to doubt my fiancée," she added defiantly.

"Why isn't she here with you now?" Agent Sinclair asked.

Once again, the client looked to her attorney.

"Ms. Pelletier is still in Paris. She intends to return as soon as possible, perhaps as early as this weekend," the lawyer replied.

The federal agents exchanged quicker glances before Agent Sinclair resumed the questioning.

"*Bon.* So, Ms. Taymore, why don't you explain to us what took place on the night of the murder?"

The door to the room opened. A tall, muscular male in a striped dress shirt, striped tie and gray slacks strode in and dropped a piece of paper in front of Agent Sinclair. The agent removed his toothpick, read the first several lines on the piece of paper, nodded to the agent and set the paper on the tabletop between him and Agent Weiss. As the tall assistant walked toward the door, Agent Weiss scanned the document for a moment then returned her gaze to the duo seated in front of her.

"I apologize," said Agent Sinclair. "The night of the murder?"

"There's not much to say. About four thirty I told Vic I was going home for the day. I did leave, but I went and had dinner in the Grove instead. Then maybe around eleven thirty or so I went back to the house and let myself in with my key. I guessed that since he had come in from the airport so late, and was so agitated, he probably hadn't set the motion detector. I was right. I went up to his bedroom and his door was unlocked, as I assumed it would be. I snuck in quietly and . . ."

She set her lips firm and raised both eyebrows. "I killed him."

Agent Sainclair reinserted the toothpick to where it had been when he began the interrogation. "So . . . you say you entered his bedroom from the upstairs hallway, is that correct?"

Ashley Taymore nodded. "Yes. That hallway is carpeted, so I knew he probably wouldn't hear me."

"Earlier, as you were approaching the house, did you come across the grass or through one of the gardens?"

The suspect lowered the left side of her head slightly as if the question seemed odd to her. "No, I stayed on the sidewalk," she answered. "And the steps."

"I see," Agent Sainclair said, readjusting the position of the toothpick. "And how many times did you stab Mr. Valenzuela?"

She looked up to the ceiling. "Twice, I think." She halted. "Maybe it was just once. But no more than twice. I'm certain of that."

At that, Agent Weiss flung herself against the back of the chair and tossed her pen onto the legal pad in front of her. Neither the suspect, nor her attorney, reacted.

"And, so where is the murder weapon, Ms. Taymore?" Agent Sainclair added impatiently. "What did you do with the knife?"

She seemed taken aback by his sudden brusqueness and confused by the question. She blinked quickly a couple of times, looked down at the tabletop.

"I . . . um . . . it's . . . um . . . it's in the bay. Before I went home, I drove over to Virginia Key. On the way back, I threw it into the water while I was driving across the causeway."

Agent Sainclair dropped his chin into his chest. "No, no you didn't, Ms. Taymore." He leaned forward and picked up the paper that had been brought in to them a few minutes earlier. "According to this, a few hours ago our agents found a knife matching perfectly the type used to murder Mr. Valenzuela in a gully several blocks from the home. Mr. Valenzuela's blood type was AB and that was the type of the blood found on the knife."

He glared first at the suspect, then at her attorney. "Would the two of you care to tell us what's going on here?"

In the anteroom, Lara shifted in her chair. "Okay, so you were right after all," she said perkily. "She had the time frame wrong, the number of stab wounds wrong . . ." She chuckled. "Did she get *anything* correct?"

Lee had an index finger pressed vertically against his lips and was thinking. "I do believe she got the name of the victim right," he deadpanned.

The architect's left foot began to tap very slowly like a metronome running out of momentum. Lara looked at her associate. "What motivates someone like her to give a false confession, Dalton?"

The architect slunk a bit deeper into his chair. "It happens more than you'd expect," he replied, "although I've never really understood why. I've read that some people do it because they have an irrational desire for attention, but Ms. Taymore doesn't really strike me as someone who falls into that category."

His foot tapping began to accelerate in intensity.

"But another frequent motivation, apparently, is the confessor's desire to protect someone else. Someone they either *know* was responsible for the crime, or someone they believe most likely committed it."

His foot came to a sudden halt.

"So, the question we now have before us," he announced, "is who does Ashley Taymore feel some need to protect?"

29

Pressed to explain herself, Ashley Taymore eventually conceded to the authorities she had fabricated her confession. But she refused to tell them why.

Confronted with the specific details of the murder, and how her version of the incident was completely disconnected from theirs, she became stoic and sullen. When they asked her if she had created her story to escape some dangerous situation, she almost imperceptibly shook her head no. Asked if she were protecting someone else, she merely stared off into space before requesting a glass of water.

"Well, she wasn't coerced into confessing, that's for certain," Lee said to Lara on their way back to their hotel that evening. "And given that she recanted at the end, she's not one of those persons who actually believes she did it."

"Which means," Lara replied, "that she probably thought someone she cares about was responsible for the murder, as you said earlier. Her fiancée?"

Lee was lightly drumming the padded cushion that encased the door handle on his side of the back seat. "Maybe," he answered . . . but not very convincingly.

**

The storms had evaporated, leaving the air thick and sweltry. Nonetheless, Lee decided he needed to walk. Ashley Taymore's behavior had him befuddled. And there was something about Vic Valenzuela's estate, and the work being performed there, that nagged at him.

He exited a side entrance of the hotel once he presumed Lara and the rest of the team had retired for the evening. He guessed it to be ten thirty, maybe ten forty-five. The moon had made an appearance, but looked like some aging movie star being filmed through several layers of gauze.

The architect chose to push away from the heart of downtown and trudge down some side streets others might find sketchy. It was his way, always had been, to connect with the reality of a city away from the sections fabricated for tourists. He never felt fearful, even at those times when he saw his path intersecting with that of someone who seemed more intrigued with him than they should be, or when he heard someone only a few steps behind him. He knew that malice smelled fear, tracked it down the way a lion stalks a gazelle.

He refused to reward a predator with such a scent.

He was also insistent he *not* dwell on his parents. What was done was done. The papers were signed, the instructions in place. Lara's comments had comforted him even more than he had expected them to. *I may not have made the best decision for my parents*, he thought, *but at least I made it with the best of intentions. And there was always that possibility the documents would never be needed . . .*

He spotted a hardware store across the street. The front window was awash with decals advertising this brand of power tools, that brand of electrical supplies. His thoughts turned to the Valenzuela home—a visual of it materialized in his mind. It looked odd to him, with the left end of the house all cluttered by scaffolding and panel vans and tarps, and the right end—the wing in which the murder had taken place— almost pristine. He knew that wouldn't have prevented one of the workers from creeping in during the night and slaughtering the coach . . . but it did mean their familiarity with—and their access to—that section of the house was far less than it would have been otherwise.

Still, the lopsidedness of it all set him on edge, for some reason.

"So, what does that, like, *mean*, Dalton? That one end of the house *has* been restored but the other half, like, *hasn't been?*"

It was a female voice. The architect swiveled around, but there was no one behind him. He checked left and right . . . not a soul.

"No, silly down *here*," the voice admonished.

Lee lowered his gaze to the sidewalk, where a charcoal drawing of a woman's face stared up at him. The face had a round head and a flat nose but no mouth or chin. Next to the visage was a crude illustration of what appeared to be a dancer, one arm outstretched, a question mark emblazoned on her torso.

"What does that lopsidedness *mean*, baby?" the illustration implored. "It's important for you to consider, you know, the *significance* of all that."

"It is?" He looked up from the sidewalk and transposed his memory of the Valenzuela mansion onto the block of office buildings directly opposite him. And the more he reenvisioned the home's facade and decorative touches, the more he considered the relationship between the construction work and the murder scene, and the more he began to ponder a particular theory, an idea that may have been percolating in a subterranean way all this time, but was only now turning into a conscious thought.

"You're right, that fact may be a lot more important than I realized," Lee said, turning his attention back to the chalk outline beneath him.

But the figure only glared back at him in silence, her expression now more menacing than helpful.

He plodded on down the sidewalk, passing first a post office that was closed for the night and then a storefront that was vacant save for several legless mannequins positioned so they could stare at those passing by. An older man on a bicycle rounded the corner ahead. He weaved widely from one side of the street to the other as he approached the architect, who decided the front fender must be bent given the *thwack, thwack, thwack* he heard every time the tire made a rotation. *I wonder if cycling under the influence is also a citable offense*, Lee thought to himself.

As the architect neared the corner from which the cyclist had appeared, he noticed someone in a dark cloak sauntering aimlessly in circles, smoke wafting lazily from an upturned cigarette. His first instinct was to cross the street, but something about the person's stance, and anticipation of him, beckoned him forward.

The person did not stop circling as he neared but the speed of the circles slowed considerably. Finally, when Lee was about fifty feet away, the individual pivoted toward him. She had long, ironed-straight blond hair parted in the center. The cloak opened slightly to reveal the top half of a black leather bustier supporting enormous, spherical breasts. She exhaled, and a long rocket-shaped plume of cigarette smoke emerged from between her lips. She had stopped circling but continued to prop the cigarette up the way a waitress holds a tray of entrees.

"Well, 'allo luv," she cooed. "Wot brings a comely gent likes you out late on a night like this, as if I don't know?" She didn't smile as she inspected him bottom to top (*most likely gauging whether I am vice or not*, Lee assumed). But the architect flashed an embarrassed smile in return, began to veer into the street but then felt a magnetic tug that kept him from stepping off the curb.

"Come over here, luv . . . I don't bite, you know." Her voice sounded huskier—and more adamant—than it had a moment earlier. Lee had one leg swung out over the curb but he finessed it back in and firmly planted his foot slightly ahead of the other. He let his gaze float over to, and on to, her breasts. Which looked so soft. So alluring. So *immense*.

He sidled slowly forward, one step at a time, until he stood perhaps three feet in front of her. The cigarette had mysteriously vanished; she reached both palms out, cradled the back of his neck and drew his face decisively toward her chest.

He nuzzled for what seemed an eternity, intoxicated by the aromatic mix of mandarin, orchid, and sandalwood. At some point, he raised his right palm and gently placed it on her left breast but she immediately clamped it there with the palm of her left hand. He continued to nuzzle, tracing long serpentine paths across the tops of both breasts with just the tip of his nose. She did not flinch once. But Lee felt a tremor that trickled along the base of his hairline then inched its way down the length of his spine. His right knee crumpled some as she deftly moved toward his left ear and flicked her tongue along the inside rim of its upper edge.

This is insane, he thought as he began to lightly pant. *This is . . . inevitable.*

She pulled back slightly to inspect him again. Maneuvered her lips, decorated in deep purple, into a sarcastic grin.

"I'm willing to bet luvvy here has a pair of red leather wrist cuffs sitting all sad and lonely-like in his hotel room somewhere, hmm?"

Lee took a deep breath in, allowed his jaw to slacken a couple of inches, assumed the look of a lad caught with his hand in the biscuit tin.

"How on earth did you know?" he whispered.

***

He darted back into the hotel several minutes before her. She arrived at his room five minutes later, her cloak buttoned up to the base of her neck in an uncharacteristic nod to modesty. Any misconception a passerby might have had that she was bringing him the traditional definition of room service would have quickly disintegrated, however, had they seen the way she sauntered in the room, like a dominatrix striding onto a sex club's catwalk.

Which, in a way, was exactly who she was that night.

"Well, would you have a butchers at *this* swanky suite?" she proclaimed in a hushed voice. She glided through the space, allowing her fingertips to graze first the top of the armchair in the living room and then the credenza just beyond it. "You one of them politico types, luv?" she asked, as she sized up the furniture and the accessories. "Me mug's not going to end up on the front page of one of them scandal sheets, is it, cause nuthin' would set me mum to bawlin' more than that."

Her tone sounded earnest. Her leer said otherwise.

Lee had hardly moved since the strumpet had claimed his suite as her domain. Hell, he had hardly *breathed* since she had entered. She continued to inspect the room the way an appraiser scrutinizes antiques. Now and then, she pressed one hand against the side of her head, smoothing the tresses that trailed to her lower back. Finally she stopped and pivoted back to her new friend.

"Well, I don't see any narkys in the shadows anywhere so I guess you're legit. Shall we get down to business, luv?"

Obediently, Lee shuffled into the bedroom, rummaging in a drawer for several seconds. When he returned, he clutched in his left hand a crumpled wad of bills, which he deposited on the top of the credenza. "That's for your . . . cab ride home," he said in a hoarse whisper.

She sidled over, quickly flipped through the bills, her purple fingernails captivating him in the process. "Right," she finally replied. "Them taxi rides been getting so *dear*, recently, they have."

The amount confirmed, she whirled around and strode confidently over to him, assumed a stance similar to the one they had taken on the street. Lee trembled some, but when he ducked his head to once again nuzzle against her, she stopped his advance by putting two forearms up between them. Then she thrust both arms forward, sending the architect toppling against the front edge of, and then back onto, the cushions of the voluptuous couch behind him. His breathing was labored, but he wasn't sure himself if it was from the unexpected topple, or the promise of sex. She undid her bustier, releasing her bosoms into the amber lamp glow above him and then she slunk toward him and upon him. Gripping both of his forearms, she pinned them back on either side of his head and mounted him, maneuvering her body in such a way that it appeared her breasts were pulsing toward and then away from him in a taunting, tantalizing sway. Briefly, she kissed his lips—actually just brushed against them, leaving a tart, almost stinging sensation that only intensified the electric charge that blazed throughout him.

She gradually moved her head over to his left, slowly extended her tongue the way lipstick departs the tube, and made a hot circular trail just below his wrist. He breathed in sharply, struggled slightly, collapsed back onto the cushions.

"You ain't going nowhere, luvvy," she commanded.

She left his forearm yearning for more, traced down his sleeve to his elbow, then along his triceps and over to his chest, which she now nuzzled as he had hers. She had lightened her grip, but he had no intention whatsoever of attempting an escape.

Moments later, they were in virtually the same position, only now on the bed. And the red cuffs he had purchased in Manhattan a year ago were securely affixed to the headboard.

"All right, the clock's going tick tock, you know," she said to him. "Let's strip those striders off of you now, shall we?"

"Those . . . what?" Lee said.

"Your striders, luv, your trouseys. I can't really rock your world if it's hidden underneath all this fabric, now can I?"

For the first time since the encounter began, Lee ventured a smile. He never associated humor with sex, had always felt the former disempowered the latter. But there was something . . . theatrical . . . about her that he found appealing. As she leaned forward to unbuckle his belt, he reached up boldly to run his fingers through her long blond tresses . . . which came off in his hand and tumbled to the comforter, revealing a reddish-brown shock that spiked in several directions and looked to have been recently hennaed.

"Oh shit, I *knew* that was going to happen!" his companion shrieked, suddenly sounding more like someone raised on the west side of L.A. than in the East End of London. "Goddamn cheap-ass wig!" she huffed as she snatched up the lifeless mane and hurled it from the bed onto the floor. She sighed heavily, took a couple of seconds to compose herself, breathed several shallow breaths. Then, turning back to Lee, she transformed back into the sultry vixen, only one that now was wearing a completely different costume and reading from a completely different script.

"Sorry about that. This role play thing doesn't always go down the way you expect to," she whispered in as seductive voice as she could muster given the circumstances.

She bowed toward his face again, knowing full well her full breasts would restore him to a state of ardor. She was right. "So, you don't mind I drop the Brit girl accent, do you?" she asked, pinning his arms back against the bed more tautly than before. He nodded his assent as she undulated her body against his, quickening the friction until she felt him stirring below. Then she lowered herself back onto her legs and made another move for his belt. Finally unclasped, it raced through the loops as if it were delighted to be set free from its restraints.

"God, nothing turns me on more than seeing a distinguished man like you writhing in submission," she said, increasing the pace of her seduction. He began to drink in her body, gliding his glance down from her breasts to her taut abdomen to her left thigh and the long, skinny birthmark inside it.

Only . . . it wasn't a birthmark after all, he realized, but a tattoo . . . of a hideous, horn-crested lizard.

Beneath her voluptuous curves, she felt her customer transform into a long, rigid sheet of plywood. She looked at his face, into his now-heavily-dilated pupils.

"What is it?" she asked, her eyes wide with concern. "Something wrong?"

30

Her name wasn't really Krystal Kandy Labra, as she had told the members of the Miami A&M football team on the night of their party. Nor was it Anna Cleavage, the name she provided to the officers who came to arrest her in Lee's hotel suite.

Her real name was Lyndsey Frantzen, and she had arrived in Miami eight months earlier by way of a brief stint in New Orleans, which had been preceded by a two-year stay in Southern California (where, for a time, she had actually had a job portraying a fairy princess at one of the area theme parks). That had been preceded by a relatively normal upbringing in one of Milwaukee's middle-class suburbs. This was her third arrest for prostitution (including one just outside the Southern California theme park not ten minutes after her shift had ended) but the federal agents who were questioning her didn't care about any of that.

"We'd like to know why you left the cabana on the Valenzuela estate, the time you left there, and where you went." Agent Sainclair looked like he was attempting to recuperate from a really bad night at a bar . . . or racetrack.

"Um, I don't know, I mean I *do* know I left there before midnight, but other than that, I guess I left there around ten, maybe ten thirty." Lee had told the federal authorities he had spotted the hooker on the street corner and suspected she might be the one they had been looking for, but became convinced when he overheard her telling another streetwalker that she had partied with the team the night of the murder. So he pretended to be an interested john to lure her to his room so they could then arrest her. She scoffed at the story, but given Lee's tenure with them, and there being no evidence to the contrary, they chose to believe him over her.

Thank heavens I was able to hide the leather cuffs before they got there, Lee thought to himself.

"And *why* did you leave the cabana, Ms. Frantzen? Mr. Culberson says you told him before he drove the other players home that you wanted to continue your . . . activities with him one on one. But that when he returned, you were gone."

"Of course he told you that," she replied. "They always say that or something like that. No, here's what really went down. He said he wanted to do something really kinky, and that he'd pay me, like, an *exorbitant* amount of money if I did it. Eight hundred dollars. Just to bleat like a sheep, or a goat, or something like that, while he was doing me from behind."

On the other side of the one-way mirror, Roberto and Liam burst out laughing. Lee exchanged an embarrassed look with Lara.

"Anyway, I hung around for a while, maybe ten minutes or so. But then I started getting nervous. I mean, for all I knew he was going to bring a cop back with him. Or not come back at all. Or even worse, come back with his coach. I mean the coach was really hot for a guy his age and all but, shit, he totally wore me out the first time around."

Sainclair stopped taking notes for a minute and began to massage his forehead with the thumb and middle finger of his right hand. Once again, Agent Weiss was off conducting research with that associate of Lee, and he was growing increasingly impatient with having to shoulder so much of this aspect of the investigation on his own.

He was also trying to recall which of his retirement plans allowed him to borrow the most money.

"So exactly what did you do, where did you go, after you left?" he eventually asked, his voice taking on a bored timbre.

She looked off to one side. "Well, I drove back to my condo. But before I did that, I just drove around for a while."

"You drove around where?"

"Nowhere in particular. Around. I was hungry but nothing sounded good." In the anteroom, Lee dropped his head to his chest. Yet another suspect who couldn't pinpoint their whereabouts around the time the murder took place.

"Can you think of anyone who would have seen you while you were driving around, Ms. Frantzen? Anyone who would remember seeing you?"

She gave the question some consideration but slowly shook her head. Then, as if she had suddenly gotten a message that said she had just won the Florida Lottery, her expression brightened.

"Yeah, wait, I think so. Maybe. My car was really filthy, so at some point, I pulled into one of those do-it-yourself car washes to dump all the crap in my front seat into one of the trash bins. While I was doing that, some police car pulled into the lot and cruised by real slow-like. I guessed he thought I was working the car wash, because I was still dressed pretty . . . well . . . you know." She flung both arms out as if to say, *Just like this.* "But once he saw I was only throwing trash away and I got back into my car, he drove off."

"Did you happen to get a look at this police officer, or maybe his license plate?" She shook her head, then sneezed.

"Excuse me," she said delicately. Then, "Um, no. He was dark-haired, I remember that. A white guy. But that's all I remember. Sorry."

"Can you estimate about what time that was?"

She looked up at the ceiling, then quickly looked back at him.

"I'm not sure but I'd guess about eleven, or eleven thirty."

Sainclair was scribbling quickly now and glancing at his watch. After a couple of minutes went by without him saying anything to her, she leaned forward.

"Are you going to book me? 'Cause if you are, I need to call a friend of mine to see if she'll feed my goldfish."

Sainclair continued to write, did not look at her.

"We're not going to book you," he said brusquely. "But we need you to remain here for another ten or fifteen minutes so we can ask you a few more questions about that evening. Then we'll let you go."

"Okay," she replied softly, adjusting the top of her bustier so she would be better covered. "Whatever I can do to help." After randomly looking around the room for a few minutes, she leaned toward Agent Sainclair again.

"Oh, and one more thing. Do you know the name of that short little guy who brought me to his hotel room? And how I might go about finding him? I mean, I know he was responsible for my getting arrested and all, but to be honest, I thought he was pretty cute."

***

They strolled beside one another along the north side of Calle Ocho, hoping to simultaneously enjoy the sights and solve a murder.

"I don't know why they still call this 'Little Havana,'" Agent Weiss said to Warren, her hands planted deeply into the pockets of her jeans. "It could just as easily be 'Little Managua' or 'Little Salvador,' you know."

"What . . . all the Cubans have left?"

She gazed across the thoroughfare to their left, shook her head. "No, not all of them. But there's maybe only half as many living here now as there were thirty years ago."

"Really?" Warren replied, somewhat distracted. He inhaled deeply. "You sure couldn't tell it from the aroma in the air. Smells like a Cuban tobacco factory to me."

Agent Weiss scratched the back of her neck and looked up at the morning sky, which was blanketed by a thin layer of white-gray clouds. "Well, sir, don't fall for that little stereotype either," she said. "These days, the tobacco sold down here is probably from either Nicaragua or the Dominican Republic."

They looked at each other and laughed lightly at the irony of it all. Warren pulled his arms around his torso and studied the sidewalk as they continued to saunter down the street. It being midmorning, the boulevard was relatively tranquil, save for the steady stream of trucks and automobiles, and for the men in neon-colored vests who squeezed in and between the vehicles, hawking an assortment of fruit drinks and waters. He sighed and peered at the windows across the street filled with placards advertising quinceañera cruises and Affordable Care Act insurance policies. Here and there, eruptions of hibiscus or bougainvillea interrupted the collage of terra cotta roofs atop buildings painted moss green or canary yellow.

"So, what do you think . . . what do we know? Seems like we have a lot of people who had either the opportunity to murder the coach, the enthusiasm to murder him, or both. Anyone jump out at you as the top candidate for 'Most Likely To'?"

She surveyed the streetscape before answering. Shook her head again. "To be honest, I'm really more concerned about what The Organization is up to, what little scheme they have planned."

She remained quiet in contemplation for a few moments before eventually resuming the thread. "They're so damned . . . bitter, you know? So ridiculously convinced that every institution out there is deceitful and hell-bent on keeping them in manacles forevermore. So adamant that the only thing the police, civic leaders, and businesses do with their time is sit around and come up with new ways to suppress the average Joe and take away his free will. I mean, they're completely delusional, yet so convinced they're not. So, when they strike, it's always something . . . overdramatic. And horrific."

She shivered once, pulled her shoulders in tight. "Something's coming. I don't know what it is, but I do know that by the time we figure that out, it might very well be too late to stop it and too awful to watch."

They strode on. From some distant window, the three-quarters and six-eighths rhythms of a guajira song served as a background score for their walk. They passed a popular American burger chain and arrived at Fourteenth Avenue and the caricature mural depicting such great Cuban entertainers as Celia Cruz and Tito Puente. Embedded in the sidewalk beneath them, massive stars like those found in Hollywood paid tribute to celebrities, including boxer Roberto Duran, singer Julio Iglesias, soap opera star Thalia, and composer Ernesto Lecuona.

"I had no idea Cuba produced so many prominent entertainers," Warren said.

"They're not all Cuban," Agent Weiss replied. "Just Latinos and Latinas with some connection to South Florida. Roberto Duran was Panamanian. And Julio Iglesias was Spanish. It's been this huge controversy—who deserves a star, who doesn't. I mean, it's actually gotten violent at times."

Just then, they were approached by a young girl pulling a wagon full of flowers. She was six, maybe seven, and she had a large pink orchid tucked behind her right ear. She beamed up at the adults, and Warren instantly recognized her expression as a ploy designed to manipulate him into buying a boutonniere for Agent Weiss. Several steps behind the girl, an older woman (the young girl's grandmother, Warren guessed) smiled and bobbed her head frequently like a nervous stage mother watching her child's first recital performance.

Agent Weiss gently shook her head and began to wave off the child, but Warren kneeled to the young girl's level and proceeded to inspect the merchandise in her wagon with tremendous care. "*¿Qué flor crees tu que es la más bonita?*" he asked her. The child wheeled around, put one finger to her chin and considered the many options she was offering.

"That one," the girl answered in English, pointing to a large red carnation close to her. "*Es muy bonita.*"

Warren chuckled, nodded, and handed the budding salesperson a five dollar bill, indicating with the wave of a hand she need not give him any change. The girl's chaperone nodded exuberantly and smiled profusely as the pair trudged on down the boulevard.

Warren turned and handed the flower to the agent. "There you are m'lady," he said in an affected British accent. Agent Weiss rolled her eyes and stuck the stem of the carnation into the front pocket of her blouse. She glanced over at him briefly then quickly veered her look down to the sidewalk, away from his smile.

"You are . . . missing your children, I'm guessing," she said quickly. His smile waned and he nodded.

"I really hate being away from them at this stage of their life," he acknowledged. "Every day, they make some fascinating new discovery, or they let some hysterical personality trait come through for the first time. Last week, the au pair told me my little one asked her if her Dah-dee was an espionage agent. She's five, and she actually used the phrase 'espionage agent'!"

He sighed slowly, looked at her, nodded. "It's tough." She nodded back.

"And what about you?" he said to her. "Ever thought about having kids?"

Her look floated away from him once again. "Sure. I *did*. All the time, but . . ." She waited a couple of beats then turned back to him. "Since I *can't* have them and—given this job—I'm probably at the very bottom of the list of great adoptive parent candidates, it's not really an issue."

She halted again, looked out into the street. "Of course, it became an issue for my ex. The deal breaker, actually." She scuffed the sidewalk with the toe of her sandal. "But, yeah, there's really nothing I want to do more than teach a little girl how to correctly enter a room with a pistol drawn or perform a palm strike on someone's solar plexus."

Warren burst out laughing and shook his head. They silently smiled at one another for several seconds, then Agent Weiss chuckled heartily once again.

"Come on, Agent Jackson," she said, pointing across the street. "Let's go play dominoes."

They waited for the traffic on Eighth Street to clear before darting across to the cluster of small pavilions in Maximo Gomez Park. She took his left hand and pulled him toward one of the tents, where the players were shielded on all four sides from the noise of the traffic and the glare of the sunlight by large, forest-green tarps. Agent Weiss pulled back one end of the tarp, and Warren was stunned to see at least twenty older men (but only one woman) rapidly shuffling dominoes onto the white tops of tables flanked by either two or four armless chairs bolted into the pavement. Most of the *abuelos* (as Agent Weiss referred to them) wore white or blue short-sleeve shirts, gray or blue shorts, and white sneakers with white socks. Here or there, a straw fedora or felt newsboy cap topped the silver mane of one of the players. Hardly anyone spoke, but the pavilion resounded with the clack of tiles being slapped onto the table by a player determined to defeat his long-time rival.

"Watch, these dudes are *serious*," she whispered into Warren's ear, nudging his left side in the process. He nodded and pressed one palm against her upper back to help her step in front of him to see the action more clearly.

An intense game involving four middle-aged men was playing out in front of them. A long serpentine trail of dominoes forming the letter P had already developed on the tabletop; one player in a cream-colored shirt with teal and coral stripes down the front held a single tile high above his head.

"It's my lucky day!" he suddenly proclaimed. His hand then plummeted and then deftly slid his last remaining domino against one of the others on the table. Instantly, his opponents all reacted with growls of disdain; two jumped up and turned away from the table, shaking their heads in disbelief.

"Wow, I don't know . . . this could be the perfect place for The Organization to recruit a few new members," Warren whispered to Hannah. She smiled, turned, and swatted him lightly on one shoulder.

"Oh my god, you're right!" she said chuckling. "I mean, the whole park is dedicated to a revolutionary, so it's the perfect breeding ground, right? And these guys get *lethal* when they're playing! So there you have it . . . Death by Dominoes."

They crumpled together in laughter, causing them both to fall back against one of the poles holding up one side of the tarp. Everyone at the tables near them turned and glowered at the duo, who scrambled to put the pole back upright. Once the support was back in place, Warren turned to Hannah, put a finger to his lips as if to say "shush," and guided her out through the side of the tarp. Back in the sunlight, they both exploded into laughter again and, doubled over, staggered their way back to Calle Ocho.

"They will never let us back in there again, *ever*," Agent Weiss said, waving one hand up and down in front of her face as she tried to regain her composure.

"No, they won't," Warren replied, still smiling broadly. "Even if you dye your hair dark, put on black lace stockings, walk in with a canvas sack filled with one hundred dollar bills, and ask them in your ditsiest voice if playing dominoes is as easy as playing Go Fish, they will not let you back in there. No way in hell."

Noon was approaching. And the heat and humidity were inching up. Warren and Hannah sauntered past the 1920s-era Tower Theater and gave some thought to ducking in to watch one of the Spanish-language films being screened that day but then decided against that. They dodged a wave of tourists who descended from a cherry-red, double-decker bus decorated with the American flag. And they navigated their way in and around the colorful ornamental roosters that adorned many of the intersections along the boulevard, remnants of a civic art project from years past.

"Why roosters?" Warren inquired.

Agent Weiss shrugged. "Someone told me it was because most Cuban men behave like banty roosters." She rolled her eyes. "*Of course,* they would choose an artistic icon that only applied to *men.*"

Window shopping became their main activity. They wandered in and out of a couple of art galleries and a cigar shop, where Warren gave serious consideration to an elegant humidor that caught his eye. "You know, Dalton has a box like this, only it's a lot smaller," he told Hannah. "I don't know why, but he brings it with him whenever he travels. I've always admired it." But the price of the container made him arch his eyebrows, so he set it delicately back on the shelf.

For several minutes, they watched an action movie being filmed on one of the side streets off Calle Ocho. Then they decided to settle in at one of the grander restaurants along the thoroughfare. Even though it was a haven for Cuban cuisine, the building mimicked a mammoth French palace in design and decor, with rectangular mirrors around the main dining room that reflected the lights cast by the ornate chandeliers suspended from above. They ducked into a table in one far corner. Each ordered a *cortadito* with evaporated milk and a *pastelito* filled with guava and cheese.

"You know, I need to get the recipe for these *pastelitos,*" Agent Weiss remarked. "In Cuba, it's almost impossible to find them with guava anymore. Too expensive. They only come with cheese."

When the server retreated, Warren looked intently at Agent Weiss. "So, really, where do you think this is going?" he said quickly.

She took a breath in, broke into a brief smile, then turned serious. "Well, I have hope the lab analysis of the clod of dirt found in Valenzuela's bedroom will give us a lot of valuable information. We should be able to detect some key trace minerals from it, and maybe some other nutrients. Even if it doesn't lead us directly to the killer, then it should at least narrow the field for us. Beyond that, I ..."

"Stop. Hannah. No."

Warren's expression was that of a father unhappy with a usually obedient daughter. "I meant *us*. Where do you think this is going? Really."

She laughed once, looked down at the table. Played with the edge of the napkin in front of her. "I don't know. I *like* you ..."

"I like you, too," he returned. "A lot. More than I ever thought I would like someone ... again. More than I ever thought ... I could like someone ... period."

She smiled weakly, played some more with the napkin. The server returned with their coffees and milk.

Warren waited for the server to move to the other side of the room. "I like you more than I can bear," he continued. "And ..."

Hannah reached out and secured one palm over his forearm. "And, you can't," she finished. "You shouldn't. *We* shouldn't. I know. Not while they still have her. Not until ... unless ..."

He nodded slowly, chewed his lower lip. Reached up and with his fingers began to slowly stroke the hand she had placed on his forearm, tracing delicate arcs and swirls both around and between her knuckles. Not once did he take his eyes off her as he gently slid one finger down the back of her hand, stopped at the wrist, and then circled it with excruciating languidness.

She leaned her torso back away from him, gently shook her head.

Warren cleared his throat. "Hannah, I don't really know what to say. I adore my kids. I love my wife, I really do ... and yet, it's been *years* since I've seen her, much less ..." His voice trickled away for a moment. He dropped his head, then looked back up at her.

"So why do I feel like I'm some horrible person for saying part of me hopes two years from now, we're still here together, trying to figure out who killed Vic Valenzuela?"

31

The agency's regional laboratory had finished its analysis of the trace of soil found on Vic Valenzuela's bedroom carpet.

"Anything revealing there?" Lee asked Agent Sainclair over the phone.

"*Wi* . . . and no," Sainclair replied. "There were no unique chemicals or nutrients found in the composition of the dirt. However, it did show an unusually high concentration of two common chemicals. Butoxypropanol and ethoxylated alcohol, to be precise."

"I'm sorry, I'm not much of a scientist," Lee replied.

Agent Sainclair chuckled. "Neither am I, Dalton. But fortunately, the agency has several employees who excel at chemistry. Butoxypropanol and ethoxylated alcohol are both solvents. They are used in many detergents and floor cleaners. Ironically, we found them in a clump of dirt, but their primary purpose is to get soil and dirt out of things."

Lee thought about that for several seconds. "But, we are assuming the soil containing those chemicals came into Valenzuela's bedroom via the murderer's shoes, right?" he asked.

"*Wi, mesye*" Sainclair responded. "That is what is so odd. Given the high concentration of the chemicals, the person who came into his bedroom that night must be someone who comes into contact with those chemicals frequently. Certainly more than once a week, I would think. One might expect to find that high a concentration of the chemicals on, say, someone's gloves. But not so much on the bottom of their shoes."

Lee was nodding on his end of the line. "Yes, that is curious," he replied.

"I was wondering, Dalton, have your colleagues discovered any more information that might be helpful to us? I'm especially eager to know what we are learning about Astrid Steinberg. And Mr. Duran."

"Yes, as a matter of fact, my colleagues texted me this morning to say they have some more interesting details. I'm convening everyone this afternoon for them to share what they know. Of course, you are welcome to join us, Mackeson."

"Ah. This afternoon? What . . . time this afternoon?"

"About four, I believe."

"Four o'clock. Hmm. Let me see." Lee could hear Agent Sainclair flipping through the pages of some sort of pamphlet or newspaper. Suddenly, there was a grunt on the other end. "Ah, no, I have . . . an appointment then. You can fill me in after your meeting, maybe?"

Lee smiled to himself. "Certainly. All right then. I'll call you this evening."

"*A pi ta!*" the federal agent replied.

"Oh, and Mackeson . . ." Lee blurted into his phone.

"Yes, Dalton?"

"Good luck this afternoon."

For a second, there was silence on the other end. Then, "Sorry?"

Lee smiled broadly. "I said, good luck this afternoon. I hope a couple of your picks come through for you."

***

Roberto glanced at his phone. It appeared this rendezvous with Isabela might be a relatively normal one. The address was a community college in the quiet, carefully planned suburb of Doral. *Quintero Hall, Room 377*, the text instructed.

If it's a college campus, I shouldn't run into too much weirdness, he thought. *At least, I probably won't run into any midgets.*

Quintero Hall turned out to be a long, rectangular building situated at one far edge of the campus. From the sidewalk, it had little personality and even less landscaping. All three stories bore windows, but neither life nor lights stirred behind any of them. It seemed more like a toy building brick that someone had dropped from the sky . . . or the first tentative pass at a structure one might design in one of those city-building video games. It didn't help that unlike all the other buildings on campus, this edifice sat at a diagonal to the sidewalk.

Maybe this isn't going to be so normal after all, Roberto thought.

He entered the building through a ramp of steps that were situated at yet another diagonal to the front of the building. *I can just imagine what Dalton would say about the design of this place*, he said to himself with a smile, feeling a bit lightheaded because of the jarring juxtaposition of angles.

The interior of the building seemed void of people. The only indication of life was an odd buzzing sound, the source of which he could not discern. Roberto found the interior design—with a cool blue-and-silver motif accented by highly polished chrome railings—pretty sophisticated for a college building. The carpet felt of high quality—a textured plush, he guessed. The numerous windows welcomed in ample natural light without blinding the building's occupants.

He trod steadily down a narrow corridor that led to what appeared to be a semicircular information desk. As he neared, he saw a bright red glow emanating from the top of it, a glow that seemed to dim and then regain brightness every few seconds. A few steps closer, he saw that it was a large button with a rounded top, similar to those used to stop an elevator in an emergency. But where that type of button extends out from the panel, this one rose two or three inches upward from the top of the desk. Next to it was a simple sign which read, in bold black letters, PRESS.

He extended the fingers of his left hand and nudged the button downward. Nothing happened, although he thought he heard the buzzing move into a lower register and thought he felt the energy throughout the building dip. A few seconds elapsed, then he heard footsteps.

Not a midget. Not a midget at all. In fact, just the opposite. Coming down the hallway in front of him was an Amazon with flowing blonde tresses and an urgency in her gait.

"Hi there! You must be Roberto. I'm Kayla. So happy to meet you. If you'll just come this way, I'll take you to the lab where you'll make your connection. I think we have everything set up for you."

Good Lord, she must be almost seven feet tall, Roberto surmised. *Maybe just over seven feet.* Her look was very Marilyn Monroe, but where the screen star exuded a demeanor that was breathy and ethereal, Kayla came across earthy and practical.

"Did you have any problem finding us here? Don't feel badly if you did. I think it was the third visit before I got the directions down pat. Of course, that won't be a problem for you since it's unlikely we'd have you back to this same location. Still, without good signage, this place can be almost impossible to find."

They entered an elevator that was waiting open at the end of the hall. Roberto still had not seen another human being, despite the fact it was around ten in the morning.

"Are classes out for the summer?" he asked Kayla.

There was a wisp of sardonic humor in her expression. "They're out for *today*," was all she said.

As the car sped upward, she turned and studied him. From high above. "You know, you have a very interesting profile from this angle," she said cheerily. "Your nose has such an interesting bend to it, did you know that? I'd love to draw you sometime. I'm actually an artist. I specialize in abstract works but to be honest, my best works are portraitures. Go figure."

She paused, studied him some more. "Yes, you'd be an outstanding model," she continued. "I'd bet your lineage is aristocratic Spanish. Either Extremaduran or maybe Castilian. Whichever, it's aristocratic, for sure. Your profile is just so very . . . *regal*."

"Thank you," Roberto said, with a somewhat forced smile. "Actually, I'm Puerto Rican." Then he remembered his father once referring to a great-grandparent who had come to the island from Spain at some point. "Well, maybe I have some Spanish in me, somewhere," he added quietly, extending his smile.

They came to the third floor and the door opened. It looked identical to the ground floor, except for the preponderance of potted plants that lined the hallway. *The better to hide surveillance equipment with*, he assured himself.

He figured the computer lab would be like the others they had brought him to over time. A sea of monitors on a row of long tables, cords curling hither and yon. But it was not. A magnificent monitor was built into the far wall, occupying it from top to bottom. A few feet away from the screen was a comfortable, contemporary love seat upholstered in a dove-gray fabric. A chrome-and-glass end table rested to the right of the love seat; in front was a matching coffee table, the top of which was clear of items (save for a small remote control device and a round, black coaster).

"Well, I believe you know what to do," Kayla said, lifting her arms in a way that indicated she had fulfilled her mandate for the day. "There's coffee and donuts and bagels over there on the table against the far wall if you want them. The bagels are from the Buena Fortuna Deli down the street, and if you haven't had any of those, you really ought to try them because they are *amazing*. Oh, and I think we put a little cream cheese over there, too, if you like that." She laughed lightly and scrunched her nose. "So, to connect with your hostage, just press the ON button on the remote and then enter on the numeric pad whatever code they sent you. It shouldn't take more than a few seconds for your person to appear."

She nodded vehemently, waved quickly, and began to step out of the room. But only the top half of her torso exited before she pulled herself back in. "Oh, I almost forgot. They told me to tell you that you had better not fuck up this time. After whatever it was you tried to pull in Manhattan, you're on some sort of probation, apparently. They told me to tell you one more slip, and you'll never see your loved one again."

She issued a quick, efficient smile toward him.

"Enjoy your conversation," she said as she turned to leave the room.

He surveyed the surroundings, checked his phone. Only about a minute remained before their appointment. He scurried over to the side table, dribbled some coffee into one of the Styrofoam cups, ripped open a package of sweetener, and tapped the contents into his beverage.

After tossing the empty packet into a shallow white bowl sitting next to the coffee carafe, he headed for the love seat, but quickly whirled around in midstride and darted back to the table.

One bagel won't hurt, he told himself. *Especially if I don't put any cream cheese on it.*

Quickly he situated himself in the love seat and, at the appointed second, pressed the ON button on the remote. The screen quivered with black and gray static, then the words "ENTER YOUR CODE" appeared in solid white letters on a pitch-black background. Out of nowhere, a voice boomed through an invisible microphone. "Provide your pass phrase, please," a male instructed.

Roberto sighed. There was nothing he detested more than articulating the phrase that he found incredibly inane and most certainly did not subscribe to.

"I am a Wayward Colonist," he obliged his host.

And there she was, for some reason looking quizzically into the lower left of the screen. She suddenly glanced up and, spotting her brother, grinned a toothy smile.

"¡Hola, 'Berto! ¿Como estas?" she said nonchalantly.

Even if it was only a few weeks that passed between the times he saw her, she seemed, nonetheless, to mature by at least a year. This time was no different.

"You look like you're old enough to drive," he joked.

She giggled. Shook her head. "Still too short," she said, entwining her fingers first one way, then another.

"Any big news?"

She shook her head again, kept entwining her fingers. Suddenly, she brightened. "They're letting me . . ." She stopped short, glanced off-screen for a flash then reoriented her focus on her brother. "I mean, I'm playing outside more. I play hopscotch. And they gave me a rope. I can jump rope now."

He continued to smile but his heart went thud. *She's ten and she's excited about having a jump rope to play with,* he muttered to himself. *How pitiful is that?*

"That's great!" he lied to her. "Maybe next time, you can show me some of your jump rope routines."

Her smile slid slowly and she looked downward again, telling him in no uncertain terms that she knew they'd never let her do that.

They shared superficial chitchat for another minute or so. Then, Roberto scooted forward to the front end of the love seat, rested his forearms on his thighs, and took on a businesslike look.

"So are you ready to play the game we talked about last time?" he asked, perhaps a little too nervously. He detected a speck of connivance behind the twinkle in her eyes. She nodded discreetly.

Good, he thought. *I've mentored her well.*

"I'll go first," he said. "*Veo, veo* . . . I spy . . . something that begins in Spanish with the letter P.

She furrowed her forehead some, her eyes darted all over the camera. She stopped when her eyes descended some on screen. "*Ahí abajo, panecillo!*" she exclaimed, pointing to the bagel in front of him. He nodded and grinned. "Yes. And it's delicious, by the way. Now it's your turn," he said. "*En español.*"

Furtively, she nodded. Fervently, he prayed.

"*Vea vea algo que empieza con 'p' y 't',*" she uttered quickly.

He thought for only a second or two. "A palm tree?" She smiled large and nodded vehemently.

Good. She was playing the game exactly how he wanted her to, precisely how he hoped she would. A palm tree helped some. But she'd have to deliver something more unique than a palm tree. That narrowed her location only to about a hundred countries or so.

"*Lo veo por allá* . . . I see it over there," he replied, pointing to some random point over her shoulder.

She nodded and giggled for him. "You are funny," she added in Spanish, knowing they likely wouldn't get upset at her use of the language if her doing so seemed lighthearted and frivolous.

"All right, my turn again. Only this time I am going to say a color. I spy . . ." He canvassed the room he was in for a second. "I spy . . . something pink."

She sent her upper teeth over her lower lip as she studied the room. It took her a few minutes before she spotted the discarded sweetener packet in the shallow container. "*Por ahí,*" she answered, pointing to his left. "That was a really tough one, 'Berto. I can barely see it."

"That's okay," he replied. "Improving your eyesight now will only pay off in your later years." She placed her hands over her mouth and giggled in delight. "Your turn again," he told her.

She thought for a minute. And for another. She looked up to the left, then down and to the right. Began to entwine her fingers once more.

"Don't take forever, Isabela. Our time is running out."

"Finally, she replied, "*Veo, veo . . . algo blanco.*"

Something white. Too vague. That could be just about anything. "A door?" he guessed. She shook her head, her lips close together. "A house?" Once again, she shook her head.

He scratched his hair, glanced at his watch. Not a lot of time left. "I don't know, Isabela. I give up."

"*Una nube* . . . a cloud, silly," she replied, giggling.

His heart sank. That was no help at all. Either she didn't understand the point of the game after all or, more likely, she had forgotten it. His expression made her disconsolate; she realized that, somehow, she hadn't delivered. "It's over there," he said, pointing haphazardly over her left shoulder. "Now, I spy something blue and round." She instantly pointed to his shirt, which bore a company logo made up of several blue circles. "I made that one too easy for you," he said. He looked at her intently, focused like a beam on her eyes. "Give me something difficult, Isabela. Something really . . . special."

She squinted at him, set firm her lips. Suddenly, he felt a brilliant chill trickle through him. For the very first time, in all the times they had let him communicate with her, he felt like he was looking at someone who both acknowledged her imprisonment . . . and detested it.

"*Vea vea una torre de color azul,*" she intoned, faking a smile so as not to raise the suspicion of whoever was monitoring her. "*Con una bola azul por encima de tres ventanas largas.*"

A blue tower. With a blue ball on top of three long windows.

She couldn't possibly have delivered a better clue.

Her look became grave again as she added, "I'll bet you will never find that, 'Berto."

He licked his lips a few times and nodded defiantly toward the screen.

"I'll bet you I will," he replied with equal intensity. "Just you wait and see."

32

"Hello. How are you today?"

The woman in the paisley scarf and thin green coat scooted down the park bench several inches and pulled close a small paper sack to make room for the new arrival she had just greeted. The newcomer briefly nodded and took a seat before gazing off at the verdant park before them.

They sat silent for several moments, taking in the late-afternoon spectacle. On their right, three young children clambered over a hulking mass of multicolored playground equipment. In the circular pond in front of them, a group of ducklings flapped their wings and occasionally emitted a strident squawk. Behind them, somewhere, a family knocked around a soccer ball.

Eventually, there was an awkward clearing of the throat and the one who had just arrived said, "I'm sorry. I didn't mean to be rude. I'm doing very well today, thank you."

The woman in the scarf studied the other for a moment, then turned back straight ahead. And waited.

After a while, the new arrival peered down at the concrete, tugged at one sleeve and said, "Apparently, I left my watch in the car. Can you tell me . . . what the . . . time is today?"

The other person breathed in sharply, looked over at her new companion. "I believe it is four." Paused. Waited for the gaze to be returned. Then, very systematically, intoned, "Four . . . after . . . four, to be exact."

The newcomer nodded energetically at the answer and smiled, but the effort at conciliation drew no response. A strong gust kicked up, tousling their hair and flapping the cuffs of their slacks. Suddenly, the family playing soccer behind them erupted in a chorus of hurrahs, causing a baby in a nearby stroller to launch into a plaintive wail. They both turned to observe the unfolding drama, but said nothing about it.

The woman in the scarf pressed the silk tight to her head, inhaled deeply and (as if carefully reciting a poem) said, "Would you please take photos of me with your phone? Can you? I am sure the newspaper published an item claiming no weather in years has been this beautiful. Hit the sack? Oh, please. Why? When, just sitting here, you want to never leave?"

The newcomer to the bench flashed a brief smile, brushed from a pants leg several small leaves that had landed there, then asked, "Please tell me . . . is it dangerous, taking this performance drug that the media call a toxin? I can't say that I'm confident it will help me to be victorious, since I'm going with such nervousness into my first marathon. The directions say avoid water . . . really flood your system with it."

The other person on the bench smiled conspiratorially at the comment but did not answer immediately. Thought about what to say. Thought how best to phrase it.

Then, she finally replied, "Is it dangerous? Yes. It makes you so tired, I'm told. Be wise and be careful." She paused briefly, then added, "Just get rest, and eat healthy, and don't you dare still be here once it's late. So, you're running in the marathon? I'm delivering the prizes for it."

The one beside her nodded like an obedient employee, then became suddenly serious.

"Sorry, I've forgotten. What will be the time when prizes arrive?"

The woman in the scarf looked down at her shoes, then back up at her companion.

"I believe it's eleven in the morning, sharp." Somewhere in the distance, a bird squawked. A woman in a white blouse and floral skirt strolled past them, paying them little to no attention. Overhead, a jet roared toward some exotic destination.

Finally, after a while, the woman wearing the scarf rose from the bench and began to stroll away.

As quietly as possible, she whispered in passing, "I assume you got all the information you needed? You're clear on what you're supposed to do next?"

The other person looked up and nodded discreetly as the contact floated past and glided regally toward one of the park's side exits.

33

He felt more confident.

No, that wasn't quite right. What he actually felt was *less anxious.*

Nonetheless, Lee felt it still was prudent to canvass his room before any meeting in which critical information about the investigation might get discussed. To sleuth for any hidden surveillance lens. Hunt for some minuscule microphone.

He massaged the bottom of each dresser drawer, swept the top of the bedroom armoire. Ran his fingers along the perimeter of the mirror that hung above the desk, peeked beneath each corner of his mattress. His cursory research into surveillance techniques told him the bathroom is often an overlooked goldmine of spycraft. So he strode across the carpet and entered the brightly lit room just off his sleeping quarters.

His eyes scanned the area bathed in fluorescence and landed like a heat-seeking missile on the toothpaste tube. He took a sharp breath in. *No one would ever think to look in there,* he convinced himself.

Nothing. Not in the toothpaste tube, in the mouthwash bottle, nor in the shampoo and conditioner kit. Even the small rectangular package containing a sewing kit appeared innocuous.

Lee breathed in deeply, glanced around the bathroom, then peered around the doorjamb to the warmly lit rooms beyond.

I can't cover it all, he told himself, *so I am just going to have to proceed on faith.*

***

Warren was the first to arrive. He appeared more melancholy than usual.

"Ah, Warren!" his boss said, clapping his hands briskly. "Everything okay? How is Agent Weiss?"

Warren glanced up sharply at his superior, then softened his expression when he realized Lee was likely just being sociable.

"Um . . . she . . . we've learned some interesting information about Ashley Taymore actually. We think we might know why she confessed."

Lee raised both eyebrows. "Ah, really! That's excellent, but why don't you save that for when we are all assembled. Here are Lara and Bree, I see."

The two women were having an animated conversation, the ardor of which verged on argument.

"I do not *cheat*, Lara. I may bend the rules a bit, but I am *not* a cheater!" She punctuated the end of her statement with an utterance that was part scoff, part laugh.

"I didn't say you cheated," Lara volleyed back, somehow sounding insistent *and* apologetic at the same time. "What I said was you are cheating me out of an opportunity to beat you the way I know I can. I meant 'cheating' as in 'depriving,' not . . . 'conniving.'"

Liam sauntered into the room, looked one direction, then another. He slunk along the edge of the others without saying anything and quietly took a chair.

Roberto, however, came barreling in, his hair on fire. "Dalton, I think I might know where they're holding Isabela!"

That shut down all other conversation in the room as everyone riveted their attention on their colleague.

"What . . . well, that's wonderful, however . . ."

"I don't know *exactly* where they're holding her, but I have it narrowed down to two or three places. At least, I'm pretty sure I have."

"How did you manage that, Roberto?" Bree asked as she repositioned herself in her chair.

Lara, sitting next to her, leaned over and whispered to her card-game rival, "Sure you have everything you need, dear? Do you have your clipboard? Your lucky scarf?"

Bree winced and swatted away her associate, who eased back into her chair, a look of self-satisfaction on her face.

"I can't . . . go into *all* the details," he answered, almost breathless. "I've been playing a little . . . game with her during our conversations. And she's given me enough specifics about what she sees from her . . ."

He stopped, unable to say the word "prison."

"Her location," he went on. "She mentioned a tower. Described it in detail. It sounds like a tower on a mosque. Blue base, with some sort of blue, ball-shaped figure on top and three windows underneath the ball. I've found only three towers like that in the world. One is in Oman, another is on some place called . . . um . . . Reunion Island, and the other is in Afghanistan. I just need one more defining image from her to figure out which one it is."

He paused, was almost panting, looked at Lee beseechingly. Lee noticed out of the corner of his eye that Irene was arriving. She seemed perkier than she had in some time. He was both pleased and surprised when she waved at Liam and took the chair next to his.

"So, Dalton, I may need to break away one more time to try to get the information I need," Roberto continued. "Is that okay?"

Lee knew his face was probably registering concern, so he pushed out a smile. "Sure, Roberto, whatever you need. Just . . ."

He saw Roberto's face fall slightly, so he chose to demur the warning he wanted to give him. The warning that even if he learned where they were holding Isabela, that didn't mean someone could immediately storm in and rescue her. That even if all of his research proved accurate, that couldn't prevent them from whisking her off to some place thousands of miles away overnight if they had the slightest indication her whereabouts were known.

"That's fine, Roberto," was all he said. "Just keep me informed, all right?"

The designer nodded, strode over to the far edge of the room, and assumed a spot in the corner next to a tall floor lamp. He crossed his ankles, wrapped his arms around his torso, and smiled. He was happy. Then, an idea came to him and he unlocked his arms and held up one hand.

"Oh, and Dalton, sorry, Margarida told me to tell you that the work on the Valenzuela house only began about three or four months ago, at most."

That brought a twinkle to Lee's eyes. So far, his theory was coming together just as he hoped it would.

"Thank you, Roberto. With that, I'm ready to hear what the rest of you have unearthed."

Lara noticed that for some odd reason, the head of The Lee Group seemed to be leading them in a voice much more hushed than usual.

"Warren, you said that you and your . . ." Everyone suddenly looked up at Dalton slightly slack-jawed, like college students who had just received word of a pop test from their professor. "I mean, you told me a minute ago that you and Agent Weiss learned why Ashley Taymore confessed?"

Nice deflect, Dalton, Lara thought to herself.

"Yes, that's right," Warren replied. "So, apparently Ashley Taymore was convinced that her fiancée had killed Vic Valenzuela. Ms. Taymore's birthday was that week, and her friend said she was going to fly in from France and take her out to dinner to celebrate. Their celebration was supposed to take place on the night Valenzuela was killed.

"Only . . . her fiancée didn't actually show up until the next day. Swore to Ms. Taymore she had sent her a text from New York saying her plane had been diverted there due to bad weather and to expect her the following day instead, but Ms. Taymore says she never received that text. When news of the murder broke, she became suspicious of her fiancée's involvement, knowing how much her fiancée detested Valenzuela after the rape she claims took place."

"But why would *Ms. Taymore* confess to the crime?" asked Bree.

"Apparently, her fiancée's parents have both passed away and the fiancée looks after an older brother who has special needs. Ashley twisted it in her mind that if she confessed to the crime, but pled self-defense along with a long history of sexual harassment from Valenzuela in her job, she had a much better chance of beating the rap than her partner would."

"I thought this woman was a graduate of Swarthmore," Lara said sardonically.

"Anyway, Hannah and I checked all the facts. The fiancée *did* board the plane in Paris and it *was* diverted to New York due to storms. She checked into a hotel near LaGuardia late that afternoon and flew down here from New York the next morning."

"So there is no way Ms. Taymore's fiancée could be the one we're looking for," Lee murmured. "But I'm wondering if we can necessarily dismiss Ms. Taymore herself. She still had every opportunity to go to Valenzuela's home and kill him, didn't she." He uttered the last sentence more as a statement than a question.

"Actually, it looks like we *can* dismiss her," Warren replied. "Remember how she said she stayed home that night and watched a movie? Well, what she forgot to mention at the time was that she didn't just *watch* a movie—she *rented* one. Or at least, *somebody* used *her* account, and *her* password, to rent a film through *her* television set that night. And then watched the film from about ten until just after midnight."

"She could have rented the film but then still go to Coral Gables and do in the coach," Irene said quietly. "She could have rented the film to create an alibi."

"Excellent point," Warren said, pointing toward the younger associate. "*Except*, the streaming company says whoever was watching the movie stopped it twice for about five minutes each time, then resumed it. Probably to go into the kitchen or the bathroom."

Lee contemplated that quietly for several seconds, then nodded emphatically. "Well, that seems to be *that*, doesn't it?" he stated.

Warren smiled mischievously.

"Guess what movie she was watching that night."

No one said a word.

"*Suspicion*," he eventually said with a chuckle. "Hitchcock."

Someone in the room groaned.

"That reminds me, what about the knife?" It was Lara. "Everything she told us about it in her confession was wrong. But were there any prints on the one found in the ravine? Or any sort of DNA that might lead us to the real killer?"

Warren shook his head. "Nothing. On that front, they were impeccable as always in concealing their tracks."

Just then, Lee's phone indicated a call was coming in. He glanced at the screen and saw it was Agent Sainclair.

"Hello? Yes, Mackeson. How are things? Right. Oh, really? Yes, well that is interesting. That doesn't necessarily clear him, however, does it? Ah . . . Oh, really? Well, that's how all these new technologies turn out to be incredibly beneficial, isn't it?"

Throughout the room, everyone was leaning forward a couple of inches in their seats in an effort to decipher the significance of the conversation. Lee had gone quiet now, listening intently but nodding his head repeatedly.

Everyone was leaning forward . . . except for Irene who, Bree noticed, was whispering to Liam behind the palm of one hand.

What are those two up to? she wondered to herself.

"All right, well, that's good to know, Mackeson. Thanks. I'll share it with the team. Oh, Mackeson? What about the large sums we discovered being transferred? Did you get any explanation for that?" The architect went silent again and stood as if he were waiting to hear the night's winning lottery numbers announced. Finally, he began to nod again.

"I see. Yes, that makes a lot of sense. All right, I'll get back to you with what I know as soon as our meeting is over." He began to return the phone to his pocket, but hesitated. "I'm sorry, what? Hialeah? Sure I can meet you there tomorrow. Why?" There was extended chatter on the other end and the longer it continued, the wider Lee's grin grew.

"That promising, eh? Okay, but won't all the background noise make it difficult for us to talk? Oh, I see. Okay, what time then? Sure, I'll meet you there. I'll fill you in then on what we've discovered."

He tucked the phone away, a smile still on his face.

"That was Agent Sainclair with some new information about Todd Cavender, the sportswriter. Apparently Sainclair's team has come across a couple of emails Cavender's friend in Alaska wrote a couple of months ago offering him the job at the salmon farm. So that part of his story definitely seems valid. More important, Sainclair's team discovered Cavender apparently went out for a run along the river the night of the murder. His sports watch tracked his run, and it didn't show him anywhere near Coral Gables between ten thirty and eleven forty-five that night."

Warren leaned forward. "What was the information about the money, Dalton? The payments Irene found Cavender making to the gambling syndicate?"

The architect took on a sly smile. "Apparently, Cavender actually knew a lot more about Valenzuela throwing football games than he let on. It wasn't just some rumor he heard secondhand and then didn't probe into much, as he led us to believe. Turns out, he was betting on the games himself. Sainclair guesses Valenzuela was feeding Cavender the information about each game."

"Probably to make sure Cavender only wrote nice things about him in his biography, I reckon," Liam added from the back of the room. "Something similar happened with one of our cricket stars in Australia a few years back. Gave his biographer some extra perkies and, what do you know, the petty larcenies he committed back when he was a teenager somehow failed to find their way into the book about *him*."

"So, then, who does that leave us with?" Lee asked. "Have we learned any more about Astrid Steinberg and her connections—financial or otherwise—with the victim?"

Liam raised one hand halfheartedly. "Not much, Dalton. Except . . . it appears that she isn't anywhere near as affluent as she lets on."

"What do you mean?" his superior countered.

"Well, all of her account balances are fairly low—under ten thousand dollars each—and she only has four or five accounts that I can find. She did own a home until six years ago, or so, but she's renting a townhome now. Credit card balances are pretty high and I'm just not finding a whole lot in the way of assets for her."

Lee mulled this information for a time. "Well, that could certainly explain why she accepted Valenzuela's check."

"But if she is so strapped for money," Lara began, "how was she able to send that money to Valenzuela's defense team?"

Lee nodded methodically. "That's a good question, Lara. Which reminds me of another question. Did we discover anyone getting upset at Valenzuela bailing from his apparent commitment to throw the games he was coaching?"

Everyone in the room slowly shook their heads.

"If anyone did tell him they were pissed at him, they didn't do it in an email or voicemail," Irene added. The room grew quiet again.

Lee began to slowly pace within a small square in front of him. "So our list of most likely candidates now includes whom?" he asked. "The coach Hayden Haas. Astrid Steinberg. The running back . . . what's his name?"

"Culberson," Bree said quickly. "Jamal."

"Right, Jamal Culberson," Lee concurred. "Them and, I guess, the hooker?"

"Not the hooker," Bree offered.

"Really?" Lara replied, leaning forward. "What a shame. I had my money on her." She paused dramatically, turned, and looked squarely at Lee. "I think Dalton did, as well."

Everyone held their breath, except Irene who couldn't help but let a sharp, high giggle escape from behind both palms.

"Excuse me?" the architect said, his face registering a hue that was somewhere between the colors found on a pale rose and a baby pig.

Lara cracked a faint smile. "I'm just saying, Dalton, that you felt Miss . . . Labra— or whatever her real name was—had an excellent shot of being the killer. Didn't you tell me that last night? Why, I could have sworn you did."

The release valve for the room opened perhaps a smidgen, but everyone continued to gawk at their superior, waiting for his response. He looked down at his shoes and bounced a couple of times on his toes. When he looked up, he was smiling.

"Yes, of course, of course I did," he said buoyantly. "She did seem to me to be a very likely candidate." He shifted his look to the right some. "So, why precisely is she *not* a suspect anymore, Bree?"

"Well, we located the patrolman she mentioned during her interrogation." She consulted her clipboard. "Police Officer Thomas Nelson. A real Dick Tracy type he was, too. Rock jaw, dimple in his chin, all of that stuff. Anyway, he confirmed seeing a woman matching the description of Miss . . . whatever, at the car wash that night. He couldn't say for sure how long she was there, but he said he passed through the staging area for the car wash twice over an eight- to ten-minute time frame and she was there both times, cleaning out her car. So he estimates she was there a total of about fifteen minutes or so. That isn't a lot of time, but given when she was at the car wash, and its location relative to Vic Valenzuela's house in Coral Gables, she would have had to drive about sixty miles an hour both ways to be our murderer.

"Also, I checked into Officer Nelson's background just to see if they might have some sort of a connection and be conspiring with one another about their story. Didn't find anything there. Nothing. Officer Nelson is as clean as a . . . police whistle." She set her clipboard back onto her lap, folded her hands on top of it, and looked up at Dalton.

"She didn't kill the coach."

The room took on a somber air. Lee frowned and noticed he suddenly had a craving for a grilled cheese sandwich. Or a bourbon. Possibly both.

He scanned the room and his eyes landed on Irene, who tried to evade his stare by ducking behind the screen of her open laptop. "Irene?" he said quietly, hoping to draw her out.

She sighed, repositioned her laptop screen a bit. "I haven't been able to find anything that helps us place where the running back was when the murder took place. I've checked streetcams, parking lot surveillance cameras both in the vicinity of Valenzuela's house and the university campus. No luck."

She stopped, took a deep breath.

"But I do have . . . something. Maybe." She was sitting more erect in her seat now, so for the first time, everyone could see her head above the monitor of her laptop. "It doesn't really tell us who killed the coach or anything, but it's . . . sorta weird I think."

"What's that, Irene?" Lee prompted.

"Well, that Duran guy—the guy with the furniture store—his story checks out, too, kind of. I mean I was able to sort of bypass a few protocols and tap into the surveillance feed of the second drugstore he said he went to that night. And sure enough, he comes out of it with a little sack in his hand, right around the time that was stamped on his receipt."

"Okay, so he actually was there when he said he was," Roberto said from the corner. "So what? The time between his two stops is still long enough for him to have gone and killed the coach, isn't it?"

"Right," Irene replied. "Only, here's the thing. It got me to thinking he sure seemed to be an expert on the location of all these drugstores. So I looked into the archives of the surveillance feeds, and interestingly enough, for four weeks leading up to the murder, Mr. Duran visited one or the other of those drugstores at exactly the same time of night, on the exact same night of the week. And each time he left the drugstore, he didn't drive back toward his home. He drove in the *opposite* direction."

"Wow!" Warren exclaimed. "Like maybe he decided to case Valenzuela's place one night each week in preparation for the kill."

"Or practice his route for the night he followed through with it," Bree suggested.

Irene looked at the rest of the team. "I mean who goes to the same drugstore at the very same time of night, late at night, on the very same night of the week, four weeks in a row?" she asked. "And then not drive straight home?"

"I'm now beginning to wonder if Mr. Duran really wanted to look at his friend's furniture that night the way he told us he did," Lee interjected. "It seems he has somewhere to go late at night that has nothing to do with furniture."

"Are you thinking we need to interview Duran again, Dalton?" Liam asked.

Lee chewed the inside of his cheek for several moments, giving his colleague's question some consideration. Slowly, a smile crept upon his face and he began to shake his head.

"No, no, Warren," he said, the smile increasing ever so gradually. "I'm thinking we need to follow Duran sometime soon to see just where these late-night escapades really take him."

34

Bree consulted the menu . . . noticed first the "Italian BLT, with Pepperoni and Peppers." *Noooooo*, was her knee-jerk response.

She sighed, flipped the page. *Okay, I get this is a boutique hotel*, she thought. *But does all of the food have to be so damned boutique, as well?* She scanned vertically down the left-hand page.

Quinoa salad with edamame and sesame seeds.

Russet potato and broccoli wrap with chickpea sprouts and black olives.

Cauliflower soup with peas and mung beans.

She squinted and frowned. Suddenly, her eyes descended on an item in the lower-right corner.

Flank steak sandwich with sweet potato fries.

Probably about as close to an Arizona meal as I'm going to find here, she told herself.

She closed the menu carefully and her mind drifted off to a lunch several years earlier with Carole. *Was it in Prescott or Wickenburg?* she wondered. It didn't matter. It was midafternoon during one of Arizona's hotter, late-summer days. They had slunk into a high-backed booth, similar to the one she was in now, one that had afforded them quiet and privacy. Which wasn't that much of a concern since there was no one else in the dining room with them. She recalled attacking the warm rolls the server had brought to them in one of those oval plastic baskets—the comfort food she so desperately needed at that time.

"He simply wasn't the one, Bree," Carole had said, clutching both of Bree's hands tightly in hers in the middle of the table. "I know it felt like he was, but he wasn't. And you know that now. And I'm sorry. I know how much this must be hurting you.

"But I sincerely hope you will try to look through the loss to see the good in this, dear. The man *hit* you, Bree. And a man simply doesn't strike a woman he loves. Certainly not more than once. Not *repeatedly.*"

Bree hadn't sobbed during Carole's words, but she had hung her head and slowly (reluctantly?) nodded along, a single tear making an inexorable trail down her cheek. She had said nothing in response.

"And we both know what this signifies for you . . . don't we?" Carole had added, squeezing Bree's hands tightly with the admonition.

With that, Bree had heaved once, removed one hand from Carole's grasp, wiped away the rapidly accelerating tear with the back of it. "I don't see . . . at all how he's similar to my brother," she had replied haltingly.

Several seconds passed. Bree recalled Carole had lightened her grip on her hands, but had continued to hold them softly. Her reliable friend had nodded gently, saying nothing for some time. Then, eventually, she had added, "I know you don't see that. Now."

Throughout their small taco salads and their flank steak sandwiches with French fries on the side, Carole had walked Bree through the many similarities as well as her subconscious choices. Emphasized to her that she had done absolutely nothing wrong, but needed to see that the abrupt end that had come to the calamitous relationship she had been in for almost three years was both a godsend to her and something she had marched headlong into. That by making different choices, she could avoid the familiar abuse and a similar heartbreak in the future.

Bree had continued to nod obligingly but wasn't quite ready to accept it. "Really though, Carole, they aren't alike *at all.* I'm not really arguing your overall point . . . I'm just having a difficult time seeing the connection in this particular instance," Bree remembered protesting mildly.

"Stanton is driven to achieve. But my brother only would do what he had to do in order to get by. Stanton had lots of friends, my brother was, like, the ultimate loner. Stanton can rummage through the cupboards, take whatever he finds and whip it into a gourmet four-course meal. My brother couldn't cook bacon without incinerating it."

She had stopped short and shaken her head rapidly like someone trying to ward off a truth she did not want to hear.

Carole took Bree's hands in hers again. "My dear, the similarities that draw us are more often shadows, fleeting reminders that we pick up subconsciously. Didn't you tell me your brother was tall and had dark hair like Stanton's?"

Bree remembered wincing a bit, acknowledging Carole was correct.

"Didn't he have a deep, resonant voice like Stanton's?" At that point, the junior architect's expression had begun to turn into one of ironic resignation.

"And Stanton is a concertmaster, correct? And your brother was . . . ?"

Bree remembered letting out a sniff at that point and openly grinning. Removing her hands from Carole's and sitting back against the booth. "A high school band instructor," she had replied, shaking her head with disbelief.

Her companion across the table had smiled knowingly. Then after a few moments, interlocked her fingers, set them firmly on the table in front of them and said, "Your brother abusing you all of those years was horrific and you continue to try to repair that trauma through someone else."

Bree recalled nodding again, only with more assuredness now. "Yes, I am. You're right," she had answered. She remembered thinking about that for a short time, then contorting her mouth slightly, looking at her friend with pity. "It's sort of . . . sick, when you think about it, isn't it?"

Carole had continued to beam at her friend with beneficence. "No, not really," she had quietly replied, continuing to regard her friend warmheartedly. "Actually, it's a sign that you still have some hope."

"Flank steak sandwich and sweet potato fries?" A plate plopped on the tabletop in front of Bree, jolting her from her reverie. She turned and quickly deduced that the server's purple lipstick was about half a shade off from the purple streak in her hair. The hotel employee stepped back slightly and regarded her patron through a furrowed brow. "Do you want some jalapeno-grapefruit sauce to go with your sandwich?"

Bree's nose twitched involuntarily. "No . . . I *do not*," she replied more abruptly than she intended to.

"Hey, no problem," the server said, backpedaling rapidly toward the kitchen.

As she chewed the first bite of her sandwich, Bree turned to look at the people promenading along the sidewalk just beyond the plate glass window next to her. She wondered what kind of abuse The Organization might be putting Carole through in her captivity. She wondered if Carole still felt that being held hostage by someone is a choice we make . . .

There was a mild commotion nearby, someone dropping into the booth next to hers. But she didn't think much about it until she heard, "So, Irene, do you think you're ready for this?"

In her right hand, Bree clutched more tightly a tissue she had pulled from her purse to wipe up a ring made on the tabletop when she forgot to set her water glass on the place mat.

"Yeah, I think so, I'm actually sort of jazzed about it now, to be honest."

"Well . . . it's good that you think you might have a passion for it, Irene," Liam was saying. "But try not to come across *too* eager. My experience is that a little aloofness can be a lot more effective." There was a short pause. "I guess 'aloofness' isn't really the right word. I meant you will be a lot more persuasive, a lot more seductive, if you come off to them as being . . . authoritative. Yeah, that's what I really meant. Authoritative."

Bree stiffened. Every internal alarm of hers was ringing wildly. Still, she knew it would be wise to just listen, try to absorb as much detail as she could before she decided to *do* anything. Elegantly, she dipped one end of a sweet potato fry into the swirl of ketchup she had squeezed onto the side of her plate.

"So here's what I want you to do," Liam said. Bree took note that all of a sudden, her colleague's tone had, itself, become more authoritative. "Come to my room about ten tomorrow night."

"Ten?" Irene replied. "Isn't that sort of late for us?"

"Yeah, maybe," Liam said dismissively. "But that's when most of them will be online."

"Okay," Irene said meekly.

"You have your outfit?"

Bree didn't hear Irene answer, but assumed she had nodded affirmatively when Liam said, "Good."

"Do you think I should be, sort of like, coy with them? Or, is it better for me to be more direct?"

There was a long pause. Bree didn't notice how far forward she was leaning in her seat.

"Well, my first response was to say 'definitely direct,'" she heard Liam answer. "But the more I think about it, you might want to take some clues from the person you are talking to. If you're really direct, some of them might find that too aggressive. But that might be exactly what another one wants. It's hard to generalize."

"Got it," Irene replied. "Customize my come-on to each customer, so to speak."

Bree heard light chuckling through the towering bank of faux-leather across from her. Slowly, she chewed on another sweet potato fry.

"Most important of all, do everything you possibly can to get them to care about you. To see you as someone they can confide in, they believe in, they come to not just admire but . . . worship. When they contact you because they can't bear to go another day without talking to you—*that's* when you know you've got them hooked."

Bree saw the server bring food to their booth and for a couple of moments, it appeared the conversation had come to an end. But then, Bree heard Irene ask a question, obviously with food in her mouth.

"Oom, what uf one uf thum wants me to go see thum, like, in person?"

Bree tilted forward even more and hoped when Liam responded he did so after he had swallowed whatever he was eating.

"Great question," he replied as clear as any television announcer. "Definitely agree to do it. It's a great way to get them to bond to you. You may feel a little awkward at first, but trust me, you'll be glad you did it once it's over." He stopped, apparently to take a bite. "If you're going to do that, though, be sure to give me a heads-up. We have our little arrangement, remember?"

The server cautiously approached, holding Bree's bill out several inches from her torso. Bree nodded, smiled at the employee, and plucked the bill from the young woman's hands. "If you don't mind, I'm going to just sit here a few minutes longer and sip my tea."

"Sure, no hurry," the server replied, studying her customer with a look that registered somewhere between curiosity and fear.

Bree sat back in her booth and took a long, deep breath. She now had more than a fleeting intuition as to what was going on with Liam and Irene. She considered how Lee or Lara might react to the situation, then decided telling either would just compound the stress both of them were already under with both their commissions around the world and the current investigation.

So she decided to take things into her own hands.

She did not notice that the tissue she had been clutching was now shredded into pieces.

35

As the Metrorail car lurched toward Hialeah, Lee was contemplating all the team had learned over the past couple of days, trying to weave a solid tapestry from the many diverse threads they had discovered.

He wasn't having much luck.

Lara had been right—his money *had* been on the hooker, both literally and figuratively. He had felt her story was the most promising of all—drifter of sorts, proven to live on the edge. Probably sent to the Valenzuela compound when the opportunity presented itself. Found her killing instinct accelerated by the way the coach treated her during the sex party. Waited until she was left alone, then slipped into Valenzuela's bedroom and butchered him almost beyond recognition.

Only, she couldn't have. The time line didn't work. The cop who saw her at the car wash didn't have a single smudge on his record (Lee had double-checked that after hearing Bree's report).

So who *had* killed this jerk of a coach? Far more important to Lee, how was it related to The Organization's plans for takeover?

The gambling angle was still a possibility, albeit a thin one. If Valenzuela had decided to end a cozy way The Organization had found to fund their activities, they might have considered it necessary to eliminate him. But as Agent Weiss had said, The Organization never seemed to be lacking for funds. *How ironic*, he thought, *that a cult harboring such anti-capitalist venom seemed, nonetheless, to possess an endless supply of capital.*

The train gently banked a curve. Out the window, Lee spotted a nursery filled with potted trees and colorful flora. That made him circle back to someone they had not given much attention to for a while—Hayden Haas. Heaven knows, the former assistant to Valenzuela had a personal motive, even without any nudge from The Organization. And he and his team had not yet been able to account for the coach's whereabouts around the time the murder had taken place. But the coach had come across docile enough, fussing over his cat palms and his daughter.

Still, it's often the quietly seething individual who is the most susceptible to their lure, Lee thought.

He wished The Organization would give them some inadvertent help. As they always had before. In Manhattan, an intercepted fax had been full of telling anagrams. In California, the time indicated on a clock in a photograph had led him to their lair. But he had no anagrams or clocks to help him decipher this case. Not yet anyway.

He reflected some more on how The Organization worked, their penchant for word games and numbers. How they prided themselves on their puns and numerology. If they told you to pay attention to the letter Z, everything beginning with the letter Z mattered much more than it might to the casual observer. If they emphasized the number 4, then every fourth letter, or word, was what you should focus on.

He considered all the data they had before them in Miami. The names of the suspects. The addresses of their homes. The streets they lived on, the number of children they had. Nothing seemed to intersect.

Maybe it's still to come, he told himself. *But if so, it'd better come soon.*

The train slowed in preparation for its arrival at Hialeah Park station. Lee stood up to move toward the front, when a short elderly woman plowed into him from behind and scooted beyond him. As she tramped past, she looked back over her shoulder and shot him a glance that thoroughly chilled him. It went beyond a normal look of determination or exasperation—it teetered, he thought, on the edge of revulsion.

"What the . . .?" Lee said, as the woman darted from the train and evaporated into the mob that milled about on the platform.

"*Some* people!" said a pudgy man in front of him whose rapidly retreating hairline was a good six inches below Lee's. "But don't take it personally, fella. This is the rudest stop on the line. I know. I come out here twice a week, and if somebody is going to knock into me, or knock me *down*, believe you me, it's going to be somebody at this stop, rushing to get a bet in on a race." The man reached into his shirt pocket and extracted something small and rectangular that was tightly wrapped in a glimmering piece of foil.

"Here, you want a chocolate? Have a chocolate. I've heard it said chocolate is a balm for the soul. It's certainly been my experience that chocolate makes the world seem like a much more hospitable place."

Lee squeezed his face at the thought of eating anything the man might have already nibbled on, but then pushed out a gentle smile.

"Thank you, that would be really *awesome*, but . . . I'm not . . . um . . . I'm . . . allergic to chocolate. Yes, quite allergic. But really, thank you anyway."

The man stared dumbstruck at Lee for a moment before shaking his head and waddling forward toward the front of the car with Lee just a few steps behind.

"Allergic to chocolate," the man muttered as he stepped off the car and onto the platform. "Wow. How does somebody like that actually get by in life?"

Within moments, Lee spotted Agent Sainclair just outside the entrance to the park, standing beside the statue honoring the 1948 Triple Crown winner, Citation. It would have been hard to miss the detective. The agent who normally was dressed sedately today was decked out in a lemon-yellow, short-sleeve shirt, a tie sporting brown and yellow chevrons, and tan, high-waisted slacks. His two-toned shoes, cocoa and brown, looked like a pair one would have expected to find in Duke Ellington's closet; atop his head was a cream-colored fedora encircled by a dark-brown band.

"Mackeson, you look so spiffy!" Lee exclaimed as he shook hands with the agent. "I hope you didn't dress up just for me."

The agent slid the toothpick in his mouth from one side to the other.

"*Non*, not just for you, Dalton," he replied. "I have no illusions that I can compete with such a Beau Brummel as you. That sports jacket, it is from Ovadia & Sons, yes?"

Lee glanced down at himself briefly, then smiled broadly at his companion. "Why, yes, it is. I picked it up the last time I was in Manhattan."

Sainclair merely nodded and flicked the toothpick up and down rapidly with his tongue. "*Wi*. I know the label quite well. Expert craftsmanship, but . . ." He clapped the architect on the shoulder. "Your income, it is much more generous than mine." He nudged Lee forward. "Come. I brought you here for a reason. I hope today to make both of us men of independent means."

Lee had always heard of the Hialeah Park Race Track but was unprepared for the architectural and visual treats it provided. From outside the gates, the opulent fountains and sumptuous balustrades evoked the palaces and casinos in the south of France. In contrast, the area on the other side of the entrances exuded southern Florida, from its Hialeah Park sign scrawled in an elegant script, to its profusion of deep-purple bougainvillea suspended like drapes on both sides of the staircases, to the colony of flamingos scattered across the race track's infield.

"It is my understanding that the first flamingos who lived here in the 1920s were imported from Cuba by the men who developed the track," Agent Sainclair said. "These flamingos, however, they were hatched and raised here. That, my friend, is why the infield is a National Audubon Sanctuary. It is the only location outside of the flamingos' natural environment where anyone has been successful reproducing them."

"Amazing," Lee replied. "How long do they actually stay here? *Do* they stay here?"

Sainclair was shielding his eyes from the sun as he peered out toward the infield. "Many will stay," he replied. "But some of them get donated to zoos or to other racetracks."

A light breeze kicked up, transporting from some nearby vendor the sweet aroma of roasted corn.

"It's going to be a good day, Dalton, I can just feel it. I have been following this one horse for some time now. Today is his day. Of that I am quite certain."

"So, are these horses that race in, like, the Kentucky Derby and the Preakness?" Lee asked.

Sainclair shook his head vigorously. "*Non!* These are quarter horses, Dalton, not thoroughbreds. They allow only quarter horses to race here now."

"What's the difference?" Lee ducked his head some, as if he expected a cuff from Sainclair's wrist. "I'm sorry, Mackeson, I'm not much of an expert when it comes to activities like this."

Sainclair smiled knowingly. "So, there *is* a topic I know more about than you!" Sainclair exulted.

Again, he shifted the toothpick to the other side of his mouth, became serious again. "Not to worry, *mon ami*. The nuances of this sport confound even those of us who have followed it for some time. The quarter horses, they are more compact than thoroughbreds. Their legs are longer and their *derrières* are more muscular. So they are more agile and more quick. As a result, they usually race shorter distances. You see them a lot in rodeos and horse shows, because they can turn and prance and dart more easily than the thoroughbreds can."

Lee nodded that he understood. He never knew so many varieties of racehorses existed. He tilted his chin toward the racing program the agent was holding. "So, which horse is it that's going to make us millionaires today?"

Sainclair smiled broadly again. "*Billionaires*, Dalton, if you're feeling especially adventurous today." He consulted his racing form. "Our ticket to prosperity, I believe, is a horse named Aquaterra."

"What makes you think *he* is going to win?"

Sainclair looked off at some distant spot in the sky and shook his head. "I don't know exactly. Something in the bones. I have been following him for several weeks now. He comes close to winning, then fades back in a race or two, then surges forward again and places second or third. I am not completely clear why, but I just have this feeling . . . that his time is not next week, or even the day after tomorrow, but *now."*

Lee mulled over what Sainclair was saying, looked across to the tote board to check the horse's odds.

Eight to one.

"How much do you recommend I bet, Mackeson? How certain are you Aquaterra is about to make a move?"

"A thousand dollars," Sainclair said almost instantaneously. "I am *that* sure." He then paused and stared deeply into the architect's eyes. "But you had best act now, my friend. *Chak jou pa Dimanche.*"

The architect gave Sainclair a puzzled look.

"Not every day is Sunday," the agent replied, stone-faced. "The luck, it will not last forever."

Lee nodded and headed off to place a bet. Along the way, he decided Haitians had a lot of colorful expressions that he didn't completely comprehend.

At the window, Lee checked the odds one more time before placing his bet. For Aquaterra, they had increased to ten to one.

"How much you betting, sir?" the woman on the other side of the glass barked.

"Fifteen hundred," Lee said without blinking.

"Fifteen hundred? On which horse?"

Lee glanced at the information monitor one more time. "The horse in lane five, or whatever it is you call it," he said.

The woman never took her eyes off of him as she counted out the bills he had slid beneath the glass.

"It's the fifth *post position*, sir," she answered. "Here's your ticket."

On his way back to Agent Sainclair, Lee went to stuff the ticket in the outside pocket of his jacket when his hand brushed up against something rectangular. He dug into the pocket and found a piece of paper that, folded into quarters, was about the size of a business card case.

I didn't have anything in this pocket earlier, he told himself.

He unfolded what appeared to be half a page of bond paper and began to read a message that appeared to have been produced on an old electric typewriter.

Thought you would have learned in Manhattan, Mr. Lee, that butting into our affairs can cost you dearly. suggest you leave at once. And oh, by the way, your comrade Mr. Bermudez had it wrong during the meeting in your suite the other day. it wasn't 'Suspicion' Ms. Taymore was watching the night we killed Vic Valenzuela. It was 'Notorious.'

"How did this . . .?" Lee said, turning the piece of paper over and over in his hand. Then the rewind button in his mind landed on the elderly woman with the malevolent glare who knocked into him as she was departing the Metrorail car. Knocked into him on *this* side of his jacket.

But the fact that they were tailing him throughout Miami didn't disturb him anywhere near as much as the fact that they apparently *were*, in fact, listening to him in his hotel room, despite everyone's assurances that they couldn't possibly be.

Where in the hell is that microphone? he thought.

He rejoined his companion just as the horses running the race he had bet on were being escorted toward the gate.

"So much for my feeling lucky," Lee grunted as he handed the note to Sainclair. The agent, who had been bouncing on his toes with excitement when he returned suddenly went flat-footed and took on a dour expression.

"Oh, *tout pa bon*, Dalton. I am so sorry. I will make sure we move you immediately to another suite. Or even another hotel, if you prefer."

Lee raised a palm. "Thanks, but moving to another hotel would probably be too disruptive at this point. Maybe another room. But I'm not even sure *that* will fix the situation, if you know what I mean."

"*Ah, wi.* I understand. These people, they are like the spiny vermin that we have back in Ayiti. They cause all sorts of torment, then they vanish for so long that, sometimes, you think they have gone extinct. But then one night, you are lying in bed, and you hear something gnawing on your footboard, and you just know . . ."

Lee took in a long, low breath and allowed the mélange of aromas coming from the bougainvillea and the roasted corn and the horses and the sweat of all the people around him to swirl together and coat both his psyche and his soul.

Eventually, he turned to his fellow investigator. "Do you have any idea what they're planning, Mackeson? Or, who it was that murdered Valenzuela?"

The agent chewed on his toothpick for a time, glanced first at his watch, then at the sun. "I am intrigued with this coach out in Kendall . . . Mr. Haas. His story seems quite . . . fantastic to me."

The assistant starters were beginning to guide the horses into their positions in the gate. The first horse slid easily into his stall but the second one seemed to be balking at the maneuver expected of him.

"What do you mean 'fantastic'?" Lee probed.

Sainclair breathed in heavily. "Maybe I am imagining, Dalton, but I smell foul smoke there. I find it very odd—he is a man who did not do anything extraordinary to get his coaching job at Miami A&M and did not do anything extraordinary to lose it, either. For many months, he tolerates an insufferable egomaniac—someone even *he* described as someone who got what he deserved—but then, after he is let go, he begs that egomaniac to rehire him. *Then*, if we are to believe what the sports reporter told Agent Weiss, he stalks Valenzuela all over the country. And does he have an alibi for when Valenzuela was murdered? Absolutely *non!*"

The agent pulled the toothpick most, but not all of the way out of his mouth and began to rub it back and forth between his clenched teeth a few times like floss. Then he plucked it out all the way like a finished lollipop, pivoted, and arced it into a trash bin behind him. Reaching into his back pocket, he produced a small linen handkerchief and used it to wipe first his lips, then the back of his neck.

"Let me tell you something, Dalton," he said as he returned the kerchief to his pocket. "We have a saying back in Ayiti for what happened between Haas and Valenzuela. *Bay kou bliye, pòte mak sonje.*"

Lee's expression dipped. "Mackeson, you know very well I don't have the faintest idea what you just said."

The federal agent smiled mischievously. "Yes, I do know that," he said briskly. "That's why I do it. I like to hold you in suspense." The agent grinned a bit longer, before relenting. "Translation, Dalton: The giver of the blow forgets, but the carrier of the scar remembers."

With that, he angled the brim of his hat toward the architect and raised both of his eyebrows for emphasis.

Lee had to acknowledge that when he looked at it that way, Agent Sainclair was probably right. Haas did seem to be an excellent suspect. Really, the only thing that had made Lee *not* consider Haas more seriously was the coach's seemingly blasé attitude toward it all. Which, he understood now, could just be a brilliant facade.

"So, are you saying you think The Organization may have planted him onto the coaching staff so he could murder Valenzuela at just the right time?"

Sainclair turned and smiled thinly at his friend. "Would you put it past them?" the detective replied.

The second horse had been tamed and inserted into the chute; horses four, five, and six were being cooperative, but lackadaisical. The buzz of the crowd amped up some as horses six and seven trotted into their starting positions. Only two more remained.

"But what about the running back? He doesn't seem to have an alibi either. Neither does Danielo Duran and Astrid Steinberg, for that matter."

The agent was looking not at Lee but at the final horses as they were being led into their positions for the race. He continued to stare back up the track as he replied, "That is true. That is very, very true. Most certainly, they are all possibilities."

But he swiveled swiftly back to the architect before concluding with, "But I would still put my money on the football coach almost as enthusiastically as I bet on Aquaterra just a few minutes ago."

A shrill bell rang, the gates lifted, and the crowd erupted as the race got underway. Sainclair remained poised, but Lee noticed the agent's right foot tapping a rapid staccato on the concrete beneath them. Within moments, the architect became enthralled with the tempo of the event and the beauty of the horses' muscularity as they heaved forward side by side, just inches apart. Suddenly, however, the clamor of the crowd and the thunder of the hooves reminded him of the chariot race scene in *Ben Hur*, causing him to burst forth with a giggle that caused Agent Sainclair to look askance at him from one side.

The crush gracefully rounded the first turn, and once the dust parted, Lee and Sainclair could see that Aquaterra had moved into the lead by a small margin. The architect elbowed his colleague. "Lookin' good, Mackeson!" he shouted.

The agent, however, remained nonplussed. "It is too early to go to the bank, my friend," he replied. "We wait, and we see."

Behind the pair, a rotund woman in a flouncy, wide-brimmed hat began bouncing up and down and screaming in Lee's ear. "Come on, Aquaterra! Come on! Bring it home for mama, Aquaterra! Come on!" Lee normally would have been riled by the woman's brashness. On this day, however, he found it somewhat charming.

The uproar intensified as Aquaterra widened his lead on the far side of the track to more than two lengths. At that point, the woman in the hat began to pound on Lee's upper back, her racing program scraping his neck. Lee glanced over at Sainclair, whose expression remained stoic but whose right arm, he noticed, was now bouncing in rhythm with the agent's leg and foot.

By the far turn, Aquaterra had taken a commanding, three-and-a-half-length lead. It felt as if everyone in the stands who was crushed by debt was signaling to the horse their need to retire it, and the horse was channeling all of their desperation into energy that propelled him forward. Now, Lee heard deep male voices urging the steed onward, like the chorus of basses aboard Wagner's *Flying Dutchman*.

Sainclair had tightened his right hand into a fist and was shaking it with vigor as the horse made the final turn. Somewhere behind them, a woman shrieked as if goosed from behind, and the air reverberated with the thudding of hooves.

Slowly, Lee raised both of his hands into a praying formation and placed them carefully over his mouth as the horses charged nearer. He felt a rivulet of sweat trickle along the side of his nose, but he dared not take time to flick it away.

And then, it happened. Like a balloon punctured by some upturned nail, Aquaterra dropped to the turf, roiling in an awkward sprawl of knobby knees and spinning flesh. The crowd moaned, then fell silent for a moment as the wall of dust kicked up by the collapse obscured their ability to see the carnage. Soon, though, several in the crowd realized the other horses were still charging the wire and that their pick was still in the race.

But Mackeson Sainclair remained riveted on Aquaterra, whose repeated stumbles suggested a fractured leg. Somehow, the jockey had rolled away from the oncoming charge and was sitting back against the far rail, seemingly safe, but decidedly shaken. The other horses sprinted past the finish line to muted hurrahs as medical personnel bounded onto the track. Lee surveyed the agent next to him, who stood frozen, one palm over his mouth.

Lee waited for the clamor to subside some, and for Mackeson to fully assess the outcome, before asking the question most on his mind. "Will you . . . get your money back, Mackeson?" the architect ventured meekly.

The agent shook his head, said nothing.

Lee sighed, placed both hands on his hips, turned to survey the area beyond the finish line, where the remaining horses and jockeys stood in a pattern of disarray.

"I am very, very, sorry, Dalton. I should never have encouraged you to place such a large bet. It was irresponsible of me to do so. Please, I hope you will accept my sincerest apology."

Lee turned back toward Sainclair and tried to read the tote board beyond him. "Uh, which horse *did* win the race, Mackeson? Can you tell?"

The agent squinted to read the numbers on the board. "Horse . . . number five, it appears." He consulted his program. "His name is Acumen."

"Oh, what do you know? That's the horse I bet on," Lee said quietly.

His companion slowly rotated his upper torso around to the architect. "What? I thought you also planned to bet on Aquaterra!"

Lee glanced down at the concrete and scuffed the ground with the bottom of his right shoe.

"Well, I was *planning* to, but I changed my mind at the last minute. I don't know, Mackeson, but once I saw the name of that other horse, I just felt it was the one I needed to put my money on instead."

36

Given what he had experienced while riding the Metrorail out to Hialeah, Lee was in no mood to take the conveyance back into downtown. Besides, this could be the perfect time to explore that idea about the work being performed at Vic Valenzuela's house that had been chewing on him from within. But he had only a couple of hours to spare.

So once he had bid goodbye to his forlorn associate, Lee hailed a cab to take him to Coral Gables and then back to his hotel. *It's not that outlandish a splurge*, he thought. The odds on Acumen hadn't been as big as those for Aquaterra, but his victory had padded Lee's bank account quite nicely nonetheless. He reminded himself he should look for some way to cheer up Agent Sainclair later on.

The cabdriver's name was Shirley and she'd been driving cabs for a living in Miami now for about nine years, she told him.

"Yeah, I loved Nevada and I won't lie to ya', I really miss the dry heat out there," she said, winking at her fare in the rearview mirror. "But I can't stand casinos, and I'm allergic to horse dander, and if you're not much into gamblin' or ridin', then there's not much reason to stay in Nevada!"

She was twice married, twice divorced, she said. Her first husband, whom she married at nineteen, had been her high school sweetheart up in Oregon. The honeymoon was already over on her twenty-second birthday when his right hook connected with her left jawbone, a punch that kept her in a brace for more months than she could remember. "I never was one of those silly young women who think their love can change a bad boy," she said. "The minute I saw that hatred in his eyes, and his fist heading for my head like a locomotive, I was already trying to figure whether I should head up north and move to Seattle or drive down south and try San Francisco."

She chose the Golden Gate City. Stayed there five years, mostly waitressing in diners and second-tier steakhouses. That's where she met Sal, her second husband, who owned a water restoration company in Houston. "That's one of those companies that goes in and gets your house back to normal after a hurricane, or after your toilet's backed up," she said. When she met Sal, his business was thriving and she was content to be the stay-at-home wife, chatting over coffee and playing gin rummy with the other wives in their cul-de-sac neighborhood only a mile or two from NASA. Thanks to her job in San Francisco, she had learned the secret to fixing a superb steak-and-baked-potato dinner, and she did her best to deliver that to her husband as often as possible.

But it turned out not to be enough, she told Lee. "You know, he never really said anything about it, but the minute we learned I couldn't have kids, that's when he started drifting away," she said. When the business seemed to occupy even more of his time, even when the price of oil dropped significantly, she just thought they were one of Houston's luckier couples. Besides, "If Sal was anything, he was industrious."

It was when her friend Naomi took her shopping at the Galleria that she learned it wasn't customers Sal was tending to after hours, but some cheerleader *maybe* two weeks beyond her high school commencement who happened to be working part-time at the very shoe store they were standing in when Naomi delivered the bombshell.

"Her," Naomi had said, pointing to a cheery, but vacant-eyed redhead lounging behind the cash register. "You want me to say something to the little tart, Shirley? Because I'll be more than happy to. You know I will. Just say the word, Shirl, and I'll give that little hussy what for." Shirley braked the cab to glance both ways before proceeding through a busy intersection.

"Well, did she?" Lee asked, leaning forward slightly in his seat.

Shirley glanced into the rearview mirror with a slight look of surprise.

Ah, she's not used to passengers actually listening to her stories, the architect noted to himself.

She sighed, assumed a slightly wistful look.

"No, no use in it," Shirley responded. "I knew it wasn't really that girl's fault. I could tell just from the way she interacted with the customers that she wasn't particularly bright. I figured it wasn't really *her* that Sal was interested in so much as her youth, if you know what I mean. And once I figured *that* out, I knew if he wasn't sneaking around with her, he'd be sneaking around with some other naïve girl under the age of twenty-five. That's when I got my things together and headed off to Vegas."

She was maneuvering the cab down southbound on Le Jeune Road now, passing the limestone facade of Coral Gables Senior High.

"That's a pretty fancy address you gave me," she said to Lee. "Excuse my saying it, but you don't look like you're dressed to attend one of those big gala balls they have out there."

Lee allowed a small grin to sneak out. She was fishing . . . and he found it . . . delightful. "No, no gala balls this evening, Shirley. However, if there were one I can assure you I'd ask you to go with me."

She let out a short cackle and looked back at him with another look of surprise. "Oh, I'm way too old for those fancy shindigs now," she said. "Sal and I used to go to a lot of the dances and cotillions they held at our country club. Sometimes he'd wear his tuxedo with the powder-blue cummerbund, and I'd put on the aquamarine necklace he brought me once from Venezuela. But that's all ancient history now."

Lee nodded. "Actually, Shirley, I'm . . ." He stopped short, realizing he needed to be cautious about how he described his plan to her. "I'm an architect, and the address I gave you is to a particular house I want to study from the street for about ten or fifteen minutes or so. I . . . may want to incorporate some of its design into a project I am working on. Can you just pull over to the side of the road where I ask you to, let me get out, wait there for a few minutes, and then take me back to my hotel after I'm done?"

A broad smile crossed Shirley's face. He knew she had just realized her fare, plus tip, was going to be a whole lot larger than she had expected.

"Sure thing. Don't you mind me. I've got my crossword puzzle and my Kenny G music here to keep me occupied . . ." At that, she held up the earbuds to a portable music player beside her in the front seat. "You study your house and don't mind me. Take all the time you need."

Five minutes later, Lee was standing about forty feet behind the cab, on a low berm that rose directly across the street from the front of Vic Valenzuela's house. The architect was relieved to see he was not too late to catch the renovators at work; two white panel vans stood stolidly in the driveway at the far left of the house—the back doors of the van closest to the street were wide open.

After a couple of minutes, two workmen in orange ball caps and gray jumpsuits emerged from the side of the mansion, strolled to the back of the van, and removed several sheets of plywood. Lee studied them as they carried the wood around the side of the house, one plank after another, for another five minutes or so. He could detect what appeared to be the top of a scaffold peeking above the back of the home's high pitched roof.

For another ten minutes, Lee observed the crew coming and going from the back patio, or yard, to the vans. One worker darted into a small side entrance at the front of the house near the driveway, but he quickly reemerged.

But *never* did a worker cross the midpoint of the front of the house, he noted, much less go anywhere near the garden area on the far right of the building, the garden in which the latticework began its ascent up to Valenzuela's bedroom windows.

Which was exactly what Lee had come there to check on.

His mind drifted off to what the chalk figure on the sidewalk had said to him that night, just before he had run into the prostitute.

What does that lopsidedness mean, baby? It's important for you to consider, you know, the significance of all that.

Lee put his hands on his hips and surveyed once again the house across the street. Near the peak of the scaffold at the back of the house, the tip of a blue plastic tarp rose momentarily, then retreated. In the front grass, next to the driveway, Lee noted the presence of several small hand tools and what appeared to be a sawhorse.

He swiveled around, walked halfway back toward the cab, stopped, and gazed across the street once more. Now he was looking more at the side of the house, which exuded the dignity and security of some downtown public library.

"Huh. Yes, that is interesting, *very* interesting," he said quietly. "We need to get a few more details about this renovation project, I think."

The sun was descending at a more rapid pace now, so Lee returned to the cab. He tapped the trunk three times so Shirley would not be startled when he suddenly opened the back door. He slid onto the faux leather seat, hiked up his slacks, and noticed his arrival had in no way distracted her from answering one of the clues in her puzzle.

"Thanks, Shirley, I think I got what I needed. You can take me back to the hotel now."

She didn't reply, just continued to look down at her crossword. *Oh right, her earbuds*, Lee reminded himself. He slid forward on the seat to tap her on the shoulder and repeat his request.

That's when he saw the rivulet of blood, trickling nonchalantly down the side of her neck.

37

These late-night shifts were the worst.

Jessica Sotomayor sat in her black-and-white, four-door cruiser at the south end of the John Preston Water Treatment Plant and asked herself why she ever took this job.

But who was she kidding? She knew what the answer was. Money. A little bit of security (maybe) for her and her three-year-old son, Damian. True, it wasn't the *real* police force job she had been hoping for. But she was committed to taking that academy exam again six months from now and, by God, she was going to pass it this time if it was the last thing she did.

For now, a security position helped her make ends meet. Barely. She was tired of taking the occasional twenty from her father, who couldn't possibly afford it given the meager pension he received from the state. She was *really* tired of waiting tables every weekend at her cousin's topless bar in Hallandale. She needed to let him know that after the end of next month, she wasn't going to be doing that anymore.

The security job wasn't all that bad, really. It was just boring as hell. Most of the time, she sat (like she was now) waiting for nothing to happen. Turning on the ignition and driving around the plant once or twice to make sure everything was okay, which it always was because, after all, who gives a damn about a water treatment plant? Most of the people in Miami didn't even know what a water treatment plant actually did, and they sure didn't know where this one was. Even the neighbors just thought of it as that huge, charcoal-and-white hulk of a building that towered inside a fence of barbed wire and employed several of their brothers, nephews and cousins.

At least this job didn't come with any real pressure. She could sit in the cruiser for two hours or more, listening to her tunes and eating the fritas she'd pick up now and then from one of the burger places in Little Havana. If she felt really daring, she'd smoke some weed, although she'd usually save that for when she was driving around the plant. That way, if she found herself headlights-to-headlights with one of the other security guards, she could flick the joint out the passenger-side window and just keep on moving.

A squawk came over her walkie-talkie.

"Officer 499, this is central dispatch. Do you see something moving up around the base of the south tower?"

She had to shake her head, the question was so unusual. "What? Where? The south tower? Hold on."

She had to roll the cruiser forward about fifty feet to get an unobstructed view of the tower the dispatcher had mentioned. Once she had a clear shot at it, she scanned the smoke-gray column for whatever the security camera back at the control center might have noticed. *It's probably a cat*, she thought. *Or maybe some large bird.* She waited a few seconds, saw nothing.

Except . . .

She squinted, thought *maybe* she had seen the outline of *something* moving horizontally across the back of the tower, illuminated momentarily by the glare of a streetlight. She waited . . . and waited . . . but nothing else appeared. That was the problem with the few incidents like this that arose. Even if you thought you saw something, it was usually something else. Or, as in this case, it was the power of a suggestion planted in your mind by someone else.

"Roger, dispatch, this is Officer 499. I don't see anything. I . . ."

But there it was again. Maybe. Crouched low against the tower's base.

A possum? An unusual shadow cast by one of the palm trees adjacent to the plant?

"499, could you go check again? We seem to suddenly be having some difficulty with our surveillance feed."

She laughed. *Problem with the surveillance feed? This is like some really bad scene from some really bad sci-fi flick,* she thought.

She exited the cruiser as quietly as possible and walked toward the nearest gate she had a key for. The metal door squeaked as she entered—*Dammit, they told me last month they were going to spray some lubricant on those hinges,* she reminded herself. Their stupid excuse? A gate that made noise might be a hindrance to a security guard, but it also might be a deterrent to someone up to no good. *Well, if someone really is up there next to one of those towers, that sure blows their theory all to hell, doesn't it?*

She crept along the dimly lit pathway that led from the gate toward the southeast corner of the plant, taking care not to step into any of the circles of light formed by the overhead streetlights. It was at times like this she wished she could be in her running shoes rather than the boots commissioned to each guard. The boots were good for navigating erratic terrain, but there wasn't much of that in this part of town. Besides, a lighter shoe would be preferable if she found herself having to chase someone.

Listen to what you're saying, Jessica. "If you have to chase someone." AT THE JOHN PRESTON WATER TREATMENT PLANT. Get real, chica.

She reached for the flashlight clipped to her belt and strode quietly toward the massive structure in front of her. Just her luck, the moon went behind a bank of clouds, limiting her visibility that much more. She guided the beam from the flashlight slowly up the side of the plant, then panned it first to the left, then to the right. Everything looked intact, nothing caught the beam. She stopped, stood still to listen.

All she heard was the occasional chorus of crickets and a cheer coming from some driveway basketball game maybe a couple of blocks away.

It's almost ten thirty and they're still playing basketball? I'll never let Damian do that, she told herself.

She waited there a bit longer, and when nothing presented itself, she sidled around the south side of the building to the west. Here she had a better view of the tower and the multitiered roof all around it. She knew someone was inside the building, hopefully watching *their* surveillance cameras, yet the plant almost seemed abandoned, given the dismal energy it exuded. She stopped again, waited, nothing.

Eventually, she let out a sigh of relaxation and turned to go back to the cruiser.

Then, she heard it. A soft scraping followed by a cascade of something. Pebbles? Dirt?

She swiveled around and caught, just in time, a glimpse of several small stones tumbling to the ground from the southwest corner of the roofline. Carefully, she pressed the button on her walkie-talkie and whispered, "Dispatch, this is 499. Spotted someone. I'm heading in toward the south end of the building. Request backup. Do you read me? Request backup."

The silence that followed seemed excruciatingly long, although she knew it was probably her heartbeat that made the amount of time that passed seem like several minutes, not several seconds. As discreetly as possible, she crept toward the building, her head tilted up, to catch some view of the person who most definitely should not be on that roof.

It was a few moments later that someone dressed completely in black jumped to the ground from the opposite corner of the building. Immediately, the figure crouched to the ground and darted across the shallow setback separating the building from the street, taking a route that had been plotted months before. The individual dropped into an opening in the ground that was just a few feet inside of the fence, turned quickly, grabbed the cover of sod that had earlier covered the trench's entrance, and replaced it as precisely as one could in less than three seconds. Then scrambled through the tunnel to a spot outside of the fence, about seventy-five yards away.

Well, that seemed to go well, the individual thought upon mounting a rickety bicycle propped up against a raggedy hedge. *Especially the part when I used those pebbles to trick the guard into thinking I was leaving the roof from their end of the building. Boy, nobody's ever used a ruse like that one before have they? Whoever that guard was, I sure hope they're not planning to join any real police force soon. The dope.*

With that, the bicycle headed south from the plant, toward the lights of the city and the spaghetti bowl of freeways that wound around and through metro Miami. The clouds that had been obscuring the moon thinned some, making the orb appear to glow behind a wispy swatch of gauze. The cyclist gazed up at the night sky and allowed a sliver of a smile to emerge.

Let's see, they told me the toxin should start affecting people's nervous systems within twenty-four hours or so, the cyclist thought. *I do hate the idea of some little children being among the first ones poisoned.*

But as the bicycle made a turn onto Okeechobee Road, and joined the crush of traffic on the highway, the cyclist sighed and shrugged both shoulders.

Oh well, the rider thought, head bobbing first to one side, then the other. *That's just the price I have to pay, I guess, if I want to be the star of The Transformation.*

38

It hadn't taken long for the ballistics experts to confirm that the bullet that severed both carotid arteries of Lee's cabdriver (her real name was Shirlene Hildreth) had come from a precision sniper rifle shot from deep within the dense foliage that lined the right side of the road.

"The good news is, she almost certainly died instantly," Agent Weiss told Lee, her right hand placed on his left shoulder. "The bad news is, they must really be pissed. For some reason, they don't want you scouting the Valenzuela mansion. So they sent up the worst type of signal flare."

She peered at the architect and squeezed his shoulder tight. "Why *were* you there, by the way?"

He shook his head slightly and smiled. "Ms. Hildreth—did she have any relatives here? I might want to pay my respects."

It was Agent Weiss's turn to shake *her* head. "No. None . . . unless you count Lula Belle, her parakeet. No siblings and no children. But several grieving friends, most of whom she knew through her condo association or from her volunteer work with the Tropical Audubon Society."

Lee nodded. "And The Organization, did they leave . . . any . . .?"

"Any confession note signed by one of the characters in *Wayward*

Colony? No. She doesn't seem to be someone who directly interfered with their plans. It appears she was just one of their . . . ancillary casualties."

Lee nodded again, took a large breath in. "I don't like the idea that my presence here could lead to . . . ancillary casualties, as you call them," he said softly.

Agent Weiss smiled at him and dipped her head, her lips tight with determination. "Look, Dalton, thanks to your help with these investigations, there are a lot fewer casualties than there would be otherwise. That's the way to look at it, if you ask me. That's the way *I* look at it. And don't you dare think anything but that, okay?"

Lee returned her earnest look, but his implied, *I'm not sure I really believe that*, rather than, *Thank you for that*.

"Want some time off from the investigation?" she asked him. "I'm sure Mackeson would be okay with you taking a day or two, if you need it."

Lee looked up at the sky, frowned. "No, no time *off*. There's too much to work through about the case, in my mind anyway." He paused, chewed some on the inside of one cheek. "But maybe . . . some time *away*. Away from downtown, from Coral Gables."

Agent Weiss nodded slowly and smiled. "Go. Work out whatever you need to. You know where to find us."

He decided to climb upon his Maicoletta and head west, toward the Everglades. But not that far. Just before he hit the Homestead Extension of the Florida Turnpike, he wheeled left and pulled onto the campus of Florida International University. He had always heard the campus architecture was innovative and intriguing, and he was instantly struck by the vibrant colors and quirky angles many of the buildings exhibited. He wanted to stroll across the grounds, absorb the contours of the structures all around him.

And think. About art galleries and furniture stores, and about football coaches who gamble on their games, and federal agents who gamble on the horses.

And about the work being done on Vic Valenzuela's home.

But given what had taken place in Coral Gables, he also wanted to be as discreet as possible. So he pulled the visor of his black baseball cap down low and donned the sunglasses that would provide anonymity.

It made sense to him that he begin by visiting the university's school of architecture, housed in an eccentrically designed cluster of buildings named for a former ambassador and renowned philanthropist, Paul Cejas. Coated in citrus-colored hues and shaped like one of the people movers that shuttle people around many airports, the primary building among the assemblage popped out like a piece of Op Art begging to be noticed. Although Lee's taste leaned toward things elegant and understated, he was delighted by the audaciousness of this quirky venue. He studied from multiple viewpoints its interconnected walkways and bridges, and deemed its spunk appropriate given its South Florida location.

I'd so love to design a home like that someday, he thought to himself.

Which got him wondering again about Vic Valenzuela's home. He was beginning to formulate an interesting theory, but he would need some more data to bring it all together, data he thought Roberto might be able to extract from Valenzuela's housekeeper. It was beginning to dawn on him that if all of the work that had been done at the house thus far had been performed at the end *opposite* the one Lee's bedroom was in, that might mean . . .

But he wasn't certain. And it wouldn't necessarily reveal all that much about who committed the murder.

But then again, he told himself, *it very well might.*

Numerous students began to spill from one of the venue's entrances, so Lee bounded off in a different direction, both to avoid a crowd and avoid being recognized. He usually loved to answer questions and entertain new ideas about his craft, but now, he thought, was neither the time nor the place.

He sauntered east, with the predictably bland Engineering and Computer Science building on one side of him and an atypically delightful parking garage on the other. *Leave it to Florida to make its parking garages palatable,* the architect chuckled to himself as he strode past the seven-story structure that (wisely, he thought) included an eyewear shop, a nutrition shop, classrooms, a computer laboratory, a convenience store, and office space along its ground floor. On a whim, he ducked into the convenience store and plucked a nectarine from a bin near the front door. *You can never get too much niacin and thiamin*, he thought as he paid for the fruit and took a quick bite from it.

He continued east, and quickly saw towering above him on his right the Wertheim Conservatory, a cathedral of glass featuring rectangular windows that tilted at random angles to allow varying amounts of light in on the plants. He gazed upward and noticed sloped roofs reminiscent of the one atop the 601 Lexington Avenue building in Manhattan, more commonly remembered as Citicorp Center. Lee was impressed that the school had doggedly rebuilt the glasshouse after Hurricane Andrew had demolished its original incarnation right before its construction was finished. He tinkered with the idea of entering the conservatory to check out the cacao trees and the bat flowers he had read were grown inside. He was also keen on seeing the pitcher plants, which captured insects and digested them on the spot. But he knew he didn't have the time to do that *and* admire all of the architecture the campus had to offer, so he decided to press on and try to come back and stop to "smell the bat flowers" some other day.

Just beyond the conservatory were the academic health centers, five interconnected buildings that looked like a set of index cards, each of which had been folded and perforated in different ways. Lee knew the buildings housed research laboratories, classrooms, and other academic installations; it was their exteriors, however, that he cared about.

Of the five, his favorites were Academic Health Center Two and Academic Health Center Four, which stood around the corner from one another. The two were similar in that they were variations on a theme of a rectangle. But where the former building was both colorful (bearing a mix of gold and blue—the school's colors) and multidimensional (a large, square panel resembling a multicolored microchip appeared to be affixed to one side of the center), the latter building was sleek and arctic, like a toppled refrigerator with a reflective frontispiece at one end.

Lee was about to move on, but found himself surprised and transfixed by the newest of the centers, Number Five. He decided after several minutes of examination that it might actually be the best of the lot. Occupying the farthest edge of the health center complex, it did not discreetly hug the corner at all. Instead, he decided it resembled a spacecraft from a science fiction film, poised on stilts and marked by wings that jutted from the center in multiple directions. Given its sharp angles and its ice-white facade, Lee presumed it would most definitely have to be a spacecraft from a Nordic science fiction film.

As he strolled along Southwest One Hundred and Eighth Street, he passed a blonde and a brunette who both wore sundresses and sandals.

"I know, can you believe it? It's getting to where I'm even terrified to eat anything in the cafeteria," said the blonde.

"Yeah, apparently it's really bad," the brunette replied nodding. "They said something like twenty or thirty people all over the city have gone to the hospital with it. And it's not some little stomach bug, either. They said some of them are, like, *critical.*"

Huh, Lee said to himself looking down at what was left of his nectarine. Several steps later, the architect leaned over and tossed what remained of the fruit into a nearby trash bin.

He walked toward the school's sprawling student center. But just before he encountered its plaza, he veered right and headed instead for the imposing Steven and Dorothea Green Library. Like a delicate stork, the multitiered structure rose high above—and looked out on—a roughly circular lake graced at its center by a fountain. Lee knew the original three-story structure closest to the lake had been augmented by the tower behind it, which housed, among other features, the university's broadcasting facilities. But the architect was more attracted to the library's serene study rooms, and he chided himself for not thinking to reserve one so he could contemplate the case, and his life, with fewer distractions.

His life. What *was* he going to do with it, he wondered? He felt far less despondent than he had in Manhattan, but a nervous static coursed through him nonetheless. He had resigned himself to the fact his parents would die soon and embracing that reality, rather than resisting it, was probably the wisest choice he could make. What was that quote from Saint Francis about having the strength to accept what we cannot change and the wisdom to recognize what we can? Something like that?

He'd always hated that saying, however. He preferred one by

Confucius: "He who conquers himself is the mightiest warrior."

But he was definitely growing tired of it always being about "himself." Only himself. And he had to concede, there weren't many matrimonial prospects queuing up outside his door. He wondered if he might relinquish this endless crusade against The Organization if he didn't have his team and their loved ones to think about. But he knew the answer to that without hesitating. He fretted over how intoxicating his tryst with the prostitute had been, yet knew he could never commit to someone, or a lifestyle that . . . *unseemly*. He worried that he might have become so fixated on the appearances that delight, that he could not focus on the substantial things that sustain.

He stopped, sniffed a couple of times. *That reminds me, I really ought to set up that dinner with Lara*, he told himself.

He had a few more buildings he wanted to examine, but his phone buzzed before he could take another step.

"Dalton, it's Warren. We've learned some interesting information about some of the people we've been interviewing."

"What have we learned?"

"Well, let's start with the gallery owner."

"Astrid Steinberg?"

"Right. Remember how we learned that she'd been sending checks to Valenzuela's defense team?"

"Yes," Lee replied, becoming more curious.

"Well, you'd sort of think that after the trial was over, those payments would have stopped. But they didn't. She kept sending them, for weeks after the verdict came in. And get this."

"There's more?" Lee asked, trying to keep his voice soft.

"There's more. She's *still* sending them. One landed in their account just a couple of days ago."

"Oh . . . *kay*," Lee replied, creasing his brow as he did so. "That doesn't make much sense, does it?"

"No, it doesn't," Warren replied.

"I'm wondering . . . if we should have some sort of surveillance put on these people. Ms. Steinberg, Coach Haas, the running back . . ."

"Already there, Dalton. I arranged for that with Mackeson this morning."

"Good thinking. Anything suspicious in their movements thus far?"

"Not really. Coach Haas has been to the plant store and dropped his daughter off at her dance class. The running back is working at a car dealership over the summer and he went over there today. But one little trip someone took this morning really raised my eyebrows."

"Who took it?"

Warren sniffed some on the other end of the phone. "Again, Miss Cool, Calm and Cutthroat . . . the gallery owner."

"Interesting. Well, she gets around a lot more than she lets on, doesn't she? No wonder she doesn't have any money. It seems she spends most of her time doing things that have absolutely nothing whatsoever to do with selling art."

"Yeah, tell me about it. So, around eleven this morning we got an alert that she had used one of her credit cards at a drugstore in Little Havana."

"Little Havana!" Lee exclaimed, ducking his head soon after to tamp down his volume. "That doesn't seem like a neighborhood she'd typically hang out in."

"That's what I thought, too. So Hannah—Agent Weiss, that is—made some calls to the police department to see if her license plate showed up this morning on any of their street cams."

"And?"

"It did. There's video of her parking her Cadillac Escalade alongside a curb just around the corner from the Durans' store."

"The Durans?" Lee thought about that for a moment. Tried to tie it to all the other nuggets of information they had. "Well, of course, they know each other from the murder trial," he responded. "But I would think they would have pretty much gone their separate ways by now. What would she have needed to say to Danielo Duran that she felt she had to say to him in person rather than over the phone?"

"Good question," was all Warren could say.

Lee sighed, looked off into the distance.

"Okay, well this is all getting pretty convoluted, but it's also making them all look pretty suspicious, if you ask me. As far as we know, they might *all* be members of The Organization, although I find that pretty unlikely. Thanks for letting me know this, Warren. Anything else?"

"Well, as a matter of fact . . ."

Warren fell silent. Lee waited.

Then, "Is everything okay between you and Mackeson, Dalton?"

Lee squinted some. "Sure. Why do you ask?"

Another silence for a few seconds. Then, "Well, maybe it's my imagination, but when I told him earlier that I intended to call you, he sort of got this grimace on his face, and then he told me to be sure and ask you how on-target your acumen was today. He seemed a little snarky when he said it."

Lee frowned and rolled his eyes. Apparently his switcheroo at the racetrack had irked Agent Sainclair more than he had realized.

"Tell him I said it's been a disappointment compared to what it was a couple of days ago and that I intend to take him to lunch or dinner soon to explain to him what that means, would you Warren?"

There was silence on the other end of the line for some time. Eventually, Warren came back on the line. "That's a lot for me to have to remember, Dalton," he said.

"Well, do your best," Lee replied hastily. "It's not essential you get it exactly correct."

The architect told his subordinate he'd be back late that afternoon and they ended the conversation. Lee thought about placing a quick call to Agent Sainclair to try and assuage the detective's bruised feelings, but decided to let more time pass in hopes they'd heal on their own.

He began to stroll west, toward the business school. Not because he had any enthusiasm for business, per se. That's what Lara was for. He was heading there because he had heard the architecture of the structures that comprised the College of Business complex was compelling. The first edifice he encountered, on his left, was the Ryder Business Building, which housed classes for undergraduate business students. The building itself did not enthrall Lee—save for a pyramid-topped, green-glass cube that pushed out from the building's center, the structure could easily be mistaken for most any galleria-style complex on most any urban street in most any Latin or Mediterranean city. What *did* capture Lee's attention, however, was what he saw when he turned to the right—a long, narrow, rectangular green space flanked on both sides by lines of palm trees that looked like soldiers marching into battle.

That green space would be EPIC for lawn bowling, Lee thought to himself, almost giddy with the idea.

He didn't linger long there, however, for his fancy was immediately captured by a massive building farther on which, from certain angles, resembled a beached whale perched atop a podium of glass. The building housed the graduate business school, and Lee chuckled when he realized how apropos that made the structure's upturned nose seem. However, he found the overall design of the building delightful, and he appreciated how the thin, flat, sand-colored panels converged and narrowed to a predominant focal point over the entrance, as well as how their neutral color was boldly offset by cherry-red and lemon-yellow accents near the base.

"Sir?"

Lee wheeled around toward the voice and discovered a dark-haired young man in a gold-colored long-sleeve t-shirt and dark blue running shorts standing a few feet from him. The clean-cut kid pointed toward the architect's feet.

"Your shoelaces are both untied. I'm worried you might trip over them."

Lee glanced at his shoes and, sure enough, both of his laces looked like wild clumps of overcooked pasta.

"Oh my. Thanks for that," he responded, squatting to retie the right shoe. "I swear, I never had this problem with shoelaces when I was growing up."

Lee expected the athlete to dash off now that the situation was being addressed, but instead he nodded and watched Lee attend to his left lace.

"Actually, it's the way you tie your shoelaces that's the problem," he said, more politely than condescendingly. The young man kneeled down beside Lee and took the laces out of his hand. "You tend to tie them like this, the way most of us learned to." The kid began to maneuver the laces precisely the way Lee did, placing the right string over the left and then looping the left string back under the right. Lee was trying his best to focus on the lesson, but what he was aware of more was the unusual mix of sweat and talc that was emanating from his new mentor.

"But you need to do it like this," the student said, reversing the order he had followed before. "There," he said with emphasis at the moment he tightened the knot. "Good to go. Don't feel bad, sir. Pretty much everybody does it wrong these days."

At that, the athlete leaped up from the ground, smiled at Lee, waved and began to jog away. Lee stood slowly and watched as his unexpected guardian angel loped off in the direction he had been heading before he had stopped to render aid to the architect. But when the jogger was only about fifty feet away, he turned around, winked at Lee, smiled and then took off again.

Lee stood there, not sure what to make of it all. Except that he was glad that his shoes now felt much more secure.

Eventually, the architect's attention drifted to the left of the College of Business complex where he saw the aptly named (for South Florida) MANGO building, another key component of the business school. Once again, he admired how the school had thought to interweave retail services along the ground floor of the building with the classrooms and offices located above. Much more traditional and rectilinear than the "beached whale" he had studied earlier, this structure nonetheless avoided being humdrum by interrupting the long, flat facade with a six-story wall of cool-blue glass.

He checked his watch and decided he needed to pick up the tempo. He had one more objective, and that was to spend some time at the Frost Art Museum at the southern end of the campus. But on his way there, his attention could not help but be arrested by something that looked like a graphic accompanying a question on a geometry professor's midterm exam.

The School of International Public Affairs (commonly called SIPA) consisted of two white slabs conjoined in the middle. But the buildings were anything but twins, as one was predominantly horizontal yet tipped up at one end, while the other was vertical yet set upon a glass-enclosed lobby. The architect considered it his favorite of all the buildings at the university, and was thrilled that it looked quirky and dynamic from whatever angle he photographed it.

He scooted down to the museum but was disheartened to learn it had just closed for the day. He had hoped to lose his cares and nerves amid the contemporary Cuban art the museum was exhibiting. He opted instead to wander through the sculpture park immediately outside the museum's main entrance.

Few of the sculptures grabbed his gut. Some were lighthearted (like the curvilinear and rusted rods one could meander under and through); some were geometric (like the notched cube of steel that balanced precariously on one corner). Still others, especially the works of Arnie Zimmerman, introduced new ways of looking at such familiar icons as a twister, a crane, and a clown. Lee found them all mildly entertaining, but none really captivated his soul.

And then he came across a simple bronze piece standing beside one of the exterior glass walls that offered a view into the museum's ground floor. Its name was River Waters it had recently been donated to the museum by the Afro-Cuban artist, Manuel Mendive. It was nowhere near as fanciful or ponderous as some of the other sculptures in the park; it consisted of an androgynous figure, seemingly constricted by its garb, its mouth contorted into an almost perfectly executed circle. Resting on its head was a fish, whose eye was as spherical as its carrier's lips.

For some reason, Lee was mesmerized.

On one level, the sculpture looked as if it were shocked by something it spied beyond the architect. But from another angle, it seemed to be marveling at some magic in the distance.

Was this person in torment, Lee wondered, or had it achieved some elusive bliss? The fact one could reach *either* conclusion from the artwork seemed to be what most spoke to him.

And then the sculpture spoke to him.

"It has nothing to do with torment, Dalton. It has nothing whatsoever to do with bliss."

The voice was cool and neutral, like a soft rushing wind. "My name says it all," it continued. "*River Waters*. What you see when you look at me, Dalton, is the embodiment of flow. What you see is the *exact opposite* of control. What you see is the flowing *with* something, rather than the fighting against it. Of trusting the waters to transport you onward rather than battling them to be someplace you're not meant to go. What you see is not at all tranquility, for a river is sometimes a torrent. And what you see is not at all anguish, for the waters often replenish us. It's just movement, Dalton. To a new place. With no guarantee of your final destination, but with trust you'll land somewhere safe and dry.

"You look at me, Dalton, and you see what you seek. You look at me and see what you miss. And have yearned for. For some time now. Ever since . . ."

"You're *right*. You're *absolutely right*," Lee interrupted. He began to bounce his right leg up and down excitedly, slap his palm on the side of his thigh. "To move on. Forward. Or sideways, even. But to flow, not struggle. Yes, you are *so, so* right. That's what I have been needing. What I so desperately *crave*, actually."

Lee noticed a couple of passersby glance at him, then avert their eyes.

He heard more.

"Don't misunderstand me, Dalton," the sculpture continued. "Flowing doesn't mean one avoids all pain. You can easily scrape your knee on a boulder. Take too much fluid into your lungs. But that's all a part of moving along. It's neither right nor wrong, it just is."

Suddenly the voice seemed to lower in timbre, took on a tone that sounded more grave.

"At the same time, Dalton, do not mistake my words. A river is sometimes a raging monster. It can easily become an instrument of harm."

"I see," the architect said, now eyeing the artwork uneasily. "I will most definitely remember that. Thank you for all you've said to me. Thank you for helping me to see things more clearly."

Another passerby slowed and gazed at Lee with curiosity. He was balding but dapper and was wearing a blue short-sleeve dress shirt with charcoal-gray slacks. The older man came almost to a stop, turned toward Lee, and watched the architect intently to see if he might be in need of assistance. Lee looked up and confronted the man's stare, but when the depth of his vision intersected with the man's concern, it was as if a film that had enveloped his brain his whole life had suddenly evaporated into the ether.

Lee smiled at the man, nodded once, swiveled away and headed off toward the lot he had parked the scooter in.

As he trudged back across the campus in the late-afternoon heat, the architect lowered his head and scrutinized the sidewalk.

Softly, he muttered, "Dalton, I'm beginning to think inanimate objects don't talk to everyone the way they've always talked to you."

39

Bree was going through all of the motions of needlepoint, but her heart just wasn't in it today.

Lara, on the other hand, was a whirling windmill of needles and yarn. She also seemed unusually conversational, Bree thought, as if all of the data and observations the older woman had quietly accumulated over the past several days suddenly needed to see the light of day.

"Well, I am pleased, Bree, that you are at least willing to admit that you fudge now and then in our card games," she said with a sardonic tone. "It takes maturity to own up to one's . . ." The firm's second-in-command paused as she pulled the needle dramatically up and through the embroidery hoop on her lap. "Imperfections," she concluded when the thread was at the top of its path.

She went silent for just a handful of seconds before resuming her recount of the investigation.

"I do think several of our suspects could benefit from some of that introspection. Take Astrid Steinberg, for example. She certainly plays the role of the sophisticated, righteous queen, doesn't she, but my instincts and some of my research tell me she has lowered her standards, and broken the law, far more often than she's willing to admit, even to herself. And, I'm not convinced that attorney who's never more than a few inches from her elbow is the most law-abiding individual, either.

"Then you have all those people who are living and working in that viper's nest of a household in Coral Gables. No matter what the evidence says, I'm not sure we can completely exonerate the assistant, who's shown herself to be anything but forthright, or even the housekeeper that Roberto has been in touch with. If anyone loves to cloak herself in mystery and suspicion, it's certainly that woman, isn't it?"

Bree started to say something, but Lara was on a tear.

"Then you have the assistant coach who was released *and* the running back. Isn't it curious that in an age of global positioning systems and relentless posts on social media, neither one has been able to account for his whereabouts at the time Vic Valenzuela was murdered?" She set her jaw and made several short, rapid movements with her fingers and the thread.

"All of which brings us back to my original premise, Bree. Which is that I am gratified *someone* around here is displaying at least a modicum of integrity."

Internally, Bree laughed at Lara's remark, but decided she didn't have the heart today to parry with her co-worker. She was more in need of a confidant, an advisor . . . the role Carole would have gladly and automatically assumed, if only she weren't being held hostage.

"Lara, there's something I need to bring up with you. I could really use your counsel."

It was as if all the molecules within the older woman had suddenly rearranged themselves and screeched to an immediate stop. She set her needlework flat on her lap, set one hand on top of it and the other hand on top of that.

"Well, of course, my dear, I'm happy to help. What is it?'

Bree looked slightly past her colleague; she knew she needed to choose her words with care. "I'm . . . more than a little concerned about the relationship that's been developing between Liam and Irene," she said tentatively. She began to add more detail, but realized she didn't really have any other details to provide.

Lara frowned some. She worried the concerns she had expressed to

Dalton earlier might be coming true. "What do you mean . . . are they becoming romantically involved? Because I do know Dalton wouldn't be at all comfortable with that."

Bree merely shook her head. "No, it's not that. At least, I don't think it's that. It's more . . ." She struggled to land on the words that would describe the hunch that was roiling around in her gut. "I get the sense . . . that Liam is trying to . . . coerce Irene into doing something. I'm not sure what it is, but it seems to be something that . . ."

She was foundering again. Then, suddenly, she found her footing. "I think it's something you most definitely would not associate with integrity, Lara."

At that, the older woman furrowed her forehead. "Oh dear," she said softly. Then, "To be frank, I have had some similar concerns myself. But do you have any proof?"

Just then, the younger woman's phone vibrated on the hassock in front of her. She leaned forward, picked it up, and was startled to see it was, coincidentally, a text from Liam. She became even more startled when she read the message, which had obviously not been intended for her.

IRENE, COME TO MY ROOM AT 9 PM. BE PREPARED TO BE YOUR MOST CONVINCING. I KNOW YOU CAN DO THIS. IVE SET THINGS UP SO AT LEAST TWO OR THREE ARE EAGER TO MEET YOU. SEE YOU THEN.

Carefully, Bree handed her phone over to her associate.

"Does this qualify as proof?" she asked, as Lara turned the phone around to read the message on the screen.

***

In Room 522, the curtains were drawn taut, all lamps were off. The only light came from the shimmering glow that emanated from a large laptop propped open on Liam's desk. The Australian sat sideways in his chair, rapped on a few keys, watched the images in front of him change, glanced at the time indicated in the lower-right hand of the screen.

Eight fifty-five.

She should be here any moment, he thought. *Finally, this adventure can begin.*

He hoped Irene would be aggressive enough to be believable. He worried she might get cold feet, or just come across too lethargic to captivate the interest of those at the other end of the webcam. They could be demanding, that group. Instantly skeptical if the conversation didn't go the way they thought it should, if the person they were talking to seemed too cool or contrived.

He asked himself if *he* would be persuaded to believe Irene if he were the one listening to her come-ons.

I'll just have to wait and see, he said to himself, tapping a few more keys on the keyboard. *I've given her every acting instruction I can possibly think of.*

He heard a rap on his door. The computer expert sat up straight, brought the screen of the laptop forward some to deflect the glow it sent out, and hopped up from his chair.

Irene stood at the threshold of his room, a zip-front suit bag slung over one shoulder. "Hey," she said, looking at him only briefly. "Let's get this show on the road before I change my mind."

He stood back as she darted into his room. "Wow, it's really dark in here, does it have to be so dark?" she asked.

He closed the door, chuckled, and crossed his arms upon his chest. "Yeah, it helps them focus on you, on your face," he said. "Besides, we don't want any details of the room giving away where we are."

She headed for the laptop and raised its screen some to give the room a little more light.

"My hearing's bad enough as it is," she told him. "I don't need to be blind as well." She pulled up—couldn't believe she had allowed *that* secret to slip out so easily. She dropped the suit bag on the bed and whirled around to him.

"You have the money, right? Tell me you *do* have the money?"

Liam nodded and strode over to the nightstand located on the side of the bed opposite from the desk. Slowly he opened it and extracted from it a large manila envelope, which he gingerly unclasped. Then he reached into it and slid out several bills that were tightly secured by a thick rubber band.

"Yes, I have the money," he said quietly. "But, of course, you're only going to get paid *after* your performance. Regardless of how successful you are, but only *after* your performance. That was our agreement, right?"

Irene studied the sheaf of bills he held upright. *Not enough to pay off my medical bills*, she thought. *But it's a decent start.*

She nodded at Liam. "Right. That was our agreement. Okay so time for me to change. Give me a few."

She grabbed the suit bag by one of the hangers poking out of it and strode toward the bathroom.

"Don't take forever," he said to her over his shoulder. "We don't have a lot of time before your first customer comes online."

***

Bree had to do some quick research. It had been more than a few years since she had jimmied her way into a locked room with a credit card. Or, for that matter, with a tension wrench set. She'd considered finding a locksmith online to mill a bump key for her. But she decided she didn't really have the time to wait for that. Liam's errant text message had said nine that night. And hiring the sort of locksmith who would agree to provide her with a bump key would completely negate the ethical reputation she had apparently built with Lara.

Not that that really mattered all that much to her.

Bree guessed their hotel had been built within the past fifteen years, so the credit card trick might not work. However, she took pride in the fact that, over time, she had mastered the art of using credit cards, gift cards—even parking garage tickets—to skulk her way into a variety of rooms whenever the situation demanded it. This, she had concluded, was one of those situations.

For some reason, even though a decade or so divided them, Bree felt a sisterly responsibility toward Irene. Maybe it was because of what had happened to the young associate at the end of their case in Manhattan. Or maybe it was because of the young woman's failing health. (Even though Irene had never confided in the rest of the team that her hearing was diminishing, it was obvious to everyone, especially to Bree.)

Or maybe it was because Irene reminded Bree of herself when she was in her twenties. Passionate and unusually bright. Riddled with a guilt she had never needed to assume. Lacking a strong, supportive ballast in her life.

Until Carole had come along, that is. Now, Bree understood that she and Irene shared the sense of powerlessness that comes from knowing someone important to you is rotting somewhere in an isolated prison and there's not a damn thing you can do to free them. Except, perhaps, nab a member of The Organization and hope you can coerce them to reveal your loved one's location.

Sitting on the end of her bed, Bree tried to decide how she wanted to approach Liam's room. She elected to go there without shoes, only cotton socks. As she figured it, if she encountered someone who found her activities suspicious, she'd come up on the spot with an excuse for her attire. *After all*, she thought, *it wouldn't be the first time someone has spotted me not wearing any shoes outside someone's hotel room.*

***

Liam drummed his fingers nervously on the desktop. There were only three or four minutes left until the first person was scheduled to come online and Irene was still banging the drawers in his bathroom and turning on the faucet. Although he at first had been supremely confident this was going to work, and would be beneficial both to him and to Irene, his assurance had started to wane shortly after he had placed the first ad.

That's just yer mum's negativity kicking you in the butt, mate, he told himself as he monitored the screen for the arrival of someone on the other end.

There were only two minutes left until show time, although it was likely, given the circumstances, that at least a couple of those who were scheduled to talk with Irene would be late for their appointments. *And they might not even show at all*, he reminded himself.

He heard the door open behind him. He swiveled around in his chair to see what all the ruckus in the bathroom had led to. Standing before him, looking more tart than a bowl full of limes, was Irene—or (as she had announced she wanted to be referred to that night) *Jade.*

The Australian slowly pushed himself up from the chair and took a few steps toward her, eyeing her up and down like an art collector inspecting a painting.

"Wow, you look . . . incredible, Irene," he finally said, a trace of huskiness in his voice. "You absolutely look the part."

***

Bree padded stealthily down the hallway, trying to appear as nonchalant as possible. In the event someone exited one of the adjacent rooms, she neither wanted to come off too furtive nor too prominent. Nervously, she fingered the edges of the credit card tucked tight in her right hand, manipulated it first one way than the other like an amulet being used to summon good luck.

As she arrived at Liam's door, she took in a deep breath. She glanced lightly over one shoulder then leaned toward the door to hear whatever she could. But knowing security cameras were probably recording her every move, she pretended to rap on the door as her head rested against it, stopping her knuckles just before they made any impact. She could hear muffled voices, almost certainly Liam's and Irene's. But their conversation wasn't intelligible and their tone seem measured and calm.

She leaned forward again, pretended to rap on the door again. Took a brief glimpse at her watch—it was eight minutes after nine. *You can't postpone this any longer,* she prodded herself. *You owe it to Irene to at least let her know you care.*

Deftly, she turned the credit card around in her hand and positioned it so she could slide it between the doorframe and the locking mechanism. Tilting downward the end of the card that was closest to her, she wiggled it some so it was perpendicular to the door. Then, she firmly drew the card toward her while tugging at the door handle.

Nothing budged. Bree bit her lip, committed to trying once again.

This time, she leaned closer to the door, maneuvered the card into the slot again, angled it downward—when suddenly the door swung open several inches to reveal Liam's frustrated face.

"Bree, what the hell do you think you're doing?" he whispered angrily.

"What . . . I . . . what?" she stammered.

Liam shook his head, creaked the door open a few more inches and slid his muscular frame through the narrow gap he had created.

"I said, what are you doing out here? Why are you trying to break into my room?"

Bree was flummoxed. She had no escape route to maneuver toward that made any sense whatsoever. So, she decided to stand her ground and reply with scorn.

"*How* did you know I was out here? Were you spying on me through some camera you had set up? What are you up to, Liam? What are you doing in there with Irene? Never mind, I know *precisely* what you are doing in there. Let me in, Liam, *right now*, or I will go straight to Dalton with this." She had managed to keep her harangue to a whisper . . . but only barely.

"Bree, it isn't at all what you think it is," Liam whispered back even more fervently. "Really it isn't. But you have to . . ."

"I don't care, buster!" Bree erupted, raising her voice from a whisper to a whine. "Let me in there now, or I'll call the police!" Somewhere at the other end of the hall, a door discreetly but noticeably opened, stayed open for a few seconds, then shut.

Liam had his fingertips up near his pursed lips in an effort to get Bree to shush.

"Okay, okay, you can come in," he said, "but you absolutely *have* to promise me something. You can't say a word. I mean it, Bree, not a word. You can come in, but don't say *anything* or you will completely destroy us."

Bree looked skeptically at her co-worker. *Okay, that sounded kind of weird*, she thought. But she eventually relented, since it seemed the only way for her to get access to Irene and possibly rescue her colleague from whatever ordeal she might be going through.

"Okay, let me in, now!" she responded, back in whisper mode once more.

Liam didn't move but instead put both of his palms up in front of his chest. And gave Bree a stern look.

"I mean it, Bree. Not. One. Word."

She set her lips in a tight line, then nodded briskly at him. His expression relaxed slightly and he turned the doorknob and reopened the door to his room.

Bree tensed when she saw how dark the interior was, but her fear lessened when she heard Irene speaking in what seemed to be a completely tranquil voice. But her spine stiffened again when she detected through the murk Irene's outfit—which comprised a skimpy pink top with spaghetti-thin straps lined with rows of silver sequins, and a skirt that could not possibly be more mini. Her hair, smushed down by a pair of oversized earphones, was coquettishly styled with oversized ponytails on either side of her head and ultrastraight bangs that covered her forehead. As Bree approached, she also noticed that Irene was wearing lipstick even more neon than the rest of her ensemble.

She shot an angry look at Liam, who quickly placed his index finger to his lips and nodded for them to move closer to Irene.

"So, how did you, like, feel about that?" the young associate said to whoever was on the other side of the screen. "It probably made you feel really lonely, didn't it?"

An almost childlike voice replied. "Yes. I felt really lonely. And scared."

Bree was confused. The voice she had just heard sounded like a girl's voice. A teenager, or someone only slightly older than that.

"Yeah, I totally get that," Irene said earnestly. "So, listen, after I made the decision to leave the house I was in, I was depressed for at least a month. Maybe two. The house starts to feel like your home after a while and the other girls feel like your sisters or best friends. It's really hard to leave all of that, especially when you know you don't have anything like that to go to. I totally get that, Jasmine."

Irene adjusted one of her straps and leaned forward toward the screen. "But the depression goes away pretty quickly, girl. *It does.* Once you get out of there and you get a real job and you start earning, like, you know, a *real* paycheck, trust me, all the sadness goes away. Well, most of it does, anyway. You start feeling a lot better about yourself and the next thing you know, other people start treating you better. You have to believe me when I say that. You do believe me, don't you, Jasmine?"

Bree couldn't make out what the other girl said, but whatever it was, it made Irene smile. And nod. The senior architect turned and squinted hard at Liam. She couldn't quite make sense of it all. But it also didn't seem anywhere near as sleazy as what she had envisioned. Liam smiled beatifically, took Bree by the wrist and gently guided her toward the bathroom, taking hold of her shoulders to steer her just outside of the webcam's range.

Once they were beyond the bathroom door, Bree crossed her arms in front of her. "So, what is this all about, Liam?" she demanded.

Her colleague sheepishly studied the tile on the floor for a moment.

"Bree, ever since my sister was abducted by The Organization, I've been trying to continue a cause that was close to her heart," he replied. "When Caryn wasn't giving tennis lessons to Australia's elite, she was working to rescue girls caught up in the sex trade across Asia. One of her clients had a niece in the Philippines who was abducted and enslaved while on vacation, so my sister took it upon herself to do whatever she could to help any of those girls who wanted to escape."

Bree nodded slowly, but then pointed back over her shoulder. "Okay, but what does Irene have to do with that?"

Her colleague put his hands on his hips and puffed out his chest some.

"Well, I got an idea, Bree. I'm actually pretty proud of it . . . now that it seems to be working, anyway. I figured if I found someone to pretend she was a former sex worker, and let them know there's a great life to be had on the other side, it could be a powerful incentive for some of them to leave the industry. Far more powerful than if either you or I tried to persuade them to leave. But I needed somebody believable. Somebody who could carry off the act of having been through what those girls are going through now, and convince them it really is a lot better on the other side.

"Then I thought of Irene. Asian background. About their age. Educated. I placed an ad in some of the online chat rooms and forums my sister told me those girls tend to frequent. Offered them the chance to speak to someone who had been in the trade but successfully escaped it."

He nodded toward the other room. "That's why she's dressed the way she is. So they'll be convinced Irene is the real deal. Even though she is really about as far from it as one can get." He laughed softly, quickly raised a fist to dampen the noise. "She's actually doing an *amazing* job, Bree. And the foundation is paying her for her time."

His co-worker shook her head, looked down for a moment, then smiled at him. "Well, aren't *you* the one, Mr. Wilding," she said with a grin. "I feel like such an idiot."

He sniffed. "No worries, Bree. You were just trying to do the right thing."

She shook her head and dropped her face into both hands. "Oh, you wouldn't believe the sordid things I thought were going on in here. The unimaginable things. I really should have trusted you more."

"Aw yeah, I can pretty well imagine," he replied. "Young girl. Older bloke. Late at night. I get it. Seems like you don't know me anywhere near as well as you thought you did, though, doesn't it?"

She looked up at him sheepishly. "Boy, you've got that right," she answered. "I hope you'll be able to find some way to forgive me. We're still teammates, after all."

Liam smiled back. "I know what you think. And I know why you think it. But, Bree it's important you understand that not all us blokes are beasts."

40

This time they convened in the gloom of night beneath an overpass formed by the Dolphin Expressway. To the casual eye, they were just a group of vagrants, huddling together to get high on crack. Aiisha chose to wear a thick sock cap, despite the fact it was early summer. Grant substituted a purple wife-beater for his purple windbreaker, but Rodney decided the striped serape he had worn before fit this occasion just fine. Dimah, Tomás, and Ramón dressed more discreetly this time, clad themselves in black and gray.

They had no need for small talk at this confab; they were assembled to throttle the plot into high gear.

"So I believe we all agree that the trial run went quite well," Aiisha said, pretending to take a hit off of a short, clear crack pipe in case some nosy bystander was tempted to get closer. She passed the pipe over to Tomás as the group murmured their accord.

"I wouldn't say at all that it went quite well," Grant spat out, causing the group to pull up for a moment. Everyone stared at him as if they truly were high on crack. He allowed his statement to float in the night air for several moments before adding, "I'd say it went *exceptionally* well," an elfin smile teasing them behind his grizzled face. Everyone else relaxed and nodded in rhythm.

"What was the final casualty count—thirty-five, forty?" Aiisha asked rhetorically. "And the health and human services department still say they are at a loss as to what caused the deaths, or how so many people came to be so ill?"

Tomás leaned forward and chuckled lightly. "I must say, our using a mutated toxin rather than a more common one was a brilliant idea," he asserted. "Was that my idea? Why, I do believe it *was* my idea." Everyone smiled at their comrade's comic routine, but in the interest of staying low-key, no one laughed.

Aiisha sat up tall on the cracked pavement, placed her hands lightly on her thighs, looked directly at the person sitting opposite her. A small fire that had been set by someone legitimately homeless was flickering a couple hundred feet behind her, bestowing her with the aura of a Nubian goddess.

"The way you executed your assignment at the water treatment facility was truly beyond our expectations," she said, bathing each word with love and gratitude. "We are forever indebted to your service to the cause, and are very impressed with the skill you displayed."

Across the way, the individual merely nodded and replied, "Thank you."

They were silent then, contemplating what would come next, listening peripherally to the cars and trucks above them.

"So, now it is time for us to turn our attention to the pièce de résistance, if you will," Aiisha said. Her tone had taken on a more businesslike timbre. "This time, the toxin will be three times the intensity of Toxin 1.0."

Her words jolted the others, who all turned and looked at her with varying expressions of disbelief.

Dimah passed along the crack pipe without partaking in the charade, decided to be the one to speak up. "Is it . . . really necessary, my sister, to . . . ?"

Aiisha cut her off. "To increase the toxicity that much?" She was glaring at her colleague, but she quickly caught herself and transformed her grimace into a taut smile. "Yes. Most certainly, it is, my sister. The panic this will cause will be much more beneficial to our takeover than the many deaths we anticipate."

"And when you say 'many,' that would be . . . ?" It was Rodney speaking now, peeking at her warily over the top of his serape.

With infinite elegance and exquisite precision, Aiisha rotated her head in his direction.

"Tens of thousands," she replied matter-of-factly. "Given the location of the treatment facility where we intend to make this drop, possibly hundreds of thousands. It will probably take a bit longer this time for the carnage to manifest."

She paused, smoothed out with one palm the fabric of her slacks, then returned her gaze to the others that encircled her.

"But widespread carnage there most certainly will be."

A crash of shattering glass just a few feet behind Tomás caused the entire assembly to start. A motorist on the expressway had tossed an empty bottle of orange soda onto the pavement below. Dimah's right hand flew to her breast as she emitted a heavy gasp. But Aiisha remained placid and regal.

"My comrades, the next few days shall be trying on all of us, our spirit will be tested like never before. We likely will encounter far more than soda bottles being hurled at us. But under no circumstances are we to waver. For the days ahead will almost certainly initiate the deliverance we've waited so long for. The dawn throughout the world of a clear, true freedom, not the current form defiled by patriotism and God. The beauty of a day when each sister can design her own destiny without considering boundaries or rules. When each brother will share gladly all that he owns . . . particularly to those of us who have unleashed The Transformation. When everyone unlocks the shackles of capitalism and tastes the sweet joy that comes with liberation.

"As it is written in *Wayward Colony*, may it be now and forever more."

"Power to the cause," the group intoned in unison.

The faint breeze that had cooled them over the past hour had switched its direction. Gradually, smoke from the distant fire drifted into their circle. An acrid smell of burning rubber, or tar, started to permeate the air. Dimah was the first to cough, Rodney followed soon after.

Aiisha nodded once and surveyed her acolytes one last time. "I view that as a signal, my comrades, that it is time for us to move, both literally and figuratively."

A proud grin erupted across her face, and she looked across the circle once more at the person she had complimented earlier. "Are you ready?" she asked, quietly and sweetly.

The person across from her coughed once lightly, nodded back fervently.

"I am not just *ready* to do this, Aiisha," came the reply. "As I was when I murdered Vic Valenzuela, I am *absolutely thrilled* to do this."

41

Sunlight streamed through the windows of Dalton Lee's suite. In the distance, an azure sea twinkled in the sunlight, beckoning one to splash and cavort.

But the architect was pacing back and forth past the window, barely aware of the postcard-quality view it offered. He wasn't gloomy, upset, angry, or despondent. But he *was* irritated.

He could feel the gears of The Organization turning, infinitesimally but inexorably nonetheless. Yet he wasn't clear at all in what direction they were moving, or just how much damage their rotation would cause. And, there wasn't much time left for the team to leap onto the mechanism and stop it from advancing, before . . .

Come on, Dalton, he scolded himself. *You can do this. You HAVE to do this. Otherwise . . .*

Briskly, he ran through the scraps of evidence that had emerged throughout the investigation. The speck of mud, saturated with solvents, found in Valenzuela's bedroom. The dagger tossed carelessly only a couple of miles from his home. The smooth footprint embedded in the garden soil directly beneath his window. The swiftness with which the killer had done the deed.

Then he concentrated on the rogue's gallery of individuals who remained on their list of most likely suspects. Why had Astrid Steinberg sent payments to the defense team well after Valenzuela had been acquitted? Where was Danielo Duran going late at night when he wasn't buying antacids for his wife? And why could neither Valenzuela's ex-assistant, Hayden Haas, nor his running back, Jamal Culberson, offer a solid alibi for where they had been when the coach was being murdered?

He knew the killer could be any of them, or none of them. Or maybe someone who was flitting along the circumference of their circle.

He wasn't sure of anything. Except that if his theory about the Valenzuela mansion proved correct, several of them could be eliminated from consideration.

That reminded Lee—he wanted to call Agent Sainclair to smooth over what had occurred at the racetrack.

"Dalton, *bonjou!*" the agent exclaimed upon answering Lee's call. "I was just about to phone you. There has been a development that my friends in Paris would describe as being, *très intéressant.*"

"*Ah, oui?*" Lee replied, quickly shaking his head at how corny he had just sounded. "I mean, Really? That's awesome." He shook his head again, he wasn't sure that had come off any better.

Sainclair chuckled for some time. Then, when he had recovered, he said, "Yes, Dalton. It is, as you just said, 'awesome.'"

Lee winced at the thinly veiled jab, but took some pleasure in noting Mackeson seemed to have emerged from his funk.

"We have finally been able to review the surveillance footage from the hotel where Hayden Haas was attending the coaching clinic," Sainclair continued.

"Ah!" the architect replied. For the first time that morning, he lifted his head and absorbed the beachside grandeur outside his window. "Let me guess—it shows him leaving the hotel in West Palm early enough to drive to Coral Gables and commit the murder?" A slight smile appeared on Lee's lips—both the news and the view outside his room had brightened his mood.

"*Non,*" Sainclair responded. Lee slumped, until the agent added, "Much better."

Lee waited, but his friend remained quiet.

"You're teasing me, aren't you Mackeson? Because of what happened at Hialeah a few days ago, right?"

"What? Oh no, *ami mwen*, I am over that. I won big last night! Almost as much as I lost with you! *Tout al byen*, Dalton, *tout al byen.*"

"Oh, I'm very glad to hear that, Mackeson. Very glad. I know how despondent you were that Acumen won that day. Just curious, what was the name of the horse that brought you this windfall?"

"Um . . . Any Moment Now. Yes, that was it. Any Moment Now. And he came from four lengths back in the home stretch!"

"That's wonderful, Mackeson. My congratulations." The architect waited. But his friend said nothing more.

"So . . . you were saying . . . about Hayden Haas?" he prompted.

"Ah, *wi!* Actually, it's not what the cameras at the hotel *show* that should intrigue us, but what they *do not show.*"

"Tell me more." Lee plucked a piece of candy from a small ceramic bowl nearby and tried to quietly unwrap the cellophane as he cradled his cell phone between his ear and shoulder.

"Well, apparently the dinner the golfers went to that night was at a Hawaiian-style restaurant about a mile from the hotel. A couple of people say they are sure Mr. Haas rode to the restaurant with them in a cab at around six fifteen. But no one can remember him riding back to the hotel with them after the dinner broke up, which was around eight thirty. And most important of all, the surveillance cameras never show Mr. Haas reentering the hotel that night. Not through the main entrance or through any of the side entrances he could have opened with his room key."

"That *is* interesting," Lee said. "I guess it's possible, isn't it, that he walked back to the hotel from the restaurant, went straight to his car in the parking lot, and left from there, with plenty of time to get to Coral Gables before the murder took place. Is the lot monitored at all?"

"A bit, but not very well. You can see the cars close to the building, but the cameras do not show you who enters or exits the lot. And you cannot see any of the cars that are parked far away from the hotel entrance. The exits from the lot used to be staffed, but they stopped doing that when they enacted some cost-cutting measures a couple of years ago."

"Mmm." Lee was sucking on the cinnamon-flavored candy now and he had to quickly constrict his throat to keep from accidentally swallowing it whole. "Well, Haas had to return to the hotel at some point, didn't he? The coaching clinic hadn't ended, had it? Do the cameras showing him returning to the hotel, say, in the middle of the night, after the murder took place? Or early the next morning?"

"No," Sainclair again replied abruptly. "The clinic had arranged for what they call a scramble golf tournament the next morning. The classes did not resume until that afternoon. Haas apparently showed up outside the hotel the next morning to wait with everyone for the shuttle bus that took everyone to the country club for the golf match, but between the time they all left for dinner the night before, to the time the shuttle showed up the next morning, he is not seen reentering the hotel. Not at all."

Lee pushed the candy far to one side of his mouth so his speech would be as intelligible as possible. "So, feasibly, he could have left the hotel around nine the night of the murder, driven to Coral Gables, murdered Valenzuela, gone to his home, changed into some golf attire, and driven back to West Palm to join the others the following morning."

"Yes. Either that, or maybe he had his clothes and golf clubs in his car, and he stopped somewhere between Miami and West Palm to change. Agent Weiss is looking into that, but Mr. Haas hasn't turned up yet on any other hotel or rest stop camera."

Lee decided to keep his responses brief because the candy was turning harsh and he wanted take it out and toss it into the trash without Sainclair noticing.

"I see," he said, striding over to a small trash can next to the television set. But as he encountered the can, his foot slammed into it, sending it crashing into the credenza the television set rested upon.

"What was that?" Agent Sainclair said. "Are you experiencing a thunderstorm there, Dalton?"

"Oh, no, it's nothing, just, um . . . never mind," the architect stammered after he had replaced the bin to its upright position and returned the phone to the control of his right hand. "So, Mackeson, would you say that another visit to Hayden Haas is in order soon?"

"Yes," the detective replied more authoritatively than usual. "I most certainly would."

***

Everyone was eager to hear the news that had prompted Lee to summon the team to his suite. Lara arrived uncharacteristically late, and far more dressed up, than she had to any previous session. Her taupe blouse matched her slacks, and the thin silver belt around her waist coordinated with her pumps and earrings.

"That's certainly a fetching outfit, Lara," Liam had said upon entering the room. "I certainly hope you have plans with someone special later today."

"No, not really," she said, her expression turning slightly downcast. Lee noticed her mood shift, and made a mental note to follow through with the invitation he had meant to extend to her a day or two earlier. Quickly enough, however, she perked up. "Actually, it's just that I wanted to look more professional given the news we've just received. It appears we've won not just one but two of the projects we had proposals out on." She turned toward Dalton and quietly said, "Milan and Macau."

The architect beamed and began to clap his hands when he saw Lara furrow his brow at him. He stopped the clap one third of the way in and, chastened, slowly lowered both arms to his sides.

"Well, it's a lovely outfit, regardless," Liam said nodding at his superior. "You look smashing." She smiled warmly and mouthed "thank you" to the Australian as Lee got the meeting underway. Quickly, he related to the team what he had learned from Agent Sainclair over the previous hour.

When Lee was finished, Warren replied, "Well, that's sounds pretty convincing to me. Do you want us to abandon our investigation into the Durans and Astrid Steinberg?"

Lee shook his head. "No, not at all, Warren. Anything but that. In fact, if I remember correctly, we were thinking about sending out a reconnaissance team to follow Mr. Duran on one of his late-night perambulations, weren't we?"

"Yes, we were," his senior architect replied. "Tonight is the same

300

night of the week that the murder took place so . . ."

"Well, then, tonight should be as good as any night, wouldn't you say? I also believe I heard there's going to be a full moon."

"Great," Warren answered. "I'm in."

"And, I'd like Liam and Roberto to go with you," Lee intoned.

Roberto cleared his throat. "Only if it's after about six, Dalton, remember? I've got, um . . ."

Dalton suddenly nodded strongly. "Right, you have one of your meetings with Isabela this afternoon, don't you?"

Roberto nodded. "But so long as it's in the evening, I'm good."

"I want to go," Bree chimed in. She turned and stared at Liam, who was looking askance at her from across the room.

"I won't interfere, I promise," she said.

Lara turned toward Liam, gave him a long sly wink, and said, "Uh-oh."

***

As the team was filing out the door, Lee called out to Lara to hang back for a moment.

"I suppose you'd like a few more details about what the clients in Macau and Milan said about our proposals," she barreled ahead, adjusting the collar on her blouse as she spoke. "Basically, both of them agreed to all of our terms, except for the client in Macau who . . ."

"Actually, Lara, it isn't business I want to discuss."

That made his *aide de camp* look up with an expression that straddled surprise and concern.

"I . . . I was wondering whether . . ." Suddenly, Lee felt his face quiver into a nervous tic of some sort.

"Yes, Dalton?" Lara took a step forward, her expression now registering more concern than surprise.

"I was wondering if . . . perhaps . . ." There was the tic again. It was subtle. A quiver for sure, not a convulsion. But still.

"Dinner," he finally blurted out. "I was wondering if you would . . . consider joining me for dinner, tomorrow night perhaps, my treat of course, for we really need to catch up because we haven't really talked much away from the investigation for several weeks now at least, now have we?" The last several phrases came hurtling out like dice tossed onto a craps table by a Las Vegas gambler in the middle of a hot streak.

Lara raised both eyebrows, pulled her head back a couple of inches. "Dinner? Why, I'd be delighted. No, we haven't really . . . done that for quite some time. Yes, I'd love . . . I mean, yes, let's do that. What time?"

Lee confirmed he'd meet her at her door, at seven. He'd of course handle the reservations. "Wear whatever you'd like, but I feel like dining somewhere especially nice. To celebrate . . . the new work."

***

After Lara had departed, Lee deftly locked the door behind her, then padded to the bedroom at the back end of his suite. Methodically, he opened the bottom dresser drawer and pushed through the random wad of dirty clothes he had tossed in there merely as camouflage (for he was much too tidy a person to actually wad up his worn clothes and store them in the drawer like that). In the back left corner, wrapped in what appeared to be a grimy undershirt, was the purple sandalwood puzzle box he kept close to him at all times.

No one could decipher why he insisted on bringing the box with him wherever he traveled. Even Lara, who could be romantic about such things, considered it a risky decision on his part.

"That's such a beautiful box, Dalton, I'd think you'd be worried sick about taking it with you to airports and hotels, where you could so easily forget or misplace it," she once lectured him.

As it turned out, he didn't really care what she thought about his little quirk. He always tucked it carefully in a piece of carry-on luggage, so if the plane went down, so would the box. And there was just no way, whatsoever, he was ever going to just leave it behind somewhere.

Wasn't. Going. To. Happen.

Painstakingly, he slid the box's bottom panel to the right, then pushed out another panel on its side. Those moves enabled him to then slide the top of the box toward him along a parallel track of grooves.

When they were investigating the murders a year earlier in Manhattan, Lee had used the box to keep safe a mysterious flash drive someone had given him, a flash drive that he'd placed on a white felt cushion. However, the true treasure the box carried within at all times was actually tucked beneath that cushion, in a long-and-narrow hidden compartment.

Gently, he lifted the false bottom of the box and stared admiringly at the rose-gold ring that glistened beneath. His father had placed it on the hand of his mother almost fifty years ago as they spooned in an isolated corner of Hong Kong Park. The minute he had heard his parents had been taken hostage by The Organization, Lee had stampeded into their home in Southern California, marched into their bedroom, and headed straight for the jewelry cabinet in the corner of his mother's closet.

So long as I have this, he had told himself, *we will all stay together*.

Now, he wondered whether Lara would like it. He felt confident she would. After all, he had noticed she often wore pale rose as an accent color.

But she can be so finicky at times, he reminded himself.

After he had conducted his exhaustive examination of the ring, and determined it to be intact, he replaced it in the box and quickly put the false bottom and felt cushion back in place.

But as he went to close the top panel of the puzzle box, something black fell from the underside, a softly textured oval with tentacles pointing out from all sides.

A spider, he said to himself. *How on earth did a spider crawl into this box?* The architect waited for the insect to crawl from its new location atop one of his wrinkled t-shirts, but it didn't move a single muscle. So Lee squeezed the spider tight between his right thumb and index finger and held it up to take a closer look. The minute he got it to eye level, his face took on a cool, pale pallor.

"Ah, no, not a spider at all," he remarked out loud. "But it is definitely, without any doubt, some sort of . . . *bug*."

42

The hotel's management was suitably mortified that a listening device had been hidden inside a possession Lee held so dear.

A quick check of the hotel's maintenance records revealed that shortly after The Lee Group had arrived, a temp agency had sent two housekeepers to the hotel to substitute for regular staffers who had called in sick. The head of housekeeping remembered that she had never seen either temp before and that one was of Asian descent, which could explain how the device got planted into a Chinese puzzle box with such a complex locking mechanism.

"We are *terribly* sorry, Mr. Lee," said the hotel manager, a dapper but weary-looking man in his late forties whose accent hinted he was originally from Venezuela or Colombia. "We combed through all of the furniture and public areas of your suite in search of a device, but we never disturb the personal effects of a guest, for obvious reasons. I truly hope you will accept our deepest apologies and we want you to know that if you'd like, we are prepared to upgrade you to our Presidential Suite for the duration of your stay, compliments of the hotel, of course."

"That won't be necessary," Lee said, feeling weary himself. "I don't hold you responsible for this. I do ask that you be extremely careful, however, in who you allow into my room. After all . . ." Lee stopped, reminding himself the hotel only knew him to be a world-renowned architect, not someone trying to thwart a terrorist organization. "After all . . . there are a lot of architectural firms who would love to steal some our projects away from us."

"Of course, Mr. Lee. I assure you no one will be allowed to enter your room without our having performed a thorough background check on them."

Lee wasn't as disturbed by the fact The Organization had been listening to him (he had reached the point where he almost always assumed they were listening to him at least some of the time) as he was by the sense of violation their interloping created. Had they hidden it in a pair of socks that would have been one thing. But to place it in *that box* . . .

As he headed back to his room, he told himself he should be grateful they hadn't discovered the ring and absconded with it in the process. The architect decided to just shrug the whole thing off. Besides, he didn't have much time before Agent Sainclair would arrive to drive them to the interview Sainclair had hastily arranged with Hayden Haas.

I wonder what sort of mood Mackeson will be in this time, Lee asked himself as he inserted his key into the card reader.

∗∗∗

As it turned out, the federal agent was neither ebullient nor pouting. If anything he was comfortably resigned to two simple facts. One, he believed they were getting close to learning who had murdered Vic Valenzuela. And, two, the responsible party would somehow be revealed in short order.

"What makes you think that?" Lee asked his companion as they headed toward the suburban expanse of Kendall.

"These killers, Dalton, they cannot remain beneath a rock forever. It is not in their DNA. They will either boast about what they've done in a place where they feel protected . . . but are not. Or, someone else who knows what they have done will decide they can profit far more by turning their friends in than by keeping their confidence." The agent

305

thrust the toothpick in his mouth far to one side, turned to Lee and punched him in the arm.

"I'm getting ready to speak Haitian, Dalton, so stay with me. Don't get all nervous, now. I will translate it for you after." Both men chuckled heartily.

"Okay, Mackeson, go ahead. What's your proverb of the day?"

The agent's smile expanded. He removed his right hand from the steering wheel and dangled it in the air so he could appropriately punctuate every word.

"*Dan . . . konn . . . mode . . . lang,*" he said slowly. He hesitated for a couple of seconds and raised one eyebrow to see if Lee was ready for what it meant in English.

"Meaning . . . ?" Lee replied, raising one eyebrow in return.

"It means, 'People who work together sometimes hurt each other.'"

The architect smiled along with his friend. But privately, he couldn't help but wonder if the adage applied to The Lee Group as well.

When the pair arrived at the home of Hayden Haas, it was the coach's daughter who answered the door.

"Oh, it's you, come on in," she said almost inaudibly as she toyed with her hair and tried to balance on the toe of her right ballet shoe.

Lee noticed this time how pronounced the girl's clavicles were; she reminded him of one of those horses that reporters find malnourished on some remote farm. He had always heard of, but could never understand, dancers starving themselves to stay thin. The poor girl in front of him, he thought, must be just such a dancer.

"Who is it, Heather? Ah, the investigators." It was Lupita, in full housekeeper attire this time, the handle of a duster tucked precariously under her left arm. She had bounded around the corner with an inquisitive look on her face; upon encountering the duo, her look changed from interested to intense. She paid special attention to Lee, stared at him disapprovingly for the attention he showed to the coach's daughter.

"I think I heard your phone chiming in your room," she said brusquely to Haas's daughter. "It's probably your dance instructor with the new schedule. They're probably going to make you practice twice a day, rather than every day. Go on. I'll take care of these gentlemen."

The girl ducked her head away from Sainclair and Lee, and glided off toward the back of the house, offering the slightest of skips every third step or so. Lupita continued to stare at Lee for a couple of moments before deciding his intentions were honorable.

"Mr. Haas just got back from the doctor's office. He hasn't been feeling very well since your last visit. Problems with . . . his back." The housekeeper uttered the words as if their previous visit was what had brought on his malady. Slowly she looked the two of them down and up, then nodded toward the upstairs portion of the house. "I insisted he take an Epsom salt bath the minute he came in. I think he's drying off now. You can go on into his office. I'll tell him you've arrived."

Without waiting for any question or reply, she swiveled around and tromped off in the direction from which she had appeared, the handle of the duster now clenched firmly in one fist.

"No, I do not wish for anything to drink, but thank you for asking," Sainclair whispered as he raised his eyebrows in Lee's direction. The architect smiled knowingly at Mackeson, but mostly because he recalled how stiff and stern the agent himself had been when they had first met one another.

The droopy foliage in the coach's office seemed to support the maid's story. Either Hayden Haas had been waylaid in his efforts to tend to his plants or he had suddenly lost all enthusiasm for doing so. Lee nudged Agent Sainclair in the arm and tilted his head in the direction of one of the room's far corners. The early tendrils of a spider web danced spritely, thanks to air from a nearby vent.

"For someone so demanding, she's not very thorough, is she?" Lee said, looking away from the agent, as if doing so somehow softened the critique.

Just then, a thinner and stiffer Hayden Haas crept into the room. His face was pulled tight, his stride was tentative. At one point, Agent Sainclair rose from his chair to assist Haas, but the coach quickly extended one arm and said, "No, I'm okay. The pain medication is kicking in. I may be slow right now, but I'm actually quite happy."

Lee scrutinized the coach and thought, *You're either putting on one hell of an act or you're one miserable excuse for a murderer.*

The coach informed them his stop beside his desk represented the end of his journey; it was much more comfortable for him to stand than sit.

"We have a few more questions about your activities on the night Vic Valenzuela was killed," Sinclair began.

The coach's face sagged, but he said, "That's fine. I can't believe you think I did it, but, fine, go ahead, fire away."

Sinclair paused, studied the man intently. "No accusations are being made, Mr. Haas. We're just accumulating information." The coach's expression made it clear he was unmoved by the agent's plea of innocence.

"You went to dinner with several of the other coaches the night of the murder, correct?"

The coach looked up at the ceiling then back down at the pair.

"Yes, that's right. Some Polynesian place. Worst mai tai I've ever had."

The agent took a breath in, then plowed ahead. "But the surveillance cameras at the hotel do not show you coming back into the hotel that night. Can you explain?"

The coach looked like someone who had just been scolded by a person they definitely viewed as an inferior. Slowly he rolled his eyes and sighed.

"Sure. I didn't like the room I was in. It was next to the elevator. Looked out over the air conditioning ducts. Plus, I was already starting to have some back issues then, and the mattress offered about as much support as a hammock. I knew the place was fully booked, so I decided to drive back down here and sleep in my own bed. Simple as that. Then I got up around five and drove back up there to accompany the coaches playing in the tournament."

"Can your housekeeper corroborate that?"

"Um . . . no. I gave her a couple of days off since I wasn't going to be here."

"What about your daughter?"

The coach sighed. "No. She told me that since Lupita was going to be gone, she decided to go stay with one of her friends that night."

Sinclair nodded, looked at his notes. "So, let me understand this. You were having some back issues that night . . . but you *walked* from the restaurant back to the hotel?"

The coach squinted. "No. What makes you think that? No, I hung back at the restaurant because I ran into a college friend I hadn't seen in several years and I wanted to catch up with him. After we were done, I took a cab back to the hotel by myself and had the driver let me out, just outside the entrance to the lot."

"How long did you stay at the restaurant getting reacquainted with your friend?"

The coach winced a bit. It appeared the drugs weren't kicking in as thoroughly as he thought. "Probably fifteen minutes. Maybe twenty. Look can we cut this short? I think I'm beginning to tense up pretty badly again."

Sainclair looked over at Lee and flipped his notebook closed. "But of course," he replied, hardly concealing his exasperation.

Haas stared at the detective and a wisp of a sneer crossed his face. "I already told you, didn't I, that there isn't really anyone out there who can prove I didn't kill Vic," he said with irritation. Haltingly, he began to head toward the door, but then slammed on the brakes. Carefully, he turned to his guests and weakly added, "But I didn't kill him."

"But you *did* stalk him, did you not?" Sainclair announced. "You followed him around the country. Spied on him and his girlfriend. Bombarded him with emails asking for your job back. Correct?"

Haas stopped in his tracks, shot the agent a look that mixed irritation with disdain.

"Yes, I did all of that," he replied in a soft but committed tone. "And you would have, too, under the circumstances. My life was falling apart thanks to one of his unpredictable moods. I figured if he could spontaneously have me fired, then he could just as spontaneously get me rehired. I just wanted to plead my case with him. But I could never get him alone long enough to listen. Now, if you'll excuse me."

"Coach Haas?" It was Lee, who had stood as the coach was crossing in front of him. "You've lost a little weight since we saw you a few days ago. Have you been ill, other than the back issue, I mean?"

The coach shot Lee a look of irony. "No. One of the great benefits of back pain is meaningful weight loss, apparently. I've probably lost seven or eight pounds since the last time you saw me. And that's on top of the fifteen to twenty pounds I've lost on purpose over the past several weeks. Who knows, if I keep this up, I might just fit back into my college football uniform."

"Well I hope you get feeling better," the architect said with a smile.

The coach looked over his shoulder at Lee as he hobbled toward the doorway leading into the front of the house.

"You and me both, brother," the coach replied. "I wouldn't wish this shit on anybody."

43

Roberto was perplexed. The location they had texted him for his rendezvous with Isabela appeared to be a demolition site. And not one that would have materialized overnight, which—given he had received their summons more than a day earlier—might have explained the mix-up.

He stood in the torrid sun and squinted at the screen on his phone. He was just a couple blocks from the North Shore Medical Center in a section of Pinewood where all the street names comprised numbers. But he was on Northwest Ninety-Seventh, and that was most definitely what his phone was telling him was the place he needed to be. And the address in front of him was most definitely a pile of rubble, topped by a big yellow loader.

Roberto peered one way, then the other, felt perspiration pooling under both arms and along the nape of his neck.

Puñeta! he thought, his shoulders slumping. *They made a mistake!*

It was a good thing he had padded his trip by thirty minutes, he told himself. That hadn't been easy to do, given he was required to take two buses and walk five blocks in the summer heat to get here. *Man, the carbon footprints people leave here driving all their big SUVs on all the multilane freeways is really obscene,* he thought.

As if his complaining had just manifested it, he heard a mammoth black SUV cruising slowly down the street toward him. Like a moment in some predictable gangster film, the car stopped alongside him and its front passenger window lowered dramatically. The driver, however, was anything but predictable—she was, instead, one of the most gorgeous women Roberto had ever seen, a Hispanic female in her early thirties with lush dark-brown hair, extended eyelashes, flawless makeup, and gold-colored hoop earrings. She leaned toward the passenger window and Roberto jumped at the voluptuousness of her breasts, which appeared to be doing their best to clamber out the top of her tight white dress.

She was not like the thick-thighed putas who walked the streets of Little Havana, nor was she like the nouveau riche princesses here who chewed gum and wore sunglasses that somehow were more garish than their homes.

This woman has class, he said to himself. *She's smart. Probably went to college. Maybe even has an MBA. She looks like that cocktail waitress in a high-end resort who actually owns the resort. She's hot, and she knows it. But she also knows she doesn't really need to use it.*

She flashed a trace of a grin and nodded at him. "Hello, Roberto," she said in a deep, alluring voice. "Get in, please."

Roberto winced, looked at the SUV, scratched the back of his head. "I . . . uh . . . usually take public transportation," he said sheepishly. "You know, the global warming thing and all."

She continued to smile but he now detected a trace of steeliness behind it. "I understand," she said, as seductively as someone can utter that short generic phrase. "But you need to get in, Roberto."

He let a shallow sigh escape before he took a couple of steps and opened the front passenger door.

She widened her smile some. "Back seat," she barked commandingly.

He heard the locks disengage and dutifully climbed into the ultracool chamber and onto the black leather seat accented with charcoal gray stitching around the edges. The door shut harder than he had intended for it to, but she just smiled at him in the rearview mirror.

Her body took his breath away. She was definitely over thirty, but

312

her form was as taut as a snare drum. She radiated a fragrance that hinted at patchouli layered with jasmine; her nail polish made the ends of her fingers look like iridescent pearls. She both monitored and mesmerized him through the rearview glass, glancing at him frequently and sliding her tongue occasionally across her upper lip.

"We'll be there in a few minutes, Roberto," she said. "The bottled water there in the seat pocket is for you. It's terribly hot today. Drink as much of it as you'd like. You want to stay properly hydrated on a day like this."

Automatically, he reached for the water and quickly uncapped it. Took one moderate swig, stopped, then took another much longer guzzle. After he recapped the bottle, he pushed himself back against the soft coolness of the leather upholstery and fantasized just how spectacular it would be to fuck her.

He allowed his eyelashes to flutter some and envisioned her disrobing above him to reveal a perfectly tan torso topped by globular tits that pulsed toward him whenever she moved. He pretended there was a discreet trail of light-brown hair that led from her navel to her snatch and that her thighs were athletic and smooth.

His eyelashes fluttered again, and she was bending over to kiss him and then mount him, the patchouli wafting into his awareness like curls of smoke taunting and tantalizing him. His breathing slowed considerably and at the very moment in his dream when she was reaching to slide him deep inside her, his eyelashes fluttered once more, and he felt the scene diffuse into a warm, amber pool of nothingness.

***

When he awoke, he was blinded by the color of coral. Although the room was almost as large as a one-bedroom suite, the ceiling and all four walls screamed dark pink. Even the makeshift desk he was sitting at—it was nothing more than a plywood counter, really—was painted the shade of the inside of a rabbit's ear.

The monitor through which he would converse with Isabela was embedded into the top of the desk, which concerned him because it meant he'd have to look down a lot. He hoped he wouldn't fall back asleep, but he found himself surprisingly lucid for someone who had obviously been drugged.

"Drink as much of it as you'd like," she had said to him. And fool that he always was for a woman with long legs, he had not only complied with her suggestion, he hadn't even questioned it.

There were no windows in this room whatsoever and the ceiling was unusually low—definitely well under eight feet. Between the low ceiling and the prevalence of pink, Roberto found a mild case of vertigo coming on.

Pull yourself together, 'Berto. This is show time, he reminded himself. He didn't want to appear too deep in contemplation, for he feared that might make them suspicious of what he was up to, but he searched his memory anyway for the geographic and architectural details he had to somehow extract from Isabela. The specifics that would eliminate a possible site or two and pinpoint for him exactly where they were holding her. He pretended to be studying a stapler at the edge of the desk—oddly, the *only* office accessory in the room. But he was repeating like a mantra the phrase he knew he needed to start the conversation.

"Think very hard before we play this game, Isabela," he would say. "*Veo, Veo* is fun only when you ask me to find something that's really unusual."

A voice jolted him out of his reverie with the stapler.

"Are you ready to proceed, Mr. Bermudez?"

He was disappointed it was not the voice of his sexy chauffeur. He wasn't even sure the voice belonged to a human, for it had a sharp metallic quality, like a robot speaking through an old tin can.

He nodded and (*thankfully,* he thought) the lights dimmed to dark, erasing all vestiges of pink. The monitor in the desktop glowed some, displayed crackles of static.

Roberto felt his stomach flip-flopping inside his rib cage now, but from nerves rather than nausea.

The static seemed endless, making the monitor seem like an old television console with bad reception. Then, in a flash, the screen went to black. The instruction, *Say Your Password* appeared on the screen."

"I am a Wayward Colonist," he intoned, more quickly than usual. *Let's get this little game over with, can we?*

The monitor flickered a few more times, and then an image of Isabela appeared, only THIS WAS NOT THE WAY IT WAS SUPPOSED TO PLAY OUT!

His little sister was bound to a simple wooden chair, a coarse chunk of dull-white fabric served as her gag. The ropes that constricted her movements looked frayed and bloody in places; her hair was tangled and wild.

But what Roberto noticed most was the look in her eyes, a manifestation of spectacular terror that made his adorable sister look absolutely feral.

It was obvious she could not see him, for her head first yanked left, then right, and her vision never connected with whatever camera was recording her.

"What the hell!" he bellowed, leaping from his chair. "Let her . . ."

"SIT DOWN, MR. BERMUDEZ! SIT DOWN IMMEDIATELY!"

It was the robot voice again, but with the undercurrent of anger, it now sounded not just metallic, but grating. He froze in midair—on one hand, refusing to submit to this tyranny, on the other conceding he had no leverage in this fight. Delicately, he lowered himself back into the seat.

"Did you actually think we were too stupid to see through your game, Mr. Bermudez?"

The voice had slowly assumed a more human timbre but remained raspy and raw. "Do you not comprehend the severity of your actions?" it continued. "We do not appreciate being taken for fools. We do not find your escapade amusing."

He nodded, not in agreement but in a valiant effort to quell his fury. "Yes, I'm sorry, very, very sorry," he stuttered, but he knew his contrition had not been convincing.

"So are we," the voice shot back. "Just so you know, we have moved your little sister to a new location. It's far more isolated and much less . . . comfortable than where she was before." A long silence ensued . . . and then the disembodied voice returned, this time bearing a more sardonic tone.

"I will give you this much credit, Roberto, your geographic guesses were close to the mark."

The taunt in the voice was more than Roberto could tolerate. "What in the hell are you going to do with her?" the designer demanded.

The room remained silent for many seconds before he received his answer. "We will leave her the way you see her for the next few weeks. Then, at the proper time, we're going to renege on our promise and start the process of indoctrination, to help her see the shining light she can bring to our cause.

"Now, it is time for you to leave, Mr. Bermudez," the voice continued, fading away as it spoke. "However, we won't be driving you back to your hotel.

"We assume you understand why you'll now be walking instead."

44

The stakeout position they would be taking that night was going to be a precarious one—sitting just around the corner from Danielo Duran's house in a 1970s-era van with a fatigue-green body and a white roof.

"No, this won't look suspicious *at all*," Bree said when Agent Weiss led them to it in the agency's back lot.

"Trust me, in Mr. Duran's neighborhood, it will fit right in," the agent said, slapping it on one side like a thoroughbred being prepped for a race. "Just don't try to drive it over forty miles an hour."

"Why not?" Bree asked, suspicion welling up inside of her.

Agent Weiss stared at Bree for a moment, chewed the inside of one cheek. "Never mind," she finally answered. "Forget I even said that."

Liam crossed his arms in front of him and leaned in toward the vehicle. "I knew a bloke who lived in the outback for two years in a van that was in a lot worse shape than this one," he said.

Bree pivoted toward Roberto and raised both of her eyebrows. "I know it compromises your commitment to 'going green' and all, but you *are* coming with us tonight, right?"

Roberto nodded, sullen as could be. "I have to. Dalton made me promise I'd keep my eyes on you."

Bree pulled back, assumed a highly offended look.

"I meant, *keep a watch over you,*" he said quickly. "That's . . . what I meant."

Warren leaned back against the side of the van. "And you?" he tossed out to Agent Weiss. "You coming along?"

She winced as if she had just stepped on a sharp rock. "I . . . really shouldn't. I've got a lot of paperwork to process."

Sensing an opportunity that ought to be seized, Bree shot out, "Oh come on, Hannah. It'll be fun. You can be in charge of watching the speedometer. It will be just like a double date."

At that, the men all coughed and scattered in opposite directions to check the pressures of the van's tires and the soundness of its engine.

***

Irene sat on the floor of her hotel room, stared at the blank monitor in front of her, and contemplated how to say what she wanted to say. What she *needed* to say.

It wasn't going to be easy.

How long had they known each other? she asked herself. She tried to tick off the years in her head and was bothered that she could not remember for sure. *Eighteen years? Nineteen?* She was sure they had already met before they had started attending primary school. She recalled some birthday party. He was turning four, maybe five. *Insane* amount of decorations. A great saeng cream cake. He, of course, completely ignored her, focused entirely on the other boys at the party. She was bored by the girls there, wanted instead to run and push and fall to the ground along with him and his male playmates.

But at the end of the celebration, he had walked over to her and thanked her for the gift she had brought him (a calligraphy set). And then he had hugged her. *That* she remembered vividly. Granted, it was a polite hug. A brotherly hug.

But still . . .

She sighed heavily, repositioned the screen to eliminate the glare caused by the late-afternoon sunlight coming in through the window, and tapped in the passcode that would connect her to the network he usually accessed. She was still amazed at how naïve The Organization was when it came to filters and firewalls. How could these jerks have succeeded in taking hostage so many people, how could they have gotten away with the atrocities they had, and yet be so cavalier toward their technology's security?

Then it struck her. An idea she had never considered.

Maybe they're not naïve after all, she said to herself. *Maybe they're allowing him to contact me, and are monitoring our conversations the whole time.*

She almost logged off, but just as her finger was poised above the key that would sever the link, there he was.

I dont know where I am but its hot as hell here, he typed.

She sniffed. *Here too.* Then, she felt a pang of guilt. *But Im sure its hotter there,* she added quickly.

A short pause. Then he typed back, *Where r u now?*

Miami. Florida. They killed a football coach this time.

A much longer pause. She picked at some pieces of lint on the carpet.

Getting close 2 figuring out who did it?

She started to type something, pulled up. *What if they really were following the conversation?*

Then a chill coursed through her as a new, more insidious idea took over. *What if this isn't even him?* she wondered. *What if it is one of them, pretending to be him?*

Not sure. Maybe, she replied. *Too soon to say.*

She realized she had been so eager to respond to his initial comment about the heat, she had forgotten to ask one of their verification questions: *Hey, what kind of cake was it your mom served at your 4th birthday party?*

An even longer pause. Nothing.

Finally . . .

Seriously? How do u expect me 2 remember a cake from that long ago?

Her heart sank. *Oh God,* she thought. She noticed one palm was beginning to sweat. She picked at another piece of carpet lint. *What do I do now?* she asked herself.

Then, another message.

But I'll never forget that stupid calligraphy set u gave me.

Her shoulders relaxed and she inhaled a huge amount of air. *It was him, after all. It couldn't be anyone else.* She had been terrified to tell anyone about that calligraphy set. Like him, she had thought it was a really stupid birthday present for a boy.

For a couple of moments they bantered back and forth about popular culture. In truth, she did most of the bantering . . . about what songs were at the top of the charts, the fact that big mustaches were popular again, mustaches like the ones you saw on men in those early porno movies. Things like that. Every now and then, he would ask a question. About the indie films that were being released. About what was happening in Vancouver and Seattle. About politics.

Never anything about her.

When a lull finally arrived, she knew she needed to let him know what was up. She decided to dive right in.

Im going deaf. I will probably be completely deaf in a year. Maybe less.

She started to add that it was Type II Waardenburg Syndrome and there was really nothing they could do about it. But she hesitated. *Would that really matter to him? And what if they really are following every word I write?*

Letters appeared on the screen.

OMG, Irene. I am so sorry. Is it cuz of that time when we were 6 and I hit u on the side of ur head real hard?

First she snorted. *Loud.* Then she rolled her eyes. It was *so* like him to make it be about *him* somehow. She started to write, *No silly.*

But she stopped herself. Thought about all the years of guilt *she* had endured. All the times she had asked herself what might have happened if she had used *her* computer to hack into The Organization's servers rather than his. If *she* were the one they were holding hostage, not him.

So she wrote instead, *Yes. Doctors said they used ultrasound and could trace the start of my defness 2 the very moment u hit me. So that means u have to pay all of my medical bills.*

After several seconds, he wrote again. *OMG, Irene. I will. I am so sorry.*

She laughed to herself. He was such a dweeb sometimes. For

someone so book smart, he could be so unbelievably gullible.

She wondered if he'd grasp that she was being dead serious when she told him that for her own well-being, she was probably going to have to break off these conversations.

45

"A town car? Really, Dalton? Just for the two of us to go have drinks and dinner? Did you run this past your CFO?"

The head of The Lee Group turned to Lara and sent her the coyest of smiles. "If the CFO wants to decline the expenditure," he replied, "the CFO can walk to the restaurant and explain to the maître d' why the CFO has sweat rings under her arms."

At that, the firm's business manager leaned her head back and guffawed mightily. Lee raised his eyebrows; Lara was simply not the sort of person who guffawed.

"Oh, Dalton, didn't you know? We Finns don't sweat," she said, the back of one hand pressed up against her lips. "Finland's climate doesn't cause us to sweat very often, so our sweat glands are highly underdeveloped as a result."

That caused Lee to chuckle once, then look down at the floorboard. *It seems to be going well so far*, he told himself.

The car was cruising north out of Brickell, where the pair had enjoyed predinner cocktails, toward their dinner destination—a seafood restaurant alongside the river, to the northwest. The city seemed unusually serene, almost how one might envision it to be if a hurricane were lurking just offshore.

I hope it isn't the calm before some other type of storm, he thought. And yet, he feared it likely was.

"What's going on in your mind, Dalton?"

Lara startled Lee with her question. He looked at her, mouth slightly open. He thought he had kept his intentions in check, had concealed his plans inside a cabinet of cool.

Lara shifted her attention out the window, to the office buildings that were whizzing past. "Oh, I know you said tonight wasn't supposed to be about business, but I can tell that the case is weighing heavily on your mind. That you have some sort of theory brewing . . ."

She paused and pushed her face closer to the window to study the angle of one office building in particular. Then, she leaned back into the seat again and continued. "My father used to get the same look on his face, go into the same mood, when he was struggling to come up with just the right solution for some client project."

Lee glanced at her, narrowed his look at her some. "Your mother never got that look?" he asked quietly.

Lara sniffed once, her face took on a nostalgic glow. "My mother had only two looks I can recall," she said, suddenly sounding very clinical. "The warm, maternal look she always gave me. And the look of muted suffering she always gave my father. Every time he walked in the door and every time he walked out the door."

Dalton turned away and breathed out discreetly. *So she isn't on to me, after all*, he thought. *But now I wonder if this was such a good idea.*

"Well, yes, there is something I am sort of working on," he finally replied. "Something about the Valenzuela mansion, and the work being done there. I think it could be . . . well, all I will say for now is that I think it could be relevant."

Lara nodded quietly for some time.

"Are we getting closer to a resolution?" she suddenly asked, a tinge of a tremor in her voice. "Because I really feel *they* may very well be." She looked at him intently and he met both her gaze and her ardor.

"I think so," he said. "I hope so. And . . . I agree. About them, that is."

The underside of the car suddenly made a grinding sound and Lee instantly recognized it as a cue that they were crossing the Brickell

Avenue Bridge. He waited until the vehicle rolled up alongside the Tequesta Family sculpture before angling his head to peer at the warrior wife who had given him such an ominous warning soon after their arrival.

However, the woman holding the child did not speak to him this time; she merely glared at him with a look of frustration, as if to say, "You have everything you need. There is nothing more I can give you."

At the Gusman Center, the car banked gently to the left onto Flagler. They cruised past the Miami Dade County Courthouse and History Miami, approached Interstate 95 like a smooth stealth bomber.

"You know, I didn't ask you what *you* think," Lee suddenly said to Lara. "I didn't ask if *you* have a theory. Either as to who did it, or to what The Organization might be up to."

Lara just sighed and looked at her lap. Smoothed her skirt, then looked out the window. They were on North River Drive now, just a few minutes from the restaurant. "The art gallery owner—what's her name . . . Stein . . .?"

"Steinberg. Astrid."

"Yes. Maybe it's just feminine intuition, but I become suspicious of anyone who projects an image of serenity when you first meet them, but becomes belligerent when confronted with information that seems unflattering. Or, worse yet, incriminating."

"That pretty much describes everyone we've encountered here, doesn't it?" Lee replied. "They've all seemed more than a little . . . ornery . . . wouldn't you say?"

She looked away, her expression took on a soft frown. He couldn't tell for sure now if she was miffed at him, or just contemplative.

Gingerly, he moved his hand over to her arm. "I trust your intuition," he said as he squeezed her wrist. "Implicitly."

After Lee had moved his hand back to his lap, after the car had slid past the pioneer-era buildings of Lummus Park and the Egyptian architecture of the Scottish Rite Temple, Lara turned and cast a brief but fervid look at her superior.

***

"I think I will start with the octopus," Lara said, continuing to canvass the menu, "and then I will move to . . ." Her eyes flitted up and down several times. "The lobster risotto, please."

The short, block-shaped male who was their server took the menu from her with a nod and pivoted toward Dalton Lee. The architect had one finger pressed against the menu and dragged it downward and across as if the entrees had been printed in Braille.

"Let's begin . . . with the roasted beets salad and then follow that up with the sea scallops," he blurted out all at once.

"Yes, sir, and someone will come by shortly with bread for you," the server replied.

Lara tilted her head to the right and admired how the shadows cast from the nearby torches made Lee look both more mature, and more boyish. It truly was at times like this that he shone. Their table, just a few feet from the water, had an impeccable view of the city skyline. And he had thoughtfully brought a light shawl for her in case the air grew chilly by the time they reached their desserts, although given the time of year, that was unlikely. She took another, more bountiful sip of the Puligny-Montrachet, felt it lap warmly through her.

"That certainly didn't take you much time," she said, her voice growing huskier from the wine.

He cast a quick smile, but it faded just as abruptly as it had arrived. "That was probably the only decision I've made in the past six months I haven't agonized over," he answered. She noticed he was fidgeting with the napkin in his lap, repositioning and reconfiguring it as if some chief of protocol was about to descend on their table and issue them a score for their etiquette. She wasn't sure whether she should be charmed, or alarmed, by his unease.

She leaned toward him. "Are you all right, Dalton?" she said at a volume just above a whisper. "You seem rather . . . uncomfortable."

He gave her a look like the one a schoolboy would give a girl if she told him she had spotted him peeing behind the shrubbery.

"All right? Sure . . . yes, I'm . . . well, I'm . . ." Suddenly, he exhaled and dropped his shoulders. "Oh, who am I kidding? No, Lara, I'm nervous as can be. I was planning to do this while we were having our desserts, but I may as well do it now."

The architect reached into the inside pocket of his blazer, pulled out a square black box, and set it carefully on the table a few inches in front of him.

"As I said before, I trust your intuition more than anyone else's. But really it's much more than that, Lara. You seem to always know the perfect thing to say at precisely the perfect time. I've come to realize that when I am struggling with something very personal, like the decline of my parents, I almost always wonder what you would do, how you would manage the situation. My appreciation for your thoughtfulness, your sense of style, has just intensified as the years have gone by. Which is why I thought now might be a good time, if I may, to ask you this."

Lee extended his hands and, with the flourish of a magician revealing an unexpected playing card, lifted the lid of the box and unveiled the ring.

Lara took a quick breath in and tensed inside. She kept her eyes affixed to Lee's, which seemed unusually cavalier under the circumstances.

"My dear Lara, this is the ring my father gave to my mother when he proposed to her more than forty years ago . . . and I was wondering . . . if maybe . . . you would take a close look at it and tell me if you think it's suitable for me to give to whomever I decide to propose to, should that day ever come."

Lara's napkin slid off her lap and onto the concrete below. She leaned heavily to one side and retrieved the napkin with two fingers, but her eyes never left those of the architect across the table. "I'm sorry . . . *what* did you say?"

"I mean, I think it's an awesome ring and all," he replied, "but I don't really know jewelry. I know buildings. I will *completely* trust your intuition on this, Lara. Your judgment is always so . . . sound. Should I propose to someone with this ring? Or do you think they would be offended?"

She bent over elegantly to inspect the diamonds, oblivious to the stranglehold she had on her napkin.

***

The vibration of her phone startled her. It was almost eleven, and Lara had been *that* close to slipping into her negligee and performing her nightly preparations for bed.

"Yes?" she said upon answering. She listened carefully. She at first was a bit irritated by the intrusion but as she listened to his pleas, her frown softened.

"Well . . . it is a bit late," she put forward.

More soft pleading on the other end. Lara clutched the top of her gown, wondered if she would relent. She had to admit, as frustrated as she had been earlier in the evening, she now was relaxed and . . . flattered.

"All right," she finally said softly. "Come on up."

She padded into the bathroom, primped her hair, and took quick steps to freshen her makeup . . . but not too much. Then she replaced her gown with a casual blouse and her most comfortable silk pajama bottoms.

Ten minutes later he knocked on her door. For some reason, she burst into a smile. She considered it a victory smile, although that was probably premature, she told herself.

"Well, I must say this is a bit of a surprise," she said after she let him in, closing the door quickly behind him. "Had you told me an hour ago this would be happening, I certainly wouldn't have believed it."

He strode in, bearing the expression of a chastened young boy. "Well, I don't know why you would say that, Lara," Liam said, scratching the back of his head. "I told you earlier I thought you looked smashing, didn't I?"

46

The conspirators were back in their GIANT HORIZON TEA office, but in a back room one needed an eight-digit code to access. The top of the cherrywood table they were seated around had been polished to a high gloss, but their attention was riveted to a simple round blip on a monitor mounted high on the wall in front of them.

They had been watching the screen for ten solid minutes in utter, profound silence. The silence that comes with anticipation tinged with apprehension. The silence that precedes what one suspects will be either an astounding success or a calamitous failure. The silence that precedes some grand yet unpredictable climax.

Will the quarter land on heads, or will the quarter land on tails? Will the dice show lucky seven, or will the dice deliver snake eyes?

The blip blinked several times, crept up the screen an inch or two, then moved right. A wide grin spread across Aiisha's face.

"The agent should be entering the water treatment facility any moment now," she murmured. "If the route from the rooftop to the tanks is what our schematics show it to be, the toxin should be dispersed into the water system within the next ten minutes or so."

The blip stayed motionless for several seconds, causing Aiisha to sit erect and lean forward with concern. But just as she was about to touch the keyboard in front of her, the blip began to move again, pulsing slightly as it did.

"The pulsing—that's our indication that the agent has entered through the roof, correct?" Grant asked.

"Yes, it is," was all Aiisha said.

It seemed to speed up and move in more random directions. Tomás and Rodney swiveled to look at the one who had commandeered the plot.

"No cause for alarm," Aiisha intoned. "That is to be expected given the location and configuration of the stairwells in that facility."

After a moment, the blip stopped. It remained stationary for several seconds. Knowing what this meant, every person around the table deeply breathed in, unconsciously pressed the palm of one hand against the smooth coolness of the cherrywood tabletop.

Everything hung in the balance now. Everything was about to be revealed.

Then, slowly but definitively, the blip turned deep forest green.

The toxin had been delivered. Very soon, The Transformation would be underway.

Like a flotilla of just-punctured balloons, the people assembled exhaled and relaxed. Someone slammed a palm to the tabletop. Dimah quietly uttered, "Power to the cause," which the others echoed in sequential order.

Still beaming, Aiisha raised one hand shoulder-high. "My comrades, although the toxin has been released, we should not be premature in our celebration," she announced. "We still have an agent who's on assignment in the field, who has yet to return to our fold. We should be sure our comrade is successful exiting the facility and makes it to our safe house in Wynwood."

The rustling subsided and everyone refocused their attention on the wall in front of them. The blip stealthily traveled to its original location, moved beyond that to a point near the building's perimeter. It then headed up the screen to a major thoroughfare and moved left.

Aiisha squinted, sat erect again. "Wait . . . our safe house is *east* of there," she exclaimed. "Why is the agent heading *west*?"

The others glanced at her, then back at the screen.

The blip sped up some, continued to travel in a westerly direction. At a prominent intersection, it turned south.

"No, that's not right!" Aiisha barked. "What are you doing?"

Three blocks later, the blip veered west yet again, then came to an abrupt stop next to what the generic map in front of them showed to be a small city park. It then appeared to enter the park and glide toward an oval-shaped pond located at its heart. There it slowed, remained motionless for a moment, then, once again, glowed forest green.

"Into a pond?" Grant barked, pivoting to look at Aiisha. "What the hell . . . ?"

But the blip was on the move once again, scooting in yet a different direction now, choosing yet another route that was taking it even farther away from the conspirators' safe house.

"Is there something wrong with the monitoring system?" Rodney asked. "Maybe it's just a technical malfunction."

Aiisha passionately tapped on the wireless keyboard, waited, watched the blip meander first one way, then another. At each body of water it seemed to encounter—at every pond, lake, pool, and canal—it halted, remained stationary for a few seconds, then glowed luminously green.

The woman charged with launching The Transformation rose slowly from her chair and raised her chin with disdain.

"No, we're not experiencing a technical malfunction," she said, a seething fury in her voice. "What we're experiencing, dear comrades, is an agent gone rogue."

47

Miserable.

Huddled in the van, they all had to agree that—thanks to the dense humidity and the fact they couldn't start the van and run the air conditioning until Duran left his house—they were miserable. All the windows were cracked a couple of inches. But in the back seat, Bree was furiously fanning herself with a paper napkin she had found on the floorboard. In front of her, Agent Weiss was pressing one cheek against the window for relief.

"I'm not . . . really clear . . . why I am doing this," she groaned. "I mean . . . even this window . . . is warm."

Liam had shown the forethought and courtesy to bring bottled water for everyone. The question was whether there would be enough to last.

"I'm ready to pour this entire bottle over my head," Warren said from behind the steering wheel.

Somewhere down the street, a door opened, and everyone in the van tensed in anticipation. But it was just some older woman letting her dachshund out to do its business.

"So, do I understand correctly that Dalton asked Lara on a date tonight?" Warren asked quietly.

"Say what?" Liam replied, suddenly sitting up straight.

"I don't think it was really *a date*," Bree said. "I think he just wanted to reward her for following up the way she has on all those client proposals we had out. She's helped bring in a lot of new business this quarter."

"That's not the impression he gave me," Warren said over his shoulder. "When I saw him earlier, he was more dandied up than I've seen him in years and he was pacing back and forth in his room like some cougar in a cage. He kept asking me whether it was still considered acceptable to pull out a lady's chair at a restaurant. I had to tell him yes *three times*."

Without moving a muscle, Agent Weiss said, "You know, your boss is sorta cute but he's also sorta weird."

"Hold up." Warren had his right hand in the air and his head cocked forward.

Around the corner, an aluminum door was a third of the way open. Moments later, Danielo Duran emerged into, and then through, the doorway, taking great care to softly shut the door behind him. He glanced over one shoulder, then sauntered toward and around the back of the dark SUV sitting in his driveway.

Liam glanced at his watch. "Ten fifty-five," he said. "Same time as before."

For several moments, the furniture store owner sat in the darkness of the front seat, his head tilted downward.

"Come on, let's get this show on the road, Señor Duran," Bree chimed from the back. "Momma and her friends here need some really cool air. *¡Ándale! ¡Arriba!*"

Roberto rolled his eyes and sighed. Wedged between Bree and Liam in the back seat, and still morose over his last episode with Isabela, Roberto looked like a petulant child in the middle of a long, cross-country trip.

"Jesus, Bree, you sound like Speedy Gonzalez," he said. "It's *¡apúrate! ¡corre!*, just so you know."

Bree gave her colleague a bored look. "Whatever," she replied. "I just want him to *move*."

"He might be reading a message from The Organization," Agent

Weiss suggested. "They may have summoned him somewhere. If that turns out to be the case, that would be really awesome for us."

Soon enough, Duran rolled the car out of the driveway and onto the street, only turning on his engine once he had headed the car in the direction he intended to go. He was half a block away before he flicked on the headlights.

"Now!" Liam said, punching the back of Warren's seat with one fist.

Keeping a safe distance, the team maneuvered the vintage van along a couple of side streets then sped up slightly once Duran pulled onto a busier thoroughfare. Only it wasn't really that busy, given it was almost eleven on a Tuesday night.

"I'll bet he's having an affair," Bree announced. "A quickie-type of affair maybe, but an affair nonetheless." With the air conditioning now chugging away, she had tossed aside the paper napkin and was acting lighthearted with Liam, reaching across Roberto to punch him in the arm.

"Anybody know where Dalton and Lara were having dinner?" the Australian asked no one in particular.

"Some seafood restaurant by the river," Roberto mumbled. "All I know is he picked it because it's supposed to be *muy romántico*."

About a mile up the road, Danielo Duran suddenly turned left from the middle lane. Warren quickly maneuvered the van to the left, but kept the blinker off so they'd be less conspicuous.

"Isn't that the convenience store where he was supposed to get the antacids for his wife?" Bree asked.

"Yup," Warren answered. "Now let's see if his wife really does have heartburn tonight." He waited for Duran to enter the shop before he backed the van into a space at the far end of the lot so they could easily watch the furniture store owner's movements.

"Exactly what do we think we're going to discover by following this guy?" Roberto seemed to have gone from morose to sour. "I mean we don't really think he's going to blindly lead us to some grand conclave of The Organization, do we?"

Agent Weiss took a swig from the bottled water that had been sitting in her lap and spun the cap some as she replaced it.

"Well, it's not entirely out of the question, Roberto," she said. "Don't forget, they haven't rolled out yet whatever it is they're plotting. We don't have a shred of evidence yet that he's part of The Organization, much less that he killed Vic Valenzuela. But we do know he was away from his house at the time of the murder. We know he doesn't have any alibi that proves he *didn't* kill Valenzuela. Maybe, for some reason, this is an especially convenient time for him to connect with The Organization. To do whatever it is they need him to do.

"It's a long shot. But who knows? Maybe we'll get lucky. Sometimes, that's precisely the thing that causes things to all work out. Crazy inexplicable luck, that is."

Just then, Duran strolled out between the automatic doors, a slice of pizza dangling toward his mouth.

"Pizza. Again," Warren said. "But no antacids. Or any other purchase as far as I can tell."

"You'd think *he* would be the one who needed antacids, eating pizza this late at night," Bree said. "And *convenience store pizza* at that." She wrapped her arms around herself and quivered from the shoulders down.

Their target climbed back behind his steering wheel and without looking once in their direction, backed his SUV out of its space.

"Now comes the interesting part," Warren said. "Will he head back home, or . . . ?"

They all watched through the pane of glass nearest them as Duran eased the vehicle toward one of the exits from the lot, waited for one car to pass, and turned . . . in the direction *opposite* the one he had come from.

"Bingo!" Liam yelled from the back seat.

For the next ten minutes, the two vehicles cruised calmly along the streets of Miami, first toward the Dolphin Expressway and then west along Northwest Seventh. After he continued west for several more minutes without turning, a small alarm went off inside Agent Weiss.

"Oh, my gosh," she said, suddenly sitting up straight and fumbling for her phone. "Is he headed for the airport?" Frantically, she punched a few buttons. "Selkirk, this is Weiss. We may have a suspect in the Valenzuela murder trying to flee the metro area. Stand by."

But as soon as she said that, Duran made a left turn *away* from the airport and into the neighborhood known as Flagami. Here the curbless streets were narrow—perhaps a car-and-a-half wide, and only skinny and scraggly grassy strips separated the street from the ribbon-thin sidewalks on either side.

"I'm afraid he might get suspicious if he sees us coming down the street behind him," Warren said, "so, I'm going to make a wild guess that he's close to his final destination and cut our engine for a minute."

Everyone wanted to complain, knowing they would soon be socked once again by the thick, muggy air.

But they remained quiet instead.

And waited. And watched.

At the next intersection, the vehicle slowly turned right, rolled slowly just beyond their point of vision around the corner. Then, they could see the glare of the brake lights indicating Duran had stopped the SUV.

"Crikey, you were right!" Liam whispered from the back seat. "Perfect timing, mate!"

"But now what do we do?" Bree said with a whine. "We can't see him from here. And if we open our doors, he'll probably hear us."

Warren drummed the steering wheel for several seconds. Then he leaned forward and craned his neck as far as he could in the direction Duran had gone. He followed that by leaning back and raising himself up in his seat.

"I have a plan," he suddenly announced. "But I need one of you to come with me."

Dead silence throughout the van. Warren pivoted his head one way, then behind him. Everyone merely stared back at the senior architect as if he had just informed them he had a highly contagious disease.

Irritated, he wheeled around toward the back seat. "Hey! Crocodile Dundee! Come on. Time for you to earn your keep."

With a roll of his eyes, Liam turned toward the door and waited for Warren to slide it open. Once the door was far enough back, he poked his head through the opening, made a slight hop toward the ground but tripped forward as he did. Upon landing, he crumpled to the pavement and grabbed his ankle.

"Aw, fuck me dead!" he whispered through gritted teeth, writhing to and fro beside Warren's shoes. "Shit!"

"Oh my god, Liam, are you okay?" Bree exclaimed from inside the van.

The Australian rolled one way then another, massaging and compressing his ankle as he did so.

Warren leaned down and put a hand on his colleague's shoulder. "Is this an act, because if it is, you don't have to go," he whispered.

Liam looked up and shook his head. "No act, mate. Hurts like shit." He took several quick breaths, pressed the ankle, and winced again. "It's not broken, I don't think, but it's pretty seriously sprained." Warren nodded and tapped lightly on the window Liam had been sitting next to. When Roberto's face appeared, the architect motioned for him to come out of the van.

"Help me get him back inside," he said quietly. It took a few minutes to get the Australian upright; even then, his left foot drooped at a sad, cattywampus angle. With each arm over the shoulder of his co-workers he hopped on his good foot as they nudged him toward the opening of the van and shoved him into the back seat.

Once Liam was comfortably inside, and Bree was ministering to his pain with aspirins from her pocketbook, Warren wiped his palms on his pants legs and looked at Roberto. "That leaves you," he said matter-of-factly. "Let's go."

Warren whirled around, but Roberto stood steadfast. "No," the designer said calmly. "I'm not doing it."

"What?"

Roberto looked down at the pavement, then directly and challengingly at his superior in the firm. "I said I'm not doing it, Warren. I'm not. I have to think of Isabela."

Warren let out a whiff of steam through his nostrils. "I understand, Roberto. But all of us have someone they're holding captive."

Roberto nodded softly at the comment, waited a few beats. Then he replied, "Maybe, but *my* someone is eleven years old and I'm pretty much all she has left in the world."

Warren's face contorted briefly. Then he shrugged his shoulders and nodded. "Okay, never mind."

As Roberto climbed back into the van, Warren assessed the

situation. He was going to need someone fairly tall and fairly strong to hoist him up onto a carport he had spotted in back of the home that was on this side of the one Danielo Duran had stopped at. A home with a For Sale sign in front of it, and not a spark of life inside.

His best option, Liam, was out for the count. Roberto was a no-go. Hannah was too short and fragile for the task.

That left just one person to do the job. He looked up and squinted into the window of the van.

As she gently massaged her co-worker's ankle, Bree felt a magnetic pull demanding her attention. She glanced out the window opposite her, where Warren was standing, hands on both hips, peering directly at her.

I wonder why Warren has such a tortured look on his face, she asked herself.

48

"All I can say is, thank God I wore flats tonight."

In an alleyway that stunk of food scraps rotting in some nearby trash can, Bree crept a few steps behind Warren. Both of them kept their bodies low to the ground, knowing home surveillance systems were probably on alert.

"Why do I think you wouldn't come up with these crazy schemes if you'd never had a career in Toronto as a cat burglar?" Bree hissed at her co-worker. "I'd better not end up the way Jayden did in Manhattan."

"Shhh!" Warren admonished. They had reached the back driveway of the house with the carport. From there, they could hear a small chorus of muffled voices speaking intermittently on the other side of the security fence that separated the house they were behind from the one Duran had stopped in front of.

Ever so slowly, the pair straightened up and pressed themselves against the towering fence beside them.

"I need to get on your shoulder," Warren whispered to Bree.

"You need to *what!*"

She was too loud. Warren placed a finger vertically against his lips. Whispered even more softly in reply.

"I need you to give me a boost so I can get up on that carport. I can see what's going on next door from there but that cypress tree will prevent them from seeing me."

Bree gave him a dubious look. "Are you crazy? I can't lift you. I can barely get my carry-on luggage into the overhead without four people coming to my rescue!"

"You don't have to *lift* me, Bree. You just have to *boost* me. C'mon. I thought you were a rough-and-tough cowgirl at heart, not some fragile Southern belle who takes to her fainting couch every time a little challenge comes her way."

Bree stiffened. To a woman raised in the Arizona high country, them were fightin' words. She thought about it for a second, then her jaw went rigid and she nodded vehemently at her co-worker. Spreading her legs several inches apart, she positioned herself with hands cupped a few feet above the ground; Warren put his left foot into the brace she had created and positioned his left hand on her shoulder. Then he looked back over his shoulder, grinned widely, and whispered, "Just imagine we're a couple of ranchers and you're boosting me over a barbed-wire fence so I can retrieve a couple of heifers Rusty McRustler stole from us a while back." Bree just grimaced and steadied herself against the soft soil next to the fence.

"Okay, on the count of three," he said looking down at her. "One ... two ..."

He propelled himself upward as Bree flung him with far more strength than he was expecting. He landed on the carport on his side, miraculously making only a subdued thud that was fortunately made even more obscure by the coincidental slam of a car door nearby.

Once he was certain he wasn't injured somehow, Warren raised himself to no more than a crouching position. Through the branches of the expansive cypress, he could detect about five people in the adjacent backyard. In the center of the expanse, flames flickered from a makeshift fire pit; scattered around the yard were several pieces of furniture. A Spanish style dresser over here, a bulky nightstand over there. A tall chifforobe in one corner; a massive dining room table in another.

So, maybe Duran's story was true after all, Warren thought. *Maybe he did come here just to inspect some shipments. But why is the furniture strewn all over the yard like that?*

The architect reached into his front left pocket and pulled out his collapsible binoculars. It was the pair he favored whenever he and the kids went bird watching in northern Ontario. Now he intended to use them to watch a different form of prey.

Peering through the lenses, he noticed that at the far left, the back of the fence stood open a few feet and a panel van was backed into the gap. The back doors of the van were open and a few smaller items remained inside the vehicle. He swung the binoculars to the right and instantly spotted Danielo Duran in an animated conversation with another, taller man Warren didn't recognize. In one hand, Duran was clutching what looked like a sheaf of small papers. It didn't sound like the men were arguing, but it did seem to Warren as though the furniture store owner was trying to make a point.

Warren swerved the lenses even farther to the right and zeroed in on three other men, who were dressed in neatly pressed jeans and designer t-shirts. One was definitely Hispanic, the others appeared to be Caucasian. They stood passively to the side but—given the short distance between them—came across like some sort of ensemble.

Why do those dudes look so familiar? Warren asked himself.

He fiddled with the focus of his binoculars, tried to find the setting that would let him see the threesome more clearly through the tree branches. They stood with their legs apart, hands clasped in front of them. Warren knew he recognized the trio from somewhere, he was *sure* of it. But not from a casual setting like this, that much he knew. And not in such casual clothing, either.

Then, it dawned on him.

That's it, he told himself. *Not t-shirts and jeans. Suits and ties.*

They seemed familiar to him because he had seen them every day on the news for almost a year—huddled together at a small courtroom table, heads often ducked in intense conversation.

Noah Weiner, Sidney Lanier, and Antonio Consuelas. The defense team of Vic Valenzuela. *And*, the men Astrid Steinberg had been dispensing significant sums to well after they had secured Valenzuela's freedom.

Why on earth are they here? Warren wondered.

Now, another person exited the back door of the house and joined the others in the small yard. The muscular young man in a tank top and jeans strolled up beside the defense team, nodded once at them, but said nothing. Warren adjusted his spyglass once again.

When the person came into focus, Warren's jaw went slack.

The new arrival was Jamal Culberson, the star running back for the Miami A&M Centurions. He lowered his binoculars to his chest and stared vacantly at the scene.

What the hell is going on? Warren asked himself.

Suddenly, the taller man who had been talking to Duran grunted, put one finger in the air, and charged off toward the chifforobe. Kneeling down by its side, the man rummaged behind it for several minutes as though he were trying to dislodge something that was permanently affixed to its backside. After a moment, he removed a panel, and thrust one arm deep into the crevice behind it. He was almost prone on the ground now, his legs pointed toward the others in the yard. Duran and the others ambled toward the man some, but generally kept their distance.

Eventually, his hand emerged with a fistful of clear plastic bags. Warren returned the binoculars to a position that would let him look through them, fiddled yet again with the focus. Duran extended the sheaf of papers toward the man, only Warren could now see that they weren't papers at all but bills of some sort. Some form of currency.

He gazed through the binoculars for another couple of seconds. Then, as if they had suddenly grown enormously heavy, he dropped them to his waist. He knew he didn't need to see any more.

He wasn't personally familiar, of course, with what he saw inside the bags. But he had no problem recognizing the substance.

Cocaine.

Warren bobbed his head in a slow, rhythmic motion. A lot of what he had just witnessed was beginning to bring a lot of other things into focus. He wasn't completely sure he knew what was going on, but he felt pretty certain that the seemingly random group of people assembled in that backyard over there wasn't so random after all.

Duran . . . Culberson . . . the three defense attorneys . . . whoever the guy was who owned that house . . . they were all in league with one another, bringing cocaine into the region and apparently using the furniture pieces Duran and his friend imported from south of the border as their "mules." And then distributing it—to who knows who and for who knows how long.

He nodded even more as other fragments of data they had accumulated during the investigation increasingly began to lock together. *No wonder Duran and Culberson couldn't say where they were when the murder was committed*, he told himself. *They were probably here that night, receiving and making a profit from the latest shipment. That would also explain the fifty thousand dollars Duran deposited just after Valenzuela's murder. It wasn't a payment for a hit on Valenzuela, but the money he had collected that night from the people who had come here to buy cocaine.*

He took a breath. *Slow down, bro'—it's all just a theory at this point*, he reminded himself. *And if even if you are right, that doesn't necessarily mean they're not connected to The Organization somehow, or that they didn't kill Valenzuela.*

But then he allowed his sensibility to once again take full rein of things. *This is the very same night of the week, and the very same hour of the night, as when the murder took place*, he reminded himself. *And the store video that night showed Duran heading in the same direction as he did tonight. So the chances of any of them being Valenzuela's killer are pretty slim.*

He broke himself from his reverie, swiftly took his phone out, and manipulated the keyboard to send a text to Hannah. STRAWBERRY MILKSHAKE it said—the code phrase she told him to use if he discovered anything that might require other agents to intervene.

Once he slid the phone back into his pocket, he gazed up at the full moon glowing majestic above him and chuckled softly to himself. As luck would have it, they had picked the perfect night to follow Danielo Duran on one of his late-night excursions. And wasn't "crazy, inexplicable luck" the phrase Hannah had used to describe how so many cases like this got solved?

Only, the case they were working on hadn't really been solved yet. It hadn't been solved *at all*.

He shook his head at the irony of it all. *Damn*, he muttered to himself. *This night would be an overwhelming success if I worked for the drug enforcement administration.*

"Pssst! What's going on up there? Can you see anything? Hurry up, would you? I have to go to the bathroom. *Real bad!*"

It was Bree, her knees squeezed together, her hands tucked between her legs, her head arched up toward him beseechingly. Warren carefully lowered himself to all fours, crawled to the edge of the carport, hung the top third of his torso over the edge and whispered, "Bree, there's a really big bush over there you can go pee behind. And you'd better be sure that's the one you use, 'cause when I tell you what I just saw up here, you're probably going to pee a whole lot more."

49

The first reports of people suffering life-threatening symptoms came in around eight the following morning. About forty people in the communities of Miami Springs and Brownsville were experiencing seizures and severe respiratory distress. Within two hours, seventeen of them had died at nearby hospitals. Nine others, too weak to get to any medical care, had collapsed and died in their homes.

The county's water department and Emergency Management Center issued a joint statement calling for calm and assuring residents that the algal blooms apparently responsible for the deaths had likely been caused by the unusually warm temperatures and still winds the city had been experiencing. And that standard water-filtration procedures should detoxify the blooms within a couple of hours. "But until then," the notice read, "citizens are advised not to drink any water from their tap."

However, by the time the media was starting to distribute that statement, another fifty individuals in Gladeview and Pinecrest were undergoing seizures and the paralysis of some, or all, of their motor functions.

Then the bottom dropped out and all hell broke loose.

More than ninety people in Merrick Park, Coral Terrace, and

Westchester called 911 in just over an hour to report a friend, family member, or co-worker who was experiencing some form of paralysis, respiratory failure or dysfunction of the central nervous system. In one case, a young couple (who themselves were experiencing severe gastrointestinal discomfort) dragged their semiparalyzed children ages six and four into the front yard and tried to flag down passing motorists to take them to a nearby medical center.

It turned out to be too late. For all of them.

Soon, reports of additional casualties were flooding in from Olympia Heights, Westwood Lakes, and University Park. It appeared the islands might be spared from the calamity, until the police department received word that more than one car traveling from Key Biscayne to Brickell on the Rickenbacker Causeway had inexplicably careened toward either a guardrail or oncoming traffic, resulting in collisions that had led to multiple fatalities.

Twenty minutes later, the very same thing took place on the causeways leading to and from Bal Harbour.

"And so it has begun," Lee announced to his team, who had come running to his suite within moments of his call. Lara and Warren, in particular, had assumed the crisis that was unfolding would cause Lee to grow glum. But it seemed instead to have jolted him into action, instilling in him an almost hyperkinetic sense of urgency.

"We have to move fast! We have to figure out who murdered Valenzuela, or at least find some wedge into The Organization, if it isn't too late!" he said almost breathless. "Warren, what has Agent Weiss told you about Duran and the others who were rounded up last night?"

"Well, it turns out my instincts were right," the senior architect answered. "Duran and his business partner have been smuggling cocaine into Florida for at least a couple of years by way of the furniture shipments they've been trucking in across Mexico and the Gulf States. A couple of the border agents were receiving payoffs to smooth the entry of the trucks. And, apparently, the Drug Enforcement Agency here is so consumed these days with stopping all the smuggling that's taking place by watercraft, the idea that someone would actually hide drugs in furniture shipments being trucked in from Mexico and Texas seemed much too quaint for them to actually take seriously.

"Anyway, Duran and his accomplice have confessed. Hard for them not to, given the evidence they were caught with. Jamal Culberson was there because he's been buying cocaine from them and selling it to his friends and teammates. And Valenzuela's defense attorneys have been quietly selling the cocaine to some of their more high-profile clients. It's very possible that's where Valenzuela got that stash of cocaine that was found in his bedroom, although we really don't have any proof of that."

Liam spoke up. "What about that dame who owns the art gallery? Valenzuela's sister-in-law. Maybe that's why she's continued to make those payments to Valenzuela's defense team, even after he beat the murder rap. I'll bet if you looked into it, you'd find she's one of their customers, too."

The logic of that idea rolled over the team like a tidal wave.

"Makes sense to me," Warren acknowledged.

On the far side of the room, Lara was frowning. "But, I'm a little confused," she said. "How does all of that tie in with The Organization? What does it have to do with why Valenzuela was murdered and what's going on out there right now?"

Warren sighed, shook his head. "To be honest, we can't see how it does," he replied. "At least, Hannah, Mackeson, and their team haven't been able to find any direct connection so far. There *could* be a connection. It's possible The Organization was funding its activities off of the cocaine sales rather than Valenzuela's gambling scheme, and that he got in their way somehow, or threatened to turn them in.

"But so far, they haven't been able to make that link. How Valenzuela's murder figures in with The Organization, and this terrorism plot . . . no one can tell."

"And yet we know it *has to* figure in with The Organization somehow," Bree offered, "because of the card they left on Valenzuela's body."

Lee was deep in thought. Suddenly, he snapped his fingers.

Well, at least he's stopped that infernal hand clapping, Lara thought.

He turned to Warren. "Did Agent Weiss find any footage of Hayden Haas at any of the rest stops between here and West Palm Beach?"

The senior architect shook his head. "No," he replied. "Every camera was working properly that morning and Hayden Haas doesn't appear on any of them. Sorry."

The team sat silent for some time. Even Lee seemed to calm down, although he kept tapping his right foot on the carpet like a telegraph operator sending out a message in Morse code. Eventually, the architect took a short breath in.

"Liam, you have a degree in marine biology, or something like that, correct?"

The Australian nodded and smiled. "Yeah, something like that," he replied.

"What do you know about these algal blooms? Do they normally cause so much harm to people?"

Liam looked past Lee for a moment to search his database on the topic. "Well, Dalton, I'm no expert on them, but I do know they don't form very often. And, yeah, they *can* be fatal to humans, but they usually aren't. And like the water department officials said, the filtration processes they typically use should kill the algae pretty quickly."

"But they haven't," Lee interjected.

"Right," Liam responded. "Which leads me to believe The Organization must have manipulated the chemistry of the algae somehow to make it so lethal. I remember reading about one algal bloom off the coast of South America a few years back that killed maybe fifty people. But I've never heard of one causing this many deaths. Ever."

Lee considered what Liam had just said, turned it around in his mind some. "I see," was all the architect said in response. He thought a bit more about Liam's explanation, then gave his employees a definitive nod.

"Well, I know all of you may think we've hit a complete dead end," he said, a slow smile crossing his lips. "But to be honest with you, I'm beginning to think quite the opposite."

***

The text message came in around two in the afternoon to the police substation in Grapeland Heights. The officer who opened the message wasn't sure if the crudeness of the grammar and the prevalence of typos were truly representative of the person who sent it, or merely an effort made to disguise an identity. After all, it wasn't like he had the title of detective or anything.

But once he read the message's contents, he was smart enough to immediately kick it up to his superiors at police headquarters:

THE TrANSFORMAtIoN IS HAPPeNInG. POwER to The CAUZE.
MORE DETHS ArE CoMInG. BUT SO ARe MoRE FREEdOMS
4 EVERYoNe
YOu CAnOT STOP THIS ReVoLUSHUN. IT Is DEStiNeD To BE.
WHeN We ASSuME CoNTrOL,
No LONgER WiLL THE TIRRANY oF FaCELESS CoRPOrASHUNS
RAIN.
NO LoNGeR WiLL ALeeT CITIzUNS MOnOpOLIsE
PrIVaTE WEalTH
EveryTHING WiLL Be FREE & EveryONE WiLL Be FreE
BuT The TOxIn Is SPrEADInG
& YOU CAnT SToP IT
& YOU CAnT STOp Me
HA HA

***

Federal agents were scrambling to link the message to the IP address associated with the phone it had been sent from, but it wasn't coming up in any of the agency's records.

"It could be a burner phone, or one from outside the country," Sainclair told Lee on a call. "We will keep looking. And we may have gotten a ping from whichever cell tower was closest when the message was sent. Agent Weiss is looking into that as we speak."

"How are *you* doing, Mackeson? This has to be extremely stressful for you."

There was a long pause on the other end. Lee imagined that his friend was taking his merry little time relocating a toothpick from one side of his mouth to the other before answering. But his instincts told him that probably wasn't the cause for the delay.

Finally, Sainclair cleared his throat and replied, "*Kon si, kon sa.* Okay, I suppose, for someone who will probably lose his job very soon."

Lee fumbled for what to say. He hated it when people delivered completely well-intended but false condolences at a time like this. He knew how the agency worked. He knew it wouldn't be well received if he told Mackeson something like, "Now, they're not going to let one little mishap like this override all your years of service."

Because both he and Mackeson knew they almost certainly *would* do precisely that.

So he instead took in a shallow breath and said, "If you need a reference, Mackeson, let me know. I will sing your praises to the rafters to anyone willing to hear them."

"*Merci, ami mwen,*" the agent responded quietly. "You are a good man. A very good man. I will call you later with what we know. *Orevwa!*"

Just as Agent Sainclair was signing off, a notification on Lee's phone was telling him that an urgent message had arrived. He opened it, sighed heavily as he read it.

THERE'S BEEN AN IMPORTANT DEVELOPMENT
WITH YOUR FATHER THAT WE NEED TO DISCUSS.
MUST MEET ASAP.
FOLLOW THE DIRECTIONS BELOW TO THE
LOCATION LISTED.
MEET ME THERE AROUND 10 TOMORROW MORNING?

Quickly he entered, "I'll be there." Pressed SEND.

That's when another notification arrived. Only this one had come from one of the many news sites he subscribed to.

"A federal emergency declaration has been issued for Miami-Dade County, Florida," it began. "More than 130 people there have died, and another 450 are in critical condition, due to a mysterious waterborne illness the origin of which has yet to be determined. Additional casualties are being reported every hour. A crew from the Centers for Disease Control is on its way to Miami to assess the situation but a spokeswoman for the agency says its laboratories have confirmed the deaths are due to some form of super algal bloom that has somehow infiltrated the city's water supply."

Lee read the notification one more time, studied every word.

So Liam's assessment had been correct, he told himself. *They did manipulate the algae somehow.*

Is there any possibility . . . he wondered.

***

"How did this get so out of whack? How could you let this happen? Have you gotten in contact with the agent? We can't allow an agent to operate unrestrained like this. It is entirely unacceptable, do you hear me?!"

On the other end of the phone, Aiisha inhaled deeply to calm herself before she responded to Grant. Except that she was not at all calm. Too many months—years, to be honest—had been invested in the planning of this initiative for it to gyrate out of control this way. There had been no indication whatsoever during the indoctrination or training that the agent would skitter off the agenda this way. Which reflected poorly on Aiisha, since it was *her* responsibility to detect such maverick behavior and rein it in long before it became a problem for The Transformation. Which it now was. *Big time.*

"I fully understand your concern, Grant," she said with all the equanimity she could muster. "I do. But we must approach this unexpected development in a strategic and measured way. No, I have not gotten a response from the agent. However, I do have a plan for addressing things."

That seemed to calm the older athlete down some. However, over the phone line, Aiisha could still hear his gears spinning.

"What type of plan?" he finally replied.

She licked her lips, placed one palm on the tabletop to steady herself some.

"Our agent is not yet aware of our unhappiness over this display of independence," she answered. "At the same time, now that we know this agent is . . . damaged . . . we most certainly need to cut our losses

350

and take this agent out of the field as quickly as possible."

Silence on the other end again. Only this time, Aiisha believed it felt more agreeable than hostile.

Eventually, in a softer voice, Grant responded. "And how, exactly, do you propose we do that?"

A flicker of a smile crossed Aiisha's face.

"As I recall, you still have a batch of the toxin, don't you?"

50

"Here. I brought you something."

Agent Weiss looked up to see Warren standing beside her desk, one arm extended.

"What is it?" she said, looking askance at the large paper cup in his hand. "I don't really do soft drinks."

"It's not a soft drink. Try it. I'm pretty sure you'll like it."

A skeptical smile on her lips, she unwrapped the straw he handed her, poked it through the slit in the lid of the cup, and drew in a large gulp. The moment she swallowed the liquid, she closed her eyes and slapped her desk.

"Are you kidding me? A *strawberry milkshake*?" she exclaimed the minute her lips left the straw.

He shrugged. "Well, given the state of the water right now, I couldn't very well bring you a coffee, could I?"

They both chuckled. Agent Weiss shook her head, twirled the straw in the slit of the cup lid, then ran the fingers of her left hand back through her hair. "Where in the hell did you find a milkshake anywhere near here? And a *strawberry* milkshake at that."

He snickered, tilted his head to one side. "There's a diner not far from our hotel. I had a feeling they could whip one up for me even if it wasn't on their regular menu. And, I was right."

He flashed a wide grin. She grinned back. "Apparently, I never told you about the horrible allergic reaction I get whenever I ingest anything strawberry, did I?"

She took another large draw from the cup, bulging her eyes as she did so. "Mmm, wow . . . that's really good," she said once she had finished.

Warren laughed heartily and pulled a chair next to her desk so he could sit at her level. Some of the milkshake had dribbled out of the straw, so he reached into the sack, pulled out one of the paper napkins the diner had stuffed there, and began to blot the excess milk and ice cream on her chin.

"There," he said when he had finished. He wadded up the napkin and tossed it into the trash bin beneath her desk. Then he cleared his throat, smiled quickly at her, turned and squinted at her monitor. "So, how's it going?" he asked. "Any luck with the cell towers? What they've done—it's horrible. Unbelievable."

"Yeah, I know. They tell me calls are coming in at the rate of more than fifty an hour. Another forty people have died. The water department is doing everything they can to contain it, but—just between you and me—they say this toxin is truly like nothing they have ever seen. Whoever screwed with this algae really knew what they were doing."

She took another brief slurp of milkshake. "I'm really worried about what might happen if people just come into superficial contact with it," she continued. "Like while taking a shower. It isn't a normal toxin, so who knows what could happen?"

He nodded but said nothing. Tapped the edge of her desk gently, kept looking at her.

"And, no. No luck yet with the cell pings," she went on. "But we're still working on it. We have some pretty savvy decryption experts in this department."

He continued to nod, continued to say nothing, continued to look at her. Eventually, she pulled her attention away from her monitor—and the milkshake in front of her—to him. Over time, she met his simple smile with one of her own. Ducked her head. Looked back up at him.

"But I'm getting this funny feeling you didn't really come here to talk about cell tower pings," she finally said. She picked up the paper cup, guided the straw into her mouth but just left it there this time, waiting for him to say something.

He glanced down for a second then looked back up at her.

"Yeah, well, maybe I've been . . . rethinking things, Hannah. I mean, this outbreak, what's going on right now . . . it's reminded me that, well, life's *really* fragile, you know? I mean, our life can end . . . *everything* can end . . . just like that. And I really love my wife and all, but I'm thinking now maybe I shouldn't, maybe I *can't* just live the rest of my life waiting . . . for . . ."

She turned back to her screen, then looked back at him. Set the milkshake down, sighed. Placed her right palm on the back of his left hand.

"Warren, you're right. Everything you just said is absolutely right," she began. "But I've been thinking about this, too. And the more I really think about it, the less sense it makes, really. I mean, even if we decided to just let our feelings drive our relationship, how would that relationship survive long-term—or even one year— when I am working here and you're based in Southern California? And when, thanks to situations like this, you could be expected to hop on a plane for somewhere half a world away the minute yet another confession from yet another character in *Wayward Colony* shows up on yet another corpse.

"It's sweet, Warren. It's incredibly romantic. I am very, very, very, *very* fond of you." She stopped and pointed toward the cup. "Especially since you walked in with that milkshake."

They both chuckled. Then she pulled up.

"But I've decided I just can't, Warren. Or, I guess what I mean is, I don't *want* to go down that road, even though I could. It's awfully tempting. But if and when we ever get to the other side of this situation, I want us to end up thinking about each other the way we were that day when we were in Little Havana. We were so . . . joyous that afternoon, so carefree.

"And we wouldn't be joyous, or carefree, if we were always hundreds or thousands of miles apart. Always consumed with trying to stop these idiots, and then wondering how to manage things if we *did* stop them for good and . . . your wife . . ."

She halted. Set her lips firm. Slowly shook her head.

"Your instincts were on target the first time, Warren." She picked up the milkshake and tilted it toward him. "I've learned they usually are."

Now it was his time to look down, but he did so in disappointment rather than shame. He knew she was right. But he really didn't want to acknowledge that.

Not now, anyway. *Maybe with a little time*, he thought. Then he silently kicked himself. *But who am I kidding?* he thought.

So he stood up, brushed off his slacks, nodded once, and softly said, "Okay, then." He began to turn away, but stopped halfway through the rotation and looked back at her, a stern look on his face.

"But before I go, there's just one thing I have to say," he intoned, one finger pointed in her direction.

She waited for him to finish. Wasn't sure she wanted him to.

He glared at her for what seemed an entire minute. Then, struggling as best he could to keep from bursting into paroxysms of laughter, he said, "I'm taking that damned milkshake back with me."

51

The midmorning sun warmed the back of Lee's neck, but not uncomfortably so. Humidity thickened the air, but it hadn't yet become oppressive. For South Florida at this time of year, it was a pretty nice start to the day.

Except that his contact was ten minutes late—unusual for someone who was punctual beyond reproach.

He sighed and studied the water as it gently lapped against the dock nearby. Its color here was more blue-green, almost a deep teal. Unlike him, it was also unusually calm.

He knew this was the right location—the directions could not have been more precise.

HEAD TO PELICAN HARBOR. PARK IN THE LOT BETWEEN THE BOATS AND THE MARINA STATION. WALK BEHIND THE STATION TOWARD THE WATER. I WILL BE AT THE PICNIC TABLE UNDERNEATH THE PALM TREE.

But there was no one at the picnic table when he arrived. So he sat down with his back toward the marina station, drummed his fingers on the weathered wooden tabletop. Somewhere, Agents Sainclair and Weiss were scrambling to identify precisely who had sent the taunting text and precisely where it had been sent from. Not far from them, scientists and engineers were rushing to reverse the carnage being caused by the toxin that had been poured in so many waterways.

But sitting beside this tranquil bay, beneath the gently swaying palms, Lee chose to excuse himself from all the chaos. To force himself—if only temporarily— to assume a posture of calm. To steel himself for whatever development his contact was about to discuss with him.

The meeting place became an oasis of serenity for him—but it didn't remain that for very long.

First, the American flag tethered to a pole nearby him began to flap with a violent vengeance. Then he heard footsteps making their way across the lawn behind him.

"I'm late," he heard the familiar voice huff. "I do so apologize, Dalton." His companion plopped down across from him, on the bay side of the picnic table. "Except that *you* are almost *always* late yourself, so . . ."

The architect nodded and exchanged a pained smile with his associate. "Traffic hold you up?" Lee queried. "It wasn't particularly bad for me."

The shake of a head. "No, it was . . . crossing the causeway. These days, I drive a lot more slowly on those things. It seems that ever since that bridge in Minneapolis collapsed, I've developed this irrational fear whenever I drive over water. I'm always worried they built the road with unreinforced concrete and that it won't hold up beneath the weight of my car. Or something ridiculous like that, anyway.

"It's nothing so overwhelming that it actually immobilizes me, but I do start to drive like someone over the age of eighty-five."

A short laugh followed the comment, but Dalton just chewed on the inside of one cheek and focused on a motorboat gently bobbing on the water a hundred feet out from shore.

The other person sighed, leaned closer to Dalton, looked down. Then, almost in a whisper, said . . . "I suspect you think you are the only one who dreads these get-togethers."

Lee said nothing, for he knew more was coming. However, he didn't expect what followed to be delivered so harshly.

"Well you're NOT!" his companion said, pulling back sharply. "Don't ever think you are! I mean, I'm never completely certain you won't just pull out a revolver and shoot me on the spot."

Lee cowered slightly—that stung. In part, because he knew there might be more than a nugget of truth to it.

The architect just sighed. "So, what bad news are you delivering *this* time?" he asked.

A short pause. "No bad news, really." Another, longer pause, then, "In fact, your parents have stabilized. Both of them. They've actually improved some since the last time we met. Given their age, they're still fragile, of course, but . . ."

Somewhere nearby, a tern squawked.

"But . . . ?" Lee prodded.

His confidant looked downward again. "Your father . . . he . . . I need to let you know that he has expressed some interest . . . in joining the transformation."

A knife sliced diagonally through Lee's intestines, then twisted in a slow, agonizing spiral. "No. You're lying. He wouldn't."

"He insists that political resistance is a tradition in your family, Dalton. That your grandfather was a sympathizer of Mao Tse-tung, and that . . ."

"No, he wasn't. That's not true. You're making all of this up."

"And that as time has gone on, and he's had more time to think about it all, he's come to fully grasp the many lies and hypocrisies that the democratic institutions and capitalist economies all over the world have hurled upon . . ."

"You are torturing him. He would *never* say that. You . . ."

A hand reached out to gently pat Lee's, which was resting at an angle on the edge of the tabletop. Although the architect was recoiling internally, he didn't exhibit a single tic.

"Come now, Dalton. I'm not saying I agree with his assessment. You know that." The speaker's hand retreated slowly.

Lee looked up at his contact. "I *don't* know that," he countered.

They considered each other for several seconds. Then, the other person reached into a coat pocket, extracted a piece of chewing gum, unwrapped it from its foil envelope, and quietly began to chew it.

"There's really no need to get so upset." The other's tone had shifted from one of comfort and concern to one of candor and objectivity.

"Your father has only made—how should I say it?—preliminary overtures toward a conversion. Nothing is official yet. He hasn't undergone any initiation or indoctrination that I am aware of. He's been far too weak for anything like that. Besides, we both know that people often say a lot of things they think they mean when they say them. Only to realize later on that what they said was . . . a *skew* of what they really meant. A fleeting shadow of the reality beneath their words. Not quite what they intended, but something they truly thought themselves committed to. But, in the final analysis, something they were not committed to *at all*.

"That could be the case here, as well. We'll just have to wait and see."

The speaker removed the chewing gum, looked around and, seeing no trash can nearby, pressed it against the underside of the picnic bench.

"So if you are going to get upset, Dalton, get upset at your father and his new . . . *slant* on things. Don't get upset with me just because I'm informing you about it. I'm just the messenger, Dalton, remember?"

They grew quiet again, took to staring up at the palm fronds above them and the blades of grass below. Out at sea, a horn softly blared the presence of some watercraft. The waves made a gentle thunk as they lapped against the pile of boulders along the shoreline; from the John Kennedy Causeway, the traffic delivered a low, steady drone.

Finally, Lee said, "I'm not going to kill you, but I still don't believe you."

His companion sniffed, leaned back from the picnic bench a couple of feet, gave some thought to the comment.

"Believe what you will, Dalton, believe what you will," came the reply. "Who was it . . . Andy Warhol? . . . who said, 'Everyone needs a fantasy'?"

With that, the other person slapped the surface of the picnic bench once, stood up, and drifted off toward the parking lot.

Lee remained at the bench for some time, contemplating the slivers of clouds in the sky and the gentle shimmer of the water beneath them. But it wasn't the news about his father he chewed on. Nor was it the criticisms he had received from someone he had always thought unflinchingly loyal. There was something else his contact had said that had caused a shift deep within him.

A shift that at first had been subtle, but over time became quite profound.

A shift that caused him to see a clue in the case he had subconsciously been aware of, but now was perceiving in a completely different way.

A shift that urged him to get to Valenzuela's house as very soon as possible. Before that clue might forever be gone.

***

As Lee approached the Valenzuela compound on his scooter, he made a point *not* to slow down too much. After what had happened with Shirley, he didn't want to look too conspicuous as he undertook his act of quick espionage. Besides, the breeze his velocity caused was helping sweep away the beads of sweat that had formed on his brow. Still, it was a hot breeze that tousled his hair and ruffled the sleeves of his shirt.

At one corner of the property stood a small grove of palm trees that temporarily blocked his view of the house. But when the scooter passed the last of the tree trunks, he had a sweeping view of the front of the mansion.

As before, the work vans occupied the driveway. Only now, the renovations had moved toward the center of the house.

But not a single centimeter beyond that point.

Which was exactly what the architect had hoped to discover.

Which was the final piece of evidence he had been seeking.

Which convinced him, without any shadow of a doubt, exactly who had killed Vic Valenzuela.

52

He received the call later that afternoon, as he sat in his armchair, finally savoring a glass of Buffalo Trace bourbon and, at last, what he hoped would be a great grilled cheese sandwich. He had convinced himself the events of the day called for a reward. When the attendant first whisked away the lid of the room service tray, he was less than sure the sandwich would be to his satisfaction. The bread looked slightly undertoasted. And he thought he detected the faintest aroma of Dijon. Which to his palate, was entirely unacceptable.

But after a couple of tentative bites into the sandwich, he decided it was really quite good. He would probably give it a B+. Maybe an A-.

No, a B+, he decided. But it was more than acceptable.

He answered the call, pushed himself deep into the armchair.

"Dalton, it's Mackeson. We were able to pinpoint the neighborhood the text message came from."

The architect sat up straight in the armchair, spoke more loudly than normal into his phone.

"Really? That's wonderful, Mackeson! Does the location help us much with the investigation?"

"Ah, *men wi*, I should say it does," his friend replied.

An eerie absence took over the call. For a moment, Lee thought someone had severed the connection.

"Are you still there, Mackeson? Did I lose you?"

He heard a slight scrape on the other end, followed by Mackeson's voice, barreling forward. "*Wi, Dalton, dezole!* I was just receiving . . . some important information from my assistant here."

Lee smiled broadly. He figured the "important information" Sainclair referred to was probably the result of a race at Hialeah.

"So . . . the location, Mackeson. Where did the text come from?"

"Right. First, *merci* for sending the message you did from your taxicab today. It was indeed very helpful to us. And, your instincts appear to have been correct. Indeed, the text message was sent from Kendall.

"To be exact, from within a quarter mile of the home of Hayden Haas."

At the other end of the conversation, Dalton Lee squinted his eyes some, peered off at a particular point far off in the distance.

"Yes. It's all very unfortunate, isn't it?" he replied. "But, yes, that is exactly what I expected you to say."

53

One would think that the formal act of bringing a member of The Organization to justice would bring great satisfaction to Lee.

But it never did.

It was a job that needed to be done, of that he was certain. He realized it usually meant the lives of thousands . . . perhaps *hundreds of thousands* . . . would be spared. Given the expert interrogation and negotiation skills of the country's federal agents, it almost always meant, as well, that one of their loved ones being held hostage would access freedom.

But did it bring him deep satisfaction? Not really.

Because he knew that for each soul about to be freed, another was about to be relinquished to a correctional system that corrected no one.

He felt that, at best, it was a draw.

"You don't have to accompany them, you know," Lara told him as they enjoyed a celebratory pot of jie tea in a quiet corner of the hotel's restaurant.

Lee studied the teapot in front of them for a moment; gave careful consideration to what she had just said. Over time, however, he slowly began to nod.

"Actually, I believe I do, Lara," he replied.

Her brow creased. "But why?" she asked. "My father has been with them for years, now. But even if he were the one that you were bringing in, I wouldn't have any interest in witnessing his arrest."

Lee continued to nod, ducked his head some to take another quick sip of the tea.

"Yes, I get that," he said, calmly placing his cup on the saucer. "But as curious as it may sound, I have this bizarre compulsion to study them when the handcuffs are being placed on their wrists. To watch their reaction. To see if there is even a glimmer of guilt, a shade of enlightenment, that overtakes them the minute they become a ward of the state.

"To watch how an uncompromising zealot for individual freedom reacts when their own freedom has been utterly compromised. Forever."

Lara's eyes darted for a moment toward the entrance to the restaurant; her lips curled into a discreet sneer. Lee raised his teacup to his lips again, but his gaze remained on his colleague across the table.

When he finished his tea, he set the cup down again and crossed his hands on the tablecloth in front of him. "Want to come with me?" he asked her.

Lara shifted her attention away from the entrance and back onto Lee, met his gaze for several seconds, then raised her chin an inch or so.

"Sure," she replied. "Why not?"

***

He parked the gray four-door sedan far enough from the Haas home so no direct connection could quickly be made. Made a quick inventory of the items in his passenger seat: sweatband, exercise watch, water bottle filled with the toxin.

Quit stalling, Gustafson, there is no time to waste.

He had decided this would be the last time he allowed others to run the show. As usual when he did that, events had spiraled toward calamity. Now was his chance to *yet again* save the day. Bring everything across the finish line. Hopefully in record time.

His scheme was by no means certain to succeed, but was very well thought out. He'd ring the doorbell. Say, "Hey, I was in the neighborhood, thought I'd bring by some of that energy drink I make that I know you enjoy so much." Engage in a little chitchat, *but not too much because I need to get out of there before too many people notice me.* Transform back into your typical weekend warrior. Get back to the car and get the hell out of there as fast as possible.

Let's do this, he thought, emerging from the car in a dead sprint.

***

They arrived at the coach's home with as little fanfare as possible—just two dark cars, both unmarked.

In the black SUV were the federal agents who would perform the arrest—an African-American male with the physique of a pro football player and a shorter Hispanic male with a lengthy scar on his forehead. In the town car were Agents Sainclair and Weiss, with Lee and Lara occupying the back seat. Both vehicles glided slowly up against the curb as close to the front of the house as possible. But all six doors flew open and then shut the moment the cars came to a stop.

They charged up the sidewalk, silent and serious. As they neared the door, Agent Sainclair quickened his stride and darted in front of the other agents. It appeared he had decided the honor of ringing the doorbell would be his. Lee and Lara lingered at the back with Agent Weiss—their customary deference to the federal authorities they were assisting.

***

Behind them, and unbeknownst to them, an older man in a windbreaker and shorts jogged around the corner nearest the home. However, for someone who gave the impression of being in the middle of a long, midday run, he had very little sweat to show for it.

Perhaps he had been hydrating himself frequently from the unusually large water bottle he held in his right hand?

As the older athlete made the corner and encountered the phalanx of cars next to the curb beside him, he pulled up slightly and used his peripheral vision to assess the group of people assembled on the front porch to his right.

Goddammit, the runner thought as he ducked his head and charged off down the sidewalk. *They got here before I could. Damn it!*

***

Sainclair assessed the others around him on the porch, nodded once, extended the index finger of his left hand, and jabbed the doorbell for one long buzz. Then retreated the hand and shoved it into his pocket.

And then waited.

Eventually, they could hear steps, and the door slowly opened. Behind it was Hayden Haas, his face drawn and forlorn.

"Mr. Haas, I believe you have been expecting us?"

The coach nodded. Meekly replied, "Yes."

He drew the door open wider, stepped back to let everyone enter. From the den, the coach's daughter pranced forward, her head bowed to the ground. When she looked up and saw all the men and women in the entryway, she pulled up. "Dad? What's going on?" she said. "Is everything okay?"

He turned to her, put out one hand. "Don't worry, honey, I'm taking care of this."

He then turned back to the agents and delivered a pained expression. "Does this have to happen right now?" he said. "Like this?"

Agent Sainclair nodded once, the agents behind him stepped forward decisively.

The coach sighed and turned. "Lupita," he called over one shoulder. "They're here."

A few beats later, the housekeeper rounded a corner, a small suitcase in one hand, a backpack hooked over her opposite shoulder.

"I guess we're ready then?" he asked.

She nodded quietly to the coach, said nothing.

The arresting officers surged forward, then pivoted to their left. Behind them, Agent Sainclair spoke in a strong clear voice.

"Heather Haas, you are under arrest for the murder of Victor Xerxes Valenzuela and for conspiring to provide material support to known terrorists," he announced.

The young girl froze, confused. But her look of bewilderment slowly transformed into an expression of outrage. She swung back toward her father and sent him a look of venom.

"You *knew* about this? And you didn't do anything to *stop* them?!"

The coach said nothing. Gripped the doorknob even harder as the agents yanked his daughter's arms behind her back and slipped her wrists into the handcuffs they had unclipped from their belts.

Lupita stepped forward with the backpack and suitcase. "I'll carry these out for her," she said quietly.

The coach blocked her progress with one arm, reached for the luggage. "No, I'll do it," he said quietly. "I'm her father. I didn't mean to put her in this situation, but I contributed to it. And I need to say goodbye to her. In more ways than one."

The agents marched the girl toward the door. Somehow, despite the shackles on her wrist, she managed to make her exit look like a balletic chassé, her back foot chasing the one in front.

As she bounced her way past Lee in the doorway, she whirled her head toward the architect and narrowed her eyes into thin horizontal slits.

"This isn't the end, you know," she said, a gravelly hollowness consuming her voice. "We're everywhere. *Everywhere.* Maybe a lot of us are in hiding, but we're all waiting for just the right moment to help people escape your ridiculous rules and regulations. The Transformation *is* going to happen. You can't stop it, even if you did stop me."

The agents bounced the college student over the aluminum threshold and onto the shallow brick porch. Just before she descended to the sidewalk that would take her to the vehicles beyond, she looked over her shoulder one last time and sneered at Lee and Lara.

"Power to the cause," she hissed, her mouth twisted into a taut, fierce smile.

***

367

Lara waited until the rest of the agents had departed the house, until Hayden Haas had shut the door behind them, until the two of them were comfortably seated in the back of the town car, before she delivered to Lee the verdict that she knew would unsettle him but that she felt he needed to hear nonetheless.

"I guess that answers your question, doesn't it, as to whether these beasts experience any guilt or enlightenment?"

Without answering, Lee turned and looked through his window at the front yard directly across from them. There, a young boy darted to and fro through a sprinkler, his face gleefully angled toward the sun.

54

"Okay, you win."

Lara had sidled up beside Lee without his realizing it. He detested people sneaking up beside him. But Lara had such a radiant smile on her face, he couldn't bring himself to take her to task.

"What did I win?" he replied drily. "A grilled cheese sandwich? A brand new car?"

She shook her head some, took a sip of champagne, turned, and nodded toward the Miami skyline, the lights of which made the nighttime cruise they were on all the more spectacular.

"It took me a while to get there," she said somewhat coyly. "But I will admit that Miami indeed has some very appealing architecture . . . here and there. I'm not at all fond of the swamps or the mosquitoes. But I will concede that the designs of many of the buildings here are really quite . . . intriguing."

Lee smiled back, sniffed, and followed her gaze to the lights of Brickell and downtown in the distance.

"You know, we can always move The Lee Group's headquarters here if you want, Lara," he said quickly. "I'll bet you would be outstanding at jai alai."

Lara dropped her smile, slumped her shoulders. "Oh, Dalton,

honestly . . ." she moaned lightheartedly. He nudged her and they stood in silence for several more moments, studying the gentle chop beyond the deck.

"By the way, did you ever finish your acrostic?" Lara asked.

Lee brightened, turned to her. "I did!" he exclaimed. "It was quite challenging, actually. Eventually, it revealed a fascinating quote by, of all people, Edna Buchanan."

Lara tilted her head and gave him a quizzical look. "I don't know of her," she said.

The architect smiled wide. "Edna Buchanan was one of Miami's greatest crime reporters," he replied, turning to look back at the city in front of them. She eventually went on to write crime novels." He pulled up short and nudged his associate once again. "Maybe that's what you will do when you retire, Lara. Write murder mysteries."

She frowned, as if a rank odor had suddenly floated up from the water. "Why on earth would I want to do something like that?" she uttered.

Lee looked at her blankly, blinked a few times. "Well, you don't have any children, any grandchildren," he said meekly. "What else would you do with your time?"

With that, Lara let out a scoff and retreated toward the center of the boat. Seeing an opening, Agents Sainclair and Weiss sauntered over and joined Lee as he took in the panorama before them. A server approached the trio with a tray of chorizo and prawn skewers; each of them delicately selected one.

"It was really kind of you to charter this cruise for all of us, Dalton," Hannah said. "And entirely unnecessary."

"I was more than happy to," he replied with a slight bow of the head. "You deserve it. We all deserve it." His eyes then descended several inches when a chunk of chorizo tumbled off a skewer and onto Agent Weiss's dress.

"Oh my gosh! Oh my gosh!" she exclaimed, turning first one way then the other in search of some form of rescue. Hearing the melee, the server bounded back toward her, provided a fistful of napkins she could use to scoop up the sausage.

Once the food had been removed, and the slight stain blotted with club soda, the conversation resumed.

"Dalton, I completely understand now why you have the reputation you do," Agent Sainclair announced. "Once again, your keen perception has saved a lot of lives."

Lee looked out at the sea and sighed.

"Not as many as I would have cared to save," he said, now slightly morose. He glanced back at his companions. "How many have . . . perished?"

Hannah Weiss reached out, clutched his forearm. "It doesn't matter. What matters is, you saved thousands of people, Dalton. Perhaps even tens or hundreds of thousands. Imagine, if we hadn't arrested Heather Haas and extracted the composition of the toxin from her associates when we did. Who knows what the eventual toll would have been?"

Lee began again to study the water. "The antidote . . . it is working?" he muttered quietly.

The two agents nodded. "Yes, slowly," Agent Sainclair replied. "And we cannot sugarcoat things. Several of those who ingested the toxin will likely contend with some minor health issues for the rest of their lives. But, yes, they are all recovering. Thank heavens."

Agent Sainclair pressed one palm against the architect's upper back.

"I must say, mon ami, if someone had told me at the beginning of all of this that it was the renovation work being performed at the Valenzuela estate that would lead us to the killer, I would have thought them high on cocaine themselves!"

Lee smiled, bowed his head again.

"Thank you, Mackeson," the architect replied. "Only, it was the renovation work that hadn't been performed that turned out to be key. It was only when I realized that the contractors were starting at one end of the house and moving toward the opposite end did it make sense to me that the trellis the killer scaled to reach the bedroom was probably still of substandard construction—and would likely only support the weight of someone very, very light. Certainly not the weight of Hayden Haas, who we knew was well over two hundred pounds when the murder took place. Or Danielo Duran or Jamal Culberson or even Astrid Steinberg."

Hannah Weiss had handed her plate to a server and was very carefully cradling a champagne cocktail. "But I find it a little hard to believe, Dalton, that it was the trellis alone that got you to zero in on the coach's daughter," she said.

He smiled once again.

"Well, that's true, it wasn't," he acknowledged. "Once I determined that the only person who could have successfully climbed up that trellis was someone who didn't weigh very much, several other things came together. I knew whoever murdered Valenzuela probably wasn't barefoot when they did it, and if they had been, then we probably would have found a footprint in the soil at the base of the trellis. So, I started asking myself what type of footwear would leave a print as smooth as the one your colleagues found in the garden, and it dawned on me that except for maybe a moccasin, a full-soled ballet slipper would be about the only other likely candidate. And given the flooring they use in a dance studio, and Heather's daily practice schedule, her slippers probably would have absorbed quite a bit of the floor-cleaning chemicals your forensics team found embedded in the clump of soil left in Valenzuela's bedroom."

"Very astute of you, Dalton, very astute," Agent Sainclair said. "In fact, her slippers still had some trace residue from those very chemicals when we tested them this morning."

"Well, thank you, but please understand it took me quite a while to get there," the architect replied. "Like you, I was so focused on the fact that Hayden Haas wasn't at the hotel in West Palm that night, I completely overlooked the fact that he told us that his daughter said to him that she had gone to stay with some friend. It never dawned on us to check out her alibi, did it?"

Hannah took a deep sip of her cocktail. "So he really did drive back to Kendall that night, sleep in his own bed, and then drive back up to West Palm the following morning?"

Lee nodded. "But there was no one at his house to verify that for us, so . . ."

Agent Weiss shook her head. "I still can't get over the fact it was her stepmother who recruited her to become a part of The Organization," she said emphatically.

"I know. It's very sad, isn't it?" Lee replied. "Sad and creepy, but then, in another way, utterly and completely logical. Heather never really had a nurturing female in her life—or much stability of any kind, for that matter—so she was an easy recruit for them to pluck. And no one knew that better than—what was the name her stepmother went by?"

"Madeline," Agent Weiss answered. "But it turns out her real name is Dimah Madwani."

"Yes, of course. When Madeline . . . Dimah . . . stepped back into Heather's life after disappearing, and then filled the girl's head with images of togetherness and family, it was probably way too much for Heather to resist, even if she wanted to. And I seriously doubt she wanted to."

Lee sighed, drank some more champagne.

"Some people do The Organization's bidding because they share the group's twisted ideology. Other people do it for the money, plain and simple. I suspect Heather did it because she so desperately wanted to belong to something that made her feel special and needed. Important, even."

With his middle finger, Agent Sainclair tapped the stem of his champagne flute. "But, the way they planted the stepmother onto the university's faculty . . . I have to say, even I didn't think they had that much . . . cunning."

"Yes, well, I don't know a whole lot about sports," Lee said, "But I do know enough about hiring practices to sense when someone is getting a job for reasons totally unrelated to their resume. That got me curious about those trustees who had been so aggressive about getting Hayden Haas hired as an assistant to Vic Valenzuela—trustees even Haas himself said he had never heard of before they contacted him. Now we know, of course, that those trustees weren't your random, run-of-the-mill university trustees—they were members of The Organization. And only when the toxin appeared in the water system did I begin to suspect that it wasn't really Haas they had been so eager to get on the staff at Miami A&M, but his wife—the chemist."

"Here's what I'm not clear on," Agent Weiss interjected, cocking her head to one side. "Did Haas know all along that his second wife was one of them? Was he in on the plot the whole time as well, and just keeping everything to himself so the family would stay together?"

Agent Sainclair shook his head. "No. The poor man apparently was completely clueless. That's how you know these people are reptiles. They do not think twice about manipulating perfectly innocent individuals who are just trying to put one foot in front of the other and lead a happy life."

Lee nodded in agreement.

"Truly, they were far more devious this time in how they advanced their plot. First, they had this Dimah pursue Haas and get him to marry her. How had he described their courtship? A whirlwind romance that she had pretty much driven from the start? Then, the Miami A&M trustees who were working for The Organization lobbied the rest of the university's board to get Haas onto Valenzuela's coaching staff. Only that was just a cover for their real objective—getting his new wife placed on the chemistry department faculty so she could use that world-class laboratory of theirs to work on the toxin after hours.

"The plan was proceeding just the way they had designed it—until Valenzuela got ticked off at Haas and went to the board to get him fired. Suddenly, the trustees who belonged to The Organization had to hustle because they knew the toxin wasn't ready yet and that if Haas lost his coaching job, his wife would most likely lose her faculty position as well. So, they went to Valenzuela privately and cut him a deal—leave Haas alone and we'll increase your salary and, (I'm guessing) overlook the fact you have been throwing games to make even more money on the side. That worked . . . but only for a while.

"When Valenzuela finally couldn't take Haas being on his staff anymore, he gave the trustees an ultimatum—either the Haas family goes, or I go. All the other trustees became worried they might lose the winningest coach in college football, so this time, those working for The Organization lost the vote. Haas got fired, his wife got fired soon after, and once she lost access to the university's laboratory, The Organization shifted the toxin's development to another location and made her suddenly disappear."

"And then, because Valenzuela had gotten in their way, The Organization made him disappear . . . only in a very different way,"

Hannah added. "It had nothing at all to do with his gambling scheme or his cocaine habit, did it? He just pulled a power play with the wrong underling at the wrong time."

"Exactly," Lee replied. He paused to study the deck of the ship for a moment. When he was finished, he looked back at the agents and grinned. "You were able to corral all of those untrustworthy trustees, correct?" he said.

Hannah nodded. "Yes, the two Hispanic trustees . . . Tomás Maldonado and Ramón Ybarra . . . they were somewhat cooperative when we went to arrest them. Not real cooperative but somewhat.

"But that Grant Gustafson, he was a real hellion, that one. Took three of our agents to chase him down and get the cuffs on him. Of course, given his family's prominence here, and the fact he was a Miami A&M track star back in the day, I'm not that surprised he'd put up a fight. Still . . ."

"I've never known a single one of them to just fall into line peacefully," Lee said, one eyebrow arched. "Don't forget—the first word in the title of the book they cherish so much is Wayward.

Mackeson began to tap one foot. "I've been wondering—what about the gallery owner, Astrid Steinberg? Did she figure into The Organization's plot at all?"

Lee shook his head. "Not really. But you can't really call her an innocent bystander, either. She did have quite a coke habit, apparently, and that was the reason why she continued to make payments to Valenzuela's defense team long after the trial was over. But it also turns out that Valenzuela had been using her gallery as a place to hide the hundreds of thousands he earned from throwing those games. Seems the two of them struck a deal some time back— he would make sure she had enough funds to maintain her gallery . . . and her drug habit . . . if she would make sure to petition the judge for a sentence of life imprisonment, rather than the death penalty, if he got convicted of her sister's murder. It was a cozy little deal for both of them.

"After he lost his coaching job, and the jury found him not guilty, he let her keep the money he had given her, but that was pretty much the end of the gravy train for her. Then, of course, the gravy train derailed completely when he was murdered."

"Brilliant work," Mackeson said, clamping a hand on Lee's right shoulder.

"Actually, Bree and Liam are the sleuths who unearthed those juicy details," Lee said, wincing some from the agent's strength. "Oh, and speak of the devils . . ."

Side by side, the pair Dalton had just mentioned wandered up to the others, wide smiles dominating their faces. Not far behind them came Roberto, Irene, and Warren, each of them dressed more nattily than Lee had ever seen them.

"Where's Lara?" he asked, craning his head first one way, then another.

Roberto was quick to respond. "She told me to tell you that she was changing into her jai alai outfit," he deadpanned.

Lee threw his head back and chuckled at the reference, just as a large tugboat about eighty yards away blared its air horn demonstrably. Suddenly, Lara appeared behind one of Lee's shoulders.

"I'm going to get you for that comment, you do realize that, don't you?" she said with a smirk. "Only, you won't know where and you won't know when."

Lee winced some, laughed once, and clinked his flute against hers. "I'm not scared," he replied, returning her look. "To be honest, I've grown rather accustomed to the ongoing suspense you provide."

As he proudly reviewed all the members of The Lee Group, the architect noticed Roberto looked somewhat glum. That reminded him . . .

"Roberto, I know how exasperated you are at Isabela's plight," he began. "You know we all share your concern about her captivity and, now, her safety. I am very confident that someday you will be reunited with her, and I am betting it will be sooner rather than later."

The designer merely nodded once at his superior, his chin resolute.

"But I do have a little announcement that I think will perhaps cheer you up a little bit. When we return to California, we'll have someone new on our staff who should make our lives a little bit easier, and our offices a whole lot tidier. I've hired Margarida—Valenzuela's housekeeper—to join us full-time. She was about to lose her position, and I thought she would be an awesome add to our team."

Roberto's frown fizzled. "That's really great of you, Dalton, thank you," he said. "I appreciate it, and I'm sure she does, as well."

At that moment, the architect felt his phone vibrating in his breast pocket. It was the call he had been waiting for . . . the call they all had been waiting for. He put the phone to his ear, realized that in the dark he had positioned it upside down. So he quickly inverted it, so he could hear the person on the other end.

"Uh-huh, I see. Yes," he droned softly. "Okay, yes. Of course. I will relay that just as soon as we hang up. Thanks for calling."

He returned the phone to his pocket, looked up to see his team hushed and tense, but looking off in scattered directions. As their chief, Lee always had mixed emotions at this stage of the game. He knew he was conveying news that would be delightful to one person, yet devastating to the rest.

"Yes, if you are wondering, that was the call. Thanks to information supplied to us by Heather Haas, one of our hostages has just been rescued."

He scanned the team one by one, settling at last on Irene in the center.

"It's Sung-min, Irene," he said quietly. "He's on a plane that left Bangkok about an hour ago. He should be back in the United States sometime late tomorrow."

"Sorry, but I don't believe it," she replied curtly, her face rigid and defiant.

Lee smiled weakly. "I certainly understand why you'd say that. I think we all understand why you'd say that. But they double-verified everything this time. It's him. Your friend is coming home."

Bree placed a palm on the shoulder of their technology specialist, who said nothing, but welled up in tears and thrust her bottom lip up over the top one.

Mackeson Sainclair moved to one side of Lee and began to pat the architect on the upper back several times. "It has been an honor to work alongside you, ami mwen," he said earnestly. "I think you are a brilliant man. And I am quite envious of the smart, committed team you have to work with."

Agent Weiss made a tsk-ing sound, put one hand on her hip. "And what am I, Mackeson, chopped liver?" she said, shaking some as she said it.

"Not at all, Hannah. I appreciate your skills as well," the detective replied. "I'm just saying I think Dalton is very wise to surround himself with a cadre of assistants who are as bright and talented and diverse as all of you are." He swung one arm out in a wide arc to indicate the other members of The Lee Group.

"As a matter of fact, back in . . ."

Lee cut him short. "Let me guess . . . there's an old saying in Haiti that fits this situation," he said, his eyebrows raised.

Sainclair laughed once, scratched behind his right ear.

"There most certainly is," he replied, straightening his posture so he would look more eloquent. It says, "Men anpil, chay pa lou."

The crowd leaned in closer, waited for the translation.

"I think it means 'Unity creates strength,' or something like that," he replied, laughing.

Even Roberto found humor in the detective's remark and joined the others in a clink of glasses and a wink at the others.

"So, I think it's time to make an official toast," Lee suddenly announced. Lara silently speculated whether her cohort would toast Mackeson and Hannah, or the hostage who had just been released, or the federal agents who had rescued the hostage, or even, perhaps, Lee's own parents.

Instead, the head of The Lee Group pivoted to the left and nodded toward the cityscape beyond the bay, a skyline whose colors and angles on this night seemed to be enhancing the architecture far more than usual.

"To this city," he exulted, raising his champagne toward the skyline. "And, to life.

"For if ever there were a city that embodies what it means to live life to the very fullest, it is, most certainly, Miami."

PLEASE

If you would, post a review of "Murder Becomes Miami" on:

AMAZON, iBOOKS, KOBO, BARNES & NOBLE or SMASHWORDS

The more reviews a books gets (regardless of the star-rating) the more people buy the book.

So thank you for getting the word out (either for or against) this novel.

If you know the author, please DO NOT mention that in your review, for it is likely to lead to your review being pulled. Other than that, however, have at it.

AND THANK YOU!

(Note: You only need to have an account with Amazon, iBooks, etc. to post a review there. You DO NOT have to have purchased the book there to post your review.)

The Cornet Group
thecornetgroup.com

Foreshadowing

The Organization may have been thwarted for the time being, but it hasn't given up on its overall strategy of helping people live flawless lives in a very flawed world. Dalton Lee and the rest of The Lee Group will realize that soon enough, when they are summoned to London's most exclusive neighborhood and discover that "Murder Becomes Mayfair" as well.

***

Please post a review of "Murder Becomes Miami"

If you enjoyed this book, we would be grateful if you would write a short review of it on the page where you purchased it. If you participate on Goodreads, we'd appreciate a review of it there as well. Your review could help other mystery lovers find the book and enjoy it as much as you did.

***

Get the Backstory

This is not the only time The Lee Group has solved a mysterious murder and deduced how the victim interfered with a takeover scheme planned by The Organization.

Learn more about the architects/detectives who make up The Lee Group, and the cult they are shadowing, in:

Murder Becomes Manhattan
murdermanhattan.com

Connect with Jeffrey Eaton via:

Facebook
facebook.com/pages/Murder-Becomes/1444718039076732

Twitter
twitter.com/murderbecomes

Google+
plus.google.com/107619016627963785581/about

YouTube
youtube.com/channel/UCdrWC7rirBf-7cKHIIYz14g

Instagram
instagram.com/murderbecomes/

Pinterest
pinterest.com/murderbecomes/

The following individuals provided invaluable insights into the content of this novel, and they have my profoundest gratitude:

Sandy Chapman
Rafael Ciordia
Julian Conway
Marty Mueller
Dustin Thibodeaux
Randall White

About the Publisher

The Cornet Group LLC was established in 2014 to bring forward intriguing perspectives and intelligent writing presented through the genre of fiction.

Learn more at:

CORNET ⬤

www.thecornetgroup.com

CPSIA information can be obtained at www.ICGtesting.com
Printed in the USA
LVOW06*0905031215

464162LV00001B/1/P